2:05 a.m.

C.M. Moore

www.trollriverpub.com

2:05 a.m.
An Ice Era Chronicle (Book 2)
Copyright © 2017 C.M. Moore
ISBN: 978-1-946454-35-5
Cover Design: William Black

Dear Reader,
Connor and Monica have worked very hard on this particular piece of entertainment. This book was brought to you by hard labor and love. Please respect an artist's work for the enrichment we try to bring you. I humbly ask that you don't outright steal this child born on paper and brought to you by love. If you come by this book by nefarious means and you are simply unable to give the change in your pocket for the purchase price, then take it with my blessing. But if you can purchase it and would like Connor and Monica to continue to bring you great books, please purchase a copy to support them.
Thank you,
Troll River Publications

Join the fun with giveaways, updates, and new release opportunities at: https://books2read.com/u/3yZkjv

Dedication:

I dedicate this book to my tiny shower. No joke. I cannot lift my arms up because they hit all sides. I have to duck to get my hair wet. Here's to a bathtub…

Acknowledgements:

To my better half, without you, this book wouldn't exist.

To those of you still hanging in there, April, Lyn-z, Sarah. I can't thank you enough for the tips, thoughts, and support!

To Whitney and Damien, you are my own personal munchkin and American Indian. Hugs.

To the Trolls in the Troll River Publishing House, you are all my heroes. Thank you for giving me direction and focus. Especially, Stephanie… 2 Dollars.

To the Saint Cloud, MN, Wounded Warrior Project Support Group, I can't thank you enough for the good-natured ribbing and the support for my writing. You guys are the best!

To Kay, I can't believe you read the sex in this. You make me laugh. Thanks for telling everyone how much you liked it. You're my one-woman fan club!

To Shelley, Amanda, Alison, and Diane, this story wouldn't be what it is without your notes, comments, and ideas. Your sharp eyes and brilliant suggestions mean so much to me.

To my daughters, Capi and Sam, both of you make me a better person. You help me to remember to never give up and you keep my imagination alive. I love all the questions you ask.

And finally, to all the readers out there… all I can say is wow, really wow. You all make my heart beat a little faster.

To all of you, thank you.

Chapter 1

Place: Old United States, Dallas TX, H.S.P.C.
Headquarters
Time: 2:05 a.m. Ice Year 36

Everyone is a little crazy, some more than others. Unfortunately, Nova fell into the "more than others" category. This was spotlighted by her current conversation with her ex. She summoned her best glare.

Nova repeated her peace mantra in her head so she didn't scream. Ah crap-sticks, she should've never told her ex-boyfriend that she would think about getting back with him. She had used the word *think*, that being the important word. How long would she stand in her apartment doorway and listen to his begging?

"I changed my mind. I do that. A lot." Nova cut off Troy's nonsense when he took a breath. She leaned her shoulder on the doorway of the apartment she shared with her sister-in-law, Clare. Her eyes flashed up to Troy's face hoping she conveyed her seriousness. Since her irises were blood-red, usually a dirty look was enough of a deterrent for men. Troy, however, wasn't budging and she knew why. He wanted a Davis. That's all she was. She wasn't Nova. She was just a nobody with the right last name.

"But two days ago, you said you'd take me back," the agent whined.

"I said *think*." That's it. Time to go. She needed to get to her bedroom before she hit him. She got a kink in her neck looking up at him and she tipped her head to the side to work out the ache. In moments like this, being the size of an elf annoyed the crap out of her.

"I thought you were forgiving. Is this because of Sky?" Troy flashed his pretty, charming smile. The one that made her want to slap him. He was a tall lanky H.S.P.C. agent and regular women thought him handsome and oh-so-fucking fascinating. Normal women thought Nova was out of her mind for insisting the break-up stay permanent. She realized all that, but the knowledge didn't sway her decision. She'd marry a sketchy rough-and-tumble harvester before she would date Troy again.

"I told you I love Sky and that he's sick. That's a separate issue." Irritation bubbled up in her stomach. She recognized that she was close to freaking out. There were items in her apartment she didn't want to break. Her father was out of superglue and her mother made her promise to work on self-awareness. She had to get away from Troy and into her room before she erupted.

"But—"

"No." Nova closed the door in Troy's face and sagged against the wood. "There is no way to peace. Peace is the way." She murmured her mantra to the empty living room as she forced her turbulent feelings to settle. Her stomach rolled and her head started to pound. As she rubbed her forehead, her eyes popped up to the grandfather clock next to the couch. It was 2:05 a.m.? Damn, what was she even doing awake? Sleep would help her reset. Time for bed. A coma sounded good right about now.

Nova crossed the thick carpet and had reached the door to her bedroom when she heard the entrance to the apartment open. She spun around. If that was Troy, she would throw a chair at him and he would deserve it. Over and over again, her dad stated it wasn't okay to toss furniture at people, but she was almost positive Gears would pardon her this time. She would tell Luna she was completely self-aware the whole time.

Her, sister-in-law, Clare tiptoed into the room toward the healing booth where Sky was quarantined. Clare apparently hadn't seen her roommate yet. Nova crossed her arms over her chest and waited for the other woman to notice her presence. Rarely was Nova overlooked. Her eyes didn't let that happen.

"You scared me!" Clare exclaimed when she finally spotted her. Her sister-in-law spun on her heels then took a dainty step back. She didn't out right jump, but at eight months pregnant hopping around was out of the question. "What are you doing up at this hour?" Clare tossed some of her thick blonde hair back from where the curls cascaded over her shoulder.

"Troy came by. He kept pounding on the door until I opened up. He was calling me Nutty-Nova like an endearment."

"You're not getting back with him, are you?" Clare's pink lips puckered like she'd eaten a tart fruit.

"No. I got up to punch him, except at the last minute sanity returned. I closed the door in his face."

"Thank goodness." She sighed as her shoulders dropped. "You're very forgiving, Nova, one of your good traits but he doesn't deserve it." Clare paused. "That's your *only* good trait, being that you're all—" Clare waved her hand up and down. Nova understood the reference to her perpetual rioting mental state. Her emotions could ascend then descend at the drop of a hat. It was a side effect of her gift, but knowing that didn't make it better.

"I know." Couldn't argue there.

"And I guess you're kind sometimes." Clare appeared thoughtful, as if this was the first time she was considering who Nova was. She should've left the room while she had the chance. Talking to Clare was like having a conversation with a mix of her parents.

"You're kind and all," Clare continued. "But he slept with everyone the year you were together. I mean it. Like, he slept with the whole H.S.P.C. Headquarters." Clare waved her arm around like Nova didn't know where they lived. Some days conversing with Archer's wife was exhausting.

"Yes, I know. Thanks for the recap." Nova rubbed her forehead. Getting back with Troy was a dreadful idea. He wanted her only because her brother was Archer Davis, the son of the famous Gears. Archer and Clare was a power couple in the H.S.P.C., and Troy had used her to get closer to the family. Besides, she had Sky. Troy had never accepted that she'd fallen in love with her patient upon first sight.

But that was neither here nor there, and Clare still hadn't gone on to her bedroom. The realization that they stood in the middle of the living room struck Nova. At two in the morning, no less.

"Why are you up? I assumed you'd be in the central lab, either that or sleeping." Clare was a slave to finding a cure for Snow Flu, so it wasn't strange to see her up at this hour. But since getting pregnant, she had an established schedule.

"I was looking for you. I tried your room earlier, but I didn't hear you and you locked the door. I thought maybe you'd taken your sleeping drug."

That was typical of Nova. She took her sleeping drug right before she got violent or manic. Right now, she should take the medication and lock herself in her room, not chat with Clare. The overwhelming emotions shimmered directly under the surface of her calm façade.

Her eyes scanned Clare, maybe Sky needed more of Nova's blood.

"That's where I'm going, but," Nova spun around and started for her room, "if you need me for Sky, I'll be there."

"No, wait." Clare's words stopped her. "Have you seen Sky?"

Nova gulped down panic.

"I checked on him two days ago." Her eyes flipped to the glass that separated the observation room from the rest of the apartment. Through the thick protective glass, she could see her sleeping patient. Part of the reflection revealed her blood-red eyes. "I thought you were with him. I went to my room after the fight with Dad."

"I was with him." Clare's voice dropped to a husky whisper.

As Nova pressed closer to the glass, her eyes widened. Sky's hair was white. None of his dark locks remained. Anger at herself shot through her blood. This wasn't phantom fury, as her family loved to call it.

She had chosen to lock herself in her room since throwing a chair at her father was unacceptable. She'd had no choice but to sequester herself, but Nova regretted every moment away from Sky. In the time of her severe mental breakdown, her favorite person had gotten sicker. What would've happened if he'd died alone? She'd never recover.

Spinning away from the window, she pinned Clare with a sharp glare.

"What happened to him?"

"He's getting worse." Tears filled Clare's eyes.

Crap-olla, she made a pregnant woman cry. Nova dropped her eyes to the floor. She might be nuts, but she wasn't mean-spirited. After she crossed the room, Nova awkwardly patted her sister-in-law like she'd seen Gears do to weeping women. If her brother were here, Archer would have given her an earful for upsetting his match. Good thing she hadn't seen him in a while.

"It's okay. You're a brilliant scientist and doctor just like my dad. You're a true healer like my mom. You'll save Sky. I know you will." Pat, pat, pat. Clare had to save him. Sky was Nova's whole world.

"I can't," she cried and buried her beautiful face into her hand. "And I made it worse."

"How?" Sky never became more ill. He had plateaued. Clare might be overreacting. Pregnancy hormones most likely got the better of her.

"A few weeks ago, I heard of someone who survived Snow Flu. No one has ever gotten sick then survived."

"Yeah, and…" Nova already knew that. Where was this going?

"Anyway, I thought the blood might be the missing piece of what I'm looking for." More tears made a path down her pale cheeks. "I figured if I could see how someone's body fought the illness, then that blood might hold the answers I need." Clare sniffled. "I'm so close. Your blood is amazing, but your gift doesn't allow you to catch Snow Flu. That's not the same as having the sickness and then surviving. You see how it's different."

"And?" Nova stopped herself from asking how this all made Sky worse.

"And I asked Archer to go into the Northern Earth Dens to bring me some of this survivor's blood. I thought the job would be simple. Find the person who survived and ask for a sample."

"Why didn't you send someone from the task force, a fully trained agent?" Nova felt more trepidation as this story developed. "Why did you ask your husband?"

"I couldn't ask an agent because Doctor Gears is the boss and he said this was hearsay." Clare wouldn't look Nova in the eye. "I didn't have enough proof to send anyone into that part of the underground area. He said going was too dangerous for agents, especially without having a real reason. He made sure no one would go. He thought I might go behind his back."

"You did go behind his back," Nova squeaked. "You sent your poor husband off on a mission that might not even be successful."

"I sent Archer. He didn't come back." Clare swallowed hard. Tears splashed on her wringing hands. "See, I made it worse."

Yeah, this totally sounded worse.

"Dad was right. You shouldn't have sent anyone in the first place!" Nova took a deep breath and tried with all her might not to holler. She reminded herself for the second time not to make a pregnant woman cry.

"I sent my brother, Dan, after Archer when I got concerned." Clare gripped her lab coat, crushing the fabric closer to her belly. "Dan contacted me. He said he'd tracked Archer down. He went to get him, but his CC broke, so he needs a new one."

"What's a CC?" Nova had a surge of curiosity. Part of her inquisitiveness made her an excellent research assistant, but part of that also got her sucked into whatever Clare was doing.

"CC is my new invention. I made the gadget for Archer. CC is a minicomputer that has all my intelligence inside of it. The device can put together everything I can put together. The computer can track people, and give other information. Archer calls it his Clare Computer or CC. The name stuck."

If Nova tried to keep up with everything Clare invented, she'd go crazy. Well, she would go *crazier*.

"So, Dan found my missing brother? And now he needs a CC?" Nova felt panic gather in her gut. She didn't need an emotional breakdown. Now was the time to listen. Gulping air, she desperately tried to stay centered. What should she do?

"I need help," Clare wailed. "And I don't have anyone. Archer is gone. I sent Dan after him, and now Dan needs CC. There is nothing left I can do to—" Clare stopped crying abruptly. The switch from tears to a predatory smile was so sharp that the action reminded Nova of her bad days. Clare eyed her like candy. "You could help me, Nova. You're my only hope."

Nova took a hasty step away from the other woman. She was familiar with Clare's devious I-have-a-plan look. True, sometimes that expression led to amazing things Clare and her father would create, but at this moment, Nova didn't trust it. Especially, with words like "only hope" thrown in.

"I'm your only hope? That's unfortunate."

"You're kind and helpful. You'd help me." That sentence was a little too final.

"I'm also manic with spurts of rage and severe clinical depression." Best to remind her sister-in-law who she was.

"That probably just a side effect of your gift." Clare shrugged like Nova's brand of crazy didn't merit her genius. "You can deliver CC. Bring CC to Dan for Archer.

It's all to help Sky. You want to help Sky, don't you? Come with me and we can just talk." Clare headed to the door.

"I don't know, Clare." Talk? Somehow, she doubted they would *just* talk.

"Come with me to the lab for a minute." Clare produced a tissue out of the pocket of her lab coat and nosily blew her nose. Nova felt unease trickle from head to toe. A part of her warned she would get in way over her head.

"There is no way to peace. Peace is the way—" she whispered to herself to calm her nerves.

"Nova." Clare cut off Nova's hushed whispers.

"What? Can't you see I'm trying to find some inner peace?"

"Don't waste our time. You don't have any. Now, will you help me?"

"This is the kind of crap that happens to me." Nova glanced once more at Sky. Only when she viewed him did she feel a tiny bit tranquil.

"Come on." Clare raised one perfectly sculpted eyebrow over her puffy eyes.

Nova paused while she considered if this was a good idea. She needed to sleep. This wasn't a good decision-making time, but curiosity took this moment to rear its head. She followed Clare out the door.

Chapter 2

He was out of the cage. A thrill shot through him. He bolted down the long water base hallway. Before he reached the end of the cement hall, Arrow glanced around. No, he was dreaming. He'd had this dream last night, and the night before. He wasn't free at all.

Arrow couldn't wake up and couldn't make the dream stop. He had to go through the whole scene all over again.

The pairs stood side by side down a long hallway. The blindingly white hall forced him to shield his eyes. As he began to walk, two men who stood to his right nodded to him. Two women stood to his left. A man and a woman blocked the path directly ahead of him. They were faceless blurry strangers. Each set of beings draped themselves around each other. As Arrow started to move, they followed him. He didn't bother to figure out who any of them were. No point. He'd tried before and failed. As he continued on, he waited for the man to speak first. That man always spoke first.

"Arrow, you must bind us together." The undistinguishable figure unwound a set of strings from his body. They appeared in front of him as if tucked inside his heart. Arrow didn't respond to the stranger's demand.

Instead, he stopped walking and faced the group. He said nothing. What could he say?

Arrow had studied these ghost-strings before. The strands had a golden, bright, glimmering hue. They came from the man's chest. Each person around him, in turn, produced similar ropes. The loose strings shone iridescent. The strands reached out to his hands. They made him feel inadequate. He didn't know what to do. Arrow absolutely didn't want to touch them.

"We have to be bound together," the woman to Arrow's left demanded as she blocked his path. She clung to another woman and a man. "We have to unite so we may produce more children. We're all dying. Snow Flu is killing the human race."

Just like last night and the night before, Arrow denied her claim. He shook his head. The human race would survive Snow Flu. They had to. Mother Earth wouldn't let humans become extinct.

The golden strings stirred. The ropes waved in the air as if blowing in a breeze. They called to him. His fingers itched.

"We cannot tie them ourselves because we cannot see them. You have the sight."

"How can you *not* see the strings?" Arrow asked. This was stupid. The strands floated right in front of their clothes. They came from their bodies! He gave a stern look to each one of them in turn. Somewhere in the distance, cynical laughter rolled like thunder.

"It's only you." A whisper of sound came from one woman that was wrapped lovingly around two men.

A new thought struck him, one he didn't have before.

"Why should I bind you?" He gestured to the two men. "Or you." He motioned to the two women. Pairs of the same sex made no sense. The threesomes were even weirder. They couldn't reproduce. He kept glancing at the faceless individuals wishing the dream was over. Maybe if he were awake, this would make more sense.

"Our heart strings must be tied together to care for the abandoned babies." The man to his far right spoke low. His tone was dark. "It will take all of us to care for the lost children. So many parents died. Snow Flu, radon poisoning, and cave-ins. Those children need us. Pairs, matches, all the different sets will protect life."

Arrow wanted to tell them no. He understood nothing about connecting heart strings. There was no way he would touch the mysterious floating ropes.

He opened his mouth to insist they had the wrong person, but he didn't get the chance. The scene abruptly changed.

Snow started to pour into the hall. Before his eyes, the walkway turned into a huge snow drift. Giant snowflakes consumed the people from every angle.

Well… this was different.

The snow swirled around his head. Flakes clung to his eyelashes. The ice slashing at his eyes made him tear up. He could hear laughter again, coming from somewhere far away. Where was the laughter coming from? He tilted his head. To his right angry storms loomed, to his left, gray clouds pregnant with cold flakes appeared ready to fall. He was lost in Adam's Tundra.

He put his head down to drive forward into the wind. He didn't know where he was headed, but he could see a blurry image up ahead. Squinting, he tried to catch glimpses of a person walking in front of him. If he could catch up to the man, maybe the stranger would show him the way.

Arrow's long black hair whipped around his face. He slipped on thick ice when he tried to shove his wayward strands back. Why hadn't he braided his hair? This was a dream, that's why.

He sloshed through the snow mounds as he tried in vain to see. He could no longer feel his feet as he sunk to his knees. He realized he wasn't wearing shoes. Two toes were missing. He recalled that he'd lost them to the freezing temperatures.

To his left, he hoped there would be less ice to navigate. As his hair relaxed on his shoulders, he thanked the Great Spirit that the wind settled. Pleased at the sudden change in weather, he looked around. The snow disappeared. Arrow glanced around a beautifully well-lit waiting room. The square was well organized and reminded him of a doctor's office. Was he with a physician because they planned to cut off more of his toes? He hoped not.

"We're waiting for you." An older woman dressed in green appeared.

Where had she come from? He'd heard her voice before, but he didn't think the memory was part of this dream. Throwing his hands up, he heaved an exasperated sigh. He would never interpret what this dream meant.

A train whistle blew. Arrow spun around. He knew what could happen if you got to close to the tracks. The train rushing past him nagged at his overwrought brain. He was supposed to be somewhere. He tried to remember the thing he was meant to do. Was it urgent? What time was it? He looked again for the woman. She might give him answers.

More laughter caught his attention, then he could see his sister clearly. He wanted to thank the Great Spirit there was finally someone he recognized.

Radiant Dawn would explain. The last time he had seen Dawn she lived at one of the water bases. She was safe with his mom. He opened his mouth to speak, but no sound emerged. When she moved her hands, a chain rattled.

Radiant Dawn wept softly. She curled into herself with her long black hair covering her dark black eyes. Tears streaked down her cheeks. Arrow studied her as if he'd never seen her before. They both had dark brown skin with a warm tint. Their skin color and hair color was a gift from their Sioux bloodline. Dawn looked like their mother. Other than the fact he was a few inches taller than her, they looked almost like twins.

He frowned when he saw her red-rimmed eyes. She whispered a prayer of help in Navajo. Did he know what she said? Yea, he did. Did he know other languages? He wanted to get closer to ask. Even if this was a dream, the scenario felt real. If he could get to his sister, then she would heal him. She'd make him whole again. She had the key.

He looked to Radiant Dawn to tell him what he should do to help her.

"No, Weaver. No." Dawn gave another heartbreaking sob.

"Dawn, it's me, Arrow." Maybe his sister couldn't see him. He yelled to her again.

As she faded into the searing light, he broke into a run. Fear gripped his entire being as she faded away. Before he could scream for help, his angel appeared.

His angel bent over him with her face lit in both sorrow and joy. She had returned to him. The fear vanished as quickly as it had come. His shoulders dropped as his despair slipped away.

Angel, as he called her, had light-brown hair with streaks of red and gold. He recognized every beloved aspect of her face. When he was awake, he thought about every inch of her body. He pictured her shoulder-length hair that lovingly curled around her oval face and her soft pale skin. She was simply pretty. Not strikingly beautiful, but pretty in a warm, comforting way. This woman was his angel even if her eyes were a demon red. Her eyes caught his breath and stole his thoughts every time he saw her. The almond-shaped eyes slanted toward her delicate brow. When tears filled them, they glittered.

Tears now shimmered in their depths. He wanted to wipe them away. His angel with demon eyes should never cry. He wondered if when she got angry, maybe those red orbs would spit fire. He smiled at her. She was never angry in his dreams. His angel was only ever sad with hints of delight at seeing him. A huge part of him wanted to see real happiness transform her face.

Arrow realized he'd never seen her smile. He looked at her eyes as the first tear gathered on her thick black lashes.

"They say 'Share moments, share life.' You're every good moment and my life, angel." He spoke to her as she floated before him. She didn't acknowledge him, she never did, but her silence didn't matter. Without her, there truly was no life within him.

"Goodbye," she whispered.

"No!" Arrow screamed as he sat up shivering with cold.

A fine sheen of sweat covered his naked body. He blinked to bring the room into focus. As he wiped at his grimy eyes, he glanced around hoping he was in a new place.

His shoulders dropped. He was still in a cage. Trapped on a water base. Nothing had changed.

Arrow rubbed his arms to warm them. The action didn't help. He stood wobbly from the mattress on the cement floor. His head leaned against the cold metal bars.

Across from him, he could see a nail with keys hanging near the door. The bars in front of him cut him off from the only exit. His cell was one half of the cement chamber. On his half of the room were a bed, a chipped toilet, and a filthy sink. On the other side of the orderly metal bars were a table with a handful of scattered papers around it, a clock, and a wooden door. That door was freedom and answers.

Arrow had sat up the last two nights trying to figure out what was beyond that door. The clock blinked 2:05 a.m. over and over again. He asked himself why he was in a room which was no better than a glorified cage. Why was he forgotten?

He wished he knew why he deserved to be locked away. He'd tried everything to open the metal bars. He'd done everything he could think of to reach the key. Nothing he did worked. No one ever came here either. Did he deserve being here, or was this a mistake?

The idea that maybe his angel was the one to lock him here had come up. She might be real. Sometimes he was sure he remembered her from his past. If she was the one who had locked him in here, then fine, but the least she could do is tell him what he had done.

Frustrated, he pushed away the thought that his angel trapped him. That couldn't be what happened. She would save him. Arrow had dreamed of her so often he was positive she would come back. He didn't believe she was a dream, but a real person like his sister, Dawn. Now, however, as time passed, he began to question his sanity.

Goosebumps rose on his skin, He looked down at his bare frame covered by sweat. Soon he would be able to count his ribs. Was he going to starve to death?

Arrow reached up to see if his long black hair was braided. When his fingers slid up, he bumped his hand against his right eye. He winced. Taking a deep breath, he tried for the twentieth time to recall how he'd bruised his skin. Only a hazy recollection of a stranger dashed across in his mind. Remembering anything was hard when his stomach felt like it digested itself.

Maybe he could come up with a memory.

Anything?

No.

He gave up.

Instead, he tipped his head into his hands. He reviewed what he did know. His name was Guiding Arrow. He was positive. His sister, Radiant Dawn was out there somewhere. She needed him. He was locked in a room with three walls and bars that stopped him from opening the door to freedom. He had the same recurring dream. That was it. That was all he could come up with.

Discouraged, he returned to his torn mattress. He sank down then pulled his legs up and leaned his head on his knees. His arm wrapped around his legs to keep what little body heat he had. He wasn't sure if he shivered because of the temperature in the room, or because of the dream.

The only other thing he knew for certain was he recognized the laughter in his dreams. The dark laughter was his own.

Chapter 3

"This is the kind of crap that happens to me," Nova griped furiously to the eerily silent halls of the water base. How the hell had Clare talked her into this? Where was everyone? Right now, she was ready to scream, cry, and basically make an ass of herself. Good thing she was alone.

Maybe she was *too* alone.

She turned another corner. The cement hallway looked the same as the last one she'd been walking down. This walkway was a bit grayer with round poured concrete cylinders holding the ceiling up, but generally, it was the same. She couldn't decide if she should keep going or turn back. Both emotions fought equally within her.

"Just get on a train and deliver this minicomputer," she mumbled. Dust floated in the air. "You'll be back before you know it." She waved her hand and the particles danced as she did a high-pitch tone to mock Clare's instructions. Making fun of Clare didn't make her feel better. Her voice echoed. Above her, she noticed a massive crack with crumbling stones.

A loud rumble caught her attention as she stepped around the next corner. Behind her, a booming crack made her jump. She spun around. The stone of the ceiling started to crash downward onto the stone floor. Panic and a sense of survival had her bolting away from the crushing rock. She didn't know how long she ran or what hallways she chose, but finally an ache in her side forced her to slow. Gulping for breath, she bent over and pressed her hands to her sides. Tears gathered on her lashes.

Again, she was once more in silence. Glancing around, she shook with fear and desperation. Part of the ceiling of this base just caved in. What should she do? What if it blocked her from getting out? Exhausted from first the train ride, followed by walking this base and now the running, she sat on the floor with a dejected plop.

Nova should've figured this was a mess from the moment she got on the train in Dallas. The crowds had been awful. The train smelled like unwashed feet. Sleep would have improved her mood, but she didn't even get an hour of rest.

The train ride was swift like Clare promised, but this was the first time the sleeping drug didn't work. She became more alert the further she went underground. Being awake was one problem, but being pent up in that tiny private room was another. For hours, all she'd listened to was the swish of the air rushing past the train cars. The never-ending whoosh had made her feel trapped.

Looking down the next hall from where she sat, she saw more stones and dirt piles. A sign said, "Do not enter." That sign would have helped a long, long, time ago, like right before she was almost flattened. Nova dug in the flowered bag secured to her hip. She drew out the hand-sized box computer Clare had asked her to deliver to her brother Dan. Resting the device on her palm, she spoke to the machine. This machine was her only source of help. She prayed that it would guide her to where she needed to go.

"CC." One upside, she pretty much got the hang of the damn minicomputer. The dark green box blinked as if the machine was excited to be of assistance. "Why is it so empty on base two? Where are all the people?"

She didn't think CC would know the answer, but so far Nova had asked the machine numerous questions, and the gadget had known answers to every one of them.

"This exact area of Water Base Two is condemned," CC's mechanical voice began. "According to my most recent data download, this water base has had several cave-ins that killed over twenty people. The H.S.P.C. council announced to all the NED dwellers that this area of the base is off limits. Would you be interested in learning about other water bases with similar problems?"

"You damn piece of plastic. You sent me to a place that's condemned?" Nova held the computer out as if the device might turn around and bite her.

CC answered, but Nova didn't listen. Her eyes scanned the cracks in the ceiling while she pictured stones pummeling her body into tiny pieces. Furious, she clutched CC to her chest as tears welled up a second time. She dashed the wetness away with the back of her hand. She wanted desperately to fall apart. She couldn't do this. She'd told Clare she couldn't do this. Why hadn't Clare listened?

"Well done, Nutty-Nova," she sniffled. "I'm going to be buried alive." Big, fat droplets rolled down her cheeks. "And I still don't have any idea where Archer or Dan is."

Nova couldn't sit in the hall of a disintegrating base. She *had* to get up. She *had* to get out of here. She should've never come here to begin with. Regret added to all the other emotions whirling inside her head.

As she rose from her spot on the floor, she decided there was no way in hell that she was continuing on this fruitless hunt. She took the next cement corridor trying to focus on where she should head next. Pausing, her eyes dropped to the map CC had on the display screen.

When CC navigated her to the rented rooms off one of the shuttle platforms, she should've gone home then. The room Archer had rented was in a scary area where everyone looked like thugs. Finally, as she'd reached the end of her journey, Dan was nowhere to be found. The only person she'd met at the end of her long ride was a cranky, old man. The old guy was no help. He simply told her the rooms were rented for a week. That was maddening enough, but then she had to convince the bad-tempered grandpa that she was related to Dan.

After finally persuading the elderly inn owner to give her a key to the room, Nova found nothing but a bag and a cryptic note. Now, because of her curiosity and that damn letter, she meandered around Water Base Two like she had a death wish.

A piece of garbage drifted by her leg. Nova jumped and stifled a scream. That was a mouse, not garbage. She glanced at CC. The note she'd spotted in the rented room said: "If you're looking for me then come here." At the bottom of the message was a series of numbers.

The figures appeared random, but after typing them in, CC stated that was an address on Water Base Two. Even though her head screamed that it was a bad idea, she had left to find the address any way.

"Turn left. You will have reached your inputted destination."

"Inputted destination my ass." Now that Nova discovered the base was condemned, she moved cautiously. She wished she'd not talked so much before. From this point on she would be mute, so she didn't stimulate an avalanche of rock.

Swearing in her head, she recalled how the old man never told her this wasn't a safe place to go. He was probably afraid of her. Big, bad, scary eyes and all.

"He probably thought, 'I hope that lady with weird eyes dies in a cave-in,'" she whispered crossly. She'd not thought about how she would die someday, but Nova didn't figure an abandoned area of underground homes was the place she wanted to be buried. Being buried anywhere sucked donkey balls, especially if she was buried alive.

Nova should've gone home when Dan wasn't there to greet her. Why had she believed she could go looking for him? Oh, that's right, because she was an idiot, a curious idiot.

After she tucked CC back into her carrying case, she spotted hand-written numbers on a metal door to her left. The note said if Dan got here, he should meet Archer at this address. Dan would have done what Nova had done.

So… if Dan was looking for missing Archer, and he said to come here, then this place was probably safe. A bark of laughter tumbled from her lips. This wasn't safe. This was an area which might cave in on her. Both Archer and Dan were nowhere around. This was about as far from safe as she could get.

"Throw in some thieves, maybe a rapist, and I'd be all set." Her hand touched the doorknob. She paused. Open or not open? Unrecognizable emotions inside of her urged her on. What was this feeling? Hope? Yes, optimism filled her. She would find Dan, then give him CC. Once Dan had CC, he could find Clare's missing husband. Soon Sky would be better. Clare insisted that everything that had happened was all for Sky. From everything that Clare had shown her in the lab, it did appear that the blood sample was imperative.

Another thunder of sound rolled down the hall. The noise made her shrink toward the door. Her eyes scanned the ceiling. She could simply check then get out of here as fast as possible.

Praying that Dan was on the other side, she turned the knob and pushed the door with all of her hundred and fifteen pounds. She was small but determined. The door didn't budge. Nova put her entire upper body to the metal to get the hinges to give. The scraping sound made her cringe. Once the opening was wide enough for her to pass, she stumbled in. The interior of the room made her heart fall to her stomach.

Empty.

The place looked as deserted as everywhere else Nova had been today. A single hysterical laugh escaped her.

A lone desk in the corner had lost two legs and tipped over. A chair missing its cushions sat on its side next to an empty work table. Absently, she scanned the room.

Nothing.

As she crossed over scattered papers on the floor, behind the door was a metal cabinet with a crowbar next to the bottom. The metal at the lower part of the enclosure looked corroded. There was a smattering of red dust on the floor.

"CC. Do you know what this room was for when the base was fully operational?"

Why did she even ask? Having an answer wasn't going to help. She wasn't a detective. She was a research assistant. *Assistant* being the important word here. Assistants required bosses. She wasn't up to solving a mystery all by herself. An H.S.P.C. agent could find Archer. A real agent should be doing this, like Dan. If Dan wasn't here, it was time to go.

She frowned when she considered what Clare would say when she returned with CC.

"Ah crap-cookies, I'm going to make a pregnant woman cry *again*." But what else could she do? What if this whole place caved in?

"I have no data on that subject. Please wait," CC announced after blinking.

"Like hell I'm going to wait."

Just as Nova had CC next to her pouch, a light flashed out of a small black box mounted to the top. Nova gasped as she held up the machine to see the top from another angle. Did this device take a picture? Black spots blocked her vision. She'd assumed the black box was a battery. Apparently, she was wrong. She *hated* when she was wrong.

When the spots in her vision cleared, the word "loading" flashed in white letters on the screen. The block lettering gave her a headache. She rubbed her forehead.

While she waited, Nova did a mental recap of what she faced. In a small way, going over her present situation gave her the illusion of control. It was an illusion, she understood that, but going over problems comforted her. Centering herself helped.

Alright. So currently, she was in a condemned part of a water base. She had no clue where Archer and Dan were. CC was her only help, but the annoying computer couldn't tell her what she needed to know. Especially if Nova didn't know the proper questions. All in all, she figured now was the time to quit.

"On the way home, I can write out an apology to Clare." Nova turned around to step toward the exit. "Then I'll hide in my room while she reads it."

As she moved past the broken desk, she paused. If Nova ever went missing, her brother would save her. Archer did piss her off as siblings sometimes do, but they loved each other. Could someone have taken him? And what about Dan? Nova shook her head. Dan was a highly trained agent. Both men had skills and a surly disposition. Dan and Archer were fighters. No one could take them. They were probably somewhere screwing around and scaring the bejesus out of Clare.

"I'm going to tell Dad that Archer made his pregnant wife cry." Nova's hands rose to the straps on her backpack. The two of them might be at headquarters this very moment. Most likely they would be laughing at her and Clare for worrying. Perhaps they gave Clare the blood sample that Archer was supposed to retrieve. Her trip was a fool's errand.

"I'm getting the hell out of here. Staying on a condemned base is what a lunatic would do." Nova began to walk to the exit as she took one last glance around. A door next to the metal cabinet caught her eye. Her curiosity stirred. The door was rough, sturdy wood. What if Dan or Archer were behind that door? She doubted it, but she could merely peek in.

Nova took a few steps closer as she put CC away in her backpack. Her eyes lifted to the broken lock next to the polished handle. The door looked like someone had used a small amount of explosives to break the latch. The wood splintered. Char marks dotted areas around the frame. Whoever had opened it before had no finesse. Someone had desperately wanted to enter. They evidently did whatever they had to, even if it meant using explosives. Using explosives, even a small amount was a bad idea on an underground base.

Curiosity moved from stirring to swirling to bubbling. Why would someone go to all the trouble to break the lock and risk getting flattened? What was on the other side?

Nova put her palm flat on the hardwood. She had lived her whole life in the H.S.P.C. Headquarters, most of the time hidden in the basement doing archival research. She'd never left HQ before. She'd never made any decisions of her own until now. This was all on her. In this moment, she wasn't an assistant. Nova was the boss.

Her hand paused a second longer. She could make some bad choices. She could find herself in deep trouble.

"This is probably why they call me Nutty-Nova." Her palm flexed. The door swung open.

Chapter 4

Was that a flash of light? Arrow stood up and rushed to the front of the cage. Hope blossomed. He waited for the light to come again. He waited on pins and needles. The flash might mean help. His eyes stared intently at the door.

Nothing.

His ears strained to recognize a familiar sound. He prayed he would hear someone.

"Hello? Help?" His voice seemed strangely loud in the cell.

Nothing.

Maybe he imagined the flash. Desperation and hunger could be causing him to lose his mind.

His eyes pierced the door. Reaching out, he grabbed the bars on either side of his head. His mouth opened to yell again for help then he froze. What if the person on the other side of the door wasn't here to help him? Maybe on the other side was the person who stuck him in here.

Arrow sighed. No sounds, no door opening, no one saving him. He was fooling himself. Leaning his forehand onto the bars, he closed his eyes. He prayed to the Great Spirit.

As soon as he heard the swish of the door opening, his eyes popped open.

Standing in the open doorway stood the angel. She didn't appear to him how she regularly looked in his dreams, but he recognized her. Those eyes, yea, he would never be able to forget them. The orbs were as dark and rich as red wine. They haunted him when he first dreamed about her.

The angel stood in the doorway gaping at him. Her jaw looked like her bottom lip might reach the floor. A grin hovered around his mouth. Her comical expression amused him. She wore ripped blue jeans and a tan sweater that made her hair seem less red-brown and more gold-brown. Her attire seemed off. The clothes of a celestial being should be grand.

When she didn't speak, he caught the fact that he stood there not saying anything either. Was she real or a vision? Words clogged his throat. She mesmerized him. In his dreams, she was merely pretty, but seeing her before him, he didn't think "pretty" did her justice. She was incredible, and she was… short.

A smile spread on his lips at her petite size. She couldn't be more than five-foot-nothing. He wanted to scoop her up. Her ruby red eyes bounce over the room. With eyes as red as that, maybe picking her up wasn't the best idea.

Reaching the end of her stunned shock, and maybe the end of her ability to stand perfectly frozen, she spoke. Her voice was exactly like in Arrow's dreams, only this time when the low tone washed over him, it brought his body heat up. If he'd been cold before, she chased that away with a few simple syllables.

"I should've fucking figured." She threw her arms up in the air as if thoroughly exasperated. "This is the kind of crap that happens to me."

She was the most enchanting thing he'd ever seen.

"I'm so happy you came to save me." He finally dug up words. He was amazed at how correct that sentence was. Arrow was so over-the-top excited to see her he could barely contain his joy. He forced himself not to skip up and down like a child receiving a present. Now that she was here, everything would be better. Even if he died here, he'd be ecstatic as long as she was with him.

"And you're out of your mind." She rubbed her forehead. "That's about right."

Arrow chose his next words carefully as he hid his amusement. He was positive she wouldn't welcome the term adorable.

"I'm not crazy."

"No one's ever crazy. It's only me, right? What the hell would I know about anything? You say I've come here to save you so that must be correct. I'm the one that doesn't remember, is that it?" While shoving some of her hair off her shoulder, she glared at him. Her expressive eyes glinted an orange-red. Around the centers, the color was amber. They whispered deep meaning to his soul.

"I remember you." He smiled a flash of his teeth.

"Let me make this clear." She crossed her arms over her chest. "Pay attention." Arrow's eyes flew up to her face. "I didn't come here to save you. I don't know you. I didn't know I would be here." She started addressing him, but then she turned to pace in front of the bars. She seemed to have forgotten he was there as she marched back and forth. "I should've known I'd meet a lunatic in a locked room. That's how this crap goes for me. This couldn't have been a smooth trip where I find Dan, then go home." She began to mumble to herself. He didn't mind the way her hips swayed. "Now what am I supposed to do?" She turned back to him.

He wanted to tell his angel to calm down, but he didn't think she would appreciate that.

Watching her pacing, he evaluated what she'd told him. She acted as if she didn't know him. That was impossible. She was the only thing he did know other than his sister.

"You didn't come for me?"

"No, I came here looking for my brother, Archer. He's missing. And I'm looking for Dan. I don't even know you." She spat the word *you* at him. He took a hasty step back from the bars.

"But I know you." If that wasn't true, then another part of his life didn't make sense. She was his angel. He was sure of that if nothing else.

"Right." Her voice dripped with sarcasm. "So, sorry that I'm late for our important business meeting. I was having tea and cookies with a group of harvesters and it went long." She shook her head.

He ignored the snarky comment. He didn't even understand it anyway.

"I know you." He remained adamant. How could he know her and she not know him? He wrinkled his brow as he tried to remember where they'd met for the first time. They met when… his memory remained stubbornly blank.

"No, you don't." Her mulishness was cute, but her tenacity made him think about everything he was certain of. It was a blow to realize he might've created an imaginary relationship.

"You're my angel with demon eyes."

That was the wrong thing to say. His angel whirled around as both her hands slapped on her hips. The red of her irises glimmered. Yes, she was positively a spitfire. He would have to remember never to call her eyes demon-like again. Either that or never refer to her as an angel.

"If you call my eyes demon again, I'll make sure you die on the other side of those bars."

Yes, definitely don't make any comments about her uniquely colored eyes.

As she scowled, he recognized her words as an empty threat. She would never hurt him. Empty or not, he felt bad. He couldn't meet her stare.

"I'm sorry. Your eyes are beautiful." He glanced up at her.

Her glare could've shot flames at him. Her eyes studied his face, so he kept his features contrite. She was the size of a pixy. He could envision her with wings. Maybe a magic wand. She was *his* angel. No matter what she said, he knew her. A part of him, deep in his soul, identified her as his other half. His match.

She threw up her hands again in agitation.

"Sweet son-of-a-fucking-polar-bear! You're out of your ever-loving mind." Her feet stomped on the stones as she returned to pacing.

He couldn't imagine a sweet angel swearing like that. He didn't even know what that meant.

"I'm happy you're here." He gave her a small smile. So, what if he didn't understand? "I was worried you wouldn't come for me." He looked expectantly at her. He didn't care what the situation was. He was simply happy. In some way, deep down, he was sure he'd been waiting for her his whole life.

"For the last time, I don't know you." Each word she uttered was louder than the last. By the end of her sentence, Arrow had backed away from the bars to the mattress. He hid his smile. He loved all the passion in her. He wondered if she yelled a lot, or if she happened to be in a thunderstorm mood just now.

She began to pace, then she halted. This time her eyes traveled over Arrow's body. He could feel her eyes drinking him in. Her eyes paused on his crotch. They grew wide. His skin heated under her gaze. If she wanted to, he'd let her stare at him forever.

"I can't think with you dressed like that."

"I'm not dressed. I'm naked."

"Exactly. Could you put on some clothes?"

Arrow hid his chuckle by coughing.

"I'm locked in a cage. I don't have any clothes. I thought you might bring me some when you came for me."

For the first time, Arrow considered what he looked like standing there. Did he look scary? Was he frightening her? He had bruises on his face. Standing here naked was probably questionable.

The more he reviewed his current situation, the more he couldn't blame her for not trusting him. If she really didn't know him, then he probably did look suspect. Who would trust a man standing bruised and naked in a cage?

She stamped her tiny foot. "I told you I didn't come to—"

Arrow cut her off. "You're right." He would placate her. Whatever she wanted to believe was fine with him. After he was freed from this cage, then they could work out how they had met before. "We don't know each other. It's nice to meet you, stranger-I've-never-met-before."

"Thank you." She sighed. She seemed to become friendlier when he agreed with her. He would have to remember that for the future.

"It really is nice to meet you, my angel." He didn't want to irritate her so much that she might leave in a furious rush. If they didn't know each other, he didn't care. She was here. She was his savior. That's all he needed. With her here, he didn't care if he was in a cage hungry and cold. She was his sunshine and a warm meal.

"Angel?" She cocked her head to the side as her eyes narrowed. He hoped she didn't think he was teasing her. Arrow picked his next words carefully.

"Do you think you could possibly, let me out? I've been here awhile, I think. I want to go with you." He smiled at her which only seemed to make her more baffled. Her head flipped back as if she was looking for someone he was addressing behind her. He didn't point out that the room was empty except for them, even though he wanted to.

"It's a bad day when I'm the sanest person in the room. Who are you?"

Chapter 5

"My name is Guiding Arrow." He smiled.

She didn't.

Her palm scrubbed her forehead. Leave it to her to meet a man in a locked room. A sexy, naked, *crazy* man in a locked room. She had to come up with what to do. First, she'd find out who he was and then… what?

He gazed at her with those damn intense black eyes that seemed to speak to her soul. All his emotions danced on display in those soulful depths. She couldn't look at him too much longer and not lose her mind. Instead, she briefly glanced at the papers spread out on the desk next to her. A couple of sentences on them poked at her.

"Guiding Arrow? Is that a stupid made-up name? Couldn't you tell me your real name? I don't see why you'd give me a fake name anyway." She spoke absently. They would never get anywhere if he started off by lying. She scanned the documents, but then her eyes strayed to his exposed sexual organs. His skin looked like tan silk.

Besides the strange surge of compassion that had appeared upon meeting him, there was another emotion that had shown up as well. Her sexual side, which was always dormant, seemed to have awoken around him as well. Maybe it was because he was naked. She licked her lips. Was she thinking about sex? She shook her head to expel the thoughts.

Nova fingered a few papers on the desk top. She would ignore him and work on solving this new problem. What did someone do with a naked man?

Her eyes flipped up to his. Wrong question, *so wrong*.

"That's my real name. You don't see me saying your name is stupid." Arrow lifted one eyebrow. "You can trust me. I wouldn't lie." A smirk pranced across his lips. How could he stand there and laugh? Didn't he realize how bad this situation was?

"'Trust me,' says the man in the locked room." Pausing in front of some of the scattered papers, she crouched down to pick up a few sheets on the floor. She recognized some of the notes jotted in neat script on the dirty articles. "You don't know my name, so you can't say if it's stupid."

Her eyes strayed back to him and traveled from the top of his naked head to his naked toes. *Crap, that was one too many "naked."*

She tried to concentrate. Long, thick, healthy black hair was intricately braided, eyes like polished black marble, white teeth, soft pink lips. Very kissable. Nova frowned. She was supposed to problem-solve, not do whatever she was doing.

"It's not a locked room. This is a cage." He gave her another heart-stopping smile. She should tell him to quit that. Couldn't he see that now was not the time to grin like a fool? She had to figure out what to do with him.

"This has four walls. This is a room. A cage would have bars on all sides," she responded while she studied the metal bars that made up the door. Cage or locked room didn't matter, what counted was why he was in there.

"You're right, my angel. This is a locked room. What's your name? I want to know while we discuss my surroundings." Another sweet smile lit his face.

Her eyes looked at the door behind her, then flipped back to the bars. Her palm rubbed her forehead. This poor man, though amiable, wasn't her problem. Her dilemma was a missing Archer and a missing Dan. Not a desirable male in a locked room with eyes that stirred lust. She didn't even have lust for him to stir, she reminded herself.

As he continued to wait for her to give her name, he leaned toward the bars. All those muscles rippled under his smooth skin. What now? Giving him her name wouldn't hurt anything, would it?

"My name's Nova."

"I could never say Nova was stupid." His voice was a husky rumble. "A name as beautiful as that is impossible to make fun of." He let a small smile kick up one side of his mouth. Was this guy for real?

She glared. She supposed someone could be daft *and* charming.

Nova tugged CC back out of her bag. Maybe the computer could help. She didn't have any other ideas.

"CC. Could you analyze the male in front of me?"

"Exact analysis cannot be done without a blood sample." The green box gave a mechanical answer.

"Figures," Nova griped. Now what should she ask?

"What is that?" Arrow asked.

Before she could answer his question, a bright flash of light made him stumble forward. Dazed, he tipped his head onto the bars. Black spots drifted past Nova's vision again. Blinking, she tried to bring the room back into focus.

"I'm going to go blind if this damn—" Nova snapped her lips shut when the minicomputer started speaking again in a clear emotionless tone.

"General Analysis is as follows. The human subject is male. His age is estimated at between twenty and thirty. His facial features, body, and skin type would dictate he is of Native American descent. The Native Americans, also known as American Indians, made up about 5.2 million in the height of their population. The current population is unknown. Male subject has loss two toes on his right foot. Uneven weight distribution has caused knee problems."

"That thing can't know if I have knee problems." Arrow rolled his eyes to the ceiling. "What is that?"

"Shush." She shook her head at the caged stranger. Time to work. She would keep her head on fixing the predicament of what to do with this guy. Leaning on the bars, she decided to do a full assessment. She needed to be more research assistant if she was going to get through this bizarre position. Her eyes needed to stay looking at CC and not on his impressive... her eyes dropped. His was much bigger than Troy's.

"Subject weights approximately a hundred and eighty pounds. He is six feet tall."

"I'm six one."

Her eyes popped to his face. His eyes twinkled. Did he catch her looking?

"Will you shut your face hole? I'm listening to this."

Arrow gave a bark of surprised laughter and the sound brought her eyes up.

"I'm pretty sure no one has ever said 'shut your face hole' to me before."

Nova had the urge to smile back. She also had the urge to smooth her hand over the hard plains of his toned chest, as well. Just some simple research on how he would like the feel of her. She frowned. What was she doing? He was a wounded prisoner, not a sexual playmate.

The researcher in her should make some guesses on how long he'd been without food. Don't look at his abs. Her eyes betrayed her. So much for her intention to keep all this clinical. She studied the toned 'v' that was beautifully muscled as it headed toward his dick a second time.

"What are you staring at?" He caught her ogling him again. Ah crap-monkey, what was wrong with her?

"I was thinking 'well cared for' is what I'd write if I was making notes." That was a close call. Now back to solving this mystery. Why would someone care for him, then leave him in a locked room in a base that was caving in? Nova wished Clare was here to help her come up with a hypothesis. What did he do before he was tossed into this room? He couldn't have been in here for long. His chest was ripped with powerful toned flesh. Even his stomach was sleek and flat, not like that of a gaunt captive.

"Subject has damage to his right eye. Swelling is occurring," CC continued. "Further testing required. An entry wound on his left thigh has a minor infection. Entry wound could have been caused by a needle injection. No other injuries can be assessed at this time. No further analysis without a blood sample."

Surprise made her head jerk down. Nova studied his thigh. CC was right. On the left side of his muscular leg, she could see a red and inflamed circle. A small hole was in the center.

Nova had given many shots to Snow Flu patients over the years. She knew an injection site when she saw one.

Her heart went out to him even though she reminded herself this wasn't her problem. Her gut twisted. Empathy wasn't a part of her emotional spinning wheel, but she was sure that's what she felt. She cared about this man's plight.

Nova spun away from Arrow and glanced at the documents on the floor. She picked up one. If he was injected with a drug, she had a pretty good guess what it could be. She recognized this formula.

She looked to Arrow. Their eyes met. Her forehead furrowed.

"What happened to me?" His deep voice turned whisper soft as he looked down at the injection site.

"Unfortunately, I think it's the Clean Slate Series."

Chapter 6

"What's the Clean Slate Series?" Arrow demanded. He could barely keep his voice calm. The idea that he'd been poisoned caused fear to take over his brain. All his happiness at seeing her and thinking he was rescued ran off.

She turned away from him. She was probably uncomfortable with his intense stare, but he couldn't help it. He was scared. What the hell happened to him? Who did this? What was in his body?

She spread out the papers on the desk in a neat row then held out her talking machine. Her hands grasped the clumsy-looking metal box. Attached at the top, was a square black case. When she held the strange item up to her face, she wrapped her small fingers around the back. Her eyes stayed glued above the desk as if the answers to all her questions floated there.

"CC. Is this the formula for CS3000?" Abruptly, the device flashed again. Nova swayed as if dizzy. Now she would answer him. She *had* to answer him.

Arrow's stomach started to roll due to the flashing light. His palms rubbed his eyes.

"This is not the formula for CS3000," the machine responded. For a moment, he relaxed, maybe she was wrong and he hadn't been injected with whatever she was talking about. "This formula is the antidote to CS2000. I calculate this formula is not finished."

His hand went to the hole in his thigh. His thumb brushed the wound.

"Tell me what CS2000 is," he commanded.

"This isn't the type of news people like to get." Nova wouldn't look at him. She picked up a few more papers studying the notes. Arrow came closer to the bars. His hands gripped them tightly on either side of his head. Why didn't she answer him?

"Am I going to die?" He couldn't die. He just met Nova. His life couldn't end until he and Nova had many long and happy years together.

"No, don't joke."

"Joke?" He was as far away from joking as he could get. "Just tell me, what is CS2000?"

Nova visibly swallowed. He didn't know her, but that wasn't a good sign when anyone did it.

"CS2000 is—" the box started to explain, but Nova pressed a button and the machine went silent.

"Why did you turn off the talking machine?" He began to prowl the tiny space at the front of the cage.

"CC will talk for over an hour about CS2000. This minicomputer is filled with information, too much, like its maker. I'll give the short version which is enough. Honest."

"'Honest,' says the woman who won't let me out of this cage." Arrows eyes narrowed. She wasn't going to give him a brush off answer. He wanted to know it all. His fingers touched the damaged skin around the injection site. He was unable to accept the hole was there.

"You're not going to die. CS2000 is part of what the H.S.P.C. calls the Clean Slate Series. This is a sequence of drugs designed to erase people's memories. The creator had a good reason for making the first drug, but over the years there've been perverted versions. CS3000 is the original. The drug removes your memories for a short amount of time. For everyone, it's a different length of time. It can help with dealing with moving underground, or for dealing with cave-ins or Snow Flu. Once the memories come back, they're not as traumatic. CS4000 removes your memories permanently. You'll never get them back."

"What about CS2000." That was the one he wanted to know about. Telling him about the others was unnecessary.

"Last is CS2000. That's the one I'm guessing you were given." She paused. "Remember *guessing* is the important word here." She shook her head. "That drug removes your memories, but you can have them back with the antidote. Antidotes are typically created out of the drug. You have to get the remedy that matches the drug, or your brain doesn't work right. I've seen the drug mess with people if given the wrong cure." She took a breath. When she finished, she peeked up at him. "Don't panic."

Damn straight he would panic. He would freak out. Someone had taken his memories. She was basically saying someone stole his past.

Arrow looked down at his leg, but when Nova didn't speak again, he glanced back at her. This woman was meant to save him so the sooner she accepted that fact, the better. Once free, she could tell him what they would do next. He believed in her one hundred percent.

"How do I get the antidote? I mean, how do I get the right cure?"

"You have to find the person who gave the original drug to you. Find them and hope they have the remedy.

Once you've got the cure, then you get injected again. After that, everything comes back. You'll be however you were before."

His face fell. The only thing he knew was his name. Terror flooded him. Air was no longer filling his lungs. He choked on his own breath. He thought it was bad enough to be in a cage, but this was much worse. Up to this point, he thought his lack of memories was due to the bruises on his face. He assumed he had a head injury, not that he'd been drugged.

"What now?" He tried to keep his voice calm, but his tone had a clear sharp snap.

"I'm thinking." Her enchanting red eyes roamed all over him. What was there to think about?

He looked at her expectantly while he waited. She would help him. He felt it in his soul.

Standing naked in a cage waiting for her to make up her mind caused anxiety to twist through his stomach.

Nova picked up a few more papers studying the notes. "Why would someone steal your memories? What do you know? Are you dangerous?"

"Why are you asking me?"

She didn't answer and instead she frowned at the desk and talked to herself. "What would Clare do?" she mumbled. "What would Gears do? What would Luna say?"

"Nova?" He tried to get her attention. Briefly, he considered her name. He'd been calling her "angel" in his head for so long that calling her by her real name felt funny on his lips.

She kept talking to herself. "Archer would tell me not to do it. I can't trust my intuition. I'm nuts."

"Nova." His voice was louder this time. Finally, her eyes jumped to his. She bit her bottom lip. He would have to make another attempt to sway her. "Nova, could you please let me out? I promise I won't hurt you. I trust you. I'm asking for your trust in return." It was odd she didn't want to free him. Couldn't she see how he would never hurt her? Couldn't she see how cold and alone he was? He needed her in so many ways. She *had* to see it.

Her palm scrubbed her forehead.

"What if someone put you in there because you're dangerous?" Her brow wrinkled. She began to move like a rubber ball bouncing back and forth. "What if the person who put you in there comes back here and finds me? That's not going to happen because I've not seen anyone on the base. Never mind about that." She paused. "But what if the person who put you in there forgot about you? What if they never come back and you starve? You dying isn't my problem. Is this my problem? Or I might feel guilty when I get home knowing that you died because I didn't let you out. I could get depressed." She stopped. "I can't deal with another bout of depression. I just got better. Then again, if I'm dead because you killed me, then I wouldn't be depressed." She spun on her heels. Her eyes looked at him again as if remembering he was here. "I can't be depressed if I'm dead? But how can I live if I'm guilty?"

Arrow wanted her to speak to him, not herself. He was right here. She seemed to ignore him, so he responded. He would join her private conversation even if he wasn't sure what she was talking about.

"They say, 'Understanding comes with time.'" The saying was all he could think of.

"What?" She kept walking. "Who is *they*?"

His mouth opened, but as soon as she looked at him with those captivating red eyes, he forgot what they'd been talking about.

"I don't know."

"I think that's an ad for *Time* magazine. I worked in archives in the basement of HQ." Nova shook her head. "You don't need to quote ads. Instead, we need to figure this out. This all comes down to who put you in there and why? Is anyone coming back here? Ever? Why did they steal your memories?"

It cheered him that she used the word "we." She would help him.

"I don't know who put me in here. And I don't think anyone is coming to get me. I think the place is caving in around me. I can hear the crumbling sounds. I need you. Help me, Nova. You're my only hope."

"Ah crap-shoot, not this again." She hugged her arms around herself. "Again, with the 'only hope.' Everyone is starting to sound like *Star Wars'* characters."

He wanted to tell her everything would be okay, but he didn't want to lie. And he really didn't know what *Star Wars* was.

"Can you remember who gave you the black eye?"

How was he going to explain that he didn't know dreams from reality?

"A man with blue eyes like the ocean hit me. I don't think he put me in here, but I believe he took my sister. I have to find my sister, Dawn. If I get out of here, I hope to find her. I remember her."

"I doubt you've ever seen the ocean, so you wouldn't know how blue it is," Nova grumbled.

The way her eyes softened made him think she cared. He loved that she tried to help him even if she was begrudging about it. "Is that all you remember? It's not much."

"I can't remember anything about how I got here or anything before waking up in this cage. All I have is strange dreams. The only thing I was sure of was that my sister needs me. I thought I knew you because you've come to me in my dreams." He glared at her when she opened her mouth.

She closed her lips.

"And I have no clothes or food. If you leave, then I'll die. I know you won't leave me here to die, angel. You're the only thing I have. You're my everything."

The silence that followed made the room seem colder somehow. There was a huge gap between them. Arrow waited for her to jump across the figurative expanse. Nova was meant to save him.

"Say something." He reached a breaking point.

"That's unfortunate. *Me* being someone's 'everything' is as bad as me being someone's 'only hope.'"

His shoulders slumped, breaking eye contact.

"Pay attention." She got his eyes to come back to her face. "I don't think I'm the right person to help you. You'll have to figure out the memory problem on your own, either that or let it go and—"

"You want me to let go of my memories?" He cut her off. "You're crazy. Letting go of my entire past isn't like letting go of a favorite shirt or pants."

"I'm not crazy," she snapped back. Her eyes blazed. "I didn't mean 'let it go' like that." Nova looked down at CC. "I'll free you, but you go your way. I'll leave first and go my way. I can't help you anymore after this. Letting you out doesn't mean I trust you. Got it?"

"Got it." Relief washed through him.

Nova studied the metal bars that made up the door.

"How do you expect me to let you out of here without a key?" Her fingertips touched the lock. "Of course, you must have some idea, you've been asking me to let you out for the better part of an hour."

Arrow inclined his head toward the door. "The keys are on the nail where you came in. I'm sure those are the keys. I pray to the Great Spirit they are."

Nova walked behind the partially opened wooden door. On a bent nail, there was a small set of keys on a metal loop. Flipping the keys through her fingers, she studied each one.

"Which one?" She held them up.

"Try them all. I'm sure one will work."

Nova returned to the door and began to fiddle with the keys. The second one was effective. The catch released. Her hands shook as the door swung open. Even scared, she didn't stop. He had to give it to her. She was brave. Her whole body tensed like he might attack her at any moment. She didn't know it yet, but he would never hurt her. Never.

Arrow swiftly stepped out of his half of the room. At last, freedom. He didn't have his memories but he was no longer caged, and that was something.

Chapter 7

He was taller than she was prepared for. She stepped back ready to run if he did anything threatening.

"See, angel?" Arrow shook his head at her as he headed toward the door she'd come through. "I'm leaving. I'm going my way." He paused at the door giving a relaxed grin. Was this all a big joke to him? An eye-catching smile graced his features just like before. "You know, you're jumpy."

"'Jumpy' says the man who was a few moments ago panicked over a needle injection." Now that she let him out, he sounded relaxed. He sounded like himself. She silently chuckled to herself. She'd never met him before, so how would she know what his usual-self was?

"I wasn't panicking."

"Potato, potatoes." She shooed him toward the other room. She wasn't going to stand here talking to a naked man all night. Half a night was her limit. Besides, anyone with a smile like his should never be allowed to be naked in the first place.

"Not potato, potatoes. More like potato, needle injection."

Nova shooed him again. Why did they debate irrelevant topics? Was he picking on her to get a rise out of her? His dopey grin indicated that's what he was doing.

Arrow headed straight into the other room. He began to scan the cabinet with the crowbar. She squeezed past him careful not to brush against his muscled back.

When she got to the door that let out into the hallway, she paused. Arrow was crouched next to the cabinet. He used the crowbar to bend the metal. She got a healthy view of all that male flesh tightening. She didn't know that butts could have dimples. After he had opened the door, he yanked out a navy-blue shirt.

"Nova, you're right. I panicked. But now that I got my freedom and a shirt, I'm alright. I don't generally worry about things. I'm a free spirit."

"How would you know?" Did he know his clothes were in there? Maybe some of his memories remained intact. He might've been lying from the beginning. She supposed if he had lied then it didn't matter. "I'm not dead, so… good enough," she mumbled to herself as she walked to the metal cabinet door. On a whim, she popped one of the keys into the lock. The idea was a hunch, but it paid off. The dilapidated door swung free.

Arrow didn't pay her any attention as he pulled on the shirt. He fished out a pair of worn boots with dirty gray socks stuffed inside of them.

"It appears you lost a few pounds," Nova commented as Arrow slipped on a pair of cargo pants. They drooped on his hips.

"Maybe these aren't my clothes. I saw them sticking out, and I thought, 'Hey, why not try *not* being naked.'" He tugged on the socks.

"Yeah, try that." Maybe he was right. These might not be his clothes. She still hadn't figured out why someone used a small set of explosives, opened a door, stole this man's memories, then left him to die. None of this mattered. She'd never see him again. What she should be solving was what to say to Clare when she returned with CC, no Archer, no Dan, and no blood sample.

When Arrow laced up the boots, she shifted around him. As she opened a hidden keypad on CC, she hesitated at the door that exited into the hall.

"How do we get out of here?" Arrow stood.

"What do you mean *we*? You do your thing. I do mine. Remember?" She typed a request for the directions to her rented room. "I can't help you anymore." She had her own problems.

"Got it." A lazy smile hung on his lips.

"Good." This time she didn't let his attractive mouth affect her. She was leaving without him. No amount of his good looks was going to change her mind. She couldn't trust him. Even if she did think him handsome, that meant nothing if he was sneaky and underhanded.

Nova paused in the doorway. Would he ever get his memories back? She sighed. Not her issue.

"I'll wait here. You can leave." He motioned to the door. "Thank you for letting me out. Nice to meet you, angel." Arrow headed over to the chair missing its cushion.

After righting the chair, he delicately perched on the edge as if he was king of the world. She seethed at his nonchalant attitude. Too bad the chair didn't break. That would've made her day.

"My name's Nova, not angel." A part of her screamed she couldn't leave him like this. She ruthlessly crushed down the flare-up of emotion. She was well practiced at that.

"Yea, goodbye, Nova." He made another wave at the door with his left hand. The gesture was regal. He nodded when she didn't start to walk right away.

Annoyed, Nova snapped her back straight then spun on her heels. Fine. If he didn't need her, then she didn't care if he had to walk about forever lost on this water base. As far as she was concerned, she'd done right by him. She was leaving before anything else happened.

Nova took one last peek behind her as she pushed the door wider. Was she hoping he would beg her to help him find his way? Glancing over her shoulder, she saw him lean back in his chair. *Beg me*, she thought over and over again. She hated how his eyes danced. She was sure no one ever looked at her as if she was hilarious. Her eyes were too scary for that.

He didn't ask her for help. He didn't beg. In her head, she swore. Well, good riddance. Nova sauntered through the original door she'd come in.

"There is no way to peace," she mumbled as she stepped out into the hallway. "Peace is the way." She wasn't looking forward to more scary cave-ins, dirt, and mice. Her feet ached simply thinking about her hike back.

Nova paused. CC had the word "loading" written across the screen. She must have not given the right request. She cleared the screen with the press of a button. She asked CC to give her navigational commands back to her rented room. Verbal cues would be easier. If CC was telling her when to turn, traveling might be faster.

CC's screen popped up directions and a map. The word "loading" scrolled across the screen again. Waiting for the damn thing to work, she tipped the device upside down. There was a small door on the bottom. As she was fiddling with the machine, Arrow jogged around the corner.

"Ha!" She exclaimed.

Arrow came to a dead halt. She didn't even try to hide her triumphant smile. Nova had been positive that he wouldn't be able to find his way out of here. If he truly had no memories, then he would need her to navigate. Seeing him made her feel better. Maybe he hadn't lied to her.

"I was right. You can't get out of here without me. You need to follow me." She put on her best mightier-than-thou face. Her smug look was ruined by having to raise her chin to look at him.

"Of course, you were right." Arrow shrugged. "I was going to follow you. I don't have any memories." He tipped his head to the side. His long braid flopped over his shoulder. "Did you think I was going to wander around here all night? I need you, angel."

Nova did like hearing she was right, but he was a tad too sneaky for her. Just as she was about to tell him that, a horrible boom reverberated down the hall. Both their eyes widened.

Arrow's face contorted to fear. A large crack in the ceiling started to break apart above their heads. Nova froze in terror. She couldn't die, not like this.

In what felt like slow motion, Arrow's arms curved along her waist. His weight propelled her out of the way of the cascading cement. As she struck the wall behind her, she wanted to tell him this was his fault. Pain sliced through her head before the words popped out of her mouth. Damn, she didn't get the chance to say, "I was right."

Chapter 8

"Turn right onto shuttle platform. Reach destination rented room twenty-two."

Arrow's eyes dropped to the computer screen in his left hand. After a second, he glanced at the smattering of dubious-looking people on the shuttle platform ahead of him. He'd seen no one on the grueling walk through the broken water base. For the first time seeing anyone was disconcerting.

As he approached the platform, he hugged Nova's unconscious body tighter to his chest. After he tightened his grip on her, he quickly hid the talking machine under the arm supporting Nova's legs. No one appeared as if they'd help them, so he shuffled on with his eyes averted. Best not to draw attention to them in any way. Using his peripheral vision, he tried to get a feel for the place.

In some ways, a lot of the individuals around them seemed worse off than he did. A man, thin as a new tree branch, slumped against one of the brick walls. The snoozing vagabond had eerie golden strings floating from his chest. The strings must be from Arrow's imagination. The rope conjured his dream, but he refused to investigate.

Nova came first. He needed a place where they would be safe for a while.

Hunger and exhaustion wrestled his shoulders toward the floor. Right now, he didn't think he had enough energy to walk much longer, but he trudged on. The machine stated he was at his destination. To his left was an open area where the shuttles could park for pick up, but currently no shuttles had arrived. Only empty train tracks sat lonely on that side. Past them, dark tunnels loomed. The rooms he was guided to must be the set of doors he spied on his right. Every few feet sat a door with a lamp that punctuated the space between them. On each door, he noticed hand-painted numbers. The numbers seemed to pick up in the twenties. He shifted Nova in his arms as he counted down to room twenty-two.

Ahead of him, an old analog clock glowed 2:05 a.m. It was past two in the morning? A hushed groan tumbled from his lips.

Arrow paused when he reached the door marked with the right number. Now to get in. This is where Nova was heading. She'd put this destination into her talking machine, so this must be somewhere safe where he could rest. He studied the dark lashes that fringed her cheeks. Would she wake up soon? He hoped she would. For most of his walk, he'd begged the Great Spirit to awaken her.

He scanned the door as he tried to figure out how to get away from the ne'er-do-well's hanging around the platform. Evidently, he needed a key. So far, most of his life seemed to revolve around requiring a key of some fashion. He wiggled Nova in his arms. If he could put her down somewhere, he could look through her pockets.

A loud groan blew past Nova's lips when he jostled her. The noise drew people's attention. This wasn't safe. He wished he could ask her where the keys were. They needed to get into the room before someone stole her bag. Saving her items and protecting an unconscious Nova, was a tall order for how weary he was.

"You! You there!" A man began to yell.

Arrow jumped then glanced around wildly. His whole body braced for a fight. His grip on Nova hardened as he wrapped his arm around her bag.

A short round man with a stock of gray hair hurried his way across the cement walkway. The elder came to an abrupt stop inches from Arrow. Did this man know Nova?

The stranger had a big cratered nose that took up most of his face. Overall, he wasn't anything special except he also had glowing strings that protruded from his chest.

Arrow stared in wonder at the thin gold ropes. Maybe he was cracked from lack of sleep or starvation. No one else seemed to notice theses ghost-like strands. He looked down at himself and Nova. They didn't have anything hanging off their chests.

"What?" Arrow glanced up.

"I said…" The old man bristled. His nostrils flared. "This is my inn. I don't take to folks hanging around my rooms. You move along." Arrow was about to point out that all he'd seen so far was weirdo's hanging around, but then the old man spoke again. "That's Crazy-Gal?"

Arrow looked down at Nova's sweet face. She looked serene, but he missed her larger-than-life personality. If she were awake, she'd give this guy hell for calling her crazy.

He looked up. The old man was waiting for an answer.

Arrow stepped back when one of the ropes swinging from his chest got close to touching him. There was no way he was going to have contact with them. The old man didn't seem to notice Arrow's discomfort.

"So?" The old man raised an eyebrow.

"So?" Arrow repeated. This man was going to think he was dumb if Arrow didn't start to pay attention.

"So, what color?" The elder demanded.

Arrow paused. What color was what? He tried to recall what the inn owner yammered on about. It was some question about did he know Crazy-Gal.

"Her eyes are red, like a sunset past the clouds."

"You, son, must be as odd as her if you think them eyes are pretty. You know, she looks like the devil. Well then, seeing as you're holding her. She's got the other key to the door. I'll be wanting that back, but I can open this for you because your hands are full. She's got a good size bonk on the head. That happens where she went off to."

Arrow sighed with relief as the old man unlocked the door. He considered asking him about the floating strings, but at the same time, he didn't want to sound insane. Going for regular was the safest choice, especially if he wanted to get some sleep.

None of this was regular as far as he could tell. As he took one more step toward the open door, he took one last look at the golden flowing strings that appeared attached to the old man's rumpled cardigan. The ghost-like strands waved as if there was a breeze. There was no wind. The man nodded to the dark room.

Arrow stepped over the threshold as the elder swung the door closed behind him.

Standing in the dark, he used the hand under Nova's knees to grope for a light switch. He found one after feeling the wall. Some of the tension left his shoulders when a soft glow appeared from a bedside table lamp.

The room was relatively small but efficient. The basic square dwelling held a bed, a small desk with a lamp and a larger table with chairs. A larger table with two chairs sat in a far corner with a covered tray in the middle. He tossed

Nova's bag on a chair. Arrow didn't care what was in the room. He was utterly drained. All he wanted was to set Nova down.

As he headed to the bed, he noticed on the opposite side of the room was the bathroom. A half-shut curtain separated the room from the rest of the chamber.

Slowly placing Nova on the bed, he then stretched out his arms. At first, he didn't think her so hefty, but after roaming down about twenty different hallways, he'd changed his mind. He grunted as he sat next to her then he set her talking machine on the bedside table.

A knock on the door had him up again. He trudged toward the interruption. He wished half-heartedly that someone was bringing him food. Food was a foolish thought, but he asked the Great Spirit all the same.

Opening the door, he hid his annoyance at the old man. His eyes flipped to the white square box the elder had in his hands. The box was about the size of two palms together.

"What can I do for you?" Arrow was fixated on the gold strings. Maybe they would go away if he slept.

"I feel guilty. I know I should've told Crazy-Gal not to go to that area of the WB."

"WB?"

"WB, you know, water base. See, I should've said something about the rocks and all, but I couldn't because she had them weird eyes. You understand. I saw the bonk on her head. I thought you might need this to patch her up. My name's Toppy." Toppy held out the box, but Arrow had no idea what he was accepting. His stomached rumbled.

"You hungry?"

Arrow wanted to scream yes, but he only shook his head. He wouldn't have been surprised if his thoughts on food flashed on his forehead in bright lights.

"I brought by dinner earlier. It's nothing fancy. It comes with the room. It's over on the table." Toppy pointed to the tray Arrow had noted when he entered. "Crazy-Gal already paid. When you rent from me, you get a room and one meal a day. You know, it's easier to talk to you. She looks mean. I think she's as scattered-brained as they come. She was talking to herself and swearing like a harvester. You should keep her asleep, but I guess that's not right either. The cold pack will work."

Because Arrow was so stupid with fatigue, he didn't defend Nova. He wanted to tell Toppy he was wrong. Nova was fantastic, but he couldn't think anymore. His stomach growled audibly again. Toppy tipped his head at Arrow's middle as if agreeing with the hunger.

"On the table." The old man shrugged before he turned around in the doorway. "You there. You!" he yelled at someone a few doors down from where they stood. "Move along."

After Arrow had closed the door, he hurried back to the bed. Briefly, he scanned the room for the promised tray. Two sturdy wooden chairs, one of which he'd thrown Nova's bag on, sat next to the table. His eyes drifted to the cement floor. Another bag was in the corner near a worn rag rug.

When Nova moaned in her sleep, the sound reminded Arrow he held the box. Opening the lid to check the contents, he saw an assortment of medical supplies. Toppy mentioned he needed a cold pack. He set the box on the bedside table then tipped the lamp so he could look at Nova better.

Arrow had no idea how hard she hit the floor when he pushed her out of the way of the falling cement. He didn't know how to heal her. Honestly, he didn't know anything, period. The idea of losing her after meeting her made his heart hurt. He needed her direction, but even once his mind was fully restored, he was sure he would still need her.

Picking up her shoulders in his arms, Arrow looked at the back of her head. The old man was correct. A bump the dimension of a good-sized rock was in the center of the back of her head. He fished out the plastic sack with the words "Cold Pack" written on the side. After following the directions, he put the plastic bag gently on the injury.

After he'd settled Nova, Arrow walked to the table and the waiting food. He thanked the Great Spirit the old man had brought it, but he was even more pleased that the elder wouldn't return. Seeing the old man only brought up the question of the strings. The ropes also brought back his recurring dream. He was too tired to figure that out. Better to abandon that issue, heal Nova, eat, and then sleep.

The tray had a circular metal cover and he lifted it off. None of the dishes looked clean, but he was past caring about that. After uncovering the first plate, he began to devour carrots, dried meat, and some type of cold mush.

In record time, he'd eaten everything but some of the meat he left for Nova. Once finished, he got up to return to sit at her side. He needed to talk to her. His hands cautiously shook her shoulders.

A huge wave of relief washed over him when her eyes fluttered. The rise of her eyelids was like watching the sun in the early morning.

"Damn, it's you." She blinked then raised her hands to her head. "Where am I?" Nova tried to sit up, then swayed, then slumped back down. That stubborn streak didn't get knocked out of her head.

"I brought you back to your room."

She blinked her eyes at him again. Now she really looked at him, but like he'd grown two heads.

"You stopped me from being crushed? You did that?" Her fingers ran over her head knocking off the ice pack. Her eyes darted around the room then landed on him.

"I pushed you out of the way. You hit your head. I'm sorry." Arrow leaned over to put the ice pack back on her bump.

"You're sorry?"

"Yea."

"You brought me back here?" Her voice held a bewildered note. Her tone irritated him.

"Yea."

"You helped me?" She sounded mystified and resigned like this was a riddle she could never solve. "Odd."

"It's not odd. You can trust me." People were generally good. Sure, he had pretended that he was okay with her leaving without him, but that was necessary. She didn't know she wanted him with her yet. "I used your talking machine to get here."

"It's a computer, not a talking machine. Call the box CC."

Of course, she would correct him. At least if she was pointing out his mistakes, she might be feeling better.

"Whatever you want me to call the box is fine." He sighed. "Anyway, CC gave me directions here." For the second time since meeting her, Arrow got to wondering what type of person Nova thought he was. Without a doubt, he would never hurt her. "You know, most people would say thank you for saving their life."

"How would you know what people do? You've no memories. Besides, I haven't decided if I should be happy you're here or not. You being with me might not be a good thing. I'm thinking about it."

"Then I'll wait." Arrow smiled at her. She was adorable.

"And stop grinning at me. I can't think when you do that."

Arrow pressed his lips together as if you couldn't pry them apart. If his smile jumbled her thoughts, he might have to use it to his advantage.

As Nova struggled to adjust herself comfortably on the bed, Arrow reached over to attend the ice pack. She slapped his hand away, then she picked up CC. The minicomputer began to spit out information on head injuries and concussions.

After a while, he got up. While stacking the dishes on the tray, he considered that Nova apparently didn't like when people argued with her. He loved arguing with her. Her eyes got a darker red when her temper flared. Would her eyes turn that rich wine color if she desired him? He would love to see her yearning make her eyes sparkle.

He pictured her wanting him. A frowned blanketed his face when it occurred to him that she could have a boyfriend or a husband. That reflection caused his frown to turn into a scowl. She might love someone. What if he would never be important to her? He turned away from the table and faced her.

"Do you have a man in your life? A boyfriend?" he blurted out. Bad timing, he got that, but she was here with him now. His future with her was uncertain. He wanted it permanent.

Her eyes widened and she paused CC.

"My head's killing me." Her eyes flipped to him while she set the box down slowly on the bedside table. "We're stuck here, but you want to know my relationship status?"

"Yea."

"I was dumped a while ago. Thanks for bringing that up. Way to kick me while I'm down," Nova muttered.

"Dumped? Does that mean he didn't want you anymore?" Arrow was dumbfounded. Who could possibly give her up? She was smart and full of life. He was positive her eyes had more passion in them than a thousand regular girls. Whoever this man was, he was a fool.

"Something like that," she grumbled. "Again, thanks."

Maybe he'd bruised her ego. He should come up with an excuse for his inappropriate timed questions. His mind went blank.

"I don't care or anything." The ice pack made a crunch sound when she held it to her head tighter. "Troy was screwing me over. It's not like I'm a total loser. I don't live in a locked room like some people. I have Sky, but I mean he's not exactly easy to explain. He showed up one day at my door, and he's special. Troy couldn't handle how I loved Sky from the moment I met him. I told Troy things would change if Sky ever got better. Troy's an ass. Sky's sick with Snow Flu. He needs me."

"I need you." There wasn't anything more than that.

"I'm helping you. Why do you care if I'm with someone?"

"I don't know." He truly didn't know how to answer that. Why was he trying to plan a future with Nova if they'd only just met? He shook that question away. Inside, deep in his gut, all he had was the firm understanding that he knew Nova. They belonged together.

"'I don't know' should be tattooed on your forehead." She closed her eyes. "I thought you were going to go your way. That's what you said you'd do. Now that you dropped me here, I need to rest so I can go home. You go your way."

"You're going home? This isn't where you live?"

"I don't live in the NEDs. I'm only here because I thought I could help find my brother Archer, but I'm giving up."

"You know they say 'Good things are just around the corner.' I'm searching for my sister Dawn." Arrow came over to sit next to her on the bed.

"Who is *they* you're talking about?"

"I don't know."

"Of course you don't." She rolled her eyes. "I think that's another ad slogan."

"Why are you giving up?"

"Because I don't know where to begin…" She pointed toward the table. "See that bag on the floor? That's all I have of my brother, Archer. Actually, I don't even know if that's my brother's bag or his friend Dan. When I got here, all I found was that bag, and a note to go where I met you. I can't exactly walk around showing people pictures of Archer and asking, 'Have you seen this guy?' I'm not an H.S.P.C. agent. I'm not trained for this." As she talked, she rubbed her forehead. "I'm going to make a pregnant woman cry."

Carefully, he reached out to stop the frantic movement of her hand. He didn't know what a pregnant woman had to do with this conversation but he decided against asking.

"This has nothing to do with you." When Nova put her arms down, her eyes caught his.

"Why are you looking for Archer in the first place?"

"I'm looking for Dan to give him the talking machine as you call it. CC is actually a sophisticated piece of equipment. Dan needs CC to find Archer. It's all too much, and I'm fucking burnt out."

"You're trying to find the man with the brown hair? His picture was on one of the screens. Is that your brother?"

"Yes, that's him." Nova picked up CC from the table again then opened the screen. "My big stupid older brother went missing." Nova flipped to a few of the pictures. When she came to one of two men together, she stopped. "My sister-in-law, Clare, asked Archer to go into the NEDs. When he didn't come home, she sent her brother Dan to find him. Now Dan is missing. All that's left is me walking around like an idiot. I'm going home." Tears gathered at the corners of her eyes. CC fell to her side as Nova slumped back on the bed.

"It's going to be okay." Arrow rubbed her arm gently. She didn't push him away but let him touch her. When he glanced down, he noticed the other man in the photo on the screen. Nova had stated this was her brother. The man in the picture had brown hair like Nova, but he didn't have her eyes. In the picture, next to him was another guy laughing. The stranger had blond hair. His eyes were as blue as the ocean.

"Who's this other man? The blond. I know him."

"That's Dan." Nova glanced at the photo. "I doubt you know him. A lot of people have blond hair. And anyway, you can't remember anything last I checked."

"I know him," Arrow insisted.

"'I know him,' says the man with no memories. Listen, I'm tired of you saying that. You don't know me, you don't know Dan, and you don't know the inn keeper or the train conductors. From here on out, how about you assume you don't know anyone. That'd be a lot easier for both of us."

"The man with the blue eyes, I know him. He hit me because—fine, I don't remember why, but I know what happened. He's with my sister, Dawn. I see him sometimes. He's with her." Agitated, Arrow got up. Nova wasn't going to talk him into believing his visions weren't accurate.

"You see him sometimes? What does that mean?"

"I can see what Dawn sees when I meditate. I see through her eyes. I've had those visions since I was a child. That's how I'll find her if I leave you. If you tell me to leave you." He could see her considering his explanation. The ideas fairly rolled past her eyes.

"I've heard of gifts like this at Headquarters." She spoke slowly as if she was making a plan. "If Dan is with your sister, Dawn, then you could tell me where they are. All you would have to do is tell me some scenery that she sees." Nova's voice filled with excitement as she continued, "Then we could go to where they are. I could leave this computer with Dan. He could find Archer." A smile lit up her whole face. "You can help me, Arrow." She frowned. "Now I'm starting to sound like a character from a movie."

"You want to come with me?" Arrow wanted to dance. When she smiled, the generous spread of her lips made his whole world shine.

"No." Her smile ran away from her face. "I want you to come with me."

"Same thing." He tipped his head to the side.

"It's not."

"Is this potato, potatoes?"

"No." Nova sighed. "If I go with you then you're in charge."

"And if I'm going with you?" Arrow grinned enjoying how her mind worked.

"Then you can silently come with me. I'm in charge but with you in tow. The important word here is *silent*."

"Got it."

She could say whatever she liked about not knowing him or not trusting him, but he could tell she'd started to change her mind. He loved seeing her stare at him as if she needed him. No matter what happened from here on out, he was happy she asked him to go with her.

"Are you going to show me where to find your sister and Dan? Yes, or no?"

"I'll go with you. I'll be silent. I'll shut my face hole." The room temperature began to drop and he needed sleep. Tomorrow she could explain what she needed to know about his visions, then he would meditate.

He was looking around for the best place to rest when her voice came out sleepily.

"Are you going to meditate now?" Her voice was soft as she adjusted her pillow under her head.

"No. I'm worn out." Arrow sighed. "I'm looking for a place to sleep on the floor. My arms are killing me from carrying you." He didn't want a huge discussion on how he needed to be in the right mindset to concentrate. He wasn't up for it.

"Arrow?" She cuddled her blanket as she closed her eyes.

"Yes, angel?"

"You can sleep next to me as long as you stay on your side of the bed. Don't get friendly. Besides, you smell like a man who was kept in a locked room."

That was the second-best sentence that had come out of her mouth all night. The first was when she said they could travel together.

"It was a cage and I never get friendly." He chuckled as he peeled back the blanket to slip next to her. As he stacked his hands behind his head, he knew that if there ever was a woman he wanted to get friendly with, it was her.

"'I never get friendly' says the man who I've already seen totally naked. You might get friendly. You don't know."

It appeared she liked to get in the last word. He smiled.

"Fine, you're right." Arrow yawned. No comment. Thank the Great Spirit above.

"Arrow?"

"Yea?" He should've known she would get in the last word.

"I've decided I should thank you for saving my life today. Thank you."

"You're welcome, angel."

"I'm no angel. I'm Nova."

Chapter 9

Yawning and half asleep, Nova didn't open her eyes. A few hours ago, her headache finally subsided. After the pain abated, she'd slept on and off. Her body was sore. She didn't want to get out of bed, yet she acknowledged she had to rise. The morning prodded her.

Tossing her hair out of her face, she rolled over. When no lingering headache plagued her, she snuggled further into her pillow. With only a few hours of sleep, she was relaxed. A part of her wanted to stay right where she was the rest of the day.

She rolled over to get comfortable. Nova intended to ignore her problems for a few more minutes. She was about to drift back to dreamland, when her hand bumped into solid male flesh. The hot male heat was like cold water splashed at her face. Her eyes darted open.

Arrow.

The caged stranger was in bed with her. He'd taken off his shirt. His body was warm and inviting right above the sheet. She began to roll away, but as soon as she moved, he murmured, "angel." His huge arm wrapped around her waist. Her breath hitched. *Please be sleeping*. She didn't want to wake him and didn't shift. Relaxation and a tranquil feeling burrowed into her as he snuggled next to her.

She frowned.

Relaxed and tranquil wasn't exactly what she felt. Around Arrow, her feelings were an unsettled yearning. Being with him was temptation incarnate. He was a drug she was dying to take. One moment she was powerful as if she could handle anything life threw at her, then in the next, she was a wayward child, searching. This desire for him, she hated the confusing feeling. She smiled to herself. She should be used to mixed emotions by now.

In her life, Nova was used to insane mood swings. She was familiar with not being able to identify why she felt a specific way, but this situation was infinitely different.

Deep inside, her need of Arrow was from a secret place, untouched and undiscovered. In the boundless emotional sea that forever washed over her, sexual hunger was new. She couldn't handle what it could mean. As soon as she would feel that passion, she ruthlessly closed down the reaction. She had no idea what could've gotten into her that she was fantasizing about having sex with him. In her limited experiences with the two men she'd slept with, she'd never thought about sex at all.

Knowing she had to get up before she embarrassed herself, she scooted carefully to make space between them. As she wiggled to get Arrow's arm off her chest, she felt his hard cock pressed into her hip. The feel of the hard length was like a hot branding iron. His swollen dick laughed at her, as if mocking the idea that she could forget her response to him.

Nova memorized the feel of his thickness and size against her thigh. Her brain instantly filled with the idea to reach down and grab the expanded shaft. She wondered what he would do if she did that. Would he push her off?

How was her hair? Was her face a mess? They both stunk of sweat and dust. They hadn't showered but had gone straight to bed. She looked terrible. What was she thinking? Besides, she was short with weird eyes.

Nova shoved his arm away and got up from the bed thoroughly annoyed at her errant thoughts.

"This isn't like me," she whispered to herself. "Wanting to have sex with a stranger. That's the kind of crap that happens to me." Arrow would probably think she had small breasts and no ass. Men had never thought her anything special. Her eyes made it worse. Her eye color had never mattered before, but now she wanted Arrow to see her as sexy. She wasn't what men wanted. Arrow would be no different.

Glancing around, she hunted for her backpack as she crushed down her insecurities. She scooped her sack off one of the chairs, grabbed CC, and stalked to the bathroom. She was irrational just like everyone told her. What did she care if Arrow never wanted her? The only reason he was here was so he could show her where to find Dan.

Angrily, she showered, then brushed her teeth. By the time she got out of the bathroom, she wasn't in a better mood as she'd hoped. Her entire head spun as a storm began to grow inside of her. She'd already dressed for the day, so she pitched her bag to the floor. If Clare were here, her sister-in-law would run. Gears would grab the glue for whatever furniture she was about to break.

Arrow slept soundly. She hated that he was peaceful when she was turbulent. Time to change that.

"Arrow, get up." She planted her feet at the foot of the bed. He only rolled over and hugged her pillow. "Do your thing." She slapped lightly at his exposed calf.

"What thing?" He didn't lift an eyelid.

The second slap at his leg made a pink mark.

One eye popped open. Just as he spotted her, he smiled. His dopey grin was warm as if he was encouraging her to get back into bed. That smile would mess with her for the rest of this trip.

"Do what you do so you can see your sister." She glared. "I want to know what she sees and if she's with Dan. I'm not even sure I believe you can see anything. Let's see you do it." Crossing her arms over her chest, she tipped her chin up. Battles were her specialty, and she was eager for one.

"I can't." His husky voice was heavy with sleep and super sexy. Damn it.

"Why not? Did you fucking lie to me?" Nova eyed him skeptically. Maybe he'd lied so he would have a place to sleep last night. That sounded like something that would happen to her. She felt tied in a knot. The knot got tighter. If Arrow lied to her, she would break his arm.

"I didn't lie. I can't because I'm dirty. My skin itches. I have to have no distractions to concentrate. Seeing through Dawn's eyes is challenging." He eyed her warily. "I need mindful meditating and you're a distraction as well."

Why was she a distraction? She wasn't doing anything. Well, maybe she was yelling, but she could probably stop that.

"Fine," she stated imperiously. "You can shower, so you don't itch. Then you show me you can see Dan. If I believe you, then you can come with me. Not me with you, you with me." She specified that last part in case he'd forgotten.

She still wasn't sure it was a good idea for him to come with her. She kept changing her mind. Her hunger for him added to her indecision.

"Got it." He sat up. The blanket slipped to his waist and she used everything inside of her not to stare. He was cute with his hair all frizzy and his eyes sleepy. His bare chest wasn't cute. Damn, it was delicious.

"I didn't use all the hot water, and here," She grabbed her towel from her bag then tossed the cloth at him. "You can use my towel." She should keep him covered as much as possible. The fabric fell to the bed between them as he yawned lazily. "In the bathroom is all the leftover crap from Archer or Dan. You can use the soaps. In that bag are some clean clothes. I'm sure there're clothes that'd fit you."

Arrow's eyes barely opened, but he nodded toward the bag. His legs swung over the side of the bed before stumbling to the bathroom.

Nova realized that she was impatient, and though she didn't want to be a shrew, she thought it might be the only way to deal with the sexual attraction. She grabbed CC and sat on the bed. Using voice commands, Nova brought up shuttle times. To get her mind off Arrow, she tried to figure out what she would ask to see. She had to come up with surroundings that would tell her where Dan and Dawn might be located. Nothing concrete came to her.

"For the love of the Great Spirit, what is this?" Arrow's booming exclamation crashed through her thoughts.

Nova's eyes popped to the bathroom.

Arrow stormed out of the bathroom naked. His hair was sopping wet. The black locks were unbraided and plastered to his shoulders. He was quite a sight to behold as he came to a halt in front of her. His hair sent drops splashing down his sculpted pecs. His tan skin glistened as rivulets of water followed each muscle. Her mouth went dry.

She was so shocked to see him naked, and in a state of pure agitation, that for a moment she lost her ability to speak. When she finally found her voice, she didn't think she sounded anything like her usual self. She cleared her throat. Twice.

"What's the matter?"

"Look at this." Arrow gestured wildly to his firm body.

Cautiously, and all too aware of her increasing blood pressure, she let her eyes travel over his solid frame. She prepared herself for an injury. He had, after all, yelled.

Nova licked her lips. She couldn't seem to stop herself from letting her eyes travel from his neck, over his obliques, down the wisp of black hair that made a trail toward his shaft. She saw nothing which indicated he was hurt. Arrow was magnificent. Her eyes finally settled on his throbbing dick. His hard cock stood straight up. The head was thick and pointed at his stomach. His member had a slightly swollen purple hue to the skin. The hot water must have made his dick even more engorged.

"Fuck you, Arrow. That's not funny. I thought you were hurt. Get dressed. Again, with the clothes." Annoyed, she stood up from the bed and grabbed her bag from where it was propped on the floor. She picked up the bag so she didn't gawk at him. Her fingers shook as she started to shake out her clothes to fold random articles.

Out of the corner of her eye, she noticed Arrow shake his head. Water beaded down his chest to drip of his nipple. Her tongue wanted to follow the trail.

"Arrow, quit joking." With the bed between them, she leaned down to grab one of the pillows. She threw the white mass at him. The pillow hit him in the face.

His stunned expression stared back at her.

"Joke? I'm not joking." His eyes widened. "What the hell is this? What did you do to me? I can't get rid of this.

I mean, it was sort of there when I got up, but I thought it'd go down. You did something to me. You did this." His voice had way more accusation in it than she thought was fair. Nova recognized the frantic tone. Over excited was an emotion she knew inside and out.

She didn't know what the problem was exactly, but he absolutely was distraught. For a brief moment, his fear registered in her brain with pounding force. She regarded him. He tried to ram his erection down. He acted as if he could force his shaft to obey. His eyes looked genuinely worried as he shifted from foot to foot.

What if that drug had messed with his head so much that he actually didn't remember what a hard-on was? Was that possible? She had a hard time believing that, but with Arrow, she was continually being surprised.

"What do I do, Nova? I can't get rid of this." More panic accompanied more shoving at his penis. Nova might've heard a catch at the end. She might laugh if he cried. It was, after all, only a bodily function.

"A hard-on isn't a big deal." An erection wasn't a problem. Well, to Arrow, a hard cock appeared to be an enormous deal.

"It's not a big deal?" He shoved his dick down again only to have it pop back up.

She stifled a giggle. "Well, it *is* big, just not a big deal. Calm down. Sit on the bed before you cry."

"I'm not going to cry. You calm down," he fired back, but he obeyed her. He sat on the bed then put his arms on his knees. His eyes stayed on her.

Nova shook her head at his nonsense. She was perfectly calm. After strolling to the bathroom, she picked up the towel off the floor, then came back and handed the cloth to him in silence. As he patted his skin dry, his eyes glared at his penis.

"This is natural. Getting hard is part of life. You eat then you shit." Nova saw Arrow look up at her. As she explained, his eyes seemed to relax. "You drink water then you pee. This is like all those bodily functions. You're fine. Maybe you don't remember." Her calm voice seemed to break through his anxiety. He nodded.

For Nova, this was a strange experience. Normally she was the one escalating situations to a fevered pitch. Never was she the one who was thinking clearly or the composed one. For a person who jumped from one extreme to another since birth, she was thrilled she was serene. She hid her proud smile.

"I'm not fine. I want to be like I was before. What do I do?" Arrow's voice had gone back to his usual deep even tone. His breathing looked more at ease. He didn't sound happy, but he also didn't sound suicidal. It was an improvement. "I can't meditate with this." He gestured again to his hard shaft as if his dick was some type of offending creature. This time she did let her smile show.

"It's not evil, Arrow. And you're *fine*." This was the strangest argument she'd ever had. Never had she had to convince a man that his penis working was an acceptable state of events. A grin hung on her lips.

"Are you laughing at me?"

"No. I'm not laughing. Do you hear any laughter?" She arranged her features into what she hoped was mild interest.

"No."

"See? I'm right. Not laughing at you." She took a steadying breath, so she didn't outright giggle.

"You're not laughing, but you're not helping. Now tell me what to do." His eyes pleaded.

For a second, she wondered what it would be like to have his eyes look at her like that, but with lust behind them.

Clearing her mind of where her thoughts headed, she shook out the shirt in her hand. She concentrated on smoothing out non-existent wrinkles. She needed to do a mundane activity while she talked, so she didn't either laugh or throw herself at him. Now was the time to use her professional research assistant voice like when she was trying to keep her cool around her family. Her calm voice is what got her out of the basement at HQ. All that practice came in handy.

"I can't believe I have to explain this." She talked more to her clothes than to him. She folded another garment. "All you have to do is expel your semen. You can do that with your hand, or you can take a cold shower. Your penis will go down again. I'm told by men that cold showers are not pleasant, so you know."

"Got it." He bounded off the bed and then disappeared into the bathroom once more.

As soon as he was out of sight, her shoulders began to shake with suppressed mirth. She bent over her bag and giggled uncontrollably into her shirt. After a few seconds, she forced herself to take a breath. It was strange being around someone who knew so little yet was also a steadying influence. When everything seemed out of alignment, and nothing was right, Arrow, of all people, kept her centered.

"There is no way to peace. Peace is the way," Nova whispered to her bag. Curious, but for some reason, that mantra seemed to ring true today. She would keep the peace here, and as soon as Arrow mediated, she would find Dan. Together they would find Dan and Dawn. She could use CC to put the whole thing together.

For the first time since this trip started, Nova began to trust her capabilities. Before long she could drop CC to Dan, then he would find Archer. When everyone was safe, she could return to Sky. Maybe this could all work out.

"You lied to me." Arrow shouted at her as he rushed out of the bathroom.

She should've never thought this could work out.

Arrow's hair was wet again. He was as naked as before. The towel was forgotten somewhere. Water clung to the tip of his nose. Furious, he shoved droplets off his face.

Arrow standing naked while freaking out was surprisingly beautiful. She didn't say that out loud. Sighing, she returned to the bathroom. The towel was on the floor. She came back to stand next to him near the bed. She handed him the nearly soaked piece of terry cloth. He balled the fabric up and put his face in the middle. His hard-on bobbed. The mushroom-top looked like it was trying to climb off his body. He was still incredibly swollen, and clearly pissed about it. When he threw the towel down, he frowned at his erection. She wanted to laugh. It wasn't as if his dick insulted him.

"The smell of this towel is making it worse. The towel smells like you." He kicked the cloth on the floor. "In the shower, all I can think about is you. You did this." His eyes stabbed at her. She could hear him silently damning her for his predicament.

"I didn't do anything to you. I'm not doing anything." She put her hands up in a gesture of surrender. "If cold water didn't work, then why don't you simply do the other thing?"

Secretly, she got aroused thinking that he was turned on by her. He admitted he liked her smell. That confession caused excitement to blossom. The idea he would want her made heat spread toward the junction of her thighs.

Troy popped into her head. The unwanted intrusion caused some of her heat to cool. Her ex-boyfriend had dumped her over Sky, but in their last fight, he told her having sex with her was like doing it with an iceberg. The jerk had beat it over her head that even though she had passion when she fought with him, in the bedroom, fucking her was like screwing a dead woman. The words had hit hard. She'd planned to never have sex again, but with Arrow, she was fast changing her mind.

Arrow was… different.

"Stop looking at me like that," Arrow demanded suddenly.

"Like what?" She opened her eyes wide. Was the red a turn-off?

"You look like you're thirsty and I'm a glass of water. Your eyes are beautiful, and there's an invitation my body wants to accept. All this makes *it* bigger." He signaled his swollen pole.

"I'm not looking at you any specific way." She was amazed he didn't get bothered by the color of her eyes. "This might be because of the drug." She had to change the subject. Nova tried to look anywhere but at him. "I'm not anything special, so this might be a side effect of the drug. My eyes are red. Most of the time people don't think of them as an invitation as you put it."

"I'm not going to fight with you about how attractive you are right now. Whatever you believe, you can just be right. I only want you to show me what I'm supposed to do with my hands. I'll do whatever to make this go away. I can't have this. I can't even get dressed."

Nova rubbed her brow. It was one thing to talk clinically about masturbation, but it was a whole other thing to show someone. She'd told men to give her a semen sample in a jar on more than one occasion, but actually describing what he was supposed to do was awkward. Doing sexual acts was private. Orgasms were either by yourself or shared with someone you were in a relationship with. This didn't seem to fall under one of those categories. She'd only ever had an orgasm alone in her room. Doing things with men tended to fall flat. She might not even be qualified to give him tips.

"Go to the bathroom. Touch your..." Nova paused then looked up at the ceiling. This was hard. She stopped herself from giggling at the pun. Arrow stared at her as if she was giving him the directions to a treasure. "Penis. If it feels good, keep doing it until..." She paused again. Embarrassment tinged her cheeks. How the hell did he *not* know this? "You finish," she ended lamely.

Scattering water off his butt as he spun, he headed to the bathroom again. Nova took a deep breath. His ass was molded to perfection.

Turning back to her clothes, she started to repack her bag. Maybe she should leave the room. She could see if the old man had food she could buy. That could be an escape. She could buy food with the money Clare gave her. She counted her cash and did the math for how much she would need to get home. She didn't want to get stranded, so no matter what, she needed to save enough for a train back to HQ.

Supposedly the train rides were free underground, but she'd learned that some of the information CC gave her wasn't accurate. Sure, trains were free, but only the short distance ones that jumped from water base to water base. If you wanted to take any train that headed straight to a particular destination, then you had to bribe your way on. She didn't want to spend two weeks riding trains to get back home. If she had to jump trains, it would take about two weeks, if not more, depending on departure times.

"That didn't work. Now what?" Arrow's voice cut through her thoughts while she was sorting through the bottles Clare had packed. Looking up, she set the miscellaneous lotions down on the bed. He was still naked and still beautifully hard. His hands fisted at his sides as his dick jutted out toward her.

"Now what?"

Her brain melted into a puddle in the back of her head. Arrow was gorgeous. The more Nova gazed at him, the more her attraction multiplied. His skin had a slight redness and every brawny inch gleamed. She could stand around all day and leer at his cinnamon skin. Crap-cakes, absolutely no leering. That was a bad idea.

"What do I do with it?" He tapped his foot.

"Do with it?" As soon as his question was posed, about twenty different ideas of things he could do with "it" danced in her head. She should curb her attraction to him. All this wasn't helping her get her rampant sexual thoughts under control. She should've left the room.

"I can't meditate with this," he stated. "I can barely think about anything else. I swear I can feel my heartbeat in the tip. This isn't healthy."

"It's healthy," she argued while she rubbed her forehead. It would be clearly out of the question to have sex with him. Even if she wanted to, it wasn't okay to have intercourse with a stranger. She had a code of conduct she lived by. One her dad had instilled in her. Besides all that, she also wasn't any good in bed. She didn't have sex with just anyone, partly because she would be a failure, and partly because it was a risk.

"If it's healthy, then now what?"

Nova paused. What should she say? Having sex was too personal. It opened her up too much.

"I need you to meditate." If he didn't, then they couldn't leave and she couldn't find Dan. The best idea would be to tell him to go back in and touch himself again. Her eyes dropped to the vein that ran up his cock. Maybe he couldn't reach a finish because of the drug.

Nova had never heard of that as a side effect before with any of the Clean Slate Series, but different people reacted to drugs differently. She simply needed to view this problem from a more serious medical perspective. She could help him reach climax and tell him her actions weren't a sexual pursuit. What they did together wasn't a relationship connection. Helping him could be what she needed to do to solve the problem.

Did she dare suggest that she help him ejaculate? The room got a few degrees hotter. She tugged on her sweater.

Arrow stared at her with all that need in his eyes.

"Please, will you help me, my angel?"

Chapter 10

His body felt as if all the blood rushed to his dick.

The blood pounded every time her eyes fell to his penis. Her red eyes seemed to gobble him up. He could smell her on his skin. She was in his brain, seeping into his core.

Arrow couldn't get her out of his head. His body refused to cooperate. He tried to touch himself the way she described, but all that happened was his skin got too tight. He rubbed and rubbed but nothing happened. This wasn't funny. Nova thought he would remember what to do, but deep down this was new to him. He was positive he'd never dealt with his body this way before.

He waited for what felt like an eternity. Nova cleared her throat.

"Please help me, angel."

"Being physical together is out of the question. You understand." She rubbed her forehead with her palm. The action was a good sign. At some point, he figured out that the gesture meant she was thinking. He didn't care what she told him to do. He'd do anything to not feel so pent up. His skin was too sensitive. There was a frenzy lurking just under his skin.

"Got it." He didn't understand, but he didn't want to say that in case it would push Nova away.

"I don't know you well enough even if there is an attraction there. I mean that's a whole different issue. I'm not that kind of woman. I do think that might be a problem at some point, but I can keep it together if you can."

"Got it." Arrow nodded. He assumed she wanted him to agree. He had no clue what she was talking about. He had a vague notion "being physical" meant something, but his head wasn't clear. Hopefully, she would come to the part where she would tell him how to get his body under control. Specific instructions would help.

"And I'm not really good at that kind of thing anyway." She talked. He nodded. "I've been told I'm cold, but this could be about me giving you a hand." She snickered. He wasn't sure why. "It could be for the cause. We both need you to meditate. No attachments or anything deeper. That's for the best because then I can go. I have to go home. It wouldn't mean anything. If you want to, then it's fine with me."

He didn't understand. What was she not good at? Was she not good at giving directions? Her facial expression was that of someone who waited for an answer. Did she ask him a question? Maybe he'd missed it.

Silence fell between them.

"Yes or no? If it's no, then you're on your own because I don't know what else you want to do."

He didn't want to be on his own in *any* way, especially now. He'd already been alone in the bathroom working to get his rambunctious body to relax. He only wanted this discomfort to go away so he could put on a pair of pants and button them without an ache. Thinking and meditation were important for both of them.

"Yes?" He phrased it as a question in hopes she would clarify what was about to happen. "I don't want to be on my own."

"Fine, then we agree. That's good because I didn't want to argue with you about this of all things."

"We don't argue." He grinned. He had no idea what they discussed, but even lost, she warmed his heart. She made him feel alive, whole, and as if everything would be okay. Since he'd met her, he had the oddest notion everything would be fine as long as they stayed together.

"Is this us not arguing?"

"Yea."

"This might be weird," she said after a minute passed.

"I trust you." He didn't say anything more. He wasn't sure what the topic was now. Was she referring to his body as weird? Maybe he should ask more questions. He wondered if she'd ever seen a man hard like this before. Her earlier comment made it sound as if what was happening to him wasn't unique. She didn't act as if this was out of the ordinary. He could see veins under the skin.

"Have you ever handled this before?" He couldn't keep the concern out of his voice.

"Handled?" She snorted. "Nice choice of words." She laughed lightly. "Of course I've *handled* this type of issue before. Maybe not directly, but I lived in H.S.P.C. Headquarters in Dallas, not under a rock. I've had two long-term boyfriends. Plus, I'm a research assistant to a brilliant scientist. I've worked with men in the clinic for the last year, and I had a few male friends in Archival Services." Her eyes scanned his body again as she sat on the far side of the bed. "I mean not worked with like this *exactly*, but I know enough. For six months, I cataloged porn." Her voice held a matter-of-fact tone as she patted the bed. "Come to bed." Nova acted as though he was crazy. He could be nuts. He'd considered the possibility.

Arrow looked at the bed. Most of that last speech made little sense to him. Maybe she planned to put him to sleep, so when he woke, his penis would be soft. He sat on the bed before he swung his feet up. He adjusted the pillow behind is head to get comfortable. The bed was too soft. His ultra-sensitive skin was much too aware of the sheet.

Nova gave him a reassuring smile as if he did the right thing. Maybe if he was flat, all the blood would go back to where it belonged. If he slept, then his heart would slow its pounding.

He put his hands behind his head to get ready to rest. Nova looked at the bottles she'd set to the side. A few of them she picked up before shoving them back in her bag.

Nova knelt on the bed next to him with her knee next to his hip. When it appeared she wasn't going to do anything, Arrow closed his eyes. He should ask her to hum a song. He wished she wasn't sitting so close. Her smell was that of flowers and warm skin. His mind conjured licking her skin, not sleeping. He didn't know where that idea came from, but it didn't help, so he banished the notion from his head.

Boring topics needed to stay front and center in his mind. Hot water in the shower was dull. Nova appeared in his head naked under the steam of water. He thrusted that picture aside. How about an ice storm? Instead, he pictured her playing in the snow, then kissing him. His dick throbbed. Snow. He could always think about that.

Her hands settled on his chest.

Arrow's eyes flew open. His hand snatched Nova's wrist tightly while shoving her away from his body. His mouth went dry as sweat popped out of his skin.

"What are you doing?" His voice came out rasping.

Her eyes stretched until they looked like red moons.

"You claimed you wanted my help. We talked about it. Did you change your mind? Because it didn't look like you did." She tugged on his grip. He let go, more perplexed than ever. "If this isn't okay, you can be on your own." She sounded unsure. Probably because of his grabby actions. Arrow considered what she had said. Her plan was to touch his chest? Had he agreed to that?

"I'm sorry you caught me off guard. You're right. I want help." Arrow hoped she wouldn't change her mind. Even though he didn't know what he'd agreed to, he trusted her. To show his faith in her, Arrow put both his hands back under the pillow. His fingers gripped his other hand so he wouldn't seize her wrist again. "Go ahead. I'll shut my face hole. I won't do anything."

"Oh, you'll do something, if I do it right." Again, her hands returned to his chest. "Breathe."

"Got it. Breathing." He realized he held his breath. He let the air out slowly. Her hands were coated with whatever she'd put on them from one of the bottles. She paused, then added more of the lotion to her fingers. The lotion smelled of flowers. Her fingers began to dance over his nipples. Air hissed out. She was right. She could make him do something.

"It's only oils. It's safe. Clare sent it along for dry skin. She's always telling me what to do and worrying about me." She slipped a finger over his nipples. "But this time it's helpful."

His breath caught a second time. Her fingers slid along his skin. Her actions seemed to send more blood rushing to the part of his body which was already on fire.

Arrow's eyes closed without his permission. With them shut, everything magnified. If this was supposed to help him feel better, it wasn't working. Nova's small soft fingers skimmed over his abs. Her hands grazed across his overly heated skin. Wherever her hands pranced, they seemed to leave a trail of sparks. He wanted to say she made things worse, but he couldn't bring himself to speak. His eyes pressed firmly shut while he tried to make sense of his raging emotions.

A part of him begged her to never stop. Another part of him wished she would want him back. He couldn't take it if she laughed at him. A feeling of being exposed before her came unbidden to his head.

He opened one eye to see how she looked at him. He didn't know what he would do if she thought him repulsive. Her head was bent. Some of her hair covered part of her face. What he could see were her luminous eyes. They'd turned a lighter red with golden amber around the pupils. The sight of them sent shivers racing down to his toes.

"I warmed up my hands. Are they cold?"

"Not cold." He groaned when she circled his belly button. His open eye watched her intently.

"This would be easier for me if you'd stop staring at me. I can't start with you looking at me, and anyway, I know what my eyes are like. I don't want you thinking about them."

Arrow was irked that she would think her eyes ugly. She had no idea how beautiful her eyes were, especially at this very second. He tried to come up with what he should say.

"Nova—"

"Close your eyes. You said you trusted me. I don't what to argue with you."

Arrow did as she asked.

Instead of explaining how amazing she was, he reclined on the pillow. What had Nova meant when she stated she hadn't started yet? Both hands now slipped past his belly button toward his cock. He gripped his hands together under the pillow.

Arrow tried to keep his mind from jumping to conclusions. She would help him. He believed her. Her fingers touched the tops of his thighs. Really, he had no other choice. He didn't have much in his mind to rely on. Her fingertips raked lightly between his legs. His legs shifted open in an involuntary action. He wanted to expose himself more to her, yet he also wanted to put his hands on his dick and hide.

None of that mattered because he felt like he couldn't move. Nova's hands made him feel as though he was caught in a trap. The bottle squeezed, then the room dropped away. Her hand settled over his straining cock. She gripped him tightly as she spread oil over the head of his dick. He stopped himself from launching off the bed. This might be heaven, or it might be hell.

With supreme effort, he kept his hips pinned to the mattress. His hands together under the pillow held to each other in a painful grip. No longer did he keep his eyes closed on purpose. Now his eyes sealed shut in ecstasy. Her other hand softly started to move down to envelop his entire shaft. Her fingers slid over his balls. A repetitive movement began as she rubbed a tender spot on the underside of his sac. A moan escaped from his lips.

Her one hand cupped his balls fully before spreading more liquid over them. Both her hands started to move in a distinctive rhythm. Was he panting? Her fingers on his balls made slow madding figure eights. Her other hand began to pump his cock. That movement killed his every lucid thought.

Up and down was all there was, with only the wet slick sounds in the air between them. Arrow wanted to beg her to stop. He hated it. He loved it, and he hated it. He was disgusted by the fact that he couldn't control any part of his body. His arms felt pinned down. His hips of their own volition pumped up toward her silky hands seeking her grip. He might die if she let go. She worked him over like clay to mold for her amusement.

Arrow mumbled a plea. She didn't respond. Moaning again, he wanted to be embarrassed that he was losing his mind right in front of her. He wanted to apologize for his strange behavior, but he couldn't speak a coherent word. Mindlessly, his hips rose off the bed. Heat spread through his limbs. His body tingled. Blood rushed. His heart pounded. He sucked down air like he'd run for miles.

"Please, angel," he begged, but he didn't know what for. He wanted to make the fire on his flesh end, yet he wanted her to touch him forever. Her hand moved faster. As if off in the distance, he could hear sounds of her fist closing over the tip. His erratic breathing wouldn't halt even when he tried to stop it. His hips bucked and thrust into her hand. Up and down.

Another harsher groan was forced from him. Words came out as garbled mush. He was coming apart. As he tried to settle his mind, he knew that controlling his thoughts was an uphill battle. He opened his eyes to tell her to let him go, but that was a mistake. She was bent over him with her hair fluttering along the sides of her face. Looking at her made his cock feel like it might explode.

Her cheeks had a pink hue to them. Her tongue darted out over her lips. Arrow gritted his teeth. With her head tipped toward his shaft, she didn't look up. Her eyes shifted to her hands instead. Concentration was etched in her brow. Her eyes were less red now and more amber, a deep, fathomless swirl of color.

Her fingers slipped along his balls to glide between his ass cheeks. The one little movement made him throw his head back. She would kill him. There were too many sensations all at once. The oil she used mixed with his scent. The aroma grew stronger. Around him, he could smell her as well. An animalist part of him grew. For a moment, the strong feelings frightened him to his core.

"Arrow, stop fighting. You're letting your body argue with me. Give in and let me win. I like to be right." Her husky words came to his ears the second before her mouth descended on him.

As soon as her lips wrapped around the head of his cock, he shuddered.

He didn't know what he was doing any longer. His mind emptied. Nova was right. She won. Whatever she wanted from him, she could have. He let go of the last bit of discipline. No longer could he keep himself in check.

Nova sucked all the way down his erection. He couldn't stop the tide. He called her name over and over again while he thrust helplessly past her lips. His cock shook and convulsed against the back of her mouth. As her tongue swished over his swollen head, he reached the heavens, then he flew above the atmosphere. The climax forced his abs to flex and his hips to shake. He rode waves of pleasure as they swept him along. He started to shiver but not because he was cold. His balls tucked themselves into her palm as if wanting an everlasting home there. She sucked the life from him.

Spent, he collapsed back to the bed with goose bumps over his flesh. His head spun. He'd never experienced anything like that before. He was positive of that. How could he be both awake and tired? He was alive, yet he'd died and gone to heaven.

She was his angel with the mouth of a demon.

"What did you do to me, angel?"

"We're not going to talk about it."

"Why?"

She didn't answer but quickly got up from the bed. She always got in the last word. Out of the corner of Arrow's eye, she disappeared into the bathroom and snapped the curtain shut.

Yawning, he waited. He pictured gathering Nova into his arms and relaxing. A picture of her on the bed naked for him to touch, winged past his brain. He waited for her to come back. Since he'd called her "angel" she would come back to correct him.

She didn't return to the room. The cold air wafted over his skin as he glanced down at his shriveling member. His penis looked normal again, except the hair around his dick was matted down and damp. He sat up gingerly. Was Nova avoiding him? Was his reaction wrong?

The water in the bathroom ran. The sounds of the sink being used gave him a feeling of loneliness. That was ridiculous. Nova was on the other side of a curtain. She was near him, yet far away. He wanted to hold her. Was he this needy before? He'd have to ask Dawn how he acted before the drug.

He smiled. It wasn't the drug that changed him. It was probably his Nova. His match.

Swinging his legs to the cold floor, a languid feeling flowed over him. He wanted a nap with Nova. There was no way he could sleep knowing Nova dodged him. It might not be a good idea to barge into the bathroom to force her to tell him what was wrong. He didn't know a lot but he knew enough not to do that.

He stood up. Nova had mentioned the bag might have some clothes. A black duffle was unzipped and left open. While he rummaged in the sack, he tried to decide how to get her to talk to him about how she'd touched him. It might be a taboo subject. The best idea was to meditate.

Dressed in a button-down flannel shirt and patched blue jeans, Arrow sat on the floor in the middle of the room. His back was to the bathroom in case she came out. Maybe it would be okay if Nova didn't come out of the bathroom. If he saw her, she would interrupt his thoughts. When he saw her later, he might come up with the right words. She'd done whatever magic to him so he could clear his mind, and right now that's exactly what he needed. Her touch had worked on him. Mostly. As long as he wasn't thinking about Nova, everything below his belly button was fast asleep.

"Angel? I'm going to meditate now." He took a deep breath and straightened his spine. His legs crossed with his shoulders relaxed. His mind became a calm pool. "We can talk about what happened later?"

No response.

No matter if his memories ever came back or not, he wanted to tell her he would remember the feel of her mouth on him until the day he died.

Chapter 11

"I want to talk about your mouth on me, angel," Arrow demanded for the second time as he followed her through the noisy crowd. The train platform was overloaded with people. She didn't want to stop moving forward to have *that* conversation. Actually, she wanted to never have *that* conversation.

"My name's Nova. It's not snow angel or angel or demon eyes," she answered him without turning around.

"I said demon eyes once." He sounded distracted. Another mass of rough-looking men passed them. The last man in the group stared at her eyes for a second then moved on. She scooted out of their way and ducked around their huge packs. They might be harvesters, but she didn't dwell on it. The chance of meeting a harvester on this trip was relatively small. They basically had their own trains.

"Fine, then I'll remember it *once*." Instead of gawking like Arrow, she hurried toward the center of the platform away from where the shuttles did drop-offs. She spun around when she realized Arrow stopped at a bench made out of plastic bottles. He eyed her when she grabbed his arm.

"People are staring at you. I don't like it."

"If people are staring at me it's only because I have weird colored eyes. I'm used to being the freak show. Now, will you please hurry up? We can't be late."

This train platform was busier than the shuttle that brought them here. The shuttle had been swift, quiet, and reasonably clean. This area was the exact opposite. Arrow hadn't spoken much when they left the room and got on the shuttle. He'd seemed content to watch the people that passed them by, but now he wanted to talk. Now wasn't a good time to chat. They had to keep their eyes and ears open as they navigated the swarm.

"It's not your eyes. Some men look at your ass, some look at your chest, and some look at you. I don't like it and you're not a freak show. You're…" Arrow trailed off.

This was a pointless conversation. If people stared, so what. She was used to their reactions by now. After she finally got up enough courage to meet people and leave the basement at HQ, she got used to the reactions. Arrow would have to get used to them too, that is if he wanted to travel with her.

They passed a few stalls that were built into the side of a tall, thick stone wall. On three sides of the train platform sat small shops. People bought, sold, and traded goods. Some type of meat hung in an open window. To her right, a woman called out that she had fresh tomatoes. Everyone was so engrossed in what they were doing no one looked up as they passed.

"You're absurd. No one is looking at me any particular way right now. Except you. You could stop that."

"How am I looking at you?" Arrow asked innocently. He wasn't fooling her.

"You look at me like you just saw your first sunset."

"You're beautiful." His eyes glittered with longing. They reminded her of black onyx.

"Could we agree not to lie to each other? So far we're getting along, and after all we've been through, I think it would be great if you didn't feed me a line."

"Feed you a line?" Arrow moved to her side while he adjusted the black duffle on his back. His eyes softened. "To be clear, I can't call you beautiful?"

"That's correct."

"They say, 'Power, beauty, and soul.'" He smiled down at her. "You're all three."

"That's an Aston Martin slogan." Nova wanted to laugh and slap him all at the same time. "Why do you keep referring to *they*?"

"*They* means that it's an expression." Arrow nodded sagely. "*They* are all I got in my head."

"I believe that." Nova glanced up at the rows of ventilation grates high above them. One had ice forming across the metal bars. The rising heat of the room melted the ice and it dripped down in a steady stream on the far side of the room. Someone had put a few potted plants under the water. The flowers flourished. The general masses parted around the leafy plants.

Her brother, Archer, had once told her that underground there were few things people treated as sacred. Plants were one of them because they produced fresh air. He would tell her about his trips to meet their father's friend Mac deep in the NEDs. Nova had always thought she would feel claustrophobic knowing she was under dirt, cement, snow, and ice, but since getting here, she didn't feel that way. The high ceilings and the grates with cool air blowing made her feel like she wasn't buried alive.

Also, all the smattering of plants was a comfort. Archer had told her she might feel oppressed and entombed. She didn't feel like that, but then again, she wasn't sure she could live here forever. A person might have to live here from birth to be used to it.

They made their way past a second bench made out of old tires then she stopped. She detected Arrow wasn't behind her and she turned to grab his arm and propel him forward. Arrow's head was tipped all the way back as he examined the high ceilings. He touched the cement columns which stood like silent protectors. She fiddled with her bag with one hand while resting her other hand on the fabric satchel that held CC.

"How do the trains work?" Arrow asked as she prodded him along. He moved as fast as an old man with Snow Flu. On his face was pure wonderment. At moments like this, she wished he had all his memories.

"Some work on magnets." Nova shoved past a fat lady in a shirt that had a cat in a top hat. "That's how the shuttles work I'm told. Some work on electric tracks. On the surface of the planet are wind generators. CC says there's plenty of electricity because of all the wind, but battery storage is more of a problem. Clare says there are lots of solutions. The H.S.P.C. works on those kinds of issues."

"How many water bases are there? Are they all numbered? So, some of them have names?"

Nova stopped walking when a man with a purple hat cut her off to chase after a child. Both the boy and man smelled like old cheese. She wrinkled her nose.

"I don't know how many bases there are. I know there are original ones built by the well-known Gears Davis and Rea MacBain. You can ask CC when we get on the train and out of this mob. I do know some of the bases coincide with what was on the surface before the ice. Where we're going is called New Boise, that's because above ground used to be Boise, Idaho. This is Yorktown. It was built as one of the first bases because their shuttle system was already in place. My dad has a friend who lives near here."

Arrow nodded. She hoped that by answering his questions, he'd start to walk faster. When he opened his mouth again, she realized that wasn't going to happen. It appeared every time she answered him, a second later he came up with a new question to ask.

"What do the signs that say, 'Snow Flu Free' mean?" Arrow pointed to a sign like that on a shop window next to a skinned rabbit. "I've seen those all over."

Nova glanced backward bumping into a teenage boy with long greasy hair. He saw her eyes then jerked away like she'd burned him.

"Snow Flu is the name of the virus that's spreading and killing people at an alarming rate." She paused for a second before shifting closer to Arrow. She kept her eyes downcast. "It kills more women and children than men. The illness is passed along in the snow when it melts. It often becomes airborne. Then the virus can be passed from person to person. Its clinical name is Snow Flu, you know, like Spanish Flu, or Black Death. People are hanging signs saying they aren't sick." She tugged on Arrows arm. Finally, he took the hint. He picked up his pace. "If there was an outbreak, people would panic."

"How many people live underground? Does everyone live on a water base? Do they have medical care to help them when they get Snow Flu?"

Nova figured she should be happy he asked all these questions instead of one's about how she touched him this morning. The problem was, it wasn't the best time to talk. They needed to focus on catching the right train while not having any of their bags stolen and not getting run over by a gang of unruly harvesters.

"I cannot possibly answer all your questions right now. We have to keep moving, or we're never going to get to our train."

Arrow stopped looking at the shop signs. Now he looked at all the people who moved in a disorganized mess before them.

"I don't like how these people look at you, Nova," Arrow began again. Nova dodged a fat man carrying a huge crate on his shoulders. Arrow hugged her into his arms and held her for a minute before she shrugged him off.

No one seemed to notice them as they wound their way toward the line where the general populace could prepare to enter the trains. She kept her eyes to the floor as much as she could. A rope divided the platform to separate the area that was supposed to keep people in a queue. The thick cord balanced on orange crates didn't work because people bunched into the area ignoring the cable.

"I swear I'm too damn short." Someone stepped on her toe. She had no idea what Arrow was talking about. No one looked at her at all. They seemed too focused on the trains. A tall woman cut her off. Arrow bumped into her back. Arrow was now studying a beefy man with orange hair who stood to their left. He caught her eyes and stared. She sighed.

As she spun around to talk to Arrow, she noticed that he stared down at her like a lovesick teenager.

"You like expressions, right? I have one for you. Stop talking and look where you're going. We have to get on train twenty-five." She held tight to her backpack straps and to CC as they headed past a few other trains where people scrambled to get on.

"That's not an expression." Arrow chuckled.

"How would you know? *They* say it."

Nova and Arrow made their way through another crowd of people exiting a water base gate. Arrow took the lead once they spotted the right train up ahead. He was big enough that he easily muscled people out of his way. That helped. Some people even moved out of his way while he sauntered. He carried the black duffle and the huge bag made him seem even bigger.

She spotted a place with a white metal sign pointing to a loading area. The floor in front of the sleeping train was marked in red paint. Arrow reached out for her hand. His fingers felt warm and steady.

"This train will take us to New Boise, WB10." She pointed to the loading area. Together they elbowed and shoved to the spot in front of the train. A human pile developed around them. Arrow tucked her under his arm.

The side of the train had two large doors that opened with a clank. People surged forward. Nova understood that when a train filled to capacity, people either had to buy a private room, if one was available, or they had to take the next train. Depending on the situation, most people didn't want to take the next train. Generally, they also didn't have any money to buy a room. According to CC, this train traveled all the way to New Boise with only two stops on the way. People appeared frantic to get a straight shot to their destination.

Arrow eyed people around them. A sudden faint grin lit his face. As she glanced up, she couldn't help but notice how handsome he was. He was so dopey most of the time that to see him looking composed was strange.

"What's the smile for?" she yelled up to him. The noise level in the room grew louder as people talked and shoved.

"Nothing."

Presently, she was caught in a crush while struggling to get on a train, so even though she was sure he lied, she let his response go. The wide doors could only accommodate so many. No one would back off. Nova gripped her bag tighter in the human sea.

They started up the two stairs that led to the train door. The mob of people calmed down as more folks got seated. Many individuals had already found a place on the train, so there was now space for her to pass through the wide doorway. The sliding metal door opened into the first passenger car. She was forced by the group behind her to follow up the stairs. Arrow brought her into the shelter of his arms a second time. He tucked her under his arm like one of the bags. She felt safe.

Inside the train car, seats with a worn diamond pattern lined both sides of the walkway. The big windows along the train were boarded up. Dim lights lit the center aisle. Men, women, and children rushed the aisle. The young climbed over the seats to claim a place to sit down.

Two women started fighting over a seat. A bearded man on her left kept yelling that he needed a spot in the back.

A serene smile was on Arrow's face as his eyes followed everyone with mild interest. He looked unaffected by the chaos, the noise, and the press of bodies around them. Nova felt overwhelmed by it all. The smell of so many bodies mixed with the heat made her stomach roll. The lights on the floor flashed unevenly making her eyes hurt. The racket was terrible. She hoped she didn't burst into tears or scream.

"How can you stand this?" She ducked her head under his arm then gripped his hand. His palm stayed steady in hers. Nova wrapped her small fingers around him as she clung to his side.

At that moment, Nova fully comprehended that without Arrow she could never have handled this. Getting on this train was an overload to her senses. She'd never been around this many people before. With him next to her a strange restfulness penetrated her rising anxiety.

"I think it's pretty." He gave a genuine smile.

"Pretty? There's nothing 'pretty' about this chaos."

She followed behind him clutching her bag under her arm. Arrow used the duffle like a shield. Her front pressed into Arrow's broad back. She spotted the same guy she'd seen earlier, the one with the orange hair. His eyes were black like the darkest tunnel and just as chilly. Maybe he did watch her. Perhaps Arrow was right. She didn't like the way he looked at her. It made her nervous.

Worried, she glanced up at Arrow to ask him if he could walk faster. They had to get through two passenger cars. Once through, they could go to the private sleeping rooms. She'd paid for one. The ticket was clenched in her fist. She held on to her scrap of paper for dear life. There was no way she could stay out here with all these yahoos.

"You don't see how pretty it is?" Arrow spoke, but his voice was so soft she had to strain to hear it above the din. A child screamed while two young boys punched each other over the seats.

"See what?" When she glanced up at him. His eyes jumped and flickered over the group.

"It's bright and alive. I can see it and feel it. The energy feels powerful." He ducked his head under a sign stapled over the doorway that led into the second car. This train car wasn't as busy so moving down the aisle became easier.

A new crowd filled all the empty spaces in the next car. She took an easy breath when she spotted the metal doorway ahead of them. A burly man in a train uniform stood in front of the door to the private rooms.

Arrow met his stern stare as he pried the ticket out of her hand. Nova tried to straighten to her full height to seem tough, but the guard just gawked at her eyes. After giving a curt nod, he glanced at the ticket, then handed the paper back to Arrow.

Arrow slid the door open so they could pass into the next area.

An audible sigh of relief blew past Nova's lips as they entered the next train car. The door closed behind them with a clank. She was shocked at how quiet the walkway was.

A narrow aisle was directly in front of them. On either side, smudges marked up white walls. Every few feet were pocket doors. The light along the center path shined steadily. Her eyes relaxed. One of the tiny pocket doors to Nova's right opened up. Inside she could see eight people huddled on the floor and two on the bed as a man scooted out of the group. He squeezed past Arrow before shuffling toward the door that led back to the busy passenger car.

Just as the exit door closed, it immediately opened up again. Past the guard slipped the man with orange hair. He stopped and let some other people pass him. He then started down the walkway behind her and Arrow. Maybe she imagined that she'd seen this guy more than once? Hairs on the back of her neck prickled.

"Arrow." Nova kept the concern out of her voice. "Our room is in the last private sleeping car. It's right before all the cargo cars."

She didn't think the orange-haired guy followed them, but she wasn't sure. He was probably trying to find his room like them, yet a feeling of foreboding crept up her spine. She wasn't sure she could trust her judgment. She was crazy after all.

Arrow passed through the next door. This area was much busier. People talked to each other in the tight hallway. A cluster of men stood in the doorways. The flow of never ending humans slowed them down to a snail's pace. Nova glanced behind them. She didn't see the man with orange hair. Her shoulders relaxed.

They both had to stop completely when two men carrying bulky bags shoved their way past them with a grunt and a few cuss words. Once stopped, Nova was forced to squeeze against the wall to not get mashed. To protect her, Arrow shifted his body against her smaller frame. As he pinned her to the wall, he put both hands up by her head. She now had his strong solid chest to look at. The sight of the smooth muscles in his neck made her want to lick the silky cinnamon skin over his collar bones.

While she tried to shift away, she cringed. No licking. She couldn't move. She was pinned entirely as more of the horde walked behind Arrow. One of the men must have hit Arrow because he flattened himself against her. When his frame pressed against her softer curves, she felt his engorged dick right below her belly button.

As she tried to scoot away, she sucked in a breath.

"Nova, will you please stop wiggling." He looked down into her eyes as his hands came down to hold her hips. "I can't move. We can't move."

"I'm not wiggling," she argued lamely. Then she looked up into those bewitching eyes, and that same feeling of being completely centered came over her. She didn't know what it meant.

"You're right. You're not wiggling. You're making me go out of my mind with wanting you. You're beautiful, my angel."

"Don't call me that." She stared at his lips.

"Beautiful or angel?"

"Both." She intended to tell him to let her go. The words never came out. She wanted to say they could move again, that there was no one behind him, but his eyes stole all her good intentions. He was absorbing all her common sense. All that was left inside of her was desire.

Her hands of their own volition slid up his chest to wrap around his neck. He growled when she started to guide his head closer to hers. One kiss. She would exorcise him from her system if she could take one little taste. One innocent kiss. Was that too much to ask? A kiss didn't need to mean anything. After she would tell him, she was only playing around.

His head dropped to follow her lead. He was only a breath away. Something inside of her felt like it wrapped around him. Nova lifted her lips to seal them together. Her eyes dropped closed as his warm lips captured her full attention. If they were in a crowded, stinky, busy, train aisle, she didn't know it any longer. All there was, was Arrow.

Nova licked the seal of his lips. He pressed his body from his knees to his chest cementing them together. She wanted more. She wished their clothes were gone. She wanted no barriers between them. Mindlessly, she used her fingers to tunnel into his braided hair then she pressed his mouth to hers. He groaned into her lips as she ground against his solid member.

Passion that she didn't even know existed blossomed inside of her, bringing her body temperature up to a fevered pitch. Her tongue ran along the seam of his lips again as she used her other hand to tug down on his jaw. Her fingers, adding pressure, was enough to get him to open his mouth.

His lips parted. There was enough space for her tongue to slip in to explore.

As soon as her tongue touched his, that knot that was always in her stomach dissipated. It was as if strings were tied around her heart. She was secured to Arrow. The feeling wasn't unpleasant, but she wasn't sure she liked it. She couldn't let go. Arrow felt like the anchor she was missing. At last, with him, everything was put into place. Her emotions always soaring and crashing finally had a base.

Arrow started to respond to her mouth. More and more his tongue began to move. He was timid at first as if testing if she would pull away. He had just started to lap at her tongue when someone jostled them. The kiss was broken. He stumbled to the side but caught the wall. Her brain had left her, but her sanity returned with a vengeance. Arrow straightened and tried to return to her arms, but she ducked out of his embrace. Had she lost her mind?

"I must be crazy." She looked down the hall away from Arrow. The hallway had emptied out. "We're going to our room. No more of that."

Nova refused to look at him. Out of the corner of her eye, she caught an expression on Arrow's face that could only be described as hurt and stunned. She couldn't face him.

As she hurried down the hall, she went back and forth on whether going to a private room was even a good idea. She was falling in love with the notion of having sex with him. Being alone with him was dangerous. She didn't feel safe in the hallway, but she didn't think she would feel safe from herself in the private room either.

"Angel, I don't want to go to the room. We need to talk first." Arrow's voice was stern. "You can't keep doing this to me." He tried to bring her back into her arms, but she shoved him off. He let her. This was the final door. On the other side was their room.

"I'm not doing anything."

Arrow grabbed her upper arm before she crossed the threshold into the last private car. She tried to shake off his hand a second time, but his grip stayed firm.

"Nova." Her name came out of his mouth like iron.

"Let go of my arm." She tugged, but damn, he was strong. "We need to settle into our private room."

"Once we do, we'll talk."

"No." She wasn't going to discuss that amazing kiss, or her unexplainable addiction to him. And she absolutely wasn't going to kiss him again. That had been a massive mistake. He'd done something to her. This was his fault. She would have to undo his spell.

"When you say 'no' do you mean not right now?" Finally, Arrow stubbornly followed her through the door. Together they walked down the next aisle.

"When I say 'no' I mean no." Another gaggle emptied out of a room. She would've bulldozed through them, but Arrow no longer helped her. He was dead weight hooked to her arm.

"Or later?" Arrow asked as they serpentined between people.

"No, not 'or later.' Not at all."

"We have to talk about what is happening between us. You're confusing me."

"'You're confusing me' says the man who's drugged," Nova grumbled. "Yeah, right. You were confused long before I got here." She and Arrow pressed their backs to the wall as a woman with nine rambunctious kids hopped by.

"This isn't about me losing my memory. You're confusing me, and you're healing me. I think I love you, but you're trying to keep me away. We have to talk." They headed down the hall stopping every few feet for people going in and out of their rooms.

"I don't have to talk, and you can't love me. I'm not for you," she replied doggedly, but she did understand. Nova understood the confusion mixed with healing. How could they feel like this about each other when they had only just met? They had only known each other a short time. That wasn't enough time to fall in love. Was it? She didn't know what love was. Love was too big of an emotion. She only understood insanity.

"Your tongue was in my mouth, angel," Arrow muttered as if her tongue was the clarifying factor in the conversation.

"We're not talking about where my tongue was. Also, we're not using the word 'love' again." Nova wasn't happy he brought up the kiss. If she closed her eyes, she could feel the way his cock had pressed into her belly. Her tummy did a funny flip-flop.

"I can say love all I want." He paused and she turned around to face him. His eyes twinkled. "Love."

What was she supposed to do? He didn't know what he was saying. When he got his memories back, their relationship would be different. What if he was married or had a girlfriend? And she had Sky. What if he asked her about Sky?

"Stop saying *love*."

"Love."

She wanted to kiss him again even now. Nova walked in front of him. She had to put some distance between them. A room alone together wasn't going to give her distance. She might be crazy, but she wasn't stupid.

"I mean it. Stop saying *love*. Either be a silent travel companion or go away. We're only a few feet from our

room, Arrow. Let's get in there and forget what happened."
Nova glanced past Arrow. An older man tried to help his
wife into a room. Next to him, the man with orange hair
graciously held the door as the elderly couple shuffled
ahead. Again, she saw Orange-Hair eyed her. Fear sliced
through her. She had assumed he wasn't following them,
yet there he was again.

"Let's get to our room now," she commanded. Nova
wasn't going to stay out in the hall a second longer. They
needed to get into their room so she could lock the door.

Rattling nerves inside of her screamed that getting into
her room was imperative. Danger was written all over the
stranger's face.

"I'm not moving from this spot until you tell me we're
going to talk about why you kissed me, and," Arrow
paused, "what you did to me this morning before I did my
meditations. I feel something deep for you, Nova. I know
you feel it too. I should be able to use the word love. It's
not fair for you to shut me out. I don't need memories to
know that."

The old couple moved out of the way. Orange-Hair
advanced. She tugged on Arrow's arm, but true to his word
he planted his feet. She slipped her hand from his as she
took a quick look up at the door directly next to her. The
hand-written number on the front was the same as on her
ticket.

The pocket door was all white with a silver box
locking the door in place. The box had rows of black
buttons. Nova glanced at the ticket then began to furiously
punch in the passcode scrawled on the paper clutched in
her fist. Arrow leaned against the wall belligerently. He
crossed his arms over his chest, then crossed his legs at the
ankles.

"Aren't you going to try to get in the last word? It won't matter because I know what I want to say. I don't care if you argue with me. This time it's important." Arrow juggled the bag on his arm. Nova glimpsed Orange-Hair snaking closer. The gap began to close. Her hands shook, making it hard to type in the last of the numbers.

"Are you so scared of talking to me that you plan on leaving me out in the hall? Why are you so afraid? You look like you're trying to run from me. I'm not your enemy. How we feel for each other is not something we can hide from. Love isn't bad. I don't know much, but I know that."

Orange-Hair was in arms reach.

"I'm not afraid of you. I think we should get into the room because—" Nova got the door open then grabbed Arrow's arm.

Just as she opened her mouth to say someone followed them, a hand clamped down on her wrist. She looked up into the black eyes of the orange-haired stranger.

Chapter 12

The man who grabbed Nova's arm had eyes that looked like stone. Arrow hadn't seen him coming. Nova's face morphed into a mask of alarm. The stranger's grip dug into Nova's arm and multiple things happen all at once.

Arrow tried to shove the stranger's hand off. Orange-Hair didn't let go. He propelled Arrow backward with the flat of his other hand. The hit struck him directly in the chest. He gasped and the pain surprised him. A large group of people poured out of one of the private rooms causing them to be smashed into the crowd. Orange-Hair had nowhere to go unless he let go of Nova. He didn't. Orange-Hair yanked a small weapon from his coat. With a vicious thrust, he vaulted him and Nova into the small private room. Arrow stumbled while he tried to gain his footing.

The room they all toppled into was sparse. On one wall was a low cot mounted with metal poles. Nova lost her balance upon entering. The flatbed was at knee height. She bumped her leg as her hand reached out for the wall. Arrow grabbed for her but he missed. Instead of a wall, he leaned against a half-open pocket door.

"Angel." Arrow fell toward the tiny toilet room. The duffle on his arm dropped to the floor as he fell to his knees.

He jumped up quickly and spun around. The room had only two doors. The one they'd entered was now blocked by the menacing stranger. Arrow could hear people in the hallway yelling loudly. The new arrival stood in front of their only escape. He stepped between Nova and the intruder.

"What do you want?" Nova stepped around him, but stayed near the wall. Arrow sized up the invader. He shifted in front of her again. His eyes dropped to the compact pistol the stranger held. He didn't know what kind of damage it could do.

"Give me the bag, and I'll leave. No one needs to get hurt," Orange-Hair growled. The way the newcomer spoke sounded educated and he was well dressed. He had on a long dark brown coat that was spotless. His shoes appeared worn but clean. Arrow's eyes jumped to his face again. He had bright orange hair and soulless black eyes. Educated or clean, it didn't matter. This was a killer and he knew it.

Arrow glanced at the weapon, then at the strings that hung limp and flat from the stranger's heart. This man was broken and truly heartless. He kicked the black duffle toward Orange-Hair.

"The other one." The stranger waved the sleek metal pistol at Nova. What were their options? To his surprise, she wasn't freaking out. Why wasn't Nova more worried about this situation? Maybe if she gave up the backpack, this guy would go away. He weighed the lost items against the weapon. Her life wasn't worth anything in that sack. She gripped her bag in her hands tighter.

"Give him the bag. The pack's not worth your life. He could kill you." Arrow spoke loud enough for her to hear him. The stranger gave a curt nod.

"Don't be stupid. Give it to me." A smug smile kicked up one side of the intruder's face.

"I'm not stupid!" She glared at him, then the stranger. She gripped her backpack harder.

"Alright." Orange-Hair raised his eyebrows like Nova was out of her mind. "Fucking crazy woman," he muttered under his breath.

"I didn't say that you were stupid and—" Arrow began.

"Great," she spat. Arrow took a step away from her. "Another person in the world who thinks I'm nuts. This is your fault."

"What?" Arrow's head snapped back and forth between Orange-Hair and an irate Nova. "My fault?"

"Him being here is your fault," Nova pointed at Orange-Hair, "because you look like you do, and you made me kiss you. You've got that sexy smile and what am I supposed to do with that? I don't normally like men and men don't like me, but you call me beautiful. You don't listen. You couldn't let what happened this morning go." Nova began to pace in the small area in front of the bathroom door.

A warm feeling washed over him. "You like my smile?"

"Of course, you would only hear that," she muttered. "This is the kind of crap that happens to me."

"What happened this morning?" The stranger asked.

Nova ignored him as she became a whirl in the small space.

"You had to talk about how I made you come this morning. All I was trying to do was help you out. And another thing," she continued. She seemed to forget they had an audience. "You can't say you love me because you don't know me. You say you love me because you don't know any better. I can't take advantage of that. What sort of person would I be if I let you walk around thinking you love me? What if you have a wife or kids? It's unfair to you. Don't you understand that?" When she finished her tirade, she pinned Arrow with a sharp look.

"You're right. This is my fault." Arrow's cheeks felt warm. He didn't know he felt about her sharing all of that with another person in the room, and not just any person either, a man holding a gun. He decided he would just agree with her.

Her eyes flashed. Apparently, she wasn't placated. Arrow took a step toward Orange-Hair. The stranger also must've seen the fury in the red because Orange-Hair took a hesitant step toward the exit.

"For your information, Arrow," she pointed at the weapon. "The pistol he's holding is called a Sear-Shot. The modified weapon normally has only two shots. Guns that could kill people were made illegal two years ago. There was a huge deal a few years back when the United Nations put humans on the endangered species list. Back when Snow Flu first reached the equator lots of people died. Most of them were women. Without women, everyone thought humans might not be able to survive and continue the species. I'm not trading my life for my bag. I'm not stupid. And I'm not crazy."

Arrow's eyes jumped to the man gripping the Sear-Shot. Orange-Hair's eyes slashed at her then he eyed her sack again.

"What does the gun do if not kill you? Why give him your bag at all?" Arrow squared his shoulders. "I could take him." Arrow glared at the stranger. The stranger sighed. If they were such an inconvenience to him, he could leave.

"Wow, I can't believe I have to explain this. I have two shots. This isn't empty." When the stranger spoke up, Arrow could tell the other man thought it was weird they talked at all. His raised eyebrows said as much. "This shoots a small poisoned dart into your body which makes you feel like you're on fire. Trust me when I tell you, you'll wish you were dead. Now hand over the bag."

"Fine." Nova paused for another second. This guy looked ready to shoot both of them. Loosening her grip, she tossed her bag onto the mixed tan tiles of the floor. The backpack stopped at the stranger's feet. He didn't bend over to scoop up the straps like Arrow thought he would.

"My dad was right, I might not have the patience for this. I swear, I have to spell it out for you. Give me the bag on your hip. I want CC." Orange-Hair ground out the last word.

Nova glanced down at the sack tied to her hip then shoved the bag behind her. Arrow felt panic rise. Out of everything they couldn't give up CC. Nova needed the machine. He needed it. CC was the whole point of this entire journey for Nova and his only way of finding Dawn.

Nova's eyes flashed to Arrow and his brow furrowed in deliberation. Was Nova thinking what he was thinking? They needed CC to find his sister. He didn't want the two of them to be withering in pain on the floor, but they also couldn't let CC go.

Slowly, Nova untied the flowered bag. Arrow's brain frantically reviewed their options. Seeing Nova in pain would destroy him. She meant way too much to him. Nova gathered CC and held out the satchel. Her hand's trembled as she started to give the bag to the stranger.

"Don't give it to him." Arrow stepped directly in front of her. He shoved her and the bag behind him as he stood between her and the pistol. He effectively blocked any shot from hitting Nova in case the stranger fired. The action surprised the intruder.

With a swift punch, Arrow hit the stranger in the face with one clean hit. Orange-Hair acted like Arrow hadn't touched him. The stranger's head snapped back then forward. Instantly, Orange-Hair threw a punch of his own. He walloped Arrow in the gut. Arrow doubled over, then stumbled back. Behind him, Nova jumped up on the cot. He tried to straighten up, but Orange-Hair punched the back of his head and drove him toward the floor. He saw stars.

As Arrow crumpled to the floor, he brought both his hands up. The swinging of his fists knocked the pistol out of the intruder's grip. The weapon clattered to the tiles. Arrow dove toward the weapon. Orange-Hair dove after him.

The invader and Arrow grappled over the gun. Arrow had his hand around the pistol just as Orange-Hair elbowed him in the ribs. He let go. When the stranger reached for it, Arrow kicked him and plowed the flat of his hand into the center of the other man's chest. The pistol was thrown outward. When the weapon hit the wall, the gun fired. The shot made a hissing sound. Nova jumped down from the cot. The dart that shot out of the weapon hit the bed frame with a high-pitched ping. Arrow wrapped his arms and legs around the intruder and struggled to pin him to the floor. The pistol slid toward the bathroom door.

The intruder flipped Arrow face down. Out of the corner of his eye, he spotted Nova inching toward the gun.

Arrow had to keep Orange-Hair distracted. He twisted onto his back, then threw his legs up and wrapped them around the stranger's thick waist. Arrow used his thigh muscles to yank the man off of him. As soon as Orange-Hair was on his back, Arrow tackled him. They rolled and whirled. Somehow, Arrow got pinned again. Now he was flat on his back and staring into those dead eyes. He couldn't lose. He had to save Nova.

Their unwanted guest sat on his chest. He could barely breathe. This guy used his thighs to try and crush Arrow's rib cage. Arrow labored for air. He grabbed at Orange-Hair's neck. His fingers dug into the corded muscles. He squeezed. Orange-Hair tried to pry Arrow's hand's off. He punched at Arrow's arm, but he wouldn't let go. His vision blurred. Orange-Hair started to turn bright red. He struck at Arrow's arms to remove the death grip on his throat. Arrow refused to give in. He wouldn't leave Nova to handle this man on her own. He'd die before he would give up.

"I've got it." Nova held the weapon out in front of her. Both men glanced up. She aimed at both of them. Arrow wasn't afraid she would hit him. He trusted her.

"Shoot him," he wheezed at her.

The stranger didn't move. He froze. Arrow didn't let go of his neck.

"Arrow let him go." Her eyes dropped to the Sear-Shot then her eyes met his. He held on. "Arrow," she yelled. "Let him breathe."

Both of them stared at her.

Arrow finally lightened his grip. He gave her his trust, he wasn't all talk. He shoved hard. With supreme effort, he dislodged the other man. Arrow gasped for breath as he wobbly came to his feet. He swayed.

Orange-Hair's eyes flipped to the gun, then in one graceful motion, he got to his feet. He straightened to his full height and appeared not out of breath. His eyes flashed to Nova's hands on the pistol, then to Arrow as if expecting him to attack. He'd fight again if he had to, even if he did think he might fall over.

"You work for the H.S.P.C." Nova made the statement as fact. "You should've announced your allegiance. I know this weapon." She held it up. "I've worked on it."

"Wow. You sound like my dad," the stranger drawled. "An agent of the H.S.P.C. wouldn't be beaten by a dumb Indian and a red-eyed munchkin."

Nova grinned. "You're H.S.P.C. alright. All you guys are swaggering assholes."

Arrow used his hand to rub his bruised arm. He didn't move from his spot in between her and the supposed agent. He noted that the guy didn't say he was an agent at all, and even if he was, it didn't mean they should trust him.

"You referred to it as CC." Nova cocked an eyebrow at Orange-Hair. Arrow waited to see if he'd deny his affiliation.

"Clare named the computer that." Orange-Hair smiled only a tiny lift to his lips. His hands lifted to rub his neck where Arrow's fingerprints had made marks. When he raised his arm, a bracelet with a set of glowing blue gears peeked out of his sleeve on his left wrist.

Chapter 13

Nova stepped off the bed as she glanced down at the barrel of the Sear-Shot. A scratched cog was carved into the handle. She recalled Clare mentioning that this agent was Gears' best friend's son. She'd never met him, since she was rarely fit company for anyone, but now that she was in his presence she felt a little in awe. Too bad she had already made an ass of herself. Leave it to her to meet someone as important as this and then act crazy.

Arrow stepped to her side. He didn't look like he trusted the agent, but she appreciated that he did as she asked. She didn't want to quarrel with him in front of the other man. Already she'd done that once, not that that was anything new for them. There was something to be said for staying in the basement of HQ for most of her young life. At least down there she only made a fool of herself in front of a limited amount of people.

Her eyes popped to the stranger.

"What's your name, Agent?" Nova motioned for Arrow to sit down on the cot, but he remained at her side. She already knew this agent's name but she decided to make him announce it. She was positive Archer told her Agent Joe had red hair.

Arrow looked like he was about to fall over, but he stubbornly stayed standing. She pointed to the cot. When he shook his head, she stopped herself from launching into why this was all his fault again. He should sit his ass down before he fell over. She held her tongue. No use bringing up that kiss again. Besides, she was partially to blame as well. Joe was in the room because she'd been so focused on not discussing their kiss.

"You both look like hell. Either sit down or leave. You know I'm not going to give you CC." Arrow smiled but didn't move. "You as well, Arrow. Sit down or get out."

His smile fell.

"How come you have CC? Who did you steal the computer from?" The agent did not tell them his name. He wouldn't sit down either. They both made her want to pull her hair out.

"I didn't steal CC. I'm delivering the machine to another agent."

"Who?" Joe's eyes slanted. He didn't look like he believed her. Jerk.

"Dan Davis," Nova retorted. To her surprise, Joe nodded like that made all the sense in the world.

After she'd said the name, the agent sat on the floor with his back to the exit. He stretched his long legs out then crossed his ankles. He was as tall as Arrow but twice as bulky. Joe took up plenty of space in the small room. Arrow finally sank to the cot. Maybe the two of them would call a truce. As far as she could tell, they were both at a draw.

"Dan probably broke his too," Joe sighed dismally.

"You broke yours?" Nova gasped. "Clare's going to kill you." This guy wasn't coming anywhere near her CC.

"I know." Joe nodded his agreement.

"Maybe even chopped up into little pieces." Nova smiled sweetly. "What name should I write on the headstone?"

Joe snorted as she perched on the cot next to Arrow. She set the weapon between them. They waited for the stranger to answer.

"You can put Joe on my coffin."

Nova smiled as she motioned for Arrow to sit further back on the bed. He scooted back then closed his eyes as he leaned his head on the wall. He looked awful. She should thank him for fighting to protect her. She had to admit Arrow always came through for her.

As she shifted on the cot to sit on one side, she kept an eye on Joe. The bed was uncomfortable where the metal bar was hooked to the wall. She positioned herself more in the middle then set her back against the wall just like Arrow. The mattress felt like foam covering the wood with a thin piece of fabric tacking the material down. When she leaned her head near Arrow, she heard more yelling in the hallway. The train lurched. Joe didn't get up. He merely adjusted his legs as the train started to move.

"You're Joseph Rea MacBain Davis." Nova spoke his name like she was worshiping him. She cleared her throat. She didn't mean for it to come out like that. Arrow's eyes popped open then slanted toward her.

"It's just Joe." Joe didn't appear to enjoy her reverence. The train lurched. The train car started to rock with a gentle rhythm as it picked up speed.

"I've heard of you." Nova picked up the gun again and stroked the barrel. "When I worked in Archival Services they told stories about you in H.S.P.C. training. Clare and Archer did too. I've even worked on some of your equipment."

"So, what?" Joe rolled his shoulders. His eyes flipped from Nova to Arrow. "I've not heard of you." He eyed Arrow. "You're a messenger? Because I know every agent."

"I don't work for the H.S.P.C. I'm with Nova. My name's Arrow." Arrow met his hard look. She felt tension crackle.

"Arrow is helping me deliver CC to Dan," she explained quickly. "It's a task Clare put me on personally. I'm Clare Davis' personal assistant. And you don't need to be a jerk."

Her trying to smooth things between Arrow and Joe was unnecessary. Arrow wouldn't move unless it looked like Joe was a threat again. Looking at Joe lounging on the floor, she decided she wasn't worried. She was thankful they weren't going to get into another physical confrontation. Arrow didn't look like he was up for it.

"I should've guessed." This time when Joe smiled, it was genuine. "You're Nutty-Nova. You're Archer's crazy sister. The one no one sees."

Nova frowned, then her eyes dropped. Of course, that's what they would say about her. She didn't know why it hurt so much but it did. She took a deep breath. Arrow rubbed the small of her back and she accepted the comfort.

Oblivious to the insult, Joe kept talking. "I should've known there couldn't be two women with eyes the color of blood." When she looked up, Joe's black eyes met hers. "Troy didn't tell me you were so..." Joe glanced at Arrow then back at her, "hot."

"Hot?" This agent thought Nutty-Nova was hot? A smile lifted her lips as she smoothed her hair.

"You shouldn't be kept in a basement at HQ." Joe's voice turned into a purr.

"She isn't Nutty-Nova. Troy's an ass. And if you keep looking at her like that I'll wrap my hands back around your neck until I squeeze the life from your body." A dark scowl blanketed Arrow's face.

She felt Arrow tense next to her. She wrapped her hand around his arm. Arrow was jealous and it warmed her.

Joe scratched his chin like he was thinking about it. "Wow, I guess I hit a button."

"Arrow you sound like a jealous boyfriend." Nova gave an exasperated laugh.

His anger seemed to cool and Arrow smiled at Joe.

"Yea. Shut your face hole, right?"

"What does that mean?" Nova turned to face him. Did he think she was going to fight with him? Nova forgot Joe was in the room as she stared into his eyes. She was going to say something more but her thoughts got jumbled. His eyes were dark and enchanting. When she looked at Arrow, everything outside of the two of them vanished.

"I'm jealous, and you like that I'm jealous. I can tell. I'd love to be your boyfriend if you're offering me the position."

Nova chuckled. She was the one who had used the term boyfriend. It was the closest thing she had said so far that referred to them being together in the future. Her hand ran up his arm. What was she thinking?

"You're not my boyfriend. I didn't mean it like that," she murmured. Over and over she tried to remind herself of the list of reasons they couldn't be together. His eyes stole her list.

"Why not? I could be your boyfriend. You got dumped." Arrow kept smiling at her.

"Dumped by Troy," Joe tossed out.

She frowned at Joe. She forgot the man was here.

"Is that what Troy told all the other agents? Did he say he dumped me? I bet they all think I'm pathetic." Nova didn't appreciate Joe's added snippet. She didn't want pity from anyone. She absolutely didn't want it from Arrow.

"Troy's an ass." Joe's comment made her smile, but before she spoke again, in one fluid movement, Joe got up from his spot on the floor. "As much as I'd love to sit here and listen to you both fight about whether you're together or not, I have to get my bag. If I can't take CC, then I'll have to get my samples and come back here to use it."

"What samples?" Nova asked.

"I've got some blood samples I want CC to check. It'll only take twenty minutes. I'll get my bag. Be right back." He looked at the door and then at Nova. "Are you going to lock me out?"

"Maybe." Nova sighed. She should. "Are you going to bring food? Do you want to make a deal with me?"

"I'm not making a bargain with you, Nutty-Nova." Joe's sentence was flat.

"Then no." Nova's eyes slanted. "You can't borrow CC. Get lost."

Arrow grinned happily. Apparently, he didn't want Joe around. She couldn't fault that. They did try to strangle each other.

"They say 'When you get it, you get it.' So, get lost like she said." Arrow wrapped an arm around her shoulder. She shook her head.

Joe cocked one eyebrow. "I take it you're keeping my pistol."

"I'm keeping it for the inconvenience you caused me." Nova rubbed her forehead. They could use it on this trip. With a Sear-Shot they wouldn't be totally defenseless.

"I don't see it." Joe nodded. He didn't appear angry about losing the weapon "I don't think the name Nutty-

Nova fits you at all. You seem on top of it. I think I'll call you Red." Joe smoothed some of his hair down. "Okay, Red, I'll bring back food. You can have my pistol in exchange for the use of CC."

Nova's eyes scanned Arrow's reaction. He shook his head. She rubbed her brow. Was this a good idea? He did break his CC, but he was an agent.

"I'll use the computer here in front of you," Joe added.

"I guess we won't lock you out then." Nova crossed her arms over her chest. He *was* Agent Joe.

"Damn." Arrow didn't even try to hide his disappointment.

Joe slid the pocket door open then waited for a few people to walk by in the hallway. "Sorry, Arrow, but it looks like your saying didn't fit after all." Joe looked smug. That's how all those agents were. "One other thing…"

"What?" she answered.

"If that kiss in the hall was any indication, I'd say you're together." With that parting remark, Joe disappeared into the hallway closing the door behind him.

Nova looked at Arrow to measure what he thought of the statement. What was she going to say now? They were trapped in this room and she couldn't escape the conversation.

"He doesn't know what he's talking about. Anyway, I'm not going to talk to you about us." She'd start with offence and see if that would work. "That's how Joe got into this room. You were so distracted, we could've lost CC. We need no distractions. We have to focus." Nova took out the medical box from inside her backpack then opened the snaps. The lip popped open. She yanked out a plastic tube of Gears' Goo. Holding the tube with one hand, she spread white cream on her fingers and dabbed at the small cut near his eye.

"I know it was my fault. I'm sorry, angel." Arrow tipped his head down as she spread more balm along another cut on his arm. His words melted her. Damn it. She hated the way he loved her.

"It *was* your fault." She didn't raise her voice. The topic didn't matter to her anymore. What was she going to do with her Arrow? She picked up his shirt and tugged the top over his head before setting it next to her. Her hands touched his chest then she pushed on his solid pecs until he dropped flat on the cot. Her head bent as she studied his bruised ribs. "If you hadn't been so stubborn and if you'd come into the room when I told you to, then…" Her head bent down to study his abs. He was beautiful. She smiled. She told him not to use that term and now she was using it.

"I know." He inhaled sharply as she poked at his ribs. It wasn't as bad as she thought. He'd be okay, but sore.

"It was your fault that I kissed you too. You're sexy, and when your eyes look at me, I forget we just met. I don't know you." She produced an ice pack from her bag then slapped the plastic bag on his knee that was swelling up. He winced. Her lips formed a pout. She wasn't sure why she was on this. She just had to get her head together and explain that chemistry was making a mess of this trip.

"You know me."

"No one in their right mind falls in love with someone because he has a gorgeous smile. Doing that would make me insane."

"You know me, angel. I'd do anything for you. I'm sorry I let you down. I should've been looking after you. I know that. I told you this morning I'd help you. I promised I'd protect you on the way to find Dan and Dawn. I'm sorry. And you're not crazy."

Nova got up off the bed then disappeared into the bathroom. Was this more of her hiding from him? Why was she such a coward when it came to Arrow? She ran his shirt under the cold water then wrung it out. The cool fabric was all she could think of for helping the damage to his body. She came back out holding his shirt.

"Thank you for saying I'm not crazy." It was amazing that when Arrow said it, he meant it. He was the only person who ever treated her with such respect. The respect was a more powerful aphrodisiac then his gorgeous smile. She folded the shirt carefully then placed the fabric on his ribs.

"That's cold."

"It'll help." As she leaned over to move the fabric to cover as much of the swollen skin as she could, Arrow caught her hands. Her eyes met his. She wanted to kiss him again. She had opened Pandora's box. This might be unstoppable and she had no one to blame but herself. She had thought *one kiss*. One kiss would never be enough.

"Angel," he breathed.

"I've decided." Her voice softened and her stomach fluttered. "That I'll forgive you. Next time you'll have to find a better time to kiss me." She spoke like it was all logic. She knew he didn't pick the time or place. She did. He didn't quarrel with her about it. Actually, a broad handsome smile spread across his face.

Draping her closer to him, he stared at her lips.

"Next time?" He drew her mouth closer using one hand on the back of her neck. She didn't pull away. Instead, she pressed closer to his body.

The door to the room slid open. Joe advanced into the small space. Nova froze in his arms.

"Wow, looks to me like you told him you were going down on him. Did you decide on being together?" Joe snickered. Nova wanted to punch him. She should've let Arrow strangle him.

"We're not talking about anything, and we're not together." Nova shoved away from Arrow then stood. This wasn't a good time to talk about this. She'd have to leave it for now.

"Before this trip is over, I might strangle you again, Joe," Arrow growled.

Nova heaved the black duffle and her backpack under the bed away from the agent. Arrow seemed to accept that the conversation about them was on hold for now. Thank God for that. She finished placing the bags under the bed before she plopped down on the cot again. Arrow moved over to accommodate her. When the floor space cleared, Joe sat in the middle of the tiles.

The agent took a small green bag off his shoulder then unsnapped the top. First, he fished out a paper sack. Joe threw the brown bag up to Nova. She caught the bag out of the air and peered inside. She removed carrots, plump tomatoes, and dried meat.

After handing the meat to Arrow, both of them started to eat while Joe began to open another small green bag. This bag had multiple straps and pockets. As he loosened straps, the bag seemed to grow. Joe knelt over the unrolled fabric. Finally, he unzipped a tiny pocket in the middle. From there he took out what looked like multiple finger-sized tubes. Each one was gray with a white top. She didn't recognize them.

"I need CC now," he asked over his shoulder.

Nova got up and scooped up the pistol that was stashed on the cot. She then pulled CC out of the bag on her hip. She crossed the tiny room to sit in front of the exit door. As Nova sat, she set the Sear-Shot in her lap then reluctantly held CC out to Joe. Silently she told him he better not bust hers. For a second, she wouldn't let the computer go. Joe waited patiently. Once the machine was in his hand, he turned back to the tubes.

Joe opened the first one by unscrewing the white top. Carefully he opened a small door on the back on CC and attached a needle.

Once Joe seemed to have CC to his liking, he spoke. "CC, I want a color analysis for Snow flu. Blood sample one."

He put the needle into the tube. Only a few minutes passed. She eyed the agent intently.

"Would've been nice if Clare told me it could do that," Nova muttered as she shifted closer and began to study Joe's actions.

"Blood sample one. Analysis positive," CC's mechanical voice declared.

"All that work for nothing," Joe spat at the bottle. He then began the process all over again. Just as before, CC stated the sample was positive.

A solid two hours later, Joe put the last of his tubes away. So much for twenty minutes. She shook with nerves. Her mantra turned into "Please don't drop CC."

Joe was in a foul mood. Every time CC's mechanical voice stated "positive," he swore. Stress wrinkled her forehead and she rubbed. When Joe finally handed the computer back to her, her shoulders relaxed.

"Wow, that's hard work guarding CC with your life, right, Red?" Joe started the elaborate process of closing his bag and putting the tubes away.

"We need CC to tell us where grapes are growing underground." Nova got up off the floor and headed to the bathroom. She needed a break. To the agent this might be just another piece of equipment, but to her this was their guide. "Besides I wouldn't want you to break it since you're good at that," she added before she disappeared into the little room.

Chapter 14

Once Nova closed the door, Arrow expected Joe to leave. After the agent finished with his bag, instead of leaving, he eyed the door Nova had passed through. Arrow should've expected he wouldn't get lucky enough that Joe might leave.

"Did she say grapes?" Joe sat back against the wall near the exit.

Arrow nodded. He wasn't sure what he should tell this agent, but he figured finding grapes wasn't a secret.

"I'm tracking Agent Dan," Arrow answered. "He's walking along fields of grapes. CC told us there were only two places where fields of grapes grow. I guess, one of them is outside of New Bosie. CC will navigate us there. When we get there, I'll see my sister who's with Dan. Nova will give CC to Dan."

"How do you know he's walking among grapes?"

"I just know." He didn't want to explain. All that would happen would be more questions he didn't know the answers to. His lack of history wasn't a piece of information he wanted to advertise.

Joe studied him. Arrow was pleased Joe let his comment be.

"I heard Dan was on Long Break," Joe remarked at length.

"He is or was." Nova opened the door to the bathroom. She'd washed her face and brushed her hair. His angel looked radiant all the time, so he was amazed that she could look even better. "It's none of your business." She gave him a sour frown before shoving her bag under the bed and setting the pistol next to him on the cot. When she sat, she regarded Joe fully. "But since Arrow can't keep his face hole shut, I'll tell you. Yes, Dan was on Long Break until Archer went off investigating an imaginary person for Clare."

"Wow, imaginary people. Isn't Clare pregnant? Troy told me Archer was with his wife while she got close to popping. Isn't that where Dan and Archer should be?"

Nova gave a bark of bitter laughter. "That's what was supposed to happen, but it didn't."

Arrow could feel her annoyance, so he reached out to lightly put his hand on her leg. She didn't push his hand off. Instead, she moved closer. She might not like that he'd shared information with Joe, but she was forgiving. He thanked the Great Spirit she was forgiving.

"Wow, I get it. You need Dan to find a roaming Archer since his wife is going berserk. Dan needs a CC to do it." Joe closed his eyes then leaned his head against the wall. "Wow, that's a real pisser." He started to arrange his bag like a pillow. Gauging the agent's actions, Arrow assumed Joe wasn't going to leave anytime soon. His heart sank.

Joe stretched his legs out, crossed his ankles, then folded his arms over his chest. His bag was a head rest. Yea, he wasn't leaving. He was sleeping. Nova had her eyes on the agent too.

After a while, she moved closer to him on the cot. Her body cuddled under Arrow's arm. His heart soared when she set her head on his chest. The train rocked them, and he enjoyed the feel of her in his arms.

"You shouldn't have told him where we're going," she whispered. "We don't know who we can trust. I know he's an agent, but we should be careful."

"They say," he whispered into her hair. "'The right relationship is everything.' I think we have to trust sometimes."

"*They* again?" Nova arranged him so that he was horizontal on the narrow cot side by side. Her back pressed up against his chest, and her ass snuggled against his crotch. He tried not to think about wanting her. Instead, he was simply happy she let him hold her. He wanted to be her warmth and pillow.

"*They* are all I got in my head." Since Nova faced a sleeping Joe, he couldn't see her reactions. Her breathing was even when he placed his hand on her belly. The feel of her chest as it rose and fell made him want to wrap around her even tighter.

"I think you just quoted a bank tagline."

"But I think it's right."

"The right relationship is everything? I don't think you know what you're saying. I trusted my first boyfriend, and he used me to hide that he wanted men. No one liked me, so I was easy to manipulate. I knew there were issues with us, but I was lonely and I ignored it. He didn't want to face the type of person he was. Neither did I." When Nova spoke, Arrow was pleased she was sharing her past with him. He hated it when she claimed he didn't know her. He wanted to know her. In fact, he wanted to spend a lifetime knowing everything about her.

He didn't comment but kept silent in the hope she would keep talking. After a short pause, she continued.

"After him, I made up my mind I shouldn't let his lies get to me. I decided the whole 'wanting to have sex with a man thing' was an isolated incident. He had his reasons, so I forgave him and attempted to move on. I went on date after date. My eyes were scary, and I couldn't keep a level emotional state no matter how hard I tried. I pushed people away and ruined relationships. Because of that, I was called Nutty-Nova. I was alone for a lot of years. Then I met Troy. I figured I'd finally found someone. I thought I knew him. I thought I knew myself." Nova sighed as she slid his arm lower to rest on her hip. "In the end, he used me like the others. Troy wanted to get close to Dan, Clare, and Archer. Archer was a new agent, plus he was strong. He's stupid mind you, but he has Clare. Clare's a genius. The two of them together are a powerhouse. Dan is her brother and he's skilled too. Both Dan and Clare were adopted young. Both of them were accepted into the H.S.P.C. with open arms."

"How did Troy use you?" Arrow tipped his head down and turned her head so he could see her face. He studied her flushed cheeks.

"Troy wanted to get closer to the Davises," she swallowed. "He didn't want me or love me. He didn't understand me or care. It was all lies. He wanted what I could do for him. That's how it always goes for me. People will use you if they get the chance. They pretend to be one way when they're someone else entirely. Don't tell me what *they* say about trust or relationships. I don't need to hear a commercial."

Arrow contemplated all she'd told him. He trusted people even though he had no reason to do so. Was he a fool, or was Nova bitter and her judgment clouded? He didn't know. He wished he had some memories he could rely on to make a decision either way.

"Did you love Troy or that boyfriend you had? Did they hurt you so much that you can never heal again? Is that why I can never earn your trust?"

Nova sat up. She turned so she could look into his eyes. Her eyes scrutinized him like he might be teasing her, but never before had he been so serious.

"I never said you couldn't earn my trust." She leaned her slim body over him. "I'm letting you be here with me. That should say a lot. But I don't want you to expect more than what I can offer. I can't give out love. I don't know how to do that. I don't even know what it is. I'm not right in the head, and sooner or later you'll find that out. I don't know why I've been stable so far, but one day, you'll leave when you see how insane I really am."

"I have practically no memories of my life, but what I do know about is love." Arrow smiled up into her eyes as she put her hands on either side of his shoulders. "I've enough love in me for the both of us. And as for trust, I'll earn it from you, angel. I promise I won't use you. I'll simply be your Arrow. No one else. I want to be with you not because you have CC and can help me, and not because I'm afraid to be on my own. I want to be with you because you're Nova. I love you."

"Even if I'm crazy?" She settled back on the cot next to him. Her eyes lifted to the ceiling. A single tear slipped down the side of her cheek.

Now Arrow leaned up so he could look down at her. He brushed the drop with his thumb.

"If you're crazy, then so am I." He bent his head to taste her waiting mouth. He had to connect with her. He was afraid he would go too far then she would move away. His lips only lightly brushed hers.

As soon as he started to lean away from her mouth, her hand reached up to wrap around his braid. She tugged his mouth back down for a deeper kiss. This time he let more of his hunger out. He slanted his mouth over hers, loving the feel of her under him.

Her acceptance of his body over hers made him feel like she was again giving him something. He believed wholeheartedly that he could win her love. He would never let her down.

She slipped her tongue into his mouth while he breathed her in. She probably already loved him, and she didn't know it yet. They belonged together. That was unmistakable from the first moment he saw her in his dreams.

"You're crazy, but I like it," Nova purred lazily in his ear as she held him.

He lifted his head to memorize every beloved detail of her face. Arrow would've kissed her again, but Joe cut into their private world. Arrow had forgotten the man was there. This guy had to go.

"Wow, man, you're the sappiest bitch I've ever listened to. I can't believe you of all people almost strangled me. Love and trust, yammer, yammer, yammer." Joe didn't open his eyes or lift his head. Arrow knew the comment was a dig at him, and he wasn't surprised.

"I get that you can't understand what I'm saying." Arrow glared even though Joe couldn't see him. "But then you would think if you didn't understand then you'd be silent. They say, 'Life beckons, choose wisely.' Maybe you should choose to remain silent."

Joe opened his eyes to mere slits. "What the hell does that mean?"

"That's from Busch's Beer." Nova frowned.

Arrow looked first at Nova, then back at Joe. Regretfully, he untangled his limbs from Nova's.

"It means you're sad and broken." While he sat up, he took the cold pack from his knee and the shirt from his body. He faced Joe. "You'll never understand love."

Joe sat up. His eyes widened. He stared at Arrow as if determined to uncover a secret hidden inside of him. Silently the two of them eyed each other. Arrow could see some part of Joe knew he told him a great truth.

"How am I broken?" Joe's voice held honest notes of desire for the answer.

What was the right way to explain?

"I see the connections. They're lifeless. Your heartstrings don't glow or dance or sway. They show no light, and the cords are no longer gold. You've no brightness in you, maybe you never had. You don't feel." Arrow didn't know how else to say what he saw. He couldn't describe the strings any other way. He'd been thinking of his dream since Nova had freed him from the cage. The last dream he'd had before Nova showed up. He understood he was gifted, that seeing the ropes was special, but he lacked the words to explain what they meant.

Joe surveyed Nova with a lift of his eyebrow.

"Arrow has a head injury, so sometimes he says things that don't make any sense." She sat up from where she was curled on the cot then shrugged at Joe.

"Just because you don't understand doesn't mean you need to make excuses for me." Arrow turned his back to Nova. She didn't get it because she couldn't see the strings. He figured out no one could see the golden ropes but him.

"You think I'm broken? You fix it." Joe leaned back on his bag while he regarded Arrow. There was a clear challenge in his tone. Arrow didn't know how to take it. Did Joe mean that? "Go on, show me."

Maybe Joe was trying to prove something either to Arrow or to himself. Maybe he wanted to make Arrow look bad. If Joe wanted to throw down a challenge, it worked. He didn't know if he could fix Joe's ropes, but he was going to try.

Arrow quickly got up off the bed, and then he dropped to the floor to sit next to Joe. He sat cross-legged. He'd no idea what to do. In his head, he reviewed his dream.

Joe scooted over while eyeing him warily. The harder Arrow worked to remember his dream, the more specific things came to him. Without knowing why, and without saying a word, he first unbraided his hair. His gift would work better if his hair could move.

Once his hair was free, he looked at the ropes resting flat against Joe's stomach. This was exciting. When he first saw the strings on the old man, he didn't want to touch them. But now during his travels with Nova, he'd seen how beautiful and alive the connections were. He wanted to feel the strands slipping through his fingers. He wanted to hold the power.

Now he got the opportunity. He figured Joe didn't believe him and wanted to prove he lied, but he decided he didn't care. This was a chance to see how the cords felt.

Arrow noted where the first few set of strings hung. He moved to a kneeling position so he could lean over Joe. The top cords looked frayed like someone had taken a dull knife to them. The fibers appeared like someone had tried to cut them, but didn't succeed. He leaned over more and reached for the lower set near the bottom of Joe's heart. When he reached out, Joe clutched at his wrist.

"What are you doing?" Joe had a death grip on his hand.

"You told me to fix it. You said 'show me' like an asshole."

Joe didn't let go of his hand.

"Nova," Arrow turned where she was crouched on the edge of the cot, "give Joe the pistol, the Sear-Shot."

"No way." She shook her head.

"Give the pistol to him, please, angel." He faced Joe to look him in the eye. "If I hurt you, then you can shoot me."

"I've officially lost my mind." Nova begrudgingly handed the pistol to Arrow, who passed the weapon to Joe. Once Arrow gave the Sear-Shot to him, Joe freed his arm.

Joe pointed the barrel at Arrow's face.

"I could hurt you with or without this pistol."

"Yea. Got it, Clown-Hair." Here was yet another person with no ability to trust.

As soon as Joe had the pistol aimed at him, Arrow studied the ropes again. He reached out slowly. He picked up the set coming from the center of Joe's chest. He didn't realize he was holding his breath until the air started to hurt in his lungs. Trying to relax, he exhaled then focused on the strings. They felt like silk in his hands. Some places weren't smooth, however. Rough bumps scraped his flesh.

Without paying any attention to Nova or Joe, he began to run his hands down the length to smooth the threads out.

As the cords glided through his fingers, the broken parts flattened out. All the rips and tears vanished. The fibers started to spin in his hands. They began to feel like they'd awakened, one at a time. He lovingly stroked the strings as his fingers coaxed the color to return.

Soon the mystical threads felt warm as they grew in color. In areas where they didn't seem sturdy, Arrow began to braid them like his hair. He used thinner strands to wind around thicker ones. The ropes easily wove together, and he petted them until they took on what he considered the right hue.

Everything on Joe's chest became brighter and brighter until the strands glowed properly. Now they looked like all the other ones Arrow had seen before. He smiled as he worked, feeling somehow stronger and warmer himself. Inside his soul, as the lines were renewed, so was he.

Arrow used both hands. Soon all the ropes from Joe's chest became well built. Joe's threads began to sway as if moving in an invisible breeze. He made one last flick of his wrist to let go so the heart strings could flow free.

As he sat back, the room came into focus. He blinked as if he'd been asleep. Joe stared at him mesmerized. Nova rubbed her palms against her head and worry made her eyes bounce over him.

"Nova what's wrong? Are you hurt?" He didn't like Nova upset. Her eyes grew to the size of saucers.

"Your eyes turned red, Arrow." Her hand rubbed back and forth. "What did you do? Your eyes were as red as mine. I thought they filled up with blood. Your hair moved by itself."

"I'm fine. Are my eye's still red?"

"No. Now they look dark-brown, less black and more brownish. They look healthy now."

Arrow turned to Joe to ask him how he was, but Joe's face showed stunned shock. He was completely frozen.

"Joe?" He said the agents name curiously. He glanced at the pistol. Joe had dropped the gun to the floor as if he'd forgotten he held the weapon.

When Joe stayed silent, Arrow started to get concerned. Maybe he should have never touched the strings. He shouldn't be playing with his gift when he understood nothing about it. Especially when he had no memories. Maybe once his memories returned then he would know about this strange occurrence.

Concerned that he had hurt Joe, he leaned back over him to shake his shoulder. Joe woke from his trance-like state and then raised his head. They stared at each other for a silent minute. Then Joe reacted in a way Arrow never expected.

Joe kissed him.

The agent reached up to hold Arrow's head before he planted his lips on Arrow's mouth. Arrow lost his balance as he tried to pull out of the other man's embrace. He threw both hands to Joe's chest and pushed. Joe let go. While Arrow wiped his lips, he got to his knees. Arrow then came to his feet in one fluid motion flabbergasted at Joe's unexpected show of affection. He wasn't sure he'd ever been kissed by a man, but he was sure he would never forget Joe.

"Can you feel it, Red?" Joe asked Nova. His eyes gleamed as they shot to Nova.

Nova shook her head, but Joe wasn't paying her any attention. Joe's eyes jumped around the room like frogs in a pond.

"Did you drug him?" Nova asked Arrow. "What did you do?"

"No. I don't know what happened." Arrow took a hasty step back as Joe put his green bag on his back. Joe's movements looked like a jig as he hopped around the room.

"I have to go." Joe laughed a joyous bubbling sound. The laughter was downright alarming. This guy had been a cold, callous H.S.P.C. agent. Now he was acting like an excited child on holiday.

"You ruined Joe." Nova gasped when Joe hugged him. She mouthed the words, "What did you do?"

Arrow shrugged. He didn't know what he did or what effects his actions had on people. Using his hands, he shoved out of Joe's bear hug. He would've liked to ask Joe, but it would have been like talking to someone who was high. He would have to wait to know since Nova didn't have any strings.

"One thing before I go. I didn't care before, but now I think I'll tell you." Joe's smile was so wide it took up his whole face. Arrow might be able to count all of the agent's teeth.

"What?" Arrow asked, but he was afraid of the answer. He hoped Joe didn't declare some undying love for him. If that happened, then he wouldn't know how to explain to Nova. Even with only these actions, he didn't know what he was going to say to her when she asked him later.

"Two months ago, there was a fire in New Boise. That CC is out of date. The fire destroyed all the grape crops. Now you can only get grapes outside of Bosstown. If you're looking for Dan, I'd start at a different WB." With that, Joe pranced out of the room leaving Arrow and Nova in stunned silence.

Chapter 15

Nova rubbed her forehead. CC spoke to her in that same monotone computerized voice that grated on her nerves.

"Bosstown is underground WB7. Do you want to know the base leader's names and where to locate them?"

Nova paused in her pacing. She returned to her backpack to count her money. After Joe left, she'd been looking into what he'd told them for twenty minutes. She didn't think he would return, so she wouldn't be able to ask more questions.

For now, it appeared everything he stated was true. Panic stalked her. She took a deep breath. CC gave her suggestions on trains and routes, but there weren't a lot of options. They would have to see what they could find once they reached the first stop. If they had good fortune, they wouldn't have to go all the way to New Boise to get another train to Bosstown.

Nova considered the trip. Any good fortune for her had been scarce since she left Clare. Her eyes jumped to Arrow. Well, she *had* found Arrow.

Keeping her eyes on Arrow, she smiled. He sat on the bed calmly eating the last of the carrots. He let her think by not intruding. He was probably trying to do what she asked, shutting his face hole. A frown replaced her smile. His silence bothered her. She wanted him to tell her what he thought. Her eyes dropped to the sprinkling of chest hair across his muscled pecs. He should tell her what he thought *and* put on a shirt. Now was not the time to kiss again or get involved with conversations of that nature.

"Are you listening to CC?" she asked. When she argued with him, that's when she came up with her best plans. She appreciated Arrow's silence while she looked things up on CC, but now she wanted him to speak. He'd help her stay centered. If he could say anything, she'd be okay with hearing it.

He nodded.

"Bosstown is in the opposite direction from where we're going." Nova began to pace in front of the bathroom. "We've hours yet before we can get off this train then we have to hope we can get on a train going back the other way. I don't even know if I have enough HOCs for another train ride. I might have only enough to go home. Private rooms are astronomical."

Arrow nodded. She heard the crunch of another carrot.

"Stop eating. Care about this, damn it. Say something!" She'd reached the end of her patience. Marching over to the bed, Nova snatched the carrot from his hand. "We need to talk. You're the one who likes to talk and ask questions."

"Nova, sit with me." Arrow took the carrot clutched in her hand then gathered the paper bag and set it aside. He patted the cot.

Frowning, she came to sit on the bed. Gradually, he coaxed her to lean back. Her head settled on his chest. She stared at the ceiling. Just being next to Arrow, touching him, made her mind tranquil. Before when she paced, her brain went as fast as this train, but now everything stopped. She absently ran her fingers over his arm making lazy circles. Goose bumps rose.

"It was actually a good thing that Joe told us about the fire. He might not have, and then we'd have gone all that way for nothing. This is a good thing. You should be happy. Relax and be happy, angel."

Nova shrugged. Her fingers made lazy circles on Arrow's arms again. She was glad they hadn't gone all the way to New Bosie, but now she had new things to worry about.

"He wouldn't have told us, except you..." She leaned up on her arms to look into Arrow's eyes. "Are you going to tell me what you did?"

"I can't explain very well. I see gold ropes or strings on people. The cords glow and move. All I did was I touched his strings. I smoothed them out." Arrow paused. "They didn't look right."

"That's why you said it was pretty on the train. You were talking about the ropes." Nova considered the way he'd watched people since they had started traveling.

"Yea. It's also partly why I was unfocused. I don't know what the ropes mean or what they do. I'm guessing at it. I hope when I get my memories back then I'll know, or maybe Dawn will tell me when we see her."

"Seeing gold ropes might be a side effect of your gift of seeing through your sister's eyes. I worked with a few scientists who study gifted people. A lot of times there are side effects to your abilities." Nova cuddled close to him again. She wouldn't be able to help him with what he described. She was gifted sure, but what Nova could do she couldn't control. She couldn't get Snow Flu, and other than her hellish mood swings, she had no side effects.

"I shouldn't have touched the ropes not knowing what I'm doing or what the strings mean. I took a risk with Joe. I won't take that risk again."

"I disagree. I think you should figure your gift out. It's important to know yourself." She resumed petting his dusting of arm hair.

Arrow chuckled. The rumble made her head bounce. "You disagree with me? Something new for us." His voice dripped with a mixture of humor and sarcasm.

Nova smiled.

"I don't have time to explain how wrong you are about everything because I have to plan a trip to WB7. You should put on a shirt. Again, with me telling you to get some clothes on. I think you stay naked on purpose." She sighed, and then tried to get up, but Arrow tugged her back down into his arms. She halfheartedly tried to rise again, but again he held her wrists.

Nova let Arrow settle her back against his chest. Her head leaned near one of his nipples and she inhaled. He smelled like hot male. Her Arrow. He wrapped one arm around her back. Maybe she wanted a few seconds of not worrying or planning. She could take a few seconds to enjoy his company. More and more, she felt like she knew him. Even if he didn't have a past to tell her about.

What would it be like if he were at home with her? What if they had met and he'd taken her on a date? She pictured him at her door, leaning on the frame waiting to take her to dinner. These ideas were fanciful. Once she was home, he would return to whatever life he had here underground.

"You said you might not have enough hawks? What do birds have to do with us going to Bosstown?" Arrow cut into her wayward thoughts. He tried to slip his hand closer to her breast.

Nova slapped his hand. He returned his fingers to her ribs. "Not Hawks, HOCs."

"You're just saying the same word over and over." Arrow rubbed his chin against her shoulder. He tugged her shirt down in the back. "Is this potato, potato?" Arrow's warm breath fanned her skin. The tickle of his chin hair made her squirm.

"HOC stands for H.S.P.C. Organizational Currency." She tugged her shirt back up. "I'm not talking about birds. That doesn't even make sense. We're underground." Nova wished he would put on a shirt. If he had put his top back on, they could seriously discuss what they should do next.

"Yea. Got it. Why do we have to have some of whatever these are?" Arrow asked, but his voice held no real concern for the answer. He dropped his hand to move around her waist. Now his fingers brushed against her belly button. His bare chest was warm against where his skin grazed her cheek.

Nova summoned all her strength and batted his hand away. She liked what he was doing so she figured she should stop him.

"HOCs are used for private train cars. They are also used for trading for things like food and clothes. Years back Canada, the old United States, and Mexico got into an argument on what money they were going to use. When it came down to the Looney versus the Dollar, the governments couldn't agree. The fighing made trading difficult on the Equator. There were so many currencies. One day the Mexican government, Canada, and the old U.S. got together and agreed to let the H.S.P.C. have money backed by their gold. Now on the Equator, you can use the Yen, the Euro, or the HOC. Here in the NEDs everyone uses HOCs." Nova sat up intending to leave the bed. If she didn't, she was worried her willpower might cave.

"NEDs?" Arrow asked while he captured her wrists again and pulled her back down. He kissed her neck. Nova moaned with his mouth on her skin. Now he kissed her shoulders. His warm lips distracted her so she was having a hard time thinking.

"It stands for Northern Earth Dens. United States, Canada, and Mexico above ground is the C.T.O.N.A., not the NEDs." She took a deep breath. Her voice sounded funny in her ears. She realized his questions made her stay in bed.

"Got it."

"I wish you had your memories back. I feel like I have to explain everything to you like you're a child." Angry that she could so easily crumble around him, she snatched the edge of her shirt to tug the top in place. Once more she attempted to rise, but Arrow grabbed her hand.

"I'm no child, Nova." Arrow placed her hand on his hard cock. She could feel the outline through the fabric. She yanked her fingers away as if she'd been burnt.

"I'm sorry." Arrow threw up his hands in a sign of peace between them. "I don't know why I did that. I do get it. Go ahead and pace. I promise I'll sit here. I remember silent is the important word." Arrow's eyes twinkled. "No getting friendly."

Nova paused in the motion of rising off the cot. She didn't know what to say. She didn't actually want Arrow to be silent anymore. What she wanted was… well, she wasn't going to admit what she wanted.

"You said before that the ropes were part of the reason you were unfocused?" She turned on the edge of the cot to face him. His skin was incredibly smooth. With his shirt off, she got a healthy view of all that touchable light-brown skin. Her mind pictured stroking his penis again. She wanted to experience all Arrow could offer her. No matter how hard she worked to shake the desire, she couldn't.

"Yea, part of it." His hands rose to re-braid his hair. The strands moved smoothly in his skillful fingers. After his hair was braided, he dropped his arms to his lap with a plop. He grinned at her. He was always willing to give her what she wanted. She wasn't sure she had ever been around anyone who was simply happy to make her happy. What was wrong with him?

"Do you see them on me?"

Arrow's gaze traveled over her body. Now she was nervous. What if her strings weren't attractive?

"I can't tell. Could you take off your shirt?" A mischievous gleam appeared in his eye. His mouth kicked up on one side.

"No." She hid her grin while she got up from the bed. She was being foolish. Standing next to the cot, she made up her mind to stop mooning over him.

Right before she would've retreated to the bathroom to clear her head, he reached over to capture her hand. His grip was warm and secure.

"I'm sorry. Please don't run away to the bathroom. I don't see the cords on you, or me. When I see through Dawn's eyes, I don't see them, either. I know little about the vision. I had hoped that once I saw Dawn, I'll have more answers."

"What was the other part?"

"What other part?"

"Why you're distracted and unfocused. You were so out of it that you didn't even notice Joe following us." Sighing she perched next to his hip then slipped off her shoes.

"I didn't notice Joe because I don't see anyone, but you. I told you, Nova. You're my angel. You're the only thing I want to look at."

Nova's eyes jumped to his. She wished she could tell how earnest he was. He always looked at her like he didn't see her creepy-colored eyes, or how short and unshapely she was. Arrow looked at her how all women wanted to be looked at.

As she sat there, she came to the realization she wasn't going to get up again. She needed to get whatever this was out of their systems. If they could spend some time sedating this powerful sexual attraction, then they could both focus better. They had a long trip ahead of them. She couldn't have Arrow looking at her with those captivating eyes of his.

A part of her whispered that this was the argument she gave herself about that "one" kiss. She ignored the solid reasoning that told her she might never get enough of Arrow. She was crazy. Crazy people didn't have to listen to logic.

"I told you not to call me, angel." Nova placed her dainty hand firmly on the center of his chest. She pressed on his warm pecs until he was flat on his back. As she leaned over him, she got a hint of his male scent. He didn't say anything. He didn't ask what she was doing. Instead, he looked at her with all the trust anyone could ever ask for.

Shyly, Nova touched his dark-toned neck and trailed her fingers along his collar bone. Her fingers slid up fluttering all the way to his jaw line. Bending her head closer, she pressed her tongue to the seam of his mouth before he could speak. Nova wouldn't let Arrow deepen the kiss. She lifted her head to look down into his eyes. Those hypnotic brown eyes turned black and swept her thoughts away. She should explain her actions, but when her eyes alighted on his face, her brain turned off and her emotions took over. She traced her fingers over his mouth. Delicately, she let her wandering hands move over his cheekbones and drift to his ears.

Like a blind woman, she explored him. When he tried to reach for her, she set his hands up above his head. He let her pin them there easily. Letting go of his wrists, her fingertips moved over him to investigate each one of his ribs. Tenderly, she let her mouth sip at his flesh. The sensation of his rapidly heating skin under her palms made her feel in command and sexually excited.

Nova swung one leg over his waist. She moved in a position to keep him beneath her. The sensation of his rigid hips teased her inner thighs with anticipation. It was intoxicating that he let her have whatever she wanted. Her heartbeat accelerated. The world had become suspended in time. Her pulse pounded through her veins in a hammering beat. Blood rushed and it warmed her cheeks.

Arrow tried to reach up to touch her a second time. She set his hands above his head again and steadied them with an eyebrow flare punctuating her control. He didn't say a word, but his eyes spoke eloquently. Those eyes pleaded. She understood what he wanted even if his request was never voiced. She wanted it all as well. Never before had she wanted to be in charge or to take control. In fact, she couldn't even remember ever wanting sex or anything remotely like this.

Knowing she wasn't going to stop, she bent her head. Her hair spilled like a curtain around his face. She sighed into his ear and bit softly on his earlobe before tracing the shell with her tongue. He shivered. Above her, he gripped the metal pole at the top of the mattress. A dizzying sensation started to saturate her stomach as she began to give in to what she'd been thinking about basically since she'd met him. She could lie to herself, but her body didn't accept half-truths.

As restraint left her, Nova stretched out full length on the small cot. Her one hand propped under her chin. With half-closed eyes, she studied him. His eyes observed her now with fixed intensity. They looked less black and were a brilliantly glazed soft brown.

"Nova… I don't know how to…" he muttered thickly. He sucked in a deep breath when she leaned over to flick her tongue over one of his nipples.

"You trust me?" Her hand lovingly ran down his flat stomach toward his midriff. She let her hand settle on the rough-haired expanse right above his pants.

"With my life."

When she met his waistband, she undid the first button, then the second, then the third. When he didn't make a move to stop her, she tugged on the heavy denim. He wiggled his legs to help lower his pants. When the fabric was all the way down to his knees, the absent cloth freed his erection like it was waiting to jump into her hands.

Before her, his penis looked bigger then she remembered. His cock also appeared harder somehow. She studied the skin that stretched tightly over the throbbing head. She'd seen his cock before and touched the thick top, but this was different. This time she was going to join him. Together they were both going to find the release they craved. There was nothing in her mind keeping her actions clinical this time. Who was she kidding? Even last time there were no clinical thoughts in her head.

Arrow hooked his thumbs into his pants to slide them all the way down to his ankles. She rolled off of the cot for a moment. When they reached his shoes, he sat up to yank off his boots and socks. Once his legs were free, she held in a giggle while he kicked his pants to the floor.

Naked, he returned to reclining on his back at the center of the cot. He had that look of trust shining in his eyes. The look was humbling and frightening. She was terrible in bed. Sure, her gay boyfriend had no idea, but Troy knew. What if she messed this up? What if she was awkward and he laughed? What if once he got his memories back, then he told her the sex had been horrible?

"I can see the questions on your face." Arrow captured her hand. He kissed her fingertips before speaking again. "Angel, whatever you want from me you can have it." He made a deep, harsh sound when he placed her hand over his cock. His tan skin flushed red. She sat next to him.

In one part of her brain, Nova was bewildered. She'd never touched a man because she wanted him sexually, and she always kept men at a distance. Also, she'd never reached an orgasm with someone, but now everything seemed to have changed. Wild quivers of sensation rushed over her at his heat. The more she gave in, in mind, in body, the stronger those feelings became.

Deliberately, she closed her hand over his straining shaft and shifted closer to him. She made a loose fist over the swollen mushroom top. As her fingers brushed over the tip, moisture beaded then traveled toward his balls. She spread the drips of pre-cum along a vein running downward then swiped at the slit at the top.

Arrow groaned deep in his throat but kept his eyes on her. She could see his eyes fighting to close with every tug of her hand.

"Nova…" Again, Arrow tried to touch her, but she pushed his hands above his head. He exhaled in a whoosh. "Let me touch you. Kiss me, angel. Can't you see what you're doing to me?"

"My eyes might be red, but I've excellent eyesight."

He gave another ragged gasp as her fingers tickled downward over his balls, then made their way back up his shaft.

"I don't know if I can do this again, like before. I want more. I'm going to lose my mind." Arrow trembled under her hands. The way he shuddered made her smile.

"I've already lost my mind." Changing her position, she maneuvered her body sideways. "Trust me, you don't need it for this."

Nova wanted him to be as swept away as she was. She'd never realized that desire like this could be as powerful as any other force in nature. She let go of him for a moment to taste his pre-cum on her fingers.

His eyes widened when she sucked them into her mouth.

Half on top of him with one leg on one side and the other leg pinning him down, his breath rasped as she began to caress him again. Absently she bent toward his mouth. Their lips met. She licked wickedly. He opened his mouth and her tongue speared in with no finesse, but he didn't seem to mind. He eagerly let his tongue duel with hers until they were both out of breath.

Ripping her mouth away, her nipples beaded against her bra. Her clothes were too tight. They needed to come off. When she lifted her body up, Arrow watched her through heavily lidded eyes. She sat up unzipping the front of her sweater. Once the top was loose, she threw the garment to the floor.

As she straddled him, she bent her head to sprinkle kisses from his throat to his chest. Her hands ran downward over his cut abs. Each rigid muscle flexed as she caressed him. Nova could see sweat appearing on his cheekbones. When he attempted to touch her again, she captured his hands then placed them over his head. He might have muttered some swear word under his breath, but she wasn't sure.

"What did you just say?"

"I said 'no good' in Navajo. I want you."

"I like being in control. Say, 'I want you.' in Navajo." Nova didn't add that she was afraid if he started to touch her, his hands might make her flustered. What if she ruined this? To get him to desire her, she needed to be thinking not just feeling. On top is where she would stay.

"Ayóó áníínishí Ayóó ánóshí." Arrow's hands reached for her thighs. His fingers slipped up her hips and tugged on the top of her jeans. "That's I love you." His dark eyes glittered then flipped to her shirt as his pupils dilated. She could see herself reflected in those erotic depths as they took in her face.

Letting her tongue out to lick some of the salty perspiration off of his cheek, heat infused her body. While straddling him, she grabbed the bottom of her dark blue shirt. The top was easily brought up and over her head. The movement tilted her ribcage high. Her slight round breasts strained against the black fabric of her bra. His breathing picked up then hitched. The little muscles of his face were taut as he kept himself motionless under her.

Nova slipped off of him then stood next to the cot.

"No." He grabbed at her, but she was out of his reach. "Wait."

He rolled over so he could keep his eyes glued to her. The worry that he might judge her for what she looked like hung to her brain, but the insecure feeling didn't stop her. Her fingers nimbly undid the button and zipper of her jeans then she shimmed them down. Next, she toed off her socks as her hands paused at her black panties. They hovered for a second before she grasped both sides to slide the black cotton to the floor.

Once she stepped out of the garments, she climbed back up on the bed then resumed straddling Arrow. The smell of her arousal filled the air around them. He didn't try this time to reach for her, but she could see he wanted to. He moved his hands to the top of the bed to grip the sheet until his knuckles turned white.

Since Nova sat on him again, his dick brushed lightly against the sprinkle of soft curls at the junction of her legs. After she unclasped her bra, the black fabric slipped off her shoulders spilling out her small breasts. The last of her clothing hit the floor. His cock bobbed into the gathering liquid heat between her legs.

Arrow had begun to breathe heavy when she first returned to sitting on his legs, but as she threw her bra to the floor, his panting sounded like he'd run for miles. Seeing him excited for her made her feel free and seductive. The combination was heady.

Nova leaned down to bite his neck simply because she could. Arrow gave a sharp pleasurable growl, and she murmured her approval. She liked the feel of her nipples rubbing along his torso as she rocked over him. She shifted, so her nipples beaded into tight buds. The sensation made her wetter.

Rubbing along him like a sleek cat, she could smell her aroma mixing with his. When she reached his mouth, this time, he parted his lips. He drew her in for a passionate kiss which stole her control. So she wouldn't rush, she pried her mouth away savagely leaving them both gulping for air. She looked down at him. His face looked very different.

Gone was the lost boy look. Gone was the vulnerable man who followed along telling her business slogans. In front of her was hard, magnificent, sexual male. His eyes became slits. His skin looked ridged and his lips were a darker shade. Desire had formed an erotic mask over his features. If she didn't know better, she would've thought he was some type of dream she had made up in her head.

When she sat up, his eyes stared at her chest. She touched her pert nipples and delicate aureoles while he watched.

"Beautiful," he whispered, shaking as if he was before a grand shrine. He tried to clear his throat. "I mean not beautiful. You're—" His voice halted. To stop him from speaking she bent her head again.

He lifted his mouth to eagerly meet hers. Nova sealed them together. She felt like her lifeblood poured into his veins. A sweet wild heat filled her until the drops spilled out onto his legs. This heat was impossible to stop. Now she knew, until he was inside of her, she would never be able to let this obsession go. She had to finish what she had started. Once they were done, only then she wouldn't yearn for him anymore. When this was over, they'd be free of each other. She wanted that, didn't she? That's how this would go, wouldn't it?

She lifted her mouth away to suck on each of his nipples in turn. His heartbeat raced loud enough for her to hear as his mouth parted to groan. His body surrendered underneath hers, reacting in a helpless response as she gently grazed his skin with her teeth. The taste of him was as addicting as any drug and twice as potent. She moved against him intimately aware of his every response. He lifted his hips to meet hers as if trying to manipulate her and gain entrance to her body.

As he thrust his hips up, his cock slipped along her clit. Each kiss from the very first built a furnace inside of her. He was sending her temperature climbing. There was only one thing she could do for the both of them. Her eyes shut.

She began sliding down his tense body like a warm serpent coiling on a rock. There was dampness on her skin as she moved. When her lips reached his navel, she ran her tongue around his belly button.

Harsh groans forced their way past his lips. He lifted his hips, so his erection bumped her chin. She'd sucked his cock once before, for only a minute, but it wasn't like that this time. This time she wanted to capture him. She paused for a moment realizing she wanted to possess him. At this second, she hated his past. She hated every other woman who had ever had him, loved him, or that he'd ever loved.

Arrow twisted toward her lips as his hands stroked her hair beseechingly. She ran her palms down his thighs before moving them apart. Her mouth sank downward to envelope his whole thick erection in one slow, tortuous suck.

"Great Spirit, that's..." He groaned again as she relaxed her throat to take all of the hard length.

A loud whimper tore from him, followed by begging that didn't even make sense. She let him slip out of her mouth. His shaft glistened with saliva. Her tongue flicked over the purple crown as he shuddered from head to foot.

He whispered to her, but the words were foreign. The mumbles sounded like he was speaking Navajo again. All the yearning in his voice reached her even though she didn't know the language. The driving hunger in his tone reached deep inside of her soul. That craving was all she could respond to.

Placing his legs where she wanted them, she straddled him once more. The ribbed column of his hard shaft bobbed as if searching for her warmth.

"Nova, please." When Arrow begged again, a fever of want consumed her. She was driven by primitive instincts. Maybe this was why she was bad in bed. Soon her body became in total command of her mind. She pressed down hard on top of him so that not even a piece of paper could be forced between them.

"Yes," Nova murmured while she lined up their bodies so he could penetrate her. She needed, and Arrow would satisfy. It was that simple.

Arrow's words were lost to her. The sounds he made sent shock waves through her core. Nothing around her was breaking through her sexual haze as she clung to him. These sexual emotions were so intense they bordered on frightening. She was posed for him to enter her and a stark surge of elation washed through her. Ever since the first time she saw him in that cell she had wanted this. There was no denying it. She was terrified of stopping and of keeping going. He had some type of power over her, yet he would do whatever she wanted.

His hands rose up above his head again and Nova realized maybe, after all, she really was out of her mind.

The train gave a mighty lurch. A screech pierced her sexual fog. With a heave, she lost her balance and was thrown off the small cot. As she hit the floor, she rolled over to see Arrow who tried to reach her as he scrambled off the bed.

Chapter 16

Arrow made a dive off the cot after Nova. Again, the train lurched. He was pitched forward onto his knees, and he hit the hard tiles. The sound of the brakes on the tracks shrieked terribly in the small space.

As he struggled to his feet, he caught Nova. He helped her to her feet gaining his own balance. His legs swayed with the decelerating train as they got their equilibrium back. He pulled her into his arms. As soon as he did, his unruly penis brushed against her belly.

A gasp passed his lips at the contact. Without thought, he shoved her against the nearest wall as he lifted her legs. She was as light as a cloud. He wanted what she'd been offering him, and he placed his hands under her ass. He didn't care what the train did. He wanted to climb inside of her and never leave. He slashed his lips over hers again and again. One hand slapped to the wall on the side of her shoulders trapping her. He used his body to anchor her, so as the train decelerated, they wouldn't be tossed anywhere again. Her legs gripped around his waist.

He kissed her as he sank back into the feel of her warm skin. She didn't stop him or run like he was afraid she would. Another squeal cut into the space as the train reduced its speed. Somewhere he might've heard a faint knock. He ignored the tapping and drank in all of Nova's lush curves under his big hands.

He let his eyelids drop while he marveled at the feel of her arms wrapping around his neck. He didn't care if she held him because she used him to keep herself from being thrown to the floor. He didn't care if she only wanted him because they couldn't stop this insatiable hunger they'd started. He didn't care about anything but her. One day she would hold him because she loved him and not for any other reason.

His body begged for release exactly like before, though he didn't know exactly what he should do. His lips sucked on Nova's tongue. What he did know was that he needed Nova. He loved her. Knowing that was enough for him. His mouth and dick pressed harder against her pliant body. If she would spread her legs a little more…

"Wow, sorry to break up the party, but I did knock. It's important." Joe's voice slammed through his sexual mist. Arrow wrenched his lips from Nova's.

Nova jumped out of his arms. He quickly turned to block Joe's view. Arrow was so saturated by Nova that he hadn't even heard the door open or shut. He had gotten distracted *again*.

Arrow guessed that Nova hadn't heard any noise as well. Ducking behind his back, she stayed hidden behind him as her voice weakly drifted over his shoulder.

"I didn't think you were coming back."

"I see that. Nice hard-on," Joe responded dryly. "You should've locked the door." A smile played about his mouth. "Amateurs."

If Joe thought this was amusing, Arrow didn't.

"Could you turn around?" Nova mumbled.

"Hum mm?" The agent tipped his head to the side as if he couldn't hear her. "What was that?"

"Now?" Nova sounded irritated. Arrow felt the same way. Was she annoyed about the intrusion or because Joe might've seen her naked?

Arrow placed his hand over his swollen dick. If Joe had seen his Nova naked, he would beat him.

"I've seen it all before." Joe openly smirked while he eyed his tormented flesh.

The mocking look made Arrow want to punch him. He would hit him, even if he stood here naked sporting a raging hard on. If Joe took even one step further into the room, then Arrow would gladly strangle the agent again. A deep feeling of rage grew at the idea that Joe saw Nova naked. He better turn around.

"She said turn around. Face the door." Arrow's voice shot out like a bolt of electricity. Arrow's eyes dropped from Joe's smirk to his ropes. The gold strands swayed, but they didn't reach toward Nova. The fact that the cords didn't want his woman helped him calm down. He took a deep breath. His other hand joined his right hand over his penis.

Joe's eyes widened. To Arrow's surprise, Joe presented him with his back.

"Indian and a munchkin telling me what to do," Joe muttered.

As soon as the agent was facing the door, Nova dashed from behind Arrow. She scooped up her backpack as she hurried, then she disappeared in a naked blur into the bathroom.

Once the door to the bathroom closed, Joe turned around. He leaned his back against the wall near the exit. His thumbs hooked into his pants pockets while he surveyed the room.

"I didn't mean to ruin your night, but it's time sensitive."

"I think I know what hate is," Arrow snapped. He tried to shove his disobedient shaft into some jeans he yanked from the floor. His cock and balls ached. They felt thick, full, and ready to burst. Could he go to the bathroom and touch himself until the pressure dissipated? He might have to try fondling himself again, so this throb would vanish. He wasn't sure he could fix his penis without Nova, but at this point, he would try anything.

"You don't hate me, but I guess I'm a cock-blocker. I'll make it up to you sometime, besides you'll want to hear what I have to say."

Arrow threw a thick long-sleeved plaid shirt over his head. He doubted he would care what Joe had to say. The only thing he cared about was Nova and him being alone, clothing optional.

Glaring at Joe, he started re-braiding his hair. The strands were a knotted mess.

"I want to know what you have to say. I doubt you'd have come back unless it was important." Nova appeared in the doorway of the bathroom.

Arrow stared.

She hadn't been in there for long, but she came out lovelier than ever. She wore a blue shirt, jeans, and sweater again. He gazed at her loving the way her short zippered sweater hugged her breasts. Were all her tops this tight? He liked the way her jeans formed her ass. His tongue licked his lips as he recalled the curves under those clothes. If he closed his eyes he could picture the black bra. He wanted all her garments off. Heat rushed to his cock. He tugged at his jeans.

Nova put her hair up in a ponytail. She ignored his trance-like state. She tapped her foot at Joe.

"Time sensitive? Spit it out." The pink tint of her cheeks as well as the way she spoke was the only indication she gave that she wasn't happy about Joe's presence. Did she want him as bad as he wanted her? He hoped so.

"I got a guy who'll get you on a train to Bosstown, except you've got to get off at this stop. You'll have to hurry. This isn't a long stay. It's only cargo pickup."

Nova became a flurry of action upon hearing Joe's offer. In a rush, she shoved all the scattered clothing from the floor into the duffle. After she made sure everything was in the black bag, she checked her backpack and CC.

"How did you talk to him?" she asked Joe.

"That's a need to know basis, and you don't need to know." Joe found her shoes and tossed them to her.

She seemed to accept that as an answer as she caught her shoes then handed Arrow a large flannel shirt. "It's cold in the tunnels."

Arrow obliged while she dug in the bag. She produced a long thin dark green jacket for herself and a long navy coat for him. He put on the coat as she threw him his boots.

"Where do we go? Also, how many HOCs will it cost me to get on this other train?" She tied up the laces of her black leather shoes.

Arrow glanced up when Joe didn't speak right away. He paused in the process of tying his own boots.

"The thing is, it's a harvester train," Joe said at last.

Nova slowed her swift movements. Her face went from happy to apprehensive in a heartbeat.

"Is that bad?" Arrow looked to Nova, then to Joe.

"Not bad," Joe shrugged, "exactly."

"Harvesters are like outlaws." Nova resumed tying her laces. "They like to steal I'm told. Most of the time they're men banished from water bases."

"That's true. They live by their own rules. If you don't keep track of your stuff, then it's anybody's game. They have their own code of conduct. Most of the time regular people don't get it." Joe handed Nova her bag. She settled it on her shoulder.

"And we're regular people, Arrow. We're the folks harvesters eat for breakfast." Gripping the straps on her backpack, Nova headed to the door.

"Breakfast of champions," Arrow muttered as he followed Nova and Joe. They stepped out into the hallway. The area seemed quieter than before.

"Where is everyone?" Nova asked.

"It's night, most people are racked out." Joe walked down the narrow aisle first, then Nova. Arrow took up the rear. "Everyone honors the train system of time. It's hard to tell night and day underground. People tend to go with what the H.S.P.C. and the train schedule says." Joe tugged out an old pocket watch. "It's 2:05 a.m."

Arrow only halfheartedly listened. No one moved in the halls, so it was easy to walk speedily through the train cars back the way they came.

"What stop is this?" Nova asked.

"The stop we're at now is a harvester stop. This is only for fresh batteries and cargo. No one would dare get off here." Joe's sentence struck Arrow. If no one would "dare" get off this train, then why did he suggest they do it?

As they reached the first open passenger car where people snoozed in their chairs, Arrow moved closer to Nova and took her hand. She squeezed his fingers. Her warm touch reassured him. The simple feel of her small fingers made his world go around. He couldn't lose her. Again, he considered meeting harvesters. Were they *that* scary?

"What do harvester's harvest? Do they grow food? Why are they outlaws?" Ahead of him, he could hear a light buzz of conversation from a few night owls. Arrow pulled Nova under his arm as a man got up to scoot by them.

"The name harvester is just a name. They're not underground farmers. Along the Ice Border, there are people who are H.S.P.C. scavengers. Scavengers pull useable items from the snow and ice where it's melting. A lot of that stuff goes directly to the H.S.P.C. to be repurposed." Nova answered him while they waited for a woman to pull a bag from under her chair. She took up most of the aisle. The three of them waited for her.

"Glaciers are always moving." Joe glanced over his shoulder. "The ice picks items up then carries it to the snout, but melting takes time."

"Harvesters were started by a group of men who wanted to go above ground to free things from the ice before the items reach the Ice Border." Nova squeezed past another man to get into the next passenger car. "The harvesters don't wait for the terminal moraine."

Joe reached the exit door, then turned around. "Going to the surface of the planet is dangerous work. You never know what you're going to get. Sometimes they get a good haul. If that happens, then harvesters make money. They trade for things they want, or for services, or for HOCs."

"Or sometimes people simply die up there." Nova scoffed. "Freeze to death or avalanche."

"Or Polar bears," Joe shrugged.

"Got it." Arrow nodded. "Harvesters pick items from the ice, then they move underground on their trains."

"It's not exactly *their* trains." Joe paused at the metal door for them to get out. He glanced around the platform, but no one seemed to notice them leaving. "It's not the harvesters who own the trains but no one rides with them because they like to gamble, fight, and they have no ties to anyone. That's why they're called outlaws. I think of them like gypsies." Joe smiled. "Never mind, you probably don't know what a gypsy is."

"I know what a gypsy is." Nova nodded. "That's a good description. Archer told me once that they've no allegiance to anyone because they always know they might die. They live for the moment or for the money."

"Why would anyone do it? Why go up there? Money's not vital." The idea was appalling. "I'd never go up to the surface and leave Nova to fend for herself. This work is selfish and reckless. I can't imagine risking death all the time for the hope of HOCs. Money's nice, but it's pointless if you're alone in the world with no one to love you."

"Wow." Joe opened the door to let them out onto the new train platform. "You're one sappy bitch, Indian."

"And you're a heartless ginger, Clown-Hair."

Joe gave a surprised bark of laughter and followed them.

Arrow stepped off the train holding Nova close. They moved down the metal stairs.

"So, why do they do it?" Nova piped up. "Is it about the money?"

"They do it because a lot of them have nothing else to live for. When you don't care about anything then why not? Some of them have been kicked off water bases for illegal activities. Some are criminals who are dodging the equator because authorities are looking for them. Some have no family and friends." Joe motioned for them to move further away from the trains toward one of the far walls. "They might not have any other options for surviving."

"It's like they say, 'When there is no tomorrow.'" Those words sounded like a saying Arrow must've heard before. He didn't think he could live by that credo, but he could picture someone else doing it.

"Wow, okay, I guess you could say that." Joe had them move to the left of the train.

"Or FedEx simply wanted people to ship with them," Nova muttered.

The train platform they stepped out onto was built of uneven stones placed together. Every few feet he could make out letters engraved in the smooth rocks. Some rocks had carved "beloved father," or a name and a date. He was disturbed by the quiet.

Joe mentioned that no one stopped here. This place looked deserted. The walls were a barren slab of cement surrounded by tracks on two sides. There were only two doors he could see. He could hear muffled noise coming from behind one of them.

Another train arrived, followed by another. He could hear animal noises in the last train's cargo hold. A small handful of men got out and worked on loading canisters. No one else emerged.

Arrow's eyes scanned the cold concrete walls. He tipped his head back to look up at the high ceilings. On the columns were dim lights which gave the space a yellowish gloomy glow. After how busy the last place was, this was an assault on his senses. A scrap of paper with the words *"Sports Illustrated"* stuck to his boot. He shook his leg. The paper floating away was the only movement in the place.

"Where is everyone?" Nova asked.

"See that door over there?" Joe pointed to a door with a picture of white squares with black dots. "That's Laying Odds. Normally harvesters stop here to get out of the train and share information on the surface, ice storms, and who died. They play Boxcar Dice or share drinks, if they snagged alcohol. That's where everyone is. If you run into anyone, don't draw attention to yourselves. Act natural. My guy will meet you. He'll help you get on the train."

"Act natural?" Arrow asked at the same time as Nova spoke up.

"What is this going to cost me?" Nova demanded.

Arrow realized Joe hadn't answered that question before. Joe's black eyes jumped to Arrow, then bounced to Nova.

"It's not going to cost you anything if you keep your head. All you've got to do is hang here until my associate shows up. Act natural, like you belong. It'll be no problem for him to get you on the train."

Nova looked as skeptical as he felt. "And where the hell will you be?"

"I've got to get back on my train." Joe nodded toward the train like they didn't know where the vehicle sat. "I gotta get to Junction City. Wow… you see, some of us have to work. We can't all go running around willy-nilly."

"Willy-nilly?" Arrow asked.

Joe ignored him.

"You might be leaving us stranded here purely so you can have my private room. These harvesters are going to come out, steal my money, then leave us. You're dumping us with a bunch of outlaws. And that's if we're lucky." Nova's assessment sounded like a premonition. Arrow agreed with her.

"Wow, way to be a downer. You wanted to go in the opposite direction. If you want to get to Bosstown, this is your chance. And I wouldn't do that to Arrow," Joe snapped matter-of-factly.

"Why?" What did it matter to him? Joe didn't owe Arrow anything.

"You changed my life." Joe ran his hand through his orange hair and looked at his boots. "I swear, this guy I know will take care of you. Now, I gotta go because my train's leaving. You can change your mind. If you want to go all the way to New Boise, go ahead." Joe made a sweeping gesture like he offered them the option of returning to their private room. That's what they should do.

Nova's eyes darted to the door into Laying Odds. Indecision walked across her face. Should they trust Joe?

He glanced at a forgotten bench propped against the wall next to Laying Odds. The seat was made out of different-sized wood logs slapped together. He pictured harvester men fighting over that bench. In his mind's eye, he saw men drinking, fighting, and filling this dismal room. Nothing about the cold walls welcomed them. A bone chilling recollection that he'd been trapped here before filled his mind.

Arrow looked at Nova. He saw everything good in the world. If they were left here, then he would have to protect her. He wasn't sure he would be able to defend Nova from a pack of men. He would try, but he didn't know if he could do it. He'd let her down when Joe snuck up on them. He didn't want to fail her a second time.

"Fine, we stay. We wait for your friend, but keep this in mind…" Nova turned to face Joe. "If I die here, Archer will kill you."

Arrow knew she meant that. Joe's quick nod made it clear he understood.

"I know Archer will kill me, that's why you're going to be fine. The harvesters aren't all bad, and you have my pistol. You have a shot left, you have brains, scary eyes, and—" He looked at Arrow. "He throws a good punch."

Listening to Joe, Arrow thought they should get back on the train. His punch wasn't good enough. The train might've been noisy, but it was relatively safe. He pictured briefly having a chance to be in the private room with Nova again. His body responded instantly. He swallowed hard to banish all memories of her naked body. He wouldn't let her down again by getting distracted.

"I don't think we should do this, angel," Arrow whispered to her. He would have to concentrate. Also, he would have to not get consumed by the sight of the ropes.

"What happened to your sayings on trust?"

Arrow shook his head. "What the hell do I know?"

"And that's why you're the silent participant on this journey. We're going to get on the harvester train with Joe's friend. We can't waste time going nowhere."

"It's not nowhere. It's a safer train to New Boise." Arrow wanted to add that he could be alone with her, but he didn't think that would help his side of the argument.

"We stay. We trust Joe." Nova's eyes flash a richer red. He shouldn't argue. He'd told her she could call the shots on this trip, and he'd promised he would help her. So far, he hadn't done a decent job of that. He was damn lucky she hadn't ditched him. Without her, finding his sister would be impossible. Nova had CC, all the money, and she was a sharp spitfire with brains.

He thought about what he had. He had a pair of poor-fitting pants, a distraction at glowing strings he didn't understand, and an over-the-top sexual attraction. Add all that up with an empty head and he knew he needed her. Whatever she wanted he would let her have it, even if it meant staying deep in enemy territory.

"Whatever you want to do, angel." Arrow sighed.

"Wow, she's got you by the balls." Joe turned to face the train, then paused. He spun back around and faced them. "Before I go, I think you need to know two other things." Joe's voice dropped low. "The first thing is that the harvesters will try to find anything you value. They'll use whatever you love against you. Generally, they act this way to extract money. So, if you say you love your coat then they'll steal it. Afterward, they ransom the coat back to you. If you overly protect CC, well you get the drift. HOCs and trading items are the only things they go after. Also, they don't like outsiders. Just don't look weak, or stupid. Feel free to lie."

"Lie?" Arrow didn't know enough truths about his life to lie yet.

Joe's serious tone had a bite to it. "You lie your asses off. Don't make it clear you care about each other."

Nova nodded her understanding, but all this reintroduced to Arrow the idea that they shouldn't be here.

"And the second thing?" Nova asked before Joe turned to leave again.

"If that sex was any indication, I'd say you're together."

Nova glared at Joe's back as he slipped onto the train.

Seeing Joe leave produced a cold sinking feeling in Arrow's stomach. As the train pulled away, Arrow stared until the last car disappeared down one of the many dark tunnels. When the train was fully out of sight, he turned to look down at Nova. She could probably see the panic in his eyes. He expected her to tease him about his fears.

"Don't worry, Arrow. I got a good feeling this is where we're supposed to be. We'll be in Bosstown in no time." She patted his arm.

"Funny because I have the feeling we've been dropped off as a meal for lions."

"You say the damnedest things." Nova cocked her head at him. "First a hawk, then a clown, now a lion? How could you know what a lion is?"

"It's a big cat with lots of hair, and it eats people alive. It's probably what harvesters are like too."

Nova's eyes crinkled as she tried not to smile. Was she internally laughing at him?

"Lion's don't eat people alive and anyway," she shook her head, "it's going to be fine." The word "fine" died on her lips and her eyes grew huge.

Arrow spun around to see what had killed her sentence. Behind him, the door to Laying Odds was thrown open. The wooden door gaped like a giant mouth. The entrance looked like it was puking up huge dangerous men.

A massive group of mostly males, all enormous, started to gush out onto the small platform. All the men laughed and talked. Some drank from different-sized bottles and staggered as they ambled about. A handful of women pushed ahead of them. Some of the people who poured out looked androgynous.

The noise level rose to an ear-splitting level. To say the group was boisterous was an understatement. Every one of them looked like a real threat. His heart kicked up its beat. If anything ever happened to Nova, he would die. He couldn't live without her. Seeing every available corner of the room fill with danger highlighted that truth.

As they both stood immobile, men swarmed the cement platform. Arrow tried to come up with a way he could protect Nova. His eyes scanned the tracks. The two trains sleepily waiting for passengers didn't look helpful. Harvesters circled them like sharks. He put his arm around Nova, then he pressed his body against the stone wall.

"Someone stick ice down my pants and call me a whore!" The shout popped over the crowd.

Arrow glanced toward Laying Odds. A 6-foot-tall, lean Asian man elbowed his way through the mass. Arrow was poised to run when the dishwater-blond stranger reached them. Arrow grabbed Nova's arm.

"Fuck me, Weaver!" The harvester punched Arrow in the arm. The hit hurt. Arrow rubbed the stinging spot on his bicep.

The Asian had slanted eyes which didn't open far, and it made him look like he was permanently glaring. His straight white teeth flashed into a broad smile which contrasted his glare.

As he fiddled with a huge pack on his back, his dark-green eyes flipped to him then to Nova. Overall, he looked cleaner than most of the other men he'd seen so far. His skin was clear and bright. His thick hair was neatly organized into a ponytail at the top of his head. He didn't seem dangerous, but the silver spike through his earlobe did make Arrow nervous.

The stranger eyed him and Nova. His eyebrows rose. Arrow peeked at Nova, then back to the blond. The harvester's eyes danced under bouncing cyebrows. He kept jiggling the enormous pack on his shoulders. The stranger wasn't much older than him, and as the staring match continued, Arrow remembered Joe's directions. Act natural and lie.

"Hey." Arrow didn't think the greeting sounded natural. Instead, "hey" came out squeaky. He wondered if the blond could tell. The stranger didn't respond. He fidgeted with his pack again.

"You know Joe?" Nova asked abruptly.

This area of the platform continued to fill up with men, so Arrow moved toward the wall not waiting for an answer. He tugged Nova closer to his side. They backed up until their shoulders pressed against the cool cement. The blond followed their retreat. As Arrow shifted to one side, a muscular black man holding an intricately carved stick walked by.

"Weaver." The black man tipped his head.

The Asian didn't seem put off by the fact they had backed away from him or by the fact Nova stared. He stayed right in front of them. He blocked Arrow's view of the strings wrapped around people. Since Arrow couldn't look around, he studied this stranger's ropes which were bright, but hung limply in front of him. Arrow had the notion the strings slept.

"So, do you?" Nova looked annoyed. "Are you with Joe?"

"Weaver." A man with a hood over his face punched him in the arm. Again, Arrow rubbed the sting.

This time Arrow nodded back then he tried to come up with a natural pose. Nova leaned against the wall with her bag hidden behind her. She shoved her hands into the pockets of her sweater. She did a better job of acting natural. He wanted to ask her why they said "Weaver" before they hit him. He recalled his dream. He'd heard the word before. Now he was curious if there was a connection.

As people passed Arrow, he wanted to tell Nova about all the strings he could see. Some of the strings were joined together. Others moved freely. He wanted to ask a hundred questions, but instead he copied her relaxed stance. He kept his mouth shut. He had to stay focused this time to protect her. No mistakes again.

"I don't know who Joe is, but fuck man, you could've told me you were on this train." The blond shifted the giant pack. "I should've known you couldn't stay away from a strip mall. I hear it's glacial. I'm so fucking done with fleam."

Arrow looked helplessly at Nova. There were so many things in that sentence he didn't understand.

"What's fleam?"

"Shitty flea market junk." The harvester frowned at Arrow. Arrow opened his mouth to ask what a "flea market" was but Nova spoke before he could.

"If Joe didn't ask you to get us on the train to Bosstown, then who are you and what do you want?" Nova's voice had a razor-sharp edge to it. Her sentence cut like a knife. Arrow thought she looked smart and tough. He thanked the Great Spirit she was with him.

"You're kind of bitchy for one so small," the other man responded. "My names Raiden Muttson, but I'm sure Weaver could tell you that." He punched Arrow's arm again.

"Could you not?" Arrow rubbed his arm and again the other man frowned at him. Two for two. Evidently, he wasn't saying the right things here.

"Raiden," Nova eyes flashed. Arrow could see how someone might think the blood-red was scary. "If Agent Joe didn't send you, then you can get lost. Weaver's with me." She inclined her head at Arrow.

Arrow guessed his name was Weaver now. He would have to ask Nova about that the first chance he got. He looked at how Raiden took to her telling him to get lost. The other man's face didn't show any reaction. The name Raiden Muttson was familiar. He wasn't going to say that maybe he knew him. He could hear Nova in his head saying he didn't know anyone, so he should shut his face hole. Instead, he considered the name Weaver. Was it a nickname? Maybe Weaver was his real name. Perhaps, Arrow was a fake name he'd given himself. He wanted to ask Raiden. Did this man know him?

None of this scene seemed familiar to him. He glanced at another man who nodded at him. Did all these people know him? Frustration filled him at his lack of knowledge over his past. Everything in his head was a mixture of dreams and reality.

"Are you talking about Agent Joe? As in the H.S.P.C. Snow-Everyone-Joe?" Raiden asked as the blood drained from his face. "Fuck me, Weaver, you leave for a few years, then you go up in life. I can't believe you know *that* Joe. I heard a few of the harvesters talk about him. Morgan-Roth says he's a heartless snowballer."

"Joe said someone would get us on the train to Bosstown." Nova glared. "If that's not you, get bent."

"Weaver can do it. Why not ask him? We've been on lots of trains together." Raiden hooked his thumb at Arrow. This guy wasn't leaving. Nova's pretend scowl was fast becoming not pretend.

Arrow was dumbfounded. What should he do? Should he take the chance and ask if they knew each other? The idea seduced him. It would be like opening a locked door if he could find someone who could tell him about his past.

He paused. Speaking up was a risk. He had promised to care for Nova. He considered the best way to put his question together.

"We're friends?" As he asked Raiden, he tried to sound nonchalant.

Raiden's smile vanished. He looked as if he had been asked a complex mathematical equation.

"No," he finally grunted out. The answer came out belligerent, then he seemed to think better of his retort. The harvester tempered his voice to less hostile when he spoke again. "I mean, I owe you and all, and you've never let me forget it, but damn, Weaver. I mean, fuck you. You know how you are." Raiden looked at Nova "Is he messing with me? He asked what fleam was."

"Maybe." Nova's eyes flipped around the room as if this conversation bored her, but Arrow knew better. She was probably searching for the person Joe claimed would help them.

"Fuck it then." Raiden nodded.

Arrow didn't know what he should say next so he kept his mouth closed. Nova started to rub her forehead.

"Why do you owe… Weaver?" Nova asked suddenly.

Maybe it was best if they didn't probe Raiden for any more information. If this man knew he'd lost his memories, then he might take advantage of that. Joe had implied harvesters would capitalize on any weakness. He leaned over to whisper that they should let this be when the harvester started speaking.

"It's not like he'd ever let me forget it, but whatever," Raiden answered. "He saved my life in a snow storm on the surface, but we're not friends. Weaver always said you shouldn't have friends. Look out for number one, right?" Raiden punched his arm. He glanced at the train. Now Nova watched him closely. "I know you only bring this up when you want something. So, fine. You don't have to fuck with me. If you want to hit the mall, I'll trek with you." Raiden spoke with a sigh like he wasn't happy. "I know you don't let me trek with anyone else." He made that statement starkly. His shoulders dropped. Arrow felt sorry for him.

"Trek?" Nova asked. Arrow moved again as someone came by and punched his arm. He rubbed where the future bruise would be. He glared at the offender. This punching thing was getting old.

"Trek on the surface, you know, face the snow. I'll tell Doug I'm going with you, but shit, I already paid him. This would've been helpful to know, like fucking, yesterday. Snowballs." Raiden would've walked away at that point, but Arrow placed a hand on his arm.

When Arrow set his hand on Raiden's wrist, the harvester's strings stirred. The cords implied a relationship. Arrow didn't know how he knew that, but he did. This guy did know him. He was positive. He might be the only person he would come across who could tell him about himself. He couldn't let Raiden walk away.

When his eyes glanced at Nova, he willed her to understand how he felt. He had a moment of indecision. The stress had him feeling like he'd stood there for hours. How much of a chance would it be if he told Raiden the truth? How mad would Nova be? Would he be putting them in danger? It would be a lot of trust in one sweep. He couldn't keep his hand on Raiden forever. Already the harvester stared at Arrow like he was insane.

"If Weaver saved your life then you would owe him. A snow storm is severe. He lost toes," Nova stated. "He could've lost even more."

Was she giving Arrow her okay?

"Yeah." Raiden's eyes drilled into Arrow's hand. "I lost part of my foot too."

Arrow let go. They needed to know. Raiden might tell him about his life. Maybe he'd know where his sister might be. If the man Joe sent never showed up, then Raiden might be their only hope of leaving here.

"What's wrong with you?" Raiden asked him.

"Raiden." He tried the name out to see if he'd used it before. The name didn't sum up any images in his brain. Sighing, he took the leap of trust anyway. He saw Nova's nod of approval, and he doggedly continued. "You don't have to trek with me if you don't want to."

"What's the catch?" Raiden put both hands on the straps of his bag.

"You can go to the surface without me, but..." Arrow took a deep breath, "if I saved your life, if you owe me, then please help get Nova and me on the train to Bosstown." Arrow paused. "Please."

Chapter 17

The inside of Laying Odds looked vastly different than anything they had seen so far. Nova followed Raiden as he led them toward the entrance of the gambling joint. They strode past a bench with two harvesters smoking. Most of the men who had exited the drinking establishment gathered around the platform. A few looked their way. She kept her eyes on the floor. Raiden didn't speak, but pushed past everyone with his huge duffle making him seem fatter than he was. There was a stunned, confused silence which hung on his shoulders, much like the pack. Arrow glowered at the people who punched his arm.

"Where are we going?" Arrow asked.

"The train won't be here for a while. Delays." Raiden opened the door to the bar. "If you want on the train, follow me." The smell of sweat and liquor slapped her in the face. She grimaced but walked in.

Nova had no idea if she made the right decision following this stranger or not. So far, everything seemed to be okay. This was a lot of faith to place on a man with a spike in his earlobe.

"Is this safe?" Arrow asked as he pressed closer behind her. His hand settled on the small of her back. The room opened up into a massive cave. The walls were carved out of the rock on three sides. Items were mounted on the walls and only a handful of lights hung from silver tape attached to the craggy roof.

"You want a drink, Mortal Combat?" A short, beefy man behind a marble counter called to Raiden as they entered. He held up a bottle and shook it. Behind him a tattered American flag hung on a looped rope.

"I think I need one," Raiden muttered more to himself then made straight for the man pouring amber liquid into a dirty cracked glass. Raiden picked up the glass then led them toward the far corner of the cavern. He hadn't answered Arrow's question, but Nova was sure he heard him. The room had only a smattering of men playing a box dice game. They lounged on the stone floor in pockets dotting the room. Some of their faces had a sinister mask under battery-powered bulbs in yellow plastic cages.

Where the rock wall and the floor met sat a low wooden coffee table. Raiden stopped and faced them. In this tucked away corner, they were under what might be holiday lights. They blinked red, then green. Raiden put his back to one of the walls as he slid his pack off his shoulders. He then threw the sack to the floor. The bag rolled. Before it stopped moving, he sat on top of the flat side. He flipped the long lapels of his coat around him. His yellow shirt, which peeked out from under his many layers, had a smiley face peeking out from the middle.

Arrow did the same thing with their duffle. He took the bag off, then plopped it on the dusty floor. He didn't speak, but with a wave of his hand, he offered the makeshift chair to Nova. She daintily perched on the duffle then leaned her head against a sign that said, "no turn on red light." Arrow sat cross-legged on the floor next to her.

Once they were seated, Nova expected more harvesters to appear in the bar, but the room stayed somewhat empty. Beyond her, tucked behind the bar, were three other doors. When some men entered the cave, they passed them before they headed across the room. Hearing the noise behind the first door, she figured the exit might take you to a busier area of men and women. With how boisterous the sounds were on the other side, she guessed it might be better to stay here where they were relatively secluded.

"I couldn't ask before with all those guys on the platform, but now we have no one to overhear us. I want to know. Who are you?" Raiden demanded once they were seated.

"I appreciated that you waited until we were in a more private spot." It would've been bad if someone overheard their conversation, and it would've been impossible for Arrow to pretend to know things with Raiden. If Raiden knew Arrow as well as she figured he did, then there would be no way for Arrow to fool him enough to get on the train. Arrow asked Raiden to get them on the next train. Now they must convince Raiden to do it and to not tell anyone that Arrow wasn't himself. She hoped they were up to the task.

"This is the best place to talk. If you want to get on that next train, spill it. Who are you?"

Arrow momentarily stopped looking around. He faced Raiden's pointed glare. Nova figured he wasn't going to take a flippant answer. She wouldn't accept a casual dismissal if she were in Raiden's place.

"Is it that obvious?" She asked Raiden.

"It's obvious to me," Raiden replied as a few men shuffled by. He dropped his voice. "He might've been able to fake it with other guys, but not me. I'm the only one who'll trek with him."

Nova didn't know if Arrow should tell him the truth or not. If they had more information on what type of person Raiden was, then they would know if they could trust him.

"Why are you the only one who will trek with me?" Arrow watched the colorful holiday lights. He looked relaxed and watching him made Nova feel at peace. Arrow lifted his hand. Gingerly, he touched the lights like they were precious gems.

Traveling with Arrow might be difficult at times, but then again without him, she wouldn't have managed to get this far. She had told him she wanted to get on the train to Bosstown. Arrow tried to make that happen. When she reviewed the trip, she realized she was the one who stated they should trust Joe and get off the other train. Arrow was behind her in everything she chose to do, so she could do no less for him. If he told Raiden about himself to find out who he was, then she would back him. At this point, she believed she could make it to Bosstown because of Arrow.

"Weaver said once I could never trek without him. He's a dickhead like that. I knew something was up when he told me I could go." Raiden shrugged. Arrow stopped looking at the lights. He probably didn't like being called a dickhead, but he didn't comment. "Weaver never used my name. He always calls me Mutt," Raiden continued as he stretched out his legs. He crossed one giant booted ankle over the other.

"He calls you Mutt?" Nova asked. That seemed an odd name for a friend.

"Yeah, I hate it, so he loves to use it. Also, Weaver never used the word 'please' in his life. Let alone using it twice in one conversation. I didn't think he even knew the word. So, who are you? You look like Weaver, you sound like him, but I've got the feeling we've never met."

Arrow remained silent.

"Arrow had a head injury." Nova hedged when Arrow didn't speak. She didn't want Arrow to sound weak. Also, telling the whole truth would only open up a whole host of other questions that neither of them had the answers to.

"Arrow's your first name?" Raiden studied Arrow now. He leaned forward. "You know I once saw you sign something A. Yazzie, but I didn't know." Raiden looked like he chewed that over. After a few seconds, he smiled. Nova had the impression that overall Raiden was fairly easy going. Good. That's what they needed.

"I'm not happy I'm a dickhead, but I'm happy I have a last name." Arrow smiled at last. "My last name is Yazzie, Arrow Yazzie." He glanced at her. "Did you hear that, Nova? I have a last name. It's a start." Raiden eyes got a tad bit bigger. "Raiden, we'd appreciate it if you didn't mention my head injury. Please." Arrow's face took on a look of deep concentration. "I don't know if we can trust you, but we're taking a chance on you. All we want to do is get to Bosstown. We don't want trouble."

Raiden grinned. His teeth gleamed. "If you don't want trouble, then that's also not like Weaver. Weaver loved trouble, fighting, and gambling. Well, that and a lot of HOCs."

"Why do you call me Weaver?"

The nickname was a topic Nova wanted to know about as well. She was glad he asked the question. She figured she would need to ask more about the man she traveled with. They would need to know about Arrow if they wanted to make it on this journey. He might have to pretend to be himself if he ran into other people who knew him. She didn't know how long the trip to get to Bosstown would take, but she did know you couldn't fool people indefinitely.

"You got the nickname because of the braid in your hair all the time." Raiden looked to Nova. "Everyone calls him that. I don't think anyone knows his name's Arrow."

"I'll call him Weaver then." Nova nodded.

"I don't like it. It's not my name," Arrow protested. "They say, 'The mark of a man.' My name is part of my mark."

Nova's brow crinkled. "I'm not even going to begin to figure out what that means. I doubt anyone ever said that. Ever." She could see Arrow about to protest again, so she put her hand up to stop him.

"That's an ad for Old Spice." Raiden cocked his head to the side. "He's quoting soap?"

"It's only for when we're around harvesters." Nova nodded to Arrow. Even with her reassurances, he moped about the name change.

"Fine, I'll be Weaver the dickhead. And then would it make us *blend in* if I call you Mutt?" Arrow dropped his head into his hand. Arrow's comment dripped with scorn.

"It'd be best." Raiden grinned.

Arrow gave an exasperated sigh. After a minute, he took a more relaxed deep breath. "I don't like the idea of being someone else."

Raiden tilted his head like Arrow had spoken in Swahili. "It's not you're being someone you're not. You're going to be someone you are." Raiden looked helplessly at her to explain that remark. Nope, couldn't help him there.

"What would you have liked me to call you? Did you want me to call you Raiden? Is that what your friends call you?"

"I don't really have a lot of friends." Raiden shrugged like this didn't matter but his tone suggested that Arrow had hit a major topic. "But if I did, I would want them to call me Raiden."

"I hope one day you'll let me call you Raiden, and we'll be friends." Arrow leaned next to Nova. He squeezed her hand briefly and stopped looking at Raiden. Instead, he inspected a faded "this way" sign.

"You'd call me by my first name?" Raiden kept scrutinizing Arrow like he had sprouted wings. "That's fucked up."

"Fucked up? I never knew him any other way." Above Nova, a few of the lights swung. They'd changed colors from red and green to blue and white.

"I like to fight and gamble? Is that what's so different about me?" Arrow spoke more to the sign then to them.

"I have to admit we trekked together for years, but I guess, I didn't know much about you. Gambling and fighting are all I've ever seen you do. Well, and tell people to fuck off."

"What about family or friends?" Arrow eyes widened. It broke Nova's heart to see him get excited. She could already tell if Arrow lived the harvester lifestyle, a family probably wasn't in the picture.

"I didn't even know you had a family. You told me once that your dad died when you were young. And you've no friends other than me, sort of. For all the years we've been together, all I've ever seen you do is gamble for money. I don't know what you wanted all that money for exactly. You never spent the HOCs anywhere. You only accumulated it."

"I wanted money?" Arrow's Adam's apple bobbed. She held his hand tighter.

"When you needed more money, like if you lost a bet, then we'd go to the surface and get fleam to sell." Raiden didn't seem to notice that Arrow was upset. "You'd often drag me on impossible expeditions I was sure we were going to die on, but we always lived. I never understood your devotion to the almighty HOC. Once your money was in order again then it was back to gambling or picking a fight or sleeping." Raiden paused. "We never talked much."

"What about my sister? Did I talk about Dawn?" Arrow had that hopeful note back in his voice. Nova winced.

"I didn't know you had a sister."

Arrow let go of her and dropped his head into his hands. Nova stroked his shoulder. Watching Arrow find out about himself was like witnessing a train wreck. She wanted to look away but she couldn't.

"What about a girlfriend or wife?" Nova couldn't help but ask. She was scared of the answer. Maybe Arrow gathered up money for a woman. Arrow's head snapped up. Maybe he wanted to know if someone might love him or miss him. Nova wanted to know that.

"Weaver can't have sex, so what would he need a woman for? It's not like he'd talk to a woman, which would mean he'd have to be nice. He isn't a nice person. Weaver's a terrible person."

Arrow and she exchanged looks. Did he say that Arrow couldn't have sex? What did that mean?

"He what?" Nova sputtered. The more she listened to Raiden, the more she got a strange image painted of the man she was with. It sounded like they talked about two entirely different people. The man she met in the locked room chatted with her, could have sex, and was okay with a woman. More than okay, he was romantic, sweet, and downright sexy. He wasn't a terrible person. Actually, her Arrow was a little dopey, but he was kind and helpful.

Plus, he had a sister, didn't he? Arrow claimed he could see through her eyes. If he didn't have a sister, then that opened up a host of new questions. Who was the woman he saw when he meditated?

"I'm sorry, but you're a terrible person." Raiden scratched at his blond ponytail. "Or you were a terrible person before. I don't know what to say. Fuck, you've been gone for a few years. I didn't think you'd come back. You got sick after that last dangerous run we had. That's when you got frost bite. You lost toes, and I don't know what else you got. I mean, snowballs, you were decent enough to carry me for miles, but I always figured you saved my ass because I was the only one who'd willingly trek with you. I guessed you'd never forgive me for my screw up." Raiden looked at Nova with an apologetic shrug. "I'm no good in a blizzard. I get lost easy, even in good weather. Sure, Weaver saved my butt before, but that last one turned him off to going through Adam's tundra with me again. Yeah, I didn't think he'd come back, and he's a terrible person most of the time." Raiden punched his bag. "Snowballs."

"Not all that. I mean go back to the sex." Nova didn't even want to go into all the other thing's he had told them. That was a lot of information to digest. The first thing she wanted to know about was the sex.

"The sex? Oh, you know, Arrow can't get his dick hard. His down below doesn't stand up and—" Raiden stared at the bag between his legs. He squirmed. "Women are pointless is all I'm saying. No need to tell you."

"Is it a side effect of my gift?" Arrow pondered out loud then looked to Nova. "You said gifts have side effects. Maybe if I use my gift a lot, I can't have sex." Arrow glanced around the room. His eyes bounced over the smattering of people. She could almost see him trying to do the math in his head. He started counting on his fingers.

Arrow looked like he tried to add up all the times he'd watched the strings.

Nova stopped the frantic movement of his hands. Her fingers squeezed his.

"You're not gifted as far as I know. Are you gifted? Do you have a sister?" Raiden looked at both her and Arrow. "Is that why you left to join The Originals? I thought they took you in because you had Native American blood is all. We'd heard that Mother was looking for The Great American Indian, whatever that meant. I was surprised they took you even with your missing toes and being sick. I heard The Originals only accept the best of the best. Pure blood and healthy, like Noah's Ark. I never knew exactly if you'd joined them, but if you were gifted, then that's why they let you in."

"What's The Originals?" Arrow asked.

Nova wanted Raiden to go back to the sex topic. Before she could cut in, Raiden's head snapped up. His eyes darkened.

"Snowballs, it's Ash Winsor." The name hissed from Raiden's mouth. All easygoing man dissolved. What was left was marble.

Nova swiveled her head around to follow Raiden's line of sight. From her vantage point, she saw three men come in the entrance. The door slammed. The three men swayed like they'd been drinking. They laughed as they walked. One man yelled something to the bartender and drinks were poured.

Furiously, Raiden whispered to Arrow, "Remember to call me Mutt. Follow my lead." He leaned closer to them. "That's Ash Winsor in the middle. Don't forget you like to gamble. You're a terrible person. Be a dickhead, got that?"

Before Arrow could respond, the three men who entered, spotted them. They forced a direct line to Arrow as if singling him out. They stepped over harvesters on the floor as if they had their sights set on them. As they got nearer, Nova studied the one in the middle. She wished there was more than hung Christmas strands. The dim lightbulbs did little in letting her see the new comers well.

As the men got closer, Nova could tell the man in the middle was about the same height as Raiden and Arrow. He was the one Raiden called Ash Winsor. Other than his height, Nova noted that Winsor had a sharp nose, chin, and round smoky-silver eyes. His hair was short, black, and slicked back on his head. The coat he wore made it impossible to tell if he was fat or thin. The jacket that hung loosely on his body was covered in multiple types of fur. The hood of the jacket had so much fur on the sides that his head appeared small on his massive shoulders.

The other two men with Winsor loomed above the harvester. They both towered over Arrow. Winsor's two buddies made Ash and Raiden look like children. One was a hefty black man with a similar coat and an enormous carved walking stick. His skin tone matched Winsor's exactly. They could be related. The other man had pale creamy white skin with shoulder-length ink-black hair. His washed-out complexion made him look like he was tired of carrying the pack on his sturdy shoulders. Both men were fierce looking, but it was evident the man in the middle was calling all the shots.

"I thought I saw a huge pile of polar bear shit, then I realized it was you, Mutt," Ash called to Raiden as soon as he stood in front of the wooden table. He spoke casually but he glared at Raiden. Nova had no idea why.

As Winsor handed his pack to the pale man next to him, Nova decided he had a handsome face except it was hard to tell with the scowl across his features. No one looked at Nova as she studied the new add-ons to the room.

That was fine by her. For once her eyes hadn't stolen anyone's attention. She might've been passed over because of the bad lighting.

"Gee, Winsor." Raiden made a point to use the man's name probably for Arrow's benefit. "I heard an avalanche crushed you. I'm sorry it didn't." Raiden hopped to his feet. He crossed his arms over his chest then stepped in front of Arrow. The pale man glared at Raiden and moved closer to Ash.

Winsor smirked. "This fucking argy-bargy with you is as much fun as playing leapfrog with a male elk. Jog off." Winsor crossed his arms to copy Raiden's stance. Raiden glanced at her. She wondered if he was silently telling her to not draw attention to herself.

"Go play on the train tracks. We're busy." Raiden took a menacing step forward. The dark-haired man next to Winsor did the same thing. It caused Nova to lean away from the two of them. She scooted as close to the wall as she could get.

Arrow got up from his seat to stand in front of her. She leaned around him. Raiden and Winsor stood toe to toe.

"How much semen do you have to drink to be this stupid? I said jog off." Winsor's eyes looked like they were trying to rip Raiden apart. The silver flashed like steel.

"There's only one thing that stops me from breaking you in half." Raiden snapped his teeth together. "I don't want two of you around. Beat it, coal-eater."

Nova prayed Raiden wouldn't leave. Both men appeared to hold their ground. She glanced at Arrow's back while the two harvesters stared eye to eye. Winsor's shadow hovered.

Arrow took a step to the side to stand directly in front of her. He must be trying to guard her, but she didn't think she needed protection. These men were fully focused on each other. She wasn't scared. The mini gathering acted like no one else was around.

"I think that stupid spike through your ear is fucking with your hearing."

A muscle in the side of Raiden's cheek ticked. "Eat a dick, you mother-fucking—"

"Down, Mutt." Arrow's voice was a low growl. He stepped between the two men. He didn't sound anything like the man she knew.

With his graceful movement, his action forced Winsor and his shadow to move back. Raiden had to do the same thing. A few men entered the bar joking and calling to the dice players, but because of the tension Nova had the feeling the room was hushed. She glanced at the man with the walking stick, but he leaned against the wall. He didn't seem to notice the conflict. Maybe Raiden and Winsor fought so much that it'd become an ordinary occurrence.

"It's a good thing blond hair isn't contagious." Winsor relaxed his shoulders. The dark-haired shadow shrugged and leaned away. No one seemed to think there was anything wrong with Arrow. That was a good thing.

"Mutt and I have business to talk over." Arrow glared. "Say what you've gotta say, then fuck off."

The "fuck off" part was terrific. She wanted to congratulate Arrow on remembering.

"Now, now, Weaver. You shouldn't bite the hand that feeds you," Winsor replied. "Muzzle your dog. This is no time to wag off. Do you want to play now or later? I say we play now while it's new fallen snow around here."

Nova had no idea what was going on. So far, she had kept up with some of the harvester terms, but this was beyond her knowledge.

"Train will be here soon," Raiden interrupted.

"I'm going to pull that ponytail off your head and shove it in your laughing gear." Winsor turned away from Raiden and faced Arrow again. "What'd you say, Weaver? Are you in?"

Arrow was silent. Crap-cans, she couldn't help him. In for what?

"Weaver isn't interested in the games. We've got shit to discuss," Raiden snapped.

Nova would have to remember to thank him for coming to the rescue. The pale man ruffled against the wall.

"All you've got coming out of your mouth is shit, Mutt." Winsor didn't even bother looking at Raiden this time.

"It's a trek to a strip mall. It's glacial." Arrow nodded like he meant it. Well done.

Winsor looked skeptical, then he laughed. His chuckle was a light sound. The tone didn't fit with Nova's assessment of his character.

"Tosh, Mutt. When has Weaver ever turned down the game to talk to you? This is a lot of new ice and we got time. No one's betting the ivories. I'll set it up. You can talk on the train. Stop snowing me. It's game time." With that, Winsor turned to trot happily toward the door that led into what Nova figured had more harvesters on the other side. More people entered the cave. They passed the three of them to go in that direction.

Nova stared wide-eyed, lost on what happened. As Winsor and the two men with him started yelling to some other harvesters about a game, they passed the threshold and out of their sight.

"Snowballs," Raiden muttered to himself as he sat back down on his bag. He drew out a multicolored cube from a side pocket. The square was small and fit easily in his hands. He kept turning the sides of the cube this way and that way. When he shuffled the cube, turning the sides, it caused the colors on all the squares to change.

Arrow sat next to Raiden, then she joined them. She waited for Raiden to explain what happened. He kept playing with the cube.

"Are you going to tell us what's happening?" She spoke when it seemed Raiden wasn't going to explain.

Raiden glanced up. He held out the cube on his palm. "It's a puzzle I found on the surface. You have to make the sides all one color by turning them and—"

"Not that! I don't give a damn about that. What was that guy Winsor talking about? What game? What's fresh ice or fresh snow or whatever?"

"Yeah, he uses fucked up terms. You get used to it after a while."

"Why don't you get along with Winsor? Do you hate him? Does his friend hate you too? You know, the tall one with the black hair?" Arrow asked.

Those were stupid questions. Who cared why they didn't like each other? The upcoming game was vastly more important than Winsor and Mutt's war.

"I don't hate him or his friends. In fact, Morgan-Roth is okay." Raiden set his cube down. "Ash and I are just sort of weirdly competitive. I don't know what the deal is. I thought maybe it's because people whisper that he's a Fletcher. Around here anyone who can call themselves a Fletcher think they get to run the place. He's got Stone with him too. Stone is that the tall anemic-looking guy. So, since he's got Stone, Ash can be a real snow squall." Raiden picked up the colorful cube again.

Nova wanted to scream that this was a useless conversation. To her surprise, she kept her temper.

"Do Winsor and I get along?" A strange look came into Arrow's eyes like he knew something he wasn't telling them.

"You gamble together. You always gamble when you're on the same train or when you meet up at Laying Odds. That's why there was no way I would be able to talk him out of it. I didn't think he'd be here, or I would've hidden you in one of the private rooms in back. There are quarters behind the bar. If you can find someone who has a key to a room, we could've gone in there."

"We'd need a key. That sounds about right." Arrow nodded at Nova. She almost laughed. Almost.

"You could've hidden us?" Nova bit back some not nice comments she wanted to make. "That's how this crap always goes for me."

Arrow reached out to hold her hand. His warm palm immediately quelled her temper.

"I'm not a slush-head." Raiden looked indignant. "It would've caused questions. People would've wanted to know why we needed the room. I didn't want to raise suspicion. I got to be careful, too. I could be tied to the tracks for bringing in outsiders. Besides, I didn't know exactly who you were. I thought our talking to more people wouldn't be a great idea. People might've figured out you weren't Weaver, and," he pointed at Nova, "you look like a vampire."

Nova had to admit he may have thought this through. "What's a vampire?"

"A vampire is an immortal human who drinks people's blood," Arrow answered while he traced, "packaged ice" on one of the signs with his other hand.

"You remember what a vampire is, but not fleam? What kind of head injury did you get?" Raiden shook his head at him.

Arrow opened his mouth, and then closed it again.

"We're not going into it," Nova announced. "Tell us about the game Winsor wants Arrow to play or gamble. That's what's important."

"It's a simple game. You won't have to talk, which is good."

"Got it." Arrow stopped touching the sign. He leaned over to whisper in her ear giving her goose bumps. "Sounds easy, angel. I can shut my face hole."

"He doesn't talk. What does he do?" She refrained from leaning into his warm mouth.

"Ash will place Weaver and two other guys in the middle of the room on a bench. You undo your pants. Ash gets some hot women or men to dance naked in front of you. It gets dirty. As soon as the music starts, the betting begins. It's entertainment for the people watching, and the betting is usually decent for you and Ash. Since Weaver can't get hard, he always wins. For Ash, Weaver is his sure thing. You see, whoever gets hard first watching the sexy dancers loses. The game is you've got to hold out, but you have to watch."

"What do you mean get hard? Like my...?" Arrow trailed off.

"Your dick stands up, or in your case, your dick doesn't stand up." Raiden looked at her like she should explain more, but she was reeling. What the hell type of game was that?

"I never get hard? Never? Never?" Arrow sounded confused. Nova was both confused as well as appalled. This wasn't a game; this was madness. No more would she ever think she was zany. From now on, the harvesters were truly out of their minds.

"Yeah, you've never been able to get it up in all the years I've known you. I don't know how Ash knows that, but he knows, so he places his bets accordingly. You must've told him once. I know it too, but no one else."

"Is that it? That's the whole game?" Nova asked.

"Never?" Arrow sputtered.

"Most of the time people always fall for it and bet Weaver will lose." Raiden shrugged. "You and Ash always sucker people to make money. In Ash-lingo, he's telling you there are a lot of new harvesters on this train. That's what he means by fresh ice. When he says fresh snow, he means new money's rolling in. You typically act super into the girls, or the guys, then Ash places the bet like he's a fool who doesn't know any better. No one else knows about the penis thing because it's a touchy subject. Anyway, it works for the two of you because Ash makes the bets. You split the money. You always play."

Raiden fumbled with his cube again. He looked like he was done with the topic. Nova swallowed.

"Never ever?" Arrow gulped.

"Who the hell came up with such a disturbing and disgusting game?" Nova asked Raiden after she digested all that information.

Raiden looked up. "Weaver did."

Chapter 18

The bench Arrow sat on was smooth polished wood. He ran his hand over the top while he studied the glossy finish. He wondered how many times he might've sat on this bench before. His finger traced the wood grain pattern.

Looking up abruptly, he spotted two other men approaching him. Earlier when the bench was placed here in the middle of the cave room, Raiden told him to sit. He did. No one seemed to notice him here because everyone milled around and talked to each other.

Now that the other two men took spots on the bench, more people stared at him and built a semicircle along the rock wall. The three of them became the center of attention.

On the furthest spot away from him, sat a young scrawny man with pimples all over his face. His eyes were glazed with excitement and his strings bobbed. The ropes had a bright sheen to them. The youth unzipped his pants as he sat. He yanked out his penis with zest. He held the fleshy pole for a second before letting his dick flop down as if he was afraid to hold it too long. The small pink member plopped limply on his worn blue pants. He leaned back as if waiting for someone to admire his cock.

The man who sat directly next to Arrow, between him and the kid, was an older guy with a receding hairline and droopy eyes. Even though his ropes twirled in front of him, he looked wiped out. The older man sat like the chore was involved. He opened his tan pants. He tugged out a longer thicker dick, but his penis was about as animated as the man was. His cock seemed to be saying "Please leave me alone so I can go back to sleep." This man's entire demeanor begged for a nap.

When Arrow had perched on the bench, he'd not opened his pants. Now, the man next to him flipped his bloodshot eyes over to Arrow's crotch accusingly.

Arrow glanced at Raiden who stood in the corner of the room next to Nova. Nova talked to him with her head bent. She looked gorgeous and furious. Raiden nodded then he gestured to the bags at his feet. As Raiden guarded the bags on the floor, he toyed with his puzzle cube.

When he caught Raiden's eye, the harvester gestured to his pants. Arrow shook his head. Raiden nodded.

Knowing that it might cause problems if he didn't produce his penis like the others, he braced himself for the awkward action. Slowly he unbuttoned his pants. He picked his own limp penis up in his hands. Feeling self-conscious, he pulled his dick out to let it be displayed in front of him on top of his cargo pants.

Oddly, no one looked at him or commented. Showing his penis was expected. It was as if he hadn't done so then he would've been out of place.

The mix of harvesters ambled around again. Instead of thinking about the strange situation, Arrow studied their ropes to get his mind off what he was doing. He could hear conversations swirling. People made bets that the younger man would "pop wood" first. He heard the term over and over again. Winsor said he was sure it would be Arrow.

Conversations and guesses flew around him. Most of the chatter he didn't understand. Since he didn't get the discussions, he considered the fact that he'd supposedly done this before. This didn't feel familiar.

When no memories came to him, he wondered what type of man he was before he'd met Nova. What sort of person was he that money would be the only thing he cared about? He glanced at Nova. From where he sat, he saw her slap the cube out of Raiden's hand.

When Raiden bent to pick the game up, she appeared to be giving him an earful. She obviously didn't like this any more than Arrow did. Warmth filled him that she didn't want him to show his body. He smiled when he saw her wildly point at him.

Meeting her had been a miracle. Since he'd met her, everything in the world was better, even this. Around her, he was always comfortable and sure. Around her, he could be naked, and it was no problem.

He sighed, then noticed the black man with the carved stick had shown up in the room. His golden strings swirled freely. He'd been looking at all the movement of the ropes. Earlier, he'd been trying to see past them to the people they were attached to. Sometimes seeing the people was impossible. He noticed the other man with the black hair had also shown up. Both men joined the circle around the bar.

Arrow kept one eye on Nova in case anything happened. Even if his pants were down, he could get to her.

As an older man with an instrument took a seat near the bench, another man joined him with what looked like two small drums hooked together. He studied the two men as they sat on the floor. The instrument was a guitar. Having even that little memory return made him smile.

When the stranger began to tune the instrument, Arrow was sure he'd seen that before.

Winsor gave a nod to the guitar player. The way Winsor gave covert looks at the two men who were with him made Arrow doublecheck that Nova was safe next to Raiden. There was something about Winsor that bothered him. He studied the way his strings swayed and stretched.

While he waited, Arrow tried to figure out what would happen next. He didn't understand why he could remember Dawn but not this. Maybe he didn't want to remember this.

"Our dancers have just arrived!" Winsor announced as he stepped into the center of the circle in front of the bench. The entrance opened with a flourish by two men. The announcement seemed off. No new trains had showed up. How could they have *just* arrived? Arrow had the feeling that whatever Winsor did, it was orchestrated for his own benefit. From what he'd gathered so far, Winsor was a cunning man. Below all those smarts, however, Arrow had the feeling he was missing something.

Arrow didn't have time to think about Winsor because the circle parted. Everyone in the room swiveled their heads to where the doors opened. Two beautiful women strode in.

Both ladies were exquisite with sharply legs, smooth curves, and swinging hips. They were a sight to behold. They looked so out of place in amongst all the grubby harvesters, Arrow had the urge to pinch himself to see if this was another weird dream.

They were dressed in simple gray skirts and shirts that matched. One of the women was all light hair with light-colored eyes. The other one was coffee colored with dark hair and eyes to match. They were exotic, but Arrow noticed little of that. What held his attention completely were the ropes which came out of their chests. The bright lines obscured his vision of most of their bodies. The golden strings were luminous as the cords shimmered.

When the women moved together giggling to each other, he could see their ropes were woven together tightly. He craned his head to the side to see more. He wanted to see how the ropes were secured at different points.

"Let's hear some music!" Winsor called out. The drum started a steady beat. The guitar had a repetitive rhythm. The music was neither too loud nor too quiet but it washed over his ears superbly. He didn't pay much attention to the ambiance or the people, but instead stared at the ropes.

"Like what you see?" the old man commented next to him.

"It's amazing." He studied the strands. They were braided like his hair.

As the two women undulated and swung their hips, their strings stayed connected. The ropes grew longer when they moved apart, but they stayed secured. Arrow leaned forward to examine the braiding when they spun closer. The women took off some of their clothes. He had the urge to tell them to stop walking around. He wanted to trace the pattern, but he kept his mouth shut and his hands on the bench.

Feeling like he wanted to learn more, he ran his hand over his own hair. He might be able to tie people together. He could braid people's ropes using this technique. He remembered what it was like to touch Joe's strings. If he connected people this way, what would the side effect be? If the girls were now clothed or naked he didn't know or care. His head was beyond whatever activities they engaged in.

His dream came back to him vividly. He was certain these two women were bound to be together. These two had found the other half of their souls. Their souls were meant to be connected no matter what happened in the outside world.

As the strings stayed tight, he considered the fact that they were both women. Wasn't the other half of a woman supposed to be a man? He reviewed the question. Gender didn't matter when two souls looked for each other. These women were blessed by Mother Earth, or the Great Spirit. This was souls belonging. The rightness of the connection showed in the way the ropes clung lovingly to each other. The ropes didn't lie.

As the two women bobbed their ass in front of the man next to him, he considered that he couldn't see his and Nova's strings, but they were similarly connected. They were tied like they were supposed to be. How to convince her of that he didn't know. Since this trip started, he'd seen no ropes on them so he wouldn't be able to explain it this way. Now that he considered it, he'd not seen anything like this specifically on anyone.

On all the trains and all the places they'd traveled, no ropes were connected like these. Some had tried to braid themselves but weren't succeeding. Were all the other men and women he saw, simply people biding their time until the right person came along?

Depression tugged at his heart as one of the women draped an arm across his shoulder. It was sad that all the people he'd seen had never found their other half. An even more disturbing thought came into his head. What if Nova had tried to connect with Troy or Sky?

One of the women brushed passed him as a horrible idea hit him. What if people found their other half, and then they severed the ropes? Could the cords be broken? He wanted to reach out to test the strength of the ones in front of him.

Loud cheers jarred him. The young man on the end of the bench had thrown his hand over his straining member. Flushed, the boy got up. All around him, money changed hands. As the betting started all over again, he noticed all the gold ropes on the people facing him. Would none of these people ever have what these two women had? He wanted to know how strong the connection was. Could they stand the test of time? How sturdy was his and Nova's cords? He glanced at Nova to make sure she was safe.

The music played on. The two girls danced together touching sweetly. They began to kiss. They blocked his view of Nova. He returned to looking at them. They seemed happy. He wanted that type of happiness with Nova, but what if because of his past, they couldn't be happy? What if because they didn't have any strings, that he could see, maybe he'd damaged their connection?

He hadn't considered that his past could be a problem. He wanted Nova. She was the most important thing in his life, and now he wished he would never find his sister. He didn't want to know about the dickhead Weaver. Maybe those memories weren't worth remembering.

Winsor laughed. A harvester shoved to the front of the circle. Two men argued. If this was what was in his head, he certainly didn't need it.

More cheers went up. The older man next to him stood more quickly than Arrow guessed he could. His cheeks were red. People began laughing. The noise level got steadily louder and floated up to the rock ceiling.

Arrow wasn't paying any attention to the crowd. He plopped his head into his hands and put his elbows on his knees. He wanted him and Nova to be together forever, but he didn't know how to do that.

He started to scan the crowd. Three men who were cheering caught his eye. Arrow stared at a set of ropes that were trying so hard to tie themselves together. The three men who watched the girls were talking. Did those guys know they were meant to be together? He wished he could get up so he could finish the braiding. He wanted to say, no matter how their life went, it would all be better when they were tied together.

"They're hot." Winsor spoke to a group on men on his left. "I picked the hottest women I could find, but Weaver likes men."

Arrow swung his eyes over to where the other man stood. Winsor's voice snapped. He quarreled with a young boy who insisted in a few seconds Weaver would pop. The pale stranger with the black hair stood like a protective guard. Arrow paid attention to the golden strings that crept from Winsor's chest.

"This song's too long," a man next to the drum player complained. Arrow's eyes jumped to him. Winsor made a bet with the drummer, but the music drowned out some of the words as the guitar got louder.

The girls moved closer to him since he was the only one left. They took up spots on both sides of him. He could smell the sweat on their bodies. He didn't like the way they smelled. It was a mixture of a sharp perfume and rich lotion. The perfume accosted his senses. He wished he could inhale Nova's flower smell.

One of the girls was in his line of sight so he couldn't see Nova. To do so, he would have to stand up. That would break the rules.

Raiden had explained that he had to sit until the music ended. One of the girls knelt on the bench next to him. She leaned in front of his face as her hand petted his shoulder. She leaned in his line of vision, so he could watch her kiss the light-haired girl. How long *was* this song?

One of the girls whispered in his ear about eating her out. That caught his attention. He'd never heard the term before. What would they eat? Were they going to eat out of the bar? Maybe on the train? He was a little hungry. He could eat.

He wondered if Nova was hungry. He should've shared more of the food Joe gave them. She was so small and delicate. Taking care of her should be his top priority. He promised her he would care for her, and when he said that, he didn't mean for this trip. He'd meant until he died.

"Get the hell off my boyfriend." The bellow cut through the group like an explosion.

Arrow would've stood up, but the girls in front of him moved so swiftly he was afraid the bench would overturn. He slapped his hands down on both sides of the wood to keep his balance. The two women in front of him scurried to grab their clothes off the floor. All other eyes shot to Nova.

The music made a dead stop. The silence was eerie. All that could be heard was the clink of a few glasses on the bar. The room had a fog of tension descend. Arrow took in the incredible sight of Nova in a full rage.

She stepped part of the way into the circle where the girls had danced. Her fists were clenched at her sides. Her eyes were a blaze of glowing red. They looked like they might light the room on fire. She was short, but at this moment, she looked huge and wild. Arrow noticed a few of the men back up. She seemed like a holocaust of fury that was about to rain down on everyone. The girls yanked on their mini gray shirts and skirts as if the chamber was already ablaze.

Arrow drank in the sight of her. He couldn't help it. He smiled.

"Are you jealous?" He was elated. He wanted to kiss her. She was so beautiful when she was mad.

Nova didn't speak. Winsor took a step directly in front of him. He now looked at Winsor's back. Arrow leaned to the right so he could see Nova. She glared at Winsor.

He wasn't going to get an answer now.

Winsor cleared his throat. "Rules state that anyone who disrupts betting before the song is finished is punished. We don't take that lightly. Punishment for this infraction is being tied to the train tracks." Winsor's voice was loud in the newly acquired silence. All around the room, murmurs of agreement fluttered.

"Is that your sick made-up rule for your sick made-up game?" Nova spat at Winsor.

"No, it's not my rule. It's your boyfriend's rule." Winsor laughed. Arrow wished he could see Winsor's face, but he could only see his back. Winsor kept talking, but he moved so Arrow could see Nova. "Don't even pretend that you're jealous," Winsor continued. "You spoke up to end the song early for your own betting purposes. If you're losing the wagers you made, then sucks to be you, but you can't mess with the rest of our gambling by pretending to be miffed. Everyone knows that Weaver travels single. He isn't into women who look like they've just feasted on a man's heart. I know you're not jealous, but if you are then you're a fool. Weaver is a loaner. No matter your paddy, you'll be tied to the tracks. No exceptions."

At the end of Winsor's speech, the crowd erupted. Someone shouted that the song was too long. All around the bar people called out that she didn't interrupt the betting at all.

People started to call out that the game should've been over a long time ago. A man behind him screamed that Ash was a scammer. Other people claimed Weaver would've gotten hard if only Nova hadn't spoken up. Others asked where the girls had gone. All the harvesters wanted the girls back to restart the game. Other's contested restarting wouldn't be fair.

Arrow glanced at Raiden to get a clue. Raiden tried to be heard as he talked over a bickering assembly. No one had grabbed her so far, but Raiden tried to convince people that Nova shouldn't be tied up.

"If she gets tied up, she'll start the tunnels on fire. Look at her eyes!" Raiden yelled. A few men quickly believed Raiden's claim. They began to agree she should be left alone.

"Underground fires killed my family," an old man yelled. "Her gift can kill us all!"

Arrow felt fear wash over him. Nova might be killed. His muscles bunched ready to run to her.

Nova didn't look at him. Instead, she talked to Winsor, but he couldn't hear her over the yelling. The fear for her kept him rooted to the spot on the bench. He remembered what Joe told him. Nova shouldn't have stated that they were together. She'd put them at risk. Now they had to come up with a way to handle this. Joe said lie.

"She'll light the whole room on fire. I've seen it." He nodded to Raiden as his friend crossed into the circle of people. Raiden stood next to the bench. If Nova ended up tied to the tracks, then he would go with her. He didn't care if he got hit by a train.

No matter what, he would stay with Nova until the very end.

"Winsor." Nova's voice had a razor-sharp edge that silenced the room. "You want to bet? Then let's bet. I bet you three hundred and fifty HOCs that I can get Weaver hard for me."

The room was so silent that Arrow could hear the squeak of someone's shoes on the floor. Arrow's eyes flew to Nova's.

All around him, Arrow heard a few whispers start. Everyone repeated the same thing. No one could have that many HOCs. The gathering sized her up now. Arrow heard someone ask where she could've gotten that money.

"I don't believe you have three hundred and fifty HOCs. Besides, we're throwing you onto the tracks." Winsor's steel-colored eyes scanned the pack for support. No one moved or spoke.

"I have the money. I can get Weaver hard unless instead, you'd like to see me light this room on fire?"

"Make the bet!" two men behind Arrow called out to Winsor.

"I want to see her do it," another man yelled. More people nodded. Arrow could see them warming up to the new wager. Nova must have been able to see the growing excitement as well. She flashed her eyes at a few people while she stood tall. She looked like a force to be reckoned with, a small force, but a force.

"If I get him hard, then I keep my money, and I'm left alone keeping my gifts to myself."

"And if you don't get him hard?" Winsor scanned the throng.

"If I don't, then you get the money. You can tie me to the tracks," she stated.

"Let's see it!" someone hollered. "She should get naked."

All around them, the room began to buzz. People were equally saying she could do it and she couldn't.

Winsor looked doubtful, but Arrow could see the way everyone was into the bet. Winsor looked concerned for the first time. His forehead crinkled.

"Maybe I just kill you, and take your money?" The threat was cold, but even Arrow could tell there was worry behind those words. Winsor was unsure. The intimidation was weak.

Nova laughed. "You think I'm that stupid? I've my money hidden. You'll never find it. Besides, do you want to take that chance? Your face will be melted off before you even get close to me."

Harvesters began to bet. A fat man with a striped shirt claimed that Winsor would accept. Others responded that he wouldn't. A handful of people must've heard about the confrontation. They spilled through the door behind the bar. The minutes ticked by.

"If I'm not his girlfriend then why are you scared?" Nova mocked. "Weaver is single, right? I look like I just feasted on a man's heart."

"I'm not scared," Winsor snapped. "Fucking nob."

Arrow realized he was on the edge of his seat. Raiden's hand appeared on his shoulder. He looked up. Raiden made a curt shake of his head then pressed him to the bench. Arrow knew his friend silently told him not to move or talk. He wanted to demand that Nova get somewhere safe.

"Standard rules. You get one song. You can't touch him from the belly button down to his knees."

Nova's eyes narrowed. "Raiden picks the song."

There was only silence in the room as Winsor tipped his head to the side.

"It's a bet."

Chapter 19

There were probably hundreds of times in her life she had lost her temper. Right now, she remembered none of them clearly. At this moment, all she could think was that she'd been justified.

In the past, she was always freaking out, most of the time about nothing, but for once she didn't consider this issue nothing. Sure, she would agree this was bad timing, but her actions couldn't be helped. Nova didn't think she had ever been jealous before, but she couldn't push the feeling down. Sitting there watching those beautiful women had made a part of her snap. She tried to remember her mantra, but she couldn't even recall one word while those women pranced before Arrow. Arrow was her man. They had no right to him.

In fact, none of these people had a right to any part of him. He didn't belong here. He was sweet and sensitive, with his dopey lost look. He wasn't to be displayed like a cut of meat. This life wasn't for him. He was meant to be at home with her, loving her. She didn't know what else Arrow should do, but she was sure he was supposed to be hers and hers alone.

Nova headed from the middle of the room to where her bags sat next to Raiden. Raiden talked to the huge man with a mammoth walking stick. The two moved apart when she approached. She took one more glance at Arrow.

He probably thought she was funny when she turned so green, but she didn't care. All she'd wanted was for the girls to stop, and damn the consequences. Except, she should've considered all the intricacies of the situation before she opened her mouth. Now she had more than she bargained for. Showing her true colors to Arrow and admitting she was jealous was a big deal. Arrow probably would say they were together now that she had indicated she wanted him all for herself. It would be hard enough to explain to Arrow how she felt, but now she had to deal with Winsor who was a much bigger issue. How the hell was she supposed to know this sick twisted game had rules like you couldn't interrupt the song? She actually agreed that the song had gone on too long.

Now that she had opened her mouth, she had to dig in and not back down. There was no other choice but to play this out until the end.

Nova crouched next to her bag then began to brush her hair to buy herself time. There was no way she was going to take off her clothes. Getting naked wasn't the answer. Or was it? The idea nagged at her. Boasting she could make Arrow get an erection was the only thing she could think of. She couldn't lose. She couldn't give up her money, her bags, and maybe even CC.

Why had she spoken up? She should've kept her mouth shut and let the song end. She shoved her brush back in her bag. She wouldn't have been able to stay silent even if she could go back in time to change her actions. Regrets were useless.

In her bag was a bottle of flower water that Clare gave her. Nova took the tiny bottle out. She dabbed the scent on her neck. Next, she applied the strawberry lip balm Clare had also sent with her. She put on the ointment as she tried to keep her hands from shaking.

"I talked to Essie. He's the drummer. I picked the longest song I could think off. The tune is not *that* long, however." Raiden's long coat swished around his legs as he walked up behind her.

Nova could barely hear him over the buzz of the crowd. The whole place was alive with betting. Since they had entered the bar, she hadn't seen a single woman around. Now that the betting had changed, women from the other room squeezed into the cavern. Everyone swarmed into the area even from the platform. Nova guessed they all wanted to see what might happen. People who claimed Weaver didn't like females came to see if Nova could make him react. Others believed he liked hot women fine, but that the ladies were simply not his type. Some stated with conviction that he got off on men.

"How long is the song?" Nova asked absently, as she took off her dark coat and stuffed the garment into the larger duffle. She made sure CC was safe, and all her bags were in order for Raiden to guard.

"The song isn't going to play until the train for Bosstown shows up, that's all I know. What's the plan? I take it you can't light the room on fire."

Nova could hear the concern in Raiden's voice. She stood up from where she squatted next to her bag then faced him. She could do this. She *had* to do this.

"There is no plan. I can't light the room on fire, but it's not a problem. I'll get Arrow to respond to me. Everyone is wrong. I'm right." She hadn't had any problem with his dick so far. There was no reason for her to be nervous. Ever since she'd met Arrow, he'd been able to show he liked her.

"I'm wrong? You think we're all wrong?" Raiden looked at her like she spoke in tongues. "How long have you known Weaver?"

Nova shrugged. At this moment, she felt like she'd known him for a lifetime. "What does this question have to do with my getting him hard?"

"I'm guessing, I've known him a lot longer than you and I'm telling you he can't get it up. When you fail, Winsor and all these harvesters are going to tie you to the tracks. They'll take your money." Raiden paused. "Do you even have that much money on you?"

Nova nodded. Raiden looked relieved and upset simultaneously.

"Why would you carry money like that with you?" He slapped his hand to the top of his head like he kept his hair from falling out. "I've never even seen money like that."

"I need that much to get home." She was now done with this conversation.

She didn't care what Raiden said about Weaver. If he wasn't going to offer her anything helpful, then there was no point in talking with him. She didn't need a doomsayer. Maybe he did know Weaver, but he didn't know Arrow. Arrow was a healthy, responsive man. Arrow was also sweet and kind, with an idyllic view of the world. Arrow was *not* Weaver. Raiden would never understand that Arrow did want her. She wanted him also. Maybe their chemistry was just that simple. This was a boy and a girl, that's all.

Nova glanced over to Arrow. He did his best not to look scared, but she could tell he was worried. Arrow stared. His eyebrows came down. His emotions were spread out for her to see. She let a small smile play on her lips. She did like when he wanted her. She liked when his body responded to her, and she liked when he talked to her or held her. Even now, she was stupidly happy he was worried about her. She'd never been a man's whole world before, but with Arrow, she decided she wanted it this way. Maybe everything would be different once he got his memories back, but for now, she didn't care if it did change at the end of this journey. For now, she loved him.

Startled at her own musings, Nova rubbed her forehead. Crap, was it possible he was right? Did she love him? Could you fall in love with someone you barely knew? She kicked her bags together.

"Look after these."

"I should be coming up with a place to hide you," Raiden responded glumly. "When this becomes a pisspot, then follow me. I'll come up with an escape."

"'When this becomes a pisspot' says the man who could've hid us from the start." Nova muttered to herself as she walked away.

Winsor talked to his black-haired friend while Arrow waited. Nova ignored Raiden and walked over to Winsor and Arrow in the middle of the room. There was something about the way Winsor looked at her that made Nova pause. Winsor bothered her on a few levels.

"You didn't drug him while I wasn't looking, did you?" Nova glanced at Arrow. His shirt hung on his shoulders loosely. His braid draped over his shoulder. He looked lost and desirable, if that combination was possible. Winsor gave a smug smile. *You'll see that I'm right*, Nova thought.

"I'm fine, my angel." Arrow smiled. Winsor glared at her. Maybe he didn't like the use of the word "angel."

"You heard it straight from his mouth. We play," Winsor barked out suddenly. He moved to the edge of the circle next to the drum player. "Drum it out, Essie."

As soon as Winsor was out of the way, the music started. Nova turned to face Arrow. What should she do now? She began to unzip her sweater. Her arms slipped out and she tossed the garment on the bench. Arrow's eyebrows drew together. He looked at the sweater than at her.

"What are you doing?"

"I was going to…" She started to lift the bottom of her shirt.

Arrow shook his head. He reached out and picked up her sweater then held the top out.

"Take it off!" a man behind her yelled.

Her hand paused for a second before she took the sweater from Arrow. Not knowing what else to do, she put her arms through the sleeves.

Both men and women started to call out.

"Take off your shirt," a woman hollered.

"She has to!" a pudgy harvester waved his arms.

Conversation flared up everywhere, but Nova ignored the catcalling. She gazed at Arrow. He looked at her like she was the only thing in the world. She loved when he stared like that. A smile kicked up one side of her face. The way his eyes caressed her made her feel like they were in their own little world.

"I'm supposed to get you hard. Do you know what that means? I'm expected to make your penis stand up like in the room when we were alone together. I'm meant to excite you sexually." Nova dropped her eyes to his flaccid cock. His eyes dropped to the junction of his legs too.

"I don't think it'll excite me if you show your body to all these people. I don't want to share you, angel. I believe you don't want to share me either." He smiled ruefully, then looked to the floor. "I know what you're going to say. We're not together but—"

"I don't want to share you either. I was jealous. I called you my boyfriend." Nova grinned at him. A tiny smile of satisfaction lifted the corner of his mouth.

"I heard." His head angled up then he stared into her eyes. "You can call me your boyfriend."

She forgot they were surrounded by betting harvesters.

"I wish we were someplace where it was the two of us. Like a water base?" he said after a few notes of the music drifted past them.

"You might be a wanted man or an outlaw, and you're not allowed on a water base." Nova straddled the bench next to him then sat with a plop.

Arrow's brow crinkled. "Do you think so?"

"I was teasing. I know you're one of the good ones, besides it wouldn't matter. Once we are at the base, I could get you in. We can have a hot shower and a warm meal. A bed..." She captured his gaze. He licked his lips.

"I'd love that. I want to hold you like we were doing in the other private room before Joe came in." Arrow turned to face her. His hands clasped the wooden bench between them.

"You were doing a lot more than holding me," Nova murmured.

"Was I? I don't remember. I have a head injury."

"Should I remind you of all the things you were doing so you remember?" She could no longer hear all the noise around them. She scooted closer.

"Yes." Arrow's eyes dropped to her lips.

Careful not to break the rules, she leaned toward him. His skin was damp from perspiration. The sweat made his shirt cling to his chest.

"When we were alone," she whispered close to his ear. "I touched all of your hot naked skin. I had all my clothes off remember?"

"I wanted to touch you too." Arrow's fingers dug into the wood.

"I was afraid if you did, I'd get out of control, but I wanted you inside of me. I wanted you to lick all the soft skin between my legs. I wanted you to taste me. I've never wanted that before, but I want it now." She leaned back enough so she could drop her eyes to his mouth. Arrow's tongue darted out and over his lips.

"Yea, that's what I want." He swallowed hard. "Can I kiss you now? You did say next time I needed to find a better time. Is this an okay time?"

"I did say next time, didn't I?" Nova laughed lightly. "This isn't a better time but well… fuck it. Kiss me."

She didn't need to ask him twice. He leaned forward, and just as before in the busy train hallway, the room dropped away as soon as their lips touched. He was a fast learner. Arrow recalled what she liked and put that knowledge to good use. He opened his mouth to let his tongue slip over her mouth. She nibbled on his bottom lip, then sank her tongue into the warm cavern of his mouth.

Knowing what he wanted, she started to move her tongue in and out of his mouth mimicking the action she wanted him to take with her body. She wished she could scoot closer to feel his chest. She wanted him holding her tightly, but she didn't want to break the rules.

He growled. Nova wound her hand through his braid and pressed her fingers into the satin skin of his neck. The movement of her hands tipped his head back. Nova knelt up on the bench to lean over him without touching anything but his lips and hair. Another growl of desire came from his throat as she deepened the kiss trying to absorb his taste.

Someone grabbed her arm. Nova opened her eyes to see Raiden shoving Winsor off. Nova tumbled off the bench. After she recovered from hitting the floor, she stood and glanced around the room. Raiden was a wall between her and Winsor. No one looked happy.

"Kissing isn't fair play," Winsor yelled over the noise.

"It is. Two months ago, one of the girls kissed Carver. I was there," Raiden snarled. "The rule is not below the belly button or above the knees. She touched only his mouth and hair."

Winsor took a step back from the bench. His head flipped to the crowd. The room was a frenzy.

"I say the song was too long," the man with the beaded beard called out. Nova nodded at him. He had stated that before.

"It only took the vampire half a minute. They didn't even have to play a full song," an older lady in the back barked. Everywhere in the room, people began calling out opinions or arguing their side. Everyone had a reason why the bet should go the other way.

Arrow stood up from the bench and took her hand. He pulled her close and tried to block her from the overexcited mass by tucking her under his arm. Raiden moved until he was toe to toe with Winsor. Just when Nova thought Raiden would throw a punch, Ash's dark-haired friend shoved Raiden backward. Ash's fierce guard took a protective stance in front of Winsor. Raiden backed off and glanced at Arrow.

"Cram your shit in your pants and follow me. We've got to get the hell out of here before this gets worse," Raiden snapped at Arrow.

Arrow heard Raiden over the rising noise level and let go of her hand. He shoved his dick into his pants as the place went wild. Someone threw a drink at the bartender. Raiden began to steer them closer to the door.

The guitar player to her right defended his playing. The guy on the drums backed him up with over the top claims that he was the best drummer in the last century. They took a few steps away from the budding brawl. They hadn't gone far when Nova noticed Ash being dragged toward the back exit.

"Fuck you, Raiden!" Winsor yelled as he was pulled away. "You damp squid!"

People surrounded them from every direction. Nova tried to gauge what it would take to get out of the cave. The mob screamed for a start over. She refused to cower. Nova flashed her eyes and two men stepped back.

"We've got to get the hell out of here." Raiden stumbled backward when a harvester pushed closer. He pointed to the door.

Outside Laying Odds, a train whistle blew.

"That's our ride." Raiden grabbed Nova's hand. They weaved between arguments and shoving matches. Behind her, she saw Arrow. He pushed through the crowd. The large black man with the walking stick had her bag. She wanted to call out, but he seemed to be tailing them. The group succeeded to get through the horde. As she passed the threshold onto the train platform, she saw someone throw the first punch.

"Put down the plow, take the refrigerator off your back, and move faster." Raiden commanded. She picked up her pace. Her short legs pumped faster.

The four of them dived onto the platform slamming the door behind them. The man with the walking stick held the door closed as they sprinted toward a waiting train.

The whistle blew a second time. Arrow lifted her over the stairs and into the train. Raiden waved them through the first car. As she dodged anyone already on the train, she made swift strides across the floor. They headed for a set of doors at the end of the metal room. Their group maneuvered around boxes, people, and dice games in progress. No one paid them any attention as they barreled through.

It was darker in the next car. Nova could barely see. She stubbed her toe on a carton but didn't dare slow. Arrow grabbed her arm.

"Crap." She ran directly into Raiden's back when he abruptly halted before the next door.

"Do you have it?" Raiden waved a hand to the man who shouldered her bags. He tossed the duffle to Arrow as he walked up on them. Arrow slung the pack over his shoulders. She took her backpack and slipped on the straps.

"I thought you were with Winsor."

"Here." The stranger patted his chest. She didn't know what that meant, but Raiden seemed to think that was a good action. He smiled.

No one had answered her question.

"Thanks, Morgan-Roth." Raiden turned back to the door.

"Isn't he with Winsor?" Nova looked at each man. No one answered. Arrow shrugged. "What does he have?"

"He has the key. Let's go." Raiden wrenched on the next handle to the sliding door. The door only opened an inch. Arrow stepped forward and helped Raiden. The two men struggled with the handle.

The man called Morgan-Roth leaned on his carved stick. He stared down at her like this running was all her fault.

Raiden finally spoke through clenched teeth when he got the door to slide free. "Morgan-Roth was told by Joe to get you to Bosstown. He's normally with Winsor, but he's switching sides for safety reasons."

Morgan-Roth's deep voice cut in. "Joe said I had to help a munchkin and an Indian. When I saw Weaver, I didn't think Joe was referring to him. Now I gathered you two are the people I'm to help. I have a private room in the next train car. You can go back there. Stay out of sight until we get to our stop."

"I'm good with that." Nova gave a curt nod.

Raiden passed through the next door. She followed behind Morgan-Roth.

"Why are you helping Joe? What does safety reasons mean?" Arrow asked as the door behind them slid closed with a grinding clank.

"He told me if I didn't help you, he'd disembowel me."

Arrow laughed, but Nova didn't think Morgan-Roth made a joke.

The next train car looked much like the one they had rode in on the way here. There was one narrow aisle with doors and padlocks on both sides of the walkway.

"The room's over here." Raiden indicated the second door. Morgan-Roth took a key from around his neck.

"My life so far seems to involve *always* needing a key." Arrow took the key from Morgan-Roth as she stepped to the door in the hallway. Arrow was on one side of her next to Raiden. He handed her the key and waited. Morgan-Roth leaned against the wall near to the next exit.

On the other train, there'd been nothing like this. Things on this train were similar, but there'd only been button locks. Before she could get the lock to pop open, a hand clamped down on her forearm.

Her head snapped up. Standing next to her appeared a livid Winsor. No one had even heard him come through the door. Everyone looked at him with wide eyes.

"I got an angry mob back there. I'll be strung up for the stunt you fucking pulled. I'm never going to be allowed into Laying Odds again."

Arrow shoved Winsor forcing him to let go of Nova's arm.

"Don't touch Nova. If you have a problem, it's with me." Arrow took a step closer to her. The tight walkway seemed charged with a wrathful energy.

"Get out of my way, Weaver," Winsor demanded. Arrow didn't budge.

Nova tried to turn the key in the lock. Winsor reached around Arrow and grabbed her hand.

"We've got business," Winsor snarled. "That's money lost."

"Don't touch Nova again. This is my last warning." Arrow threw Winsor's hand off a second time.

Nova had never heard Arrow get angry before. His fury was all the more frightening because he didn't raise his voice. In fact, his tone was so soft it could've been a whisper.

"I rule the trains, Weaver, or have you been gone so long that you've forgotten? Do you think you're sunshine now that you have a vampire to fuck?" Winsor's eyes gleamed like melted mercury.

Behind Winsor, the door opened again with another terrible grinding sound. The black-haired man with the huge pack entered making the hall seem even smaller.

"Stone." Winsor's eyes never left Arrow as he spoke. "Pitch Weaver off the train. Give him to the riot."

"You made a bet. You lost." Raiden defended them.

"I did no such thing. I said the vampire could have her money. I never said anything about Weaver. I'm thinking to soothe my headache, it might be best to fling Weaver to the harvesters back there. I think the vampire and I will get to know each other while they rip you apart." Winsor grinned like he'd come up with the best solution. "You're a hot piece of ass." He eyed her. "After I cover your eyes, you can show me what you do to get Weaver so hard, unless…" Winsor gave a parody of a smile. "You want to pay me all your HOCs to go away. For the right price, I could piss off."

"Is that a threat?" Nova asked.

"I don't threaten. I state facts." Winsor, maybe to make a point, grabbed her arm again. His hand was small, but his fingers were muscular. His fingers dug deep into her skin.

Arrow glanced at the hand on Nova's arm.

Winsor might have touched her simply to prove he wasn't afraid of Arrow, but the second his hand was on her, everything changed.

It was as if the train itself held its breath. Nova felt like someone had immediately sapped her energy. She stood frozen to the spot. Her bones became both weightless and heavy.

Before her, some invisible force, like a wind, began to move Arrow's hair. His black locks started to unbraid. The strands separated out and floated like black streamers in a breeze. He held his hands up as his eyes turned a blood-red.

No one moved. Maybe they couldn't. She couldn't move if she wanted to. Her whole body was lead welded to the floor.

Arrow held both his hands up with his palms facing outward. He took a single step back. His back stiffened rim-rod straight as his hair fluttered around his face. The magical wind picked up.

As his hands started to move with purpose, he made deft strokes through the air. There was a supernatural silence. The train became whisper soft.

As Arrow's hands made some type of pattern in the air, then just as abruptly as it had started, it ended. Arrow's hands dropped to his sides. His hair fell perfectly straight down his back.

All at once, everyone moved. Stone backed up a few paces. He wrapped his arms around his middle then turned and left the hallway shaking. The door slid shut.

Morgan-Roth wiped sweat from his brow. He gasped. "I've never not been able to move before."

Raiden and Winsor turned as white as ghosts. Both of them, in unison, clutched their chests much like Nova had seen a heart attack victim do.

"What did you do to me?" Winsor's voice trembled.

Raiden didn't speak at all. He only gaped at Arrow.

"I told you not to touch her. I promised to protect Nova. I warned you." Arrow shook his head.

"I'll leave. Just fix whatever it is that you did to me." Winsor snapped his head around frantically. Some of his slicked back hair fell around his ears. "Put me back the way I was. I'll go. I promise."

Winsor curled into himself. He wrapped his arms around his middle like Stone had done. He leaned over like he might vomit. Nova took a step away from him in case he did.

"I'm not going to change what I did. I've bound you to Raiden. You'll not be able to leave his side. You don't know it, but the heart strings don't lie. If I were you, I'd be working on figuring out how to add Raiden into your life instead of attempting to take our money and kicking us off the train."

"What?" Raiden bellowed.

Nova put her hands over her ears.

"Did you say the rest of my life? I don't want Winsor for the rest of my life! I don't want anyone. You're a terrible person," Raiden sputtered. "Nothing about you has changed."

"I'm sorry, Raiden, but Winsor is part of your other half. Your match. I hope in time you'll work it out with *her*."

The word "her" had a strange effect on everyone including Nova. She couldn't place it before, but now she could see what had bothered her. Winsor's features were just a little too delicate. Her hands a bit too small. No matter how big a coat she wore, she couldn't hide the dainty wrists or her slim fingers.

Morgan-Roth must have already had this piece of information. Nova saw him heave an agitated breath. He was probably wondering where his loyalties should be placed. Morgan-Roth was most likely supposed to protect her secret. Indecision lit his eyes.

Raiden took two leaps past Arrow and her. His abrupt movement backed Winsor up against the wall. Winsor's eyes flashed around the walkway like a trapped animal. She had nowhere to move in the tight space. Raiden's one hand struck the side of the wall next to the door. With his other hand, he shoved his fingers under the hem of Ash's furry coat. As soon as his hand disappeared, Winsor slapped him. His jaw dropped. The stunned expression on his face made Nova think he hadn't believed Arrow before.

Raiden backed up. He gaped at Winsor slacked jawed. Before anyone could say anything, Raiden turned on his heel and bolted through the door.

As soon as the door closed behind Raiden, Winsor burst into tears. Both men looked terrified.

"Please, Weaver, fix it," Winsor bawled. Nova could only barely understand her as she wept. "I didn't mean anything. I was only acting like I'm tough. I have to keep my place here. No one will respect me otherwise. I'll be raped again. I have to be like this or the harvesters might figure me out. You don't know how bad it is. I can't be with Mutt. Oh God, please."

"Ash. It's okay." Morgan-Roth scrubbed his hands over his face. "Get a hold of yourself."

Winsor cried harder. Huge, fat tears streamed down her face. She wasn't a pretty crier. Her cheeks and her nose turned blotchy red as her eyes started to swell.

"It's not okay. I'm the best harvester there is, but no one would trade with me if they knew I was a woman. People thinking I'm a Fletcher won't protect me. I'm sure of it. Raiden will tell everyone. He might tell Stone. Please, Weaver."

Arrow glanced at Nova, but his face showed only that he couldn't or wouldn't change anything. Morgan-Roth's eyes were wide. Maybe he had never seen his fearless leader cry before. Nova felt like a worm.

"That's not true. I bet the men would respect you even if they knew." Nova spoke up when neither of the men said anything. "If you're a good harvester, gender won't matter. You have Stone and Morgan-Roth with you. Morgan-Roth trusts you even though he knows you're a woman. Trading and HOCs is the only thing that matters to harvesters."

Nova quoted her last sentence from Joe as she tried to soothe the distraught woman. She felt sorry for her. Ash looked like they had shot her puppy.

"Plus no one will touch you. I'm sure your men will protect you. Raiden will help you too, once you get to know him." Nova grasped at anything she could think of. She looked again at both Arrow and Morgan-Roth hoping they would agree. She didn't know if what she said was true. She knew nothing of the harvester lifestyle, but she couldn't stand here while this woman cried. She wished they would speak up and help.

"But… but… Mutt hates me." She wailed louder. Nova patted the weeping woman's shoulder.

Morgan-Roth cringed. That might be an accurate statement. Nova couldn't come up with a rebuttal.

"He doesn't hate you," Arrow murmured. "For the rest of the train ride, you can talk to Raiden. You can ask him to keep your secret. I'm sure you can convince him not to tell anyone. Until this train gets to Bosstown, Nova and I will be in this room. If all goes well for us, then when the train stops we can talk about separating you."

The word "separating" brightened Winsor. She brushed the tears from her face. She still looked like she'd been crying, but Nova was thankful the tears slowed.

"I'll go talk to Mutt now. I'll tell him that you'll undo it." She practically ran past Nova and Arrow. She snapped her fingers at Morgan-Roth. "Since I can see you've switched sides, you can go get Stone. Have him come to my private room. I'll find Mutt. I'll get him, and we'll both be in that room. Then you can make sure nothing happens to Weaver." She paused before going after Raiden and glared at Arrow. "Nothing will happen to you on this train, but I swear if you tie me to Mutt for the rest of my life, I'll figure out a way to make yours a living hell." Winsor sounded more like herself again. Her threat was oddly reassuring.

Nova liked Winsor much better when she tossed out threats than when she cried.

Arrow nodded solemnly as if accepting what Winsor said. Maybe he preferred the threats over the crying as well.

"May I give you some advice?" Arrow motioned for Nova to turn the key. Nova got the door to Morgan-Roth's room open. A muted white light automatically came on overhead.

"What?" Winsor tapped on the exit door impatiently.

"Don't call him Mutt." Without looking back, Arrow ushered Nova into the private room.

Chapter 20

The private room had the same layout as the last train with a cot mounted on the wall and a room with a toilet and sink. But this room had a few differences that captivated Arrow. On every wall were mounted objects and signs from the surface. On the cot were thick blankets with mounds of fabric and furs.

The room was bright and colorful. Arrow leaned against the door and stared at a gold-leafed clock blinking 2:05 a.m. He put the duffle down on the floor before he rested against the closed door. He exhaled relief as he took a moment to tame his jumbled emotions. Mentally spent, he was happy that he was finally away from everyone. The silence of the room was welcoming to his jingling nerves.

Nova entered and placed her bag and his duffle under the raised cot. She unfolded one of the blankets and covered the fabric pile. She made a place on the bed as if giving him time. He appreciated that. When she was done with the bed, she turned around to gaze at him.

"Do you want to talk about what happened?" Her tone washed over him like a warm shower of serenity. Even though he didn't deserve her, he thanked the Great Spirit for her anyway. Without her, he would have never been able to make this trip to find his sister.

"It's just… I shouldn't have done that. I was out of control. I lost my head when Winsor touched you. I wasn't thinking, and I acted crazy…" He faltered at a loss for explanations. He didn't have the right words for what had come over him. He'd behaved recklessly. Now he didn't know if he could ever untie Winsor from Raiden. Those ropes were way more complicated then he thought.

He knew nothing of his gift, yet he'd used the power anyway. The first time he got angry, he'd ignored his wise decision not to use his ability until he understood it more. What was worse was Raiden had paid the price for his actions. Raiden didn't deserve what Arrow had done to him. What if Winsor made his life hell? Winsor had a complicated life and the strings told him that story. Raiden had helped them. Arrow should've been a friend to him and left him alone.

He wanted to excuse his actions, but his guilt wouldn't let him. It was true, the ropes had wanted to connect as if they belonged together, but what he did wasn't acceptable. He didn't have the right to mess with other people's lives. The ropes should have tied together naturally, or not, depending on their destinies. What did he know about who should be together? Especially since he couldn't even get his own life figured out. Tying them together had been rash. Guilt doubled. He hoped Nova would understand. Maybe Raiden was correct. He was a terrible person.

"You were out of control you say?" She pretended to seriously consider that, but her eyes shone. "Oh, like, for example, yelling, 'Get off my boyfriend' and creating a riot in a bar full of harvesters?"

A smile grew inside his heart. "Yea, like that."

"You like advertisement sayings? There is an ad that goes 'Power is nothing without control.'" Nova gave him a soft understanding smile. "I've lost my temper and been irrational so many times I can't even count it anymore. I lose control." She took off her shoes, then her socks before climbing up on the bed of blankets.

"Emotions are hard to keep in check." A strange warmth blossomed in his chest.

"Tell me about it." She chuckled.

Maybe Nova understood as no one else could. She understood what it was like for him to not understand himself, or even the world around him. For him, living like this would only be until he got his memories back, but he realized for her, it was all the time. A new respect for her filled him. She navigated life taking on whatever was hurled her way. Nova did it with real strength.

"They say, 'There is no way to peace. Peace is the way.'" He didn't know where that came from, but that idea seemed true with Nova. She was both peace and the way. She was sanity in a world of insanity.

"They do say that. That's an advertisement for World Peace Day. I say it when I'm struggling." She spoke into the quiet space around them as she arranged the fabric as a pillow. "Sometimes you do things that are crazy or out of control, then you have to let them go and forgive. After that, you have to find the next peaceful moment. I think that's the path. That's how I live." She knelt on the center of the blankets.

"Since I've met you, all I've seen is that you're strong and in command. I think you're smart and tough. I'm glad I'm with you. You're my way." As he looked at her, it was as if it all didn't matter to him anymore. Nothing mattered but Nova.

"I have been pretty stable on this trip, but all I know is if I do crack, all I can do is take it as it comes, then forgive myself for my weaknesses. We have to forgive our mistakes and our failings."

"You're right. I can't go over all my mistakes. I'd prefer to have every peaceful and wonderful moment I can have with you. Being alone with you seems to be a rare opportunity." A steady warmth infused him.

"I'm always right." She grinned. "And I positively can't go over all my mistake or else we'd never get off this train." Her eyes got wide like they'd be trapped on the train indefinitely. Her look of mock fear made him chuckle. She had that ability when he was with her. When he stared into her eyes, the world dropped away, and it was only the two of them. He turned around to lock the door then removed his boots and socks.

"I wouldn't mind being trapped here with you... that is if it could be only the two of us, with no interruptions?" He let all his hope to have her chase away everything past this room. He let her see it all shining in his eyes. He didn't care if he seemed needy. He *did* need her. She would make the world make sense again. Nova was the answers to all the unasked questions inside of him.

"No interruptions like a mob of harvesters?" Nova sat up on the cot so she could move closer to him.

"No women pretending to be men." Arrow took a step to stand in front of the bed.

"No planning what to do next?" Nova scooted so she was directly in front of him with her knees on either side of his thighs. Her thighs squeezed his hips. "No CC or HOCs or H.S.P.C. agents."

"No Dawn or Dan or..." His voice grew raw. He wanted nothing but Nova and him together. "No Troy or Sky."

Nova leaned toward him. He could smell her scent of flowers again.

"No anyone," she whispered. "But you."

He inhaled deeply. He had no idea how Nova did that. The train had smelled like dusty metal and dirty men, but she smelled like flowers.

Once again, like when they'd been alone before, he experienced the dual sensations of fear and excitement. Both relaxation and stimulation floated over him. The mix of emotions was a heavy combination. Each feeling shimmered in the tiny secluded room. He could hear the beating of her heart, but then again, the pounding might be his.

Nova reached out to touch his hair lightly with a few fingers. His locks swished around his shoulders. His hands rose to braid the strands, but she stopped him, and he let his hands drop. With his arms down, her fingers strolled down his neck. His skin felt too hot and too tight. She wrapped a blanket of sensuality around him. He wasn't sure what he should do. He hoped she didn't try to stop him from touching her. He was pretty sure he wouldn't be able to stop doing anything this time.

Running his hands up her arms gently, he waited to see her reaction. He checked whether she might push him away. She only sighed. Where she knelt in front of him, she was about the same height as him standing before the cot. She tugged on his hair and brought his lips to hers. He wrapped his arms around her as soon as they kissed.

There was no breaking away, or even hesitation, from either of them. This is what Arrow had waited for. Maybe from the moment they had met, or maybe from the moment they were born. He wasn't sure nor did he care. Her soft skin was satin in his hands. His own skin felt overly sensitive. He sank into the wet hunger of her mouth, while he eagerly tried to press into her curves. His thighs bumped the cot. There were too many clothes. She was always just out of his reach. He needed to get closer, but he wasn't sure how and not scare her. His head started to swim as his blood pressure rose. Her hot tongue slipped in and out of his mouth.

The kiss went on until he couldn't remember anything else. If there had been a world outside of this room, he didn't know. Nova lifted her mouth away. Her breath teased his ear.

"No interruptions, no stopping."

"Yea, angel." He wanted to laugh or cry. All his emotions tumbled together. "No stopping." He desired her to the point of pain.

Nova tugged on his hand while she scooted over so he could climb onto the cot. She made room for him while he knelt next to her. As soon as he was on the cot, they locked against each other again immediately. They shared more heart-pounding kisses which made him feel like flying.

Noises of the train fell away as if they were on their own private cloud of passion.

As they kissed, her hands ran over his shoulders then down his back. As he struggled out of his coat, her fingers glided under his shirt to stroke his stomach. Yanking his shirt over his head, he inhaled sharply as she touched his nipples. If he could've spoken, he would've begged for more. She shifted against him as frantically as he felt. Her fingers unzipped and unbuttoned all of her clothes until she was down to only her underwear. Stupidly, he tried to help her, but his fingers were slow and their dexterity gone.

As soon as she got her sweater and shirt off, however, he helped her remove her bra. His hands finally stopped shaking. With her breasts barred to him, he cupped both— one lush globe in each hand. He touched them tenderly, reverently, not sure what she wanted, but willing to do anything to please her.

Upon hearing her sigh, he gained more confidence. Listening to her breathy gasp was like his favorite song on repeat. He wanted to make her feel what he felt. Her breasts were small. They fit perfectly in his hands. He liked how he could cover them completely and feel the beat of her heart like a drum in his palm. She guided his head down to her breast. This time, he was thankful she let him touch her. He'd wanted to do this so badly on the last train. A giddy sensation made his stomach flutter. Her dusty-pink nipple was taut and looked like it waited just for him.

Inhaling deeply, he nuzzled her soft skin. When she lightly tugged at his hair, he understood the silent command. He opened his mouth to lick at the begging tip then latched onto her skin. Nova cried out against him as she arched. He felt powerful to make her react so strongly. His fingers played with the waistband of her panties. They needed to come off.

Arrow shifted to her other breast as her hand dipped into his pants. When had she opened his fly? Now her fingertips brushed the inside of his legs. As she gripped his erection, a spiral of passion swept down his entire body. They needed her to finish what they'd begun back on the other train. His skin throbbed with stark yearning. She slipped her fingers along his shaft as if toying with him. He wanted to pull away to make the torment end. At the same time, he bucked his hips forward so she would touch more.

"Do you want to make me crazy, angel?" His words came out in short pants as he tried to force her hand to tighten on him. If only she would ease the ache.

"Yes, just like me." She shoved his pants off urgently, and he helped her get them to the floor. He'd already lost everything else he wore, but he didn't remember how that happened. As soon as he was naked, he knelt back in front of her hard, gulping for air and ready for whatever she wanted.

"You're right. I'm crazy for you."

For once she didn't try to get in the last word. She simply slipped off her underwear. The moment was scary and magnificent all at the same time. He didn't want to disappoint her, but he wasn't going to stop because of his lack of knowledge.

As if in slow motion, she bent her head to kiss him lightly on the lips. The touch wasn't nearly enough, but before he could draw her into his arms, she moved so she could place kisses down his neck. Her hot wet mouth floated down to his shoulders then to his chest. When she stopped at each of his nipples, he shivered. She continued to follow some type of path along his skin.

Reaching out to her shoulders, he skimmed his fingers along her skin toward her spine. When her kisses reached his stomach, he let his eyes close. He leaned back as her tongue licked playfully first right above his hard cock, then she nuzzled the skin between his legs.

He planned to reach out to grab her to make her stop. His intent was to tell her he wanted to touch her, but he didn't. Instead, he opened his eyes again. He wasn't sure if he wanted her bent over in front of him. He wanted to hold her. The second before he opened his mouth, her tongue reached the head of his dick. All his thoughts vanished. He bucked his hips up groaning. She licked him as she moved her mouth from his tip down to the base. He felt the swish of her tongue all the way to his toes. His head fell back. His bones quit their job. Was she going to do what she'd done to him that first time in the room? He felt like he wouldn't last for even a second if that were true. Even now he might be close to exploding.

"It's your turn now."

His eyes popped open. Nova leaned back. She no longer knelt, but sat before him with her legs slightly spread. Her legs were bent at the knees. Licking his lips, he cleared his head enough to remember what she'd done.

He tipped forward to place a light kiss on her mouth. Then he pressed kisses down her neck, smelling her unique scent. He let himself feel all the parts of her body he'd wanted to touch before and couldn't. His mouth travelled over her chest to her nipples and she wiggled for him. All her movements fascinated him. He explored her belly button, and the soft skin which led to the small triangle of hair between her legs.

As her hand combed lightly through the small mound of damp curls, he saw her uncover a little nub of pink flesh. She used her fingers to circle the spot as she moaned lightly. He swallowed his feelings of inadequacy. Now would be a good time to have a memory or two.

"Nova, I don't remember."

Nova's red eyes hugged him. The look she gave him was humbling, but also made him feel like he could conquer the world.

"I trust you. Touch me like you want to. If I want you to stop, I'll tell you."

Air whooshed out of his lungs. He wanted to bring her exquisite pleasure. She should feel all the things he felt. To know she trusted him with her body was a heady aphrodisiac.

Dipping his head, he licked tentatively at the lips she exposed. He was surprised at her reaction. She tipped her head back and moaned for him.

Feeling braver, he bent his head to discover all of the flesh between her legs. He savored the flavor of her in his mouth. Lazily, he licked then sucked at every piece of turgid flesh. He uncovered what made her pant and moan out his name. She wiggled her hips beneath his mouth as hunger grew in her eyes. Arrow placed his hands on her thighs to hold her still.

Lifting his head, he looked up at her. His mouth was slick with her cream. Her taste burst on his tongue. Isn't that what she's told him when they sat on the bench? She said she wanted him to taste her. If he'd known this is what she'd meant, he would've gotten hard the second after she said it.

After Arrow tipped his head, immediately, she wrapped her arms around his neck. She held him so tight he struggled to breathe.

"I've never come with anyone, but it doesn't matter. I want you."

Arrow had no idea what she meant when she used the word "come." She'd used the term before but it wasn't ringing any bells. Was that important? He didn't dare comment in case he said the wrong thing. The one thing he did understand was that she wanted him.

When he didn't say anything, she yanked his body hard toward her then fell backward onto the bed. He pinned her. Arrow tried to hold a part of his weight up so he wouldn't crush her, but the feel of her beneath him was heavenly. His arms gave. He wasn't even sure what he was doing anymore. Mindlessly, he blanketed her with his body. He kissed her chin, her throat, her ear. He let his mouth move wherever his lips wanted.

Her nails dug into the thick muscles of his ass while she licked his neck. He felt her teeth on his shoulders nibbling him. Nova shifted in his arms and her legs spread wider. Her heels rested on the back of his calves as her eyes turned a dark red. The red orbs were heavy with craving.

Slowly, as if his body knew what he should do, he brought his cock closer to the junction of her legs. His shaft nuzzled the welcoming curls. An animal part of him, which was dormant or forgotten, came to life.

Inch by inch, he entered her warm channel. Her slit, made even wetter by his mouth, opened like flower petals. Nova arched her back as their bodies joined. Moving carefully at first, he felt the pressure in his balls build. He slipped in and out, shallow thrusts. Then he got greedy. He drove forward until he was deeper inside of her, until he was buried all the way to his balls.

He loved the feel of their bodies with nothing between them. No clothes, no outside world, nothing to separate them. He was completely inside of Nova which was where he should be.

Entranced in the moment, he felt her hips squirm and buck. She silently demanded he move. He matched the rhythm she created. Together they rocked back and forth. He drove more deeply until she belonged to him totally, just as he belonged to her.

With Nova under him, he lost himself in the blossoming frenzy that developed between them. Nothing else mattered except the intensity of the exquisite pleasure. His hands slid beneath her ass. He lifted her to fit her even more tightly to him. He wanted to force his shaft into her very core. She accommodated him and opened her legs even wider for his hips.

In a sexual haze, he tried to understand the strange feeling growing inside of him. Ripples of pleasure cascaded over him. Thoughts vanished. Nova stiffened under his body. The muscles inside of her kneaded his cock. She shuddered in his arms while she cried out saying his name over and over like a prayer. His head spun. His balls tightened to his body. He trembled from head to toe.

His whole body shook as some overwhelming and unexpected response overtook him. His body was no longer his to control.

Instinctively, he flexed his hips pressing her harder into the cot. A wild hot wave of power pumped through him like a living creature swimming in his veins. He bucked once, then twice, and then emptied his entire life and soul into her for safe keeping.

Chapter 21

This might be the best dream she had ever had. She never remembered her dreams, but this dream she wanted to hold on to forever. Nova swore there was a hot insistent hand on the side of her legs. She could also feel soft hair brushing the inside of her thighs. All of it was divine.

She murmured her approval, but the sound of her voice didn't sound like she was in the dream world. She shifted, then felt a pulsating heat between her legs. The fiery touch was like a jolt of electricity. In a second, she realized she wasn't dreaming. Her eyes opened. The blanket moved between her legs.

Arrow.

She opened her mouth to tell him to quit messing around, but then his lips wickedly sucked on her clit. Her hips came off the cot.

"Arrow what are—" she began. His fingers began to probe her slick channel, then they worked deep inside her body. "So fucking good," she ended.

She opened her thighs more and more. Her hand reached out to hold his head tightly between her legs. Exhilaration flooded her, then heat, then energy, and then the stars. Those bursts of sharp light flashed against her eyelids as his digits pumped in and out. As her legs began to shake, she started to grind shamelessly on his face. Her whole body burned up in a stunning heat. As the orgasm subsided, she dissolved back on the bed like a piece of ice that melted in lava.

Arrow appeared in her line of sight leaning over her. His hair was braided again perfectly. Her juices dripped down his chin. His lips glistened, and his eyes shone dark black as he licked his lips. He was gorgeous.

"Good morning, angel." He smiled like a fool in love. She wanted to tell him to knock it off, but she couldn't bring herself to. She felt like he looked.

"It's morning?" She didn't even remember sleeping. All she remembered was the amazing sex, then his arms around her. She must have passed out. She'd never fallen into such a deep sleep without drugs. Then again, she had never had an orgasm with a man before, so she didn't know what she should've expected. Maybe falling asleep after sex was normal. Maybe waking up to find a man between your legs was normal too. She doubted it, but with Arrow, she wouldn't have wanted this morning to be any other way.

Arrow pushed the blanket down to nuzzle her breasts. He kissed and sucked until amazingly she started to get aroused all over again. What was wrong with her? She'd never felt this sexually demanding before.

"Arrow, what are you doing?" The question came from both her emotional side as well as her physical side. She felt so close to him. The connection scared her. At the same time, she didn't want this to end even though she knew better. His dick brushed her hip. If only her head was as clear as her body. Her body always knew what it wanted from Arrow.

"If I were your boyfriend then I'd wake you that way every morning." He ran his hands along her side as if he couldn't get enough. His fingers tickled her ribs as he fluttered along.

"Arrow we can't have sex all day." She used a stern voice, but the tone wasn't all that convincing. "We have to get up. The train is going to stop today in Bosstown, remember?" She was sure he remembered, but she threw the sentence in for emphasis.

Arrow nodded before giving a sigh. "I know. I've been up for a while already. I talked to Morgan-Roth. He told me we only had a few more hours."

Nova thought he shouldn't be sad about that information, and she shouldn't be sad either. They should both be excited that this trip would be over soon. She pictured Arrow jumping for joy when he had all his memories back. He should be giddy with the prospect of getting off the train. He could get his life back. She would return to her life as well. She liked her life. She wanted to get back to her family, Sky, and her work.

A frown appeared across her brow. She did want to go home, but the idea of a home without Arrow made her stomach hurt.

"It's good you've already been up for a while. Now, since you're wide awake, you can meditate before the train stops. You've enough time." She spoke about the mundane to hide from the tougher topic of the future. She couldn't go over the should-haves, or could-haves. Going over anything deeper would be excruciating.

"I already did that." His hands were busy again. He combed his fingers through the tiny tuff of curly hair between her legs. She couldn't think with his hands so close to her clit.

"I don't want to leave this bed, angel." His eyes searched hers. She understood what he conveyed to her. Once they left this bed, there was so much they didn't know. After they got up, they would have to think and do. This world of sensations, of soft fabric and naked skin, would be over for good. There would be things they'd have to talk about. She would have to say the words she didn't want to say. Being cocooned here with him was what she wanted to hold on to.

"Maybe we could stay in bed for a bit longer. Besides, you wouldn't be able to get dressed with this." She reached under the blanket and unerringly found his erection. She squeezed, then pumped him hard in her fist.

He groaned then moved to settle himself between her legs. He was a fast learner. He remembered exactly where to touch her with his fingers to make her wetter. Once he had her panting, he entered her with one sure slow flex of his hips.

As soon as he was fully inside of her, he put his hands on either side of her shoulders. He gazed down while he made shallow thrusts that weren't deep enough to satisfy her. She quivered under him trying to get him to move faster and sink deeper.

"More," she moaned as her eyes closed on their own

"Nova?" When he whispered her name, her eyes jumped to his.

"What?"

"I love you." He didn't wait for her to say it back, but instead, he bent his head to take her mouth in a deep scorching kiss.

His mouth was blazing, intense, and tasted like her wetness. The power, which always seemed to accompany his kiss, returned. The passion rushed through her limbs like a storm. Her bones seemed to soften while her breathing turned ragged.

She reached up to touch his hair, then his cheeks. He had a day's growth of whiskers. The rough hair tickled her fingertips. He turned his head to kiss her palm as he moved his hips in and out slowly. She wanted him to speed up, but she also wanted this to never end. His body rocked against hers as solid as granite, yet as malleable as clay. She molded his ass in her hands then petted the lower part of his back along his spine. Pulsating heat snaked through her body but his hips wouldn't speed up. He groaned.

He couldn't keep the slow rhythm forever. He would give in soon. She wrapped her legs around his waist. He pressed her further back into the cot, lifting her ass with both hands. Just as he plunged deeper and he fanned the flames of her climax, he stopped. He drew back stilling his hips. His sexy eyes studied her. She'd heard the term bedroom eyes before, but she never knew what it meant. Now she understood.

"Say you love me, Nova. I don't care if you lie to me. Say it."

Nova was so close to exploding. Her climax was right there. He kept her somehow at a pinnacle, about to go over the edge. He held her orgasm hostage for the words. She didn't want to lie, but the truth was too painful. The chances of a future were slim to non-existent. They were from different worlds. Didn't he get that so much could happen once he got his memories back?

"I love you, Arrow." The words were ripped from her with a sob. Arrow yanked her tighter to him until there was nothing surrounding her but him. She concentrated on gulping air, so she wouldn't cry. He gripped her painfully while he buried his face in her shoulder. Then his hips drove into her with the speed she craved.

Arrow was no longer soft or reserved. He began to pound her swiftly. The flex of his hips had her channel squeezing his cock. Her explosion stole her breath, her voice, and her ability to think.

Another climax magically came over her again. The power gripped her and wouldn't let go. She rode waves as they coursed through her again and again. She felt Arrow's dick swell inside of her body. Somewhere the stars were aligned, and the world was perfect. Her whole life came to a halt. Everything came down to this one flawless moment.

He shuddered holding her bound to him as he groaned. His back arched and bowed. He ejaculated, calling her name with a shout before he collapsed next to her and the pleasure started to subside.

After a few seconds passed, he shifted. His dick slid out of her tender channel. It felt lonely to have him missing from her. Why should she miss his body? Over the years, she identified that she wasn't right in the head. For that reason alone, she tried hard to use logic whenever she could. Now would be a good time to use some reason. Or at least some common sense. They were only together for a short trip. She would have to be the one who kept her cool and told it like it is.

She untangled her body from his, and then rose. He gave a sort of noise which sounded like a cross between an accepting sigh and a complaint. Ignoring him, she headed into the tiny toilet room. She washed using the bit of water that trickled out of the rusted tap.

Okay, so she hid from the conversation. When she realized what she was doing, she took a deep breath. It was time she faced him. Now was the time she told him that they had no future. They were going their separate ways and it was a reality she couldn't change. They didn't know each other well. There were too many factors he wasn't considering. He shouldn't be tossing out the word "love." Neither one of them could back up a declaration like that. She, for once, would be the level-headed one. This was a new position she didn't want, but she had to.

Ready to face him, she opened the door from the bathroom. Arrow sat on the bed with his pants on. He'd not put on a shirt. She wished he had. He looked good enough to eat. She liked his narrow hips and the muscles of his chest. He might look even better once he put on a few pounds. She pictured him having dinner with her at home. She could see him perfectly in her life as if the place for him was there waiting.

She thought about caring for him. She could look after him. If he wanted, she could help him get a better job. He didn't need to return to harvesting. She shook her head while she banished those ideas from her mind altogether. No use wanting what she couldn't have. Peace is the way. Maybe what that meant was she had to make peace with this situation. The sex had been wonderful but now it was over. She had to move on and find Dan.

Once she got home, she'd probably start going off the handle again. The first time she lost her cool in front of Arrow, she was sure he wouldn't be able to deal with her outbursts. He'd panicked at a needle injection for heaven's sakes. He would faint if he saw some of the things she did. If he witnessed one of her episodes, he would be long gone. She also had Sky to think of. He would never understand her love and devotion for Sky. Arrow would leave once he understood what it took for her to care for Sky. Her life wasn't pretty. She had no room for him.

What they were doing was simply a vacation from the real world. It was time they returned to reality.

She was ready to speak, to say all the things on her mind, but maybe she should put clothes on first. She felt

Arrow's eyes hungrily roam over all her naked flesh. She shivered but not because she was cold.

Nova crouched next to her bag quickly. With rapid movements, she dressed. If he noticed she moved swiftly, he didn't remark on it. Thankfully.

"Angel, we have to talk about what's next. There is a lot we have to go over. I can see things are different. Is it because of me? Do you want to talk about that first?" Arrow finally got up from where he sat. He reached out to pull her into his arms.

She should just say her piece. Rip it off like a bandage. Now was the time to speak up before she lost her nerve. He pulled her to his chest, and she was grateful she wasn't looking into his eyes. She stared at a few of the black hairs around his nipple.

"It is different. I lied when I said I love you. I don't love you." There, she lied to him. The sentence even sounded like she meant it. She peeked up at him to see how he took her deception. She braced herself for the pain of her rejection which would come next.

"I didn't mean we were different." Arrow gave her a half-smile and then cocked his head to the right. "I wasn't referring to us. I was talking about how you look. Can you see okay?"

"Oh." She swallowed hard. "See?" She waited for him to say something about not loving him, but that same half-smile stayed in place.

"Do you have a mirror in your bag?"

She nodded dumbly then fished a small round mirror out of her backpack. She held the small glass circle out to Arrow.

"I don't want it. You might want it, to look at yourself."

Nova tipped her head, puzzled. What did she care about how she looked? She glanced down at her dark-brown corduroy pants then the green shirt she wore. She looked like normal. Her hair was in a ponytail. That was the same. Was this his way of not talking about how she didn't love him? Maybe he didn't want to get into a fight with her.

She held up the palm-sized mirror to gaze at her reflection. As soon as her face appeared in the small circle, she forgot everything she'd been thinking. Her eyes were brown. She stared. There was a little red on the edges and around the irises, but they were mostly brown. Her eyes were a red-brown like her hair. Her jaw dropped open.

Her eyes flew to Arrow then back at the mirror. She did that two more times until finally Arrow took the mirror from her hand.

"My eyes are normal."

"Yes."

"They're brown."

Arrow nodded. She took a deep breath. All her life she had wanted normal eyes so people wouldn't stare at her. She gazed at Arrow. Did he give this to her? Did he change her? She gulped. She didn't have the answer to this. She wished she had Clare here so she could ask her what she thought.

She grasped the mirror from Arrow and held it up again.

"Your eyes are very pretty. It doesn't matter what color they are. You'd be beautiful no matter what."

"I told you not to call me beautiful." A smiled hung on her lips. Damn, but she loved this dopey man.

"I forgot. I have a head injury." He reached around her to put the mirror back in her bag. Nova could tell he didn't mean that. He remembered, but he enjoyed calling her beautiful. When he looked at her again, he seemed more somber. "I also wanted to talk to you about what's next."

She nodded and her smile faded. Here it was. Now they would talk about how she didn't love him. She steeled her heart for the conversation. She could take it. She and Troy had broken up. She hadn't even shed a tear. She'd thrown some things at him, but she'd been strong. Then again, she didn't feel anything for Troy. Troy never made her feel like Arrow did, but just the same, she could say goodbye to Arrow. She could live without him.

"Yes. What's next?" Her heart hurt at the idea of being without him. She didn't want to live without him, but it was for the best. She had responsibilities at home. Her life didn't include a lost harvester.

"I have to tell you about what I saw during my meditation. I don't want to. You're not going to like what I have to say."

"What?" Nova perked up. She happily disregarded all thoughts about their future. Instead, she clung to the new topic.

"I could see clearly through my sister's eyes, so there were no mistakes this morning. Dan looks injured maybe knocked out." Arrow sounded apologetic like he was the one who hurt Dan. His eyes were troubled.

Nova started to rub her forehead. Dan being hurt was a big problem. What if Dawn didn't care for him properly? They needed to get to them.

"It'll be okay," she muttered more to herself than Arrow.

They would be in Bosstown in a few hours. They could find them. She could get Dan medical attention. Once she was with Dan, then he could tell her where to find Archer maybe. Everything would work out once she was with Dan.

Even if Dan were injured, he was still a smart, savvy H.S.P.C. agent.

"It gets worse."

Nova's head snapped up. "What could be worse than Dan hurt?"

"They're on a train like this one. I saw the room clearly. Dan and Dawn are in a room like this with all the weird signs on the walls. The only difference is there's no bed."

"Is the train moving?" Nova began to pace. If the train was on the move, they could be anywhere.

"I don't know."

"Do you think a harvester knocked Dan out?" So far, from what she'd seen of the harvesters, she was sure they were capable of it.

"I don't know."

"Are they in Bosstown?" Maybe he could see that.

Arrow shrugged again before he drew her into his arms. She rested her head on his chest to take the comfort he offered.

"I'm sorry. I don't know more."

Two emotions were at war within her. On the one hand, she was worried. This wasn't good news. She should be scared for Dan and she was, but on the other hand, this meant the trip would continue. They could be together longer. They could have more nights like last night. Dan's injury was a stay of execution.

As soon as the idea she could stay with Arrow popped into her mind, guilt struck her. Sky needed her. She had to get home for him. Clare needed her as well. Her sister-in-law would be having a baby soon. Clare needed her brother and her husband. It would be selfish to want to keep riding trains just so she could have sex. She buried her head more into Arrow's chest, then inhaled his scent. It wasn't only sex she wanted.

She wrapped her arms around him to hold tight. It would be too complicated to bring him home, yet here she was eager for the trip to continue. She didn't think they could blend their lives together, but she wanted a longer period of time with him. Great. She was crazy.

Nova leaned back so she could look into his eyes. She had screamed, thrown things, broken furniture, and hurt people. She'd been happy at the top and suicidal at the bottom. Yet for all that, right now what she wanted with Arrow might be the real craziest thing she had ever done.

"It's going to be fine, angel. All of it."

Arrow tipped her chin so he could kiss her. It was a soft kiss, over before it started. He kept looking down at her. When he used the words "all of it" she knew what he meant. He meant what she said about not loving him. His sentence implied profound feelings that she couldn't think about. They had to hunt for Dan and Dawn. Helping Clarc was where her mind needed to be.

"It'll be fine." Nova tugged herself out of his arms then started to pace. "I know that." She walked back and forth in the tiny confines of the room. Arrow moved to sit on the cot. He tucked his legs under him. "We need to find Raiden before we get off the train." The idea started to take shape in her head. "Raiden might know about some of the trains. He's ridden them so maybe he could tell us which train we are looking for."

"You want to ask Raiden about the other harvester trains?"

She nodded.

"Why not ask CC?"

"Because we already learned CC's information is out of date. Remember, Joe told us that?" Nova crinkled her brow. She'd already considered that. "We start with Raiden. We'll ask Morgan-Roth where he is. If Raiden can't help us, then we ask CC."

"Why not ask Morgan-Roth?" Arrow winced like the idea made him uncomfortable. "I think we should ask CC now or maybe ask someone else." He stared up at the ceiling. Nova couldn't believe this was the topic he wanted to argue about.

"We agreed on your being a silent companion. You're with me, not me with you." She reminded him. "I say we talk to Raiden before the train stops. That's what we are going to do. It's the best idea."

"I don't want to face him. I feel bad about tying him to Winsor. Winsor's ropes are mixed up and..." Arrow reminded her of a frightened child. "Never mind."

She gave him an understanding smile.

"If you feel sorry, then simply offer to untie them." She smiled broadly at that idea. "In fact, offer to fix them if they answer all my questions about the trains."

"I'm not going to trade fixing what I did to them for information. Besides, I don't even know if I can undo it." Arrow gave her a fierce frown. It was evident he didn't like her new idea. He grabbed a shirt out of the duffle.

"You can do what you want," Nova exhaled her frustration, "but I'm going to go see him."

Arrow shoved his arms through the sleeves. Seeing Raiden bought her time. They wouldn't have to talk about the love thing until much later. Happiness swelled inside that she didn't have to face that yet.

"I take it by the antsy way you're hanging by the door you're ready to leave." Arrow picked up the duffle off the floor. He handed her the backpack.

When he was completely dressed, he threw the duffle over his shoulder making his coat flap.

"We have to talk to him before the train stops or we might not catch him."

His hand rose to the center of the door so she wouldn't be able to open it. The look in his eyes was burning. The intese stare caught her by surprise.

"I get you want to find him, but you know we'll have to talk about how you said you don't love me. I'm not going to forget."

All the happiness she had before deflated.

"I…" She struggled while all the words deserted her.

"We don't have to talk now, but we will soon."

"Soon… kind of." She hedged.

"I want to say something to you before we go after Raiden."

She pushed at his hand holding the door shut. His arm dropped to his side. Whatever he wanted to say she told herself not to comment on it. She didn't want to say words she might regret.

When he didn't speak right away, she looked over her shoulder with her hand back on the door.

He caught her eye then finally spoke. "You love me. I know it. If I had a banner, I'd hang it, and it would say, 'Arrow is right.'" Smiling, he opened the door to let her out into the hallway.

Chapter 22

Morgan-Roth didn't even look up when they entered the next train car. He stood in the hall flipping Raiden's cube puzzle in his hand. He had one full side yellow, but the rest of the block was a mix-match of colors.

"We need to talk to Raiden," Nova said in lieu of a greeting.

"No, we don't," Arrow called out behind her. "Do you know about the trains? Have you been on all of them?"

Nova glared at him but waited for Morgan-Roth to speak.

"I haven't been on all the trains." Morgan-Roth gestured to the door that was two down from where they stood. "You'd have to ask Raiden about that."

Nova wasted no time in heading straight there. When she reached the door, she didn't hesitate. She knocked one sharp rap before slapping her hands to her waist. Arrow wanted to tell her again that maybe they should ask CC, but he figured he was too late now. Maybe he would be lucky and Raiden wouldn't answer. Maybe Morgan-Roth was wrong, and he was somewhere else on the train. Arrow figured he should apologize and unbind them, but then again, he wasn't sure he could. The ropes had wanted to be tied. Half of the thick heavy strands hugged Raiden.

Arrow waited for the door to open, feeling on edge. If he told the truth, that he didn't know how to unlink them, they would both be mad all over again. They were probably fuming. He shouldn't have done this to Raiden. He didn't care how Winsor felt, but with Raiden, he owed the man. Raiden had helped them, then Arrow had screwed him over. Maybe he was a terrible person.

"Come in," Raiden called on the other side of the door. Nova quickly slid the door open and rushed inside. He trudged after her, wincing all the way.

What greeted him on the other side of the door was unexpected.

The room was like the one they had just left. The space had all the signs on the walls, the cot, and a room connected with a toilet. No aspect of the basic area was what had his attention. What caught all his focus was Raiden.

Raiden sat in the middle of the cot wearing only tiny, incredibly tight yellow shorts. The mini shorts looked like they were painted on and molded to his balls. The fabric had smiley faces winking at him.

When he and Nova entered, Raiden scrambled to grab whatever he could find to cover himself. His hand landed on his jacket. He threw the coat over his crotch.

"I thought you were Morgan-Roth coming to use the toilet again." His blond hair was loose and tucked behind his ears. Using one hand, he tried to pat the strands down. His other hand held his coat to his groin.

"We didn't mean to interrupt you, but we have some questions. It's important."

Nova didn't miss a beat. She sounded calm, like seeing him mostly naked was fine with her. Arrow didn't like that she was looking at Raiden. An overwhelming burst of jealousy flashed inside of him. He clamped the emotion down and was about to ask where Winsor was, when the door from the toilet opened.

Winsor stepped out and paused. Her eyes glared at seeing them. Arrow could understand her reluctance to step further into the room. He felt like an intruder. She stopped in the doorway dressed in Raiden's shirt. The top fell to mid-thigh and was the one he wore before.

She tugged on the hem then glared at Raiden like this interruption was entirely his fault.

"I didn't want to bother you, but we've a few urgent questions for Raiden before the train pulls into Bosstown," Nova explained.

Didn't she care about their state of undress?

He kept quiet wishing the floor would open up and swallow him whole. This was too awkward for him. They were trespassing, and Winsor and Raiden were probably angry. He would be pissed if the situation was reversed. He should've used more caution when it came to his gift. The ropes should decide.

"Why should Raiden help you?" Winsor stepped further into the room. "You're a wanker." Her tongue appeared to be as caustic as ever. "We've no reason to help either of you. You ruined decent HOCs" She spat at Nova. "And you tied us together."

Winsor crossed to the cot then climbed up next to Raiden. Her silver eyes slashed at both of them. Raiden rolled his eyes at Winsor's sharp comments. He threw part of his coat over her legs. Arrow noticed that without all her layers of clothes, Winsor was clearly all woman. She was shapely. He figured he should've seen her gender sooner. She was the same height as Raiden, but that is where any similarities stopped. With the shirt she had on, there was no confusion anymore. He could see the outline of her ample breasts and voluptuous hips.

Raiden studied him. He glared when Arrow's eyes followed Winsor's curves. Arrow realized he'd crossed a line.

"Yeah, Weaver. I think after what you did, I don't owe you anything. Get out," Raiden snapped tersely. Arrow's eyes dropped to the floor.

"I can understand how you might be upset. Weaver came to say he was sorry and to separate you," Nova piped up. She smiled generously. Arrow wanted to tell her he couldn't untie them, but the words were cut off when both Raiden and Winsor spoke at the same time.

"Separate us?" Raiden's eyes flipped to Nova, then to Winsor, then landed on him.

"Right now?" Winsor's eyes flipped between him and Nova as she frowned.

"We wanted to ask you some questions." Nova nodded. "I thought we could trade. Harvesters like to trade. You could tell me what I need to know, and after Weaver could untie you. He'll make everything like it was before when you hated each other."

Raiden scowled. Arrow didn't know what to make of that. Raiden should be happy with the idea of not being with Winsor anymore.

"What questions?" Winsor asked immediately.

"I was looking for a particular harvester train that has rooms like this train." Nova waved her hand around the room. "Except the space doesn't have a cot or any sort of bed." She paused. "Right, Weaver?"

"Yea, it's a private room with no bed," Arrow agreed. "And about the unbinding—"

"I can't answer that." Raiden cut him off. "I've never been in the private rooms until now. When you and I trekked together, we never needed one. Besides, it was too hard to find anyone with a key. But…" Raiden looked pensive, "I can tell you *Sloop* and *Catboat* don't have any private rooms at all. It's all cargo with a couple of passenger cars at the front."

"That's true. Also, *Ketch* and *Clipper* have some, but they're new, so they don't have anything in them," Winsor tossed out. "No signs or fleam from the surface on the walls yet."

"I didn't know the trains were named." Nova rubbed her forehead. Arrow knew they were ships. He didn't know how he knew that, but he remembered that piece of information clearly. "What's the name of this train?" Nova asked.

"This is *Bilander*," Arrow said automatically.

"That's some head injury." Raiden sounded amused.

"We can't help you," Winsor spoke in a rush. "The only other two trains you might be talking about are *Frigate* and *Windjammer*."

"Why don't you go look inside both of those trains when you get to Bosstown? They'll both be there," Raiden added.

"They will?" Nova raised her eyebrows then glanced at him. The look in her eye declared that this was a shot of good luck for them. He felt like it was good, yet once they were with Dawn and Dan, it would be harder to talk about what was next for them as a couple.

"Why are those trains in Bosstown?" A part of him hoped they were lying. If the trains were not at that stop, then he could have more time with Nova.

Raiden responded to the question first. "Most of the harvesters were heading to Bosstown in the first place. All the trains are either there or will be there. The above ground access there is nearest to the strip mall that popped above the ice enough for us to get in. I'm going with Ashley, I mean Winsor." Raiden said the last part about Winsor with a sort of softness to his voice he'd not noticed before.

"We're not going to the strip mall," Winsor stated suddenly like this was a new conversation presented. Instantly, Arrow had the feeling that they had been put in the middle of a spat. He expected the fireworks they had seen the first time Raiden and Winsor ran into each other on this train.

"Why not?" The softness in Raiden's voice didn't disappear like Arrow thought it would.

"Stone and I know where there's a whale mart. We're hunting it down. I got a hook in Water Base Azul for toothpaste. This is the mammoth haul. It's straight up glacial." Winsor smiled at Raiden like she'd forgotten they had an audience.

"What does glacial mean?" Nova wondered aloud.

"It's big." Winsor didn't even look at Nova, or him. She kept her eyes on Raiden.

Arrow was lost following their slang. He looked to see if Nova listened to this, but she rubbed her forehead. Just as he was about to ask what a whale mart was, Nova spoke up.

"Arrow could untie you, so you don't have to trek together." Nova sounded overly bright. Arrow lifted one eyebrow.

"We told you everything we know. We've nothing to trade with now." Winsor tipped her head shyly at Raiden. "If we can't buy our way out of this I guess we'll have to work it out. I mean, I'm skint."

"I'm broke." Raiden sounded relieved. "You're right, Ashley. We'll have to stay this way for now." Raiden nodded slowly. "Tough break."

Winsor joined his nodding.

Arrow caught on to what Nova was doing. She could tell they didn't want to be separated, so she used disconnecting them like a threat. They had told her everything she wanted to know.

"I'd only unbind you if you paid me," Arrow commented dryly.

Nova gave him a conspirator smile. Winsor and Raiden were probably not even close to admitting they wanted to stay bound. It made him think of his conversation with Nova. She wasn't ready to admit she wanted to stay with him either. She did want to stay with him. There was no question in his mind about that.

"I'm broke," both Raiden and Winsor said in unison.

"We have to go." Nova inclined her head to the door. "After you get your toothpaste, and if you find Weaver, then he can spilt you up. But I don't know where he'll be."

"It's a risk I'll have to take." Raiden shrugged. "Besides, by then I might be lost on the surface frozen to death. I figure I have a better chance of dying in a blizzard than I do of ever making money."

Winsor gazed at Raiden. "I never get lost. I can find my way through any storm or any amount of snow." When Winsor glanced at Arrow, she gave him a frown. "But once I get all that money, I tend to blow it on…" She looked around the room. "The ivories. It might be awhile until we get enough money together."

"We can't help you then." Nova reached for the door. "Come on. These guys are stuck together. We have to go."

Once out in the hallway again, Nova smiled at him. He couldn't help but grin back.

"I have the feeling Raiden and Winsor will be dodging you for the rest of their lives. I hope you're okay with that."

"Got it." He nodded. "I actually feel better to see them happy. I was afraid we'd walk in on them killing each other."

"They were half naked. There's no way they were fighting with each other."

"They could've been arguing. You'd argue with me even if you were completely naked."

"No, I wouldn't."

"Yea, you would. You were ready to argue with me about how we shouldn't be together, and you didn't even have your clothes on this morning."

"I put my clothes on then talked to you. See? I'm right."

"If I'm ever right, I'm going to get a big banner and make you hang it from the ceiling."

"I'll do that."

The train made a high-pitched screech. Ahead of Arrow and Nova in the hall, they saw Morgan-Roth appear. They had to get off the train. Maybe once everything was settled they would work out their issues.

"This is Bosstown." Morgan-Roth closed the small gap between them. Nova held her hand out to the wall to steady herself. Again, the train made more noise. The great machine gave a sputter. "You'll be on the train platform outside the entrance to the water base." As he commented, he leaned heavily on his walking stick.

Nova nodded. Arrow hoped he wasn't going to run into anyone angry about the betting. If Ash had gotten on the train others could have as well. He didn't want to get into an altercation outside on the platform, or even on the train.

"Is there another way off the train?" he asked.

Morgan-Roth shook his head. "Don't worry about it. Once the game stops, harvesters tend to let it go. It's simply entertainment. Besides, most of them are back at Laying Odds."

"Thanks." He felt like he should say more to Morgan-Roth. Even if he only helped them because of Joe, he was grateful.

Morgan-Roth looked surprised by his thanks, then he stared hard at his walking stick.

"Morgan-Roth," Nova broke into the awkward silence. "You wouldn't know where the two trains…" She glanced at him. "*Frigate* and…"

"*Windjammer*," he supplied.

"Where they're parked or anything like that?"

Morgan-Roth's brow crinkled as once again the train gave a lurch. They all had to sway to keep balanced on their feet.

"If *Frigate* is here already, then it's on the far end of the tracks. It always parks there because it's so much bigger than some of the other harvester trains. I don't know about *Windjammer*. I don't even know if it's here yet. It could park anywhere around."

The final screech signified the train had come to a complete halt. Around them, some of the doors opened up. In the hallway, people with huge bags made their way off the train.

He and Nova gave a swift goodbye to Morgan-Roth then followed all the men and women off the train. As they walked along, they discovered the harvester was right. If anyone remembered them they didn't say anything. The entertainment was over. Most people didn't even notice their leaving. Everyone was on a mission to get off the train and onto the next. Only a handful of men slept, lounged, or played dice.

As soon as they stepped onto the platform, Arrow got the notion he'd been at this water base before. His head felt like it swelled with memories which were just out of his reach. He wanted to figure out what it was about being here that was so familiar.

He glanced around while he followed Nova. His eyes took in the mass of people. The place was a swarm with a mix of harvesters, traders, and even a few respectable people from the water base. The dealers, who sold food outside the gates to the base, looked like people he'd seen before. Even the base guards near the huge gates looked familiar.

All along the massive platform were trains. Some had families getting off, some had harvesters, and some were cargo only. He couldn't tell if they were delivering or picking items up. He saw a man with what looked like part of a fence walk by. Nova stopped to wait until he passed.

"Do you know where you're going?" he asked her as his head snapped back and forth to take in all the interesting sites.

"Yes. I can already tell that train down on the end must be *Frigate*. It's huge. We'll go and check it out."

Arrow looked to where she pointed. He spotted a train twice as long as the others. A mixture of items was strapped to the top. Crates and boxes dotted the loading area.

"We're going to get on that train, then look around. If Dan and Dawn are on it, then we'll give CC to Dan. You can talk to Dawn. You might get all your memories back."

He grabbed her arm to stop her swift strides. "After that, are we saying goodbye?"

"No, not yet." He could hear the smile in her voice. He let go of her arm and followed her again.

"What if they aren't here?"

"Then we'll get on the water base, have a hot meal, a shower, and get some sleep. We'll get some rest until

Windjammer shows up. We can ask about that train, like when it'll be here."

Arrow had the absurd realization he was more excited for a hot shower and Nova in bed than getting his memories back. Fuck his memories. He hoped Dawn wasn't on *Frigate*.

He began daydreaming that maybe after she curled sleepily in his arms, she would be ready to listen to reason. He was prepared for all the things she was going to say. If she stated that they couldn't have a future because of her having extreme emotions, he would say he'd accept all sides of her. If she stated that they should part because he was a harvester, he would tell her he didn't care about that work. Screw being a harvester. Maybe he could learn a new job. If she brought up Troy or Sky, then he would say he would learn to live with whatever men were in her life before him. Maybe he could even talk to Troy or Sky. If either of these guys could see how much he loved Nova, how he needed her, maybe they'd back off.

"This is it." Nova made a stop at the first set of doors to the train. She put a foot up on a bolted piece of wood that acted as a step.

"Wait." Arrow grabbed her arm. "I want you to promise me that no matter what happens, once this is all done with, that you and I will talk. Promise me that you'll give us a chance. I want a future with you, angel."

"Maybe we can talk about a future together, but I'm never getting you an 'I'm right' banner." She smiled at him.

"Got it."

Chapter 23

"I wish there were more lights on in here," Nova whispered to Arrow as he followed her. They made their way through the dark and dirty train cars one at a time. She was happy to find this train was much like the one they had just been on. Her grasp of the layout was better, and it was easier to navigate in the dimly lit interior.

As they trotted along, she noted that the only difference between *Frigate* and the other trains was, this one was bigger with more cars. That and it was also strangely empty. All the items that might have been on it, had been unloaded. Train car, after train car, they walked past different-sized empty crates or huge metal boxes with nothing in them. With every door they passed through, she hoped they would reach the passenger cars, but they kept hitting cargo.

She turned around when Arrow slowed down. He stared at a forgotten sign on the ground. It read, "This is not a sign." He glanced up. The flickering low lights from the floor gave his face a sinister look. She shook off the feeling of foreboding, which started to steal her nerve, and pressed on to the next door. She hoped by the time she got to the private rooms there would be better visibility.

"Finally." She exhaled with relief when she opened the next siding door. They were now in the area with private rooms on both sides.

The hallway had lights overhead that tinted the walls yellowish. On both sides of them were doors exactly like in the last train.

"We have to check all the rooms for Dawn and Dan."

Arrow stopped her with his hands placed softly on her elbows.

"I don't like it here." His voice held notes of trepidation. She understood. She felt anxiety in her gut also. There was something wrong about this train. She gently brushed his hands off of her. This was no time to get panicky. She was probably imagining her fears anyway. She was rarely balanced after all.

"It only seems weird because it's empty. We've gotten used to the noise." Nova was whispering, but she didn't know why. She tried to speak at a regular volume. Her shoulders relaxed. "Now, all we have to do is check the rooms for Dawn and Dan. If we find them, then we help them. I can give Dan CC."

"And if we don't find them?"

"We wait on the water base until the other trains come in. We check them all if we have to. It's too late to back out now. Besides, if Dan is hurt, then we have to help him. I owe it to Clare not to get cold feet now." Nova was determined. That determination must have come through in how she spoke because Arrow inclined his head.

"If your feet are cold then I'll warm them up."

She realized she didn't want this to end. She didn't want her trip with Arrow to be over. They stood there. Finally, she clamped down on her worries for the future. There was no point in thinking about that. She tried to open the first door to her left. It was locked.

"I guess we need a key."

"We always need a key." He chuckled. The light notes of his voice instantly made her feel calm.

"We check them all, just in case one's open." Nova turned to gaze at the front of the train car then the back. She didn't know how many passenger cars with private rooms there were.

"They say, 'It's all inside.' We'll get in."

Nova laughed. "*They* don't say that. That's a J.C. Penny advertisement. I think you picked up slogans harvesting."

"Who's J.C. Penny?"

"Never mind." She started down the hallway and tried one door after another. Most were locked. Only two opened. The rooms they inspected confirmed there were no cots or beds, which signified they might be on the right train. They moved on to the next passenger car. As they did, she called out for Dan. Arrow joined her as they walked. Every so often, they would call out both Dan's and Dawn's names.

They had just opened the door to the second car when in front of them they heard a rattle coming from one of the rooms. A few feet ahead of them, Nova saw a tiny woman step out of one of the private rooms. She didn't look like a harvester. In fact, she looked like a female from a water base. Her pale-blue slacks and orange sweater had flowers crocheted on the front. Her curly black hair was back in a loose bun. Other than the fact she was delicate looking, the only feature Nova noted was a scar along her neck. The mended flesh looked like a necklace.

As soon as the strange women took a step out from the room, Nova felt Arrow grab the back of her coat. His grip stopped her from advancing. What was his problem? This woman wasn't Dan or Dawn. She was also nonthreatening. It was impossible to be frightened of someone with crocheted flowers on their shirt.

"Hello, Weaver." Her voice was casual with a light Spanish accent. She rolled her "r's." Her smile at Arrow was a minor lift of her lips.

"Teagan," Arrow replied.

"It's nice that you finally joined us." The woman nodded "Mother and I have been waiting all day. She expected you sooner, but no worry, she brought your antidote."

Nova turned around then frowned at Arrow with confusion. Was this his sister? His sister's name was Dawn, not Teagan. Teagan had referred to Mother. Was his mother here? Was she family?

"This way." Teagan motioned to the door she had come out of. She didn't acknowledge Nova in any way which added an unreal feel to the situation. This woman was so tame, like a beaten down animal, yet she made warning bells go off in her head.

"Here, Weaver." The little woman waved when neither of them moved. Reluctantly, Arrow stepped around her. This time it was Nova's turn to grab him.

"Arrow, wait." A huge part of Nova nagged that this was dangerous.

"It's okay. I know her. This time I really do. She knows me." He gave her a reassuring nod, but it did nothing to waylay Nova's doubts. "It's like they say, 'Just do it.' I'm going to take a chance."

"Great, now we are on to athletic shoes." She let go of his arm so as to not get into an argument. Together they moved closer to the private room.

Nova's growing apprehension expanded like a balloon in her belly. As soon as she peered into the private room, she understood why. Inside her head she could hear herself scream. No sound came out, but her eyes widened. The sight before her stole her breath.

On the floor of the private room was a woman who looked much like Arrow. She had the same hair and eyes, but she'd been beaten. Her eyes were red and her cheeks were tear stained. Her tan skin looked ashen. All over her face, bruises stood out. She knelt on the floor with both hands shackled to a huge clear container. Inside the plastic box was a comatose man folded into the fetal position.

Gaping, Nova realized the battered figure in the box was Dan. She would've turned to run, but as she took a step, she spotted another box directly behind her. In the plastic holder was Archer similarly arranged. She recognized him instantly. Vomit rose to her throat. Both men appeared dead. She tried to take a steady breath so she wouldn't hyperventilate.

Nova spun around as her eyes flipped to Arrow. He did the same thing she did. He stared at Dawn and both the men smashed into boxes.

"What is this?" he asked the woman he'd called Teagan. He took a step toward her menacingly. "Let my sister go. We're leaving."

Teagan didn't back up. One dark eyebrow rose. "We have your memories. Don't you want them?"

"Fuck my memories." Arrow reached out to grab Teagan but before he had a hand on her, a voice stopped him.

"We've been waiting for you." A different woman came through the door from the toilet room. This lady was in her early forties, Nova guessed. She was dressed in a simple green floor-length skirt and a matching sweater. Her face was both vacant and aware. She was both robust and fragile.

Nova had the feeling she was meeting a real live chameleon who could change for whatever setting.

"You're from my dream," Arrow whispered.

"Mother." Teagan gave a bow. The young woman gave the impression like a queen had entered the room.

Arrow glanced at her, but Nova didn't understand much of this either. The only thing she had figured out was they were trapped. Teagan stood in front of the only exit.

The woman referred to as "Mother" gracefully stepped in front of Arrow.

Teagan grabbed Nova's shoulders. Her grip was like iron. The little woman pressed Nova close to the box that held Archer. There wasn't much space in the room and she stumbled, but Teagan's hold was firm.

"Let go of Nova." Arrow reached for Teagan, but Mother slipped between them. He hesitated.

"Get off—" Nova couldn't finish her demand. Teagan let go of her shoulders and wrapped one hand over her mouth. The other arm wrapped around Nova's body. She squeezed.

Powerlessly, Nova stared as Mother produced a needle from her pocket then inserted it into Arrow's neck. His hands came up for a second like he might stop her, but then they dropped to his sides. Confusion was written on his face.

After Mother drew the needle from his skin, she wiped her hands on a piece of fabric from her skirt pocket. Daintily, she tossed both the fabric and the needle to the floor.

Teagan was slowly squeezing the life out of her. Nova shoved the woman's hand off her mouth. She struggled to blindly throw herself from the room, not knowing what to do, but Arrow got her attention.

He placed his hand on his neck. His eyes closed as his fingers covered the injection site. He looked like he might be dizzy. He swayed.

"Arrow?" Nova saw blood on the rag. Again, she tried to bolt. She reached out for Arrow desperately, but Teagan wouldn't let her touch him. Teagan wrestled both of Nova's hands behind her back. Teagan's hands were so strong that it felt like she might crush Nova's wrists.

Mother wasn't paying any attention to Nova's inept fight. Instead, she looked at Arrow as if he were a small lost child. She began to pet his hair. Her other hand reached out to steady him. Her features were serene and caring.

Nova tried again to get out of Teagan's iron hold. Desperation made her yank with strength she didn't even know she had, but it was no use. Dawn began to cry. Arrow's sister shrank back.

"Arrow?" Nova called out to him again. Now he leaned heavily on Mother. He wasn't pushing her away. Why wasn't he fighting her? Why wasn't he helping them escape?

"No, please," Dawn wept. Arrow's sister tried to stand. Dawn's struggle caught Mother's attention. She gave a smile to Dawn, then let go of Arrow. Arrow leaned heavily on the wall next to the door. Nova tried again to grab him. Teagan bent her arms back until Nova thought they might break.

"Shhh, now." Mother reached out to pat Nova's cheek. Mother's eyes were full of a dark fascinating haunted wisdom. She could have stared for hours. With an unhurried movement, Mother lifted chains much like the ones on Dawn from on top of the box that held Archer's limp body. Mother handed them to Teagan. Teagan forced Nova's hand out in front of her. With a sickening click, Teagan secured the cuffs to Nova's wrists.

Nova's eyes dropped to the metal which dug into her skin.

"You see, we must do what is best for the world. The H.S.P.C. is our doom. When they rule us fully, only misery and perversion will be left. I see the future. The Originals must have the cure to Snow Flu. The H.S.P.C. must not have it." Mother, being slightly taller than Nova, tipped her head down showing off two gold front teeth.

While Nova was distracted, Mother hooked the chains on her wrist to the clear coffin that held Archer. Mother's actions brought Nova down to her knees. When she tried to stand, Teagan kicked the back of her legs, making them buckle.

"I don't understand. You can't do this to me. Arrow?" She called to him again as she wrenched on the cuffs. "You can't do this." Angling herself around, she tried to see if Archer was alive. Terror took over her brain. She yanked with every ounce of strength she possessed. Her tugging did nothing but make the chains rattle. "Arrow, help me."

Mother, with that same bland smile, slapped her across the face. Nova saw stars. The pain silenced her. Strangely, focusing on the blood in her mouth helped clear her head. She had to think. Of all the times not to lose her cool, this was the one.

"Shhh now." Mother smiled like Nova was a naughty child.

Nova ripped at the chains. Short loops hooked to the container keeping her on her knees. She was stuck bent over the clear coffin, exactly like Dawn.

"What the fuck is this? Let me go." She looked around. Why wouldn't Arrow do something? "Arrow, what the hell is wrong with you? Help me!"

Arrow leaned on the wall until Teagan came over to yank him into her embrace. She held Arrow like his weight was nothing.

"Weaver, are you feeling up for a walk? We're going to the water base to rest. Then we'll go somewhere safe." Teagan talked to him in quiet tones. He blinked twice as if waking from a dream.

"Mother?" His eyes looked around the room with a general sweep. They landed on the woman in green.

"We missed you. Now that you're here, we have much to do. I've good news. Your sister is no longer needed." Mother straightened to her full height.

Arrow nodded his agreement. His eyes jumped to the boxes.

"We don't need Dawn?" His eyes fell to his sister weeping softly, then to the chains. Nova couldn't believe he was so relaxed about the situation. His demeanor spoke of not caring about anything.

"We don't need her anymore. I realized she causes more problems than it's worth. I've found another full-blooded American Indian like you." Mother's voice held absolute authority. "Our new member will help us fulfill our destiny."

Her pleasant actions were at odds with the entire bizarre conversation. Nova tried not to hyperventilate.

"Arrow," Nova snapped. How could he ignore her? He should be fighting to get out of this room, not standing there leaning on Teagan. Couldn't he see what a horrible position they were in?

Arrow's eyes dropped to her. His brow crinkled in confusion. A lost puppy look was on his face. That dopey lost look she recognized.

"We're leaving Nova?" He addressed the question to Mother, not to her. Again, Nova tugged on the chains. The chains made a scraping sound on the thick plastic. If she were free, she would hit him. *Hard.*

"Yes. We must leave them like I always do," Mother stated simply. "The men have Snow Flu. Now is the time for us to go."

Nova gasped. Did Archer and Dan have Snow Flu? The thought was gruesome. Who in their right mind gave someone Snow Flu, then stuffed them in a box to die while locking another person to the container. She couldn't believe they planned to leave her here. She was also stunned that Arrow was in complete cooperation. His eyes seemed glazed over. Maybe he didn't understand her plight. How could he not understand what was happening?

"I'll explain it all in great detail once we are on our way. Soon you'll be feeling like yourself again," Mother soothed.

Arrow, to her overwhelming shock, nodded his agreement.

"Arrow, you can't leave me," she yelled at him, losing her barely grasped control. Inside her heart pounded at the idea he planned to leave her chained to Archer. She didn't even know if Archer was dead or passed out. "Arrow, you can't do this. You love me." Tears stung her eyes. A single sob escaped her lips.

Arrow's eyes leapt again to Mother for direction.

"Come along. I'm excited for you to meet your match. Your conpar is everything you'll need. We'll have our cure." Mother motioned to the door.

Arrow leaned on Teagan. Teagan wrapped her arm around his waist. With her other hand, Teagan plucked the sack off of Nova's shoulders. Nova's muscles screamed with pain. Teagan handed the pack to Arrow. Arrow smiled like he was getting a gift. He hugged the backpack to his chest.

Without another glance at her or Dawn, Teagan took the duffle from where Arrow had let it fall to the floor. She put the duffle on her back. Again, the whole thing felt insane to Nova.

"Arrow?" Another sob passed her lips. He didn't even look at her. "You can't fucking do this. What the hell are you doing?" Nova yanked at the chains. They rattled again. This couldn't be happening. She started to scream and curse at him. Anything to get through to Arrow.

Dawn placed her head on the clear box. She whispered nonsensically to Dan. Nova briefly looked at her container with Archer squeezed inside. The rise and fall of his chest signified he was still alive. She pressed her lips into a grim line as Arrow followed Mother and Teagan out of the room. The door closed.

"Arrow." She screamed his name again and again until her throat was raw. She strained to listen for sounds of them out in the hall. She expected him to reappear. He would save her.

When nothing more happened, and it was clear he wasn't coming back, she felt like time stopped. Her brain, not able to handle the enormity of the circumstances, quit processing. She shouted for help while she jerked on the cuffs.

She was losing her voice as she tried to pull as hard as she could on the chains. Blood began to drip from her wrists down her arms. Red drops smeared on the container.

Feeling defeated, she finally collapsed to the floor. After crying for what felt like years, a mumbled sentence from Dawn caught her attention. Nova lifted her head.

"No one is going to get on this train. No one's going to hear you."

Nova glared. Her fist swiped at her tears. There must be a way out of this. She had to get her head together. She wished she could ask Dan or Archer what they would do. They would have an answer.

She used her hand to bang on the lid.

"Archer!" she yelled. "I'll get you out." She needed to open the box. Her head bent to look at the lock and the hinges. Her fingers tugged at the seams. "Wake up!"

"Don't," Dawn begged. Nova glanced up at the pleading in her voice.

"They might have an idea. I might be able to wake him." Nova pulled again on the metal cuffs. She tried once more to open where the box was sealed. "I'll get them out."

"If you open the case, you'll release Snow Flu into the air. Before Dan passed out, he made me promise I wouldn't let the boxes be opened. He told me he could accept his death, but not mine or that of others," Dawn explained through more tears. She sputtered out the last of her sentence.

Her explanation slicked through Nova's brain. Nova was immune to Snow Flu so she hadn't considered what it would mean to open these boxes. Now she understood.

"Why would they do this?"

"If we open the case, we release Snow Flu on this train." Dawn's words slipped from her lips between sobs. "The virus will kill us, and all the people who come in here to help us. The flu will be in the air. It could spread to the water base. Who knows how many will die then? If we don't open the case, then the person inside dies when they run out of air." Dawn caressed the top of the case.

Nova looked down at Archer. So, her brother would die in there, or she could let him out and everyone would die. And if he was given Snow Flu, he would die no matter what. Snow Flu didn't take long to kill someone. Nova thought about how fast Snow Flu could spread. She kept her eye on his breathing, but it was hard to tell how much air he had left. He was scrunched into the clear container. His knees were in his chest. She felt the lump in her throat.

"Why would Arrow do this to me?" Nova's voice was a harsh whisper. She didn't think Dawn heard her, but Dawn answered her with a scathing response.

"Mother does this because it buys her time to get away. She leaves her victims with the unholy dilemma of kill others or let someone die. And Weaver," Dawn spat. "I don't know what game he was playing with you, but he's a terrible person. He was probably using you to get here. He, Mother, and Teagan, consider themselves Official Family. They're the leaders of The Originals. He's their American Indian, Mother is English, and Teagan's from Spain. The Originals all have different bloodlines to make perfect people." Dawn said the word "perfect" with venom.

"But you're his sister? You're his family, not them."

"I'm nothing to them." Dawn wiped some tears from her cheeks with the back of her hand. "I haven't seen Weaver for most of my life. We only lived together when we were young. Our mother was Sioux and our father was Navajo, but even if they were both American Indians they had nothing else in common. They were constantly at war with each other. They could barely communicate with us. We had to learn to speak Navajo to talk to our father. Our mother spoke only English.

"When we were ten they split up. I lived with our mother until she died two years ago. Weaver lived with our dad. I didn't know what happened to Dad or Weaver. In fact, Weaver showed up only a short time ago. Mother had a plan to take over the H.S.P.C. She needed me as well as Weaver. She says she can see the future, but she's insane. And Weaver, he's a willing puppet. They kidnapped me because Mother needed another American Indian."

"He wouldn't do that." Nova's stomach rolled.

"Yes, he would. After they put me in a cage, I fought. Mother had Teagan create a memory drug so I'd go along with them willingly. They thought they could control me better if I had no idea who I was. The day they were to give me the drug, I wrestled with Mother. I got the needle. I injected Weaver. Teagan grabbed me, but then Dan burst in. He fought Teagan. He saved me." She gave a heartbreaking smile at Dan unconscious in the case. "Mother and Teagan got away. Dan trapped Weaver and left him in the cage I'd been kept in. I'd hoped Weaver was dead." The anger and pain in Dawn's words were palpable in the air between them.

Her story painted a distorted picture of the man Nova had met and fallen in love with.

"But Weaver didn't die. He got out of that locked room." Nova was painfully aware of the role she had played in that.

"Yes. He got out somehow. Mother and Teagan couldn't go back to where he was so instead they used this other agent as bait so Dan would come for him. His name's Archer." Dawn nodded to the box Nova was attached to. "They made sure it was easy for Dan to find Archer. When Dan and I showed up to help Archer, they trapped us. Mother and Teagan knew Weaver would look through my eyes and follow the one thing he recognized. Mother could see it in the future. They counted on it."

"I can't believe this." Nova felt ill. This was wrong. Dawn was wrong. Arrow wasn't like this. He wouldn't go along with a plan to kidnap his own sister and keep her for some insane woman. He cared about people, about her. He was kind, helpful, and understanding. He wouldn't give someone Snow Flu and let them die. This was too cutthroat for her Arrow.

"Believe what you want, but you're the one cuffed to a dying man. We're probably going to die too. We're going to starve to death here," Dawn finished. It appeared like Dawn wasn't going to try to convince Nova of anything. Arrow's sister was only stating facts. Facts Nova refused to believe.

"Arrow told me—"

Dawn cut her off sharply "If he told you anything different and you believed him, then you're crazy."

Chapter 24

Teagan's arms around his waist were so tight he had the feeling of being a prisoner. She no longer held him to support him. She made sure he couldn't run away. He was captured.

Arrow knew this as well as he knew his own name.

In his head, he reviewed everything he knew about Mother, Teagan, and all of The Originals. His head filled with his childhood and how his father was strict on him speaking Navajo. His father had been a serious man, but had been kind to him. He remembered how they both fell apart when his mother left with Dawn.

Back then, he had felt nothing about the scenario, but now he missed his mother. He missed his sister. He was lonely as a child, then later as a man. Feelings about all sorts of things came into sharp focus while Teagan led him through the train. He was so cold in his teen years, unable to give love or to receive it. His father had become as cold as he. As he headed into his late teens, his father died.

He never went to his father's funeral. When his mother passed, he'd not gone to hers either. All of his memories crystallized as he was dragged between Teagan and Mother. He felt oddly like a different person. He couldn't understand why he hadn't cared about his family before, but no matter the past, now he cared. He'd only ever felt sort of hollow inside, but now he was concerned about the people he loved. He no longer felt empty.

Teagan and Mother kept him between them as they stepped onto the train platform. Some harvesters joking and laughing passed them. Their banter brought memories of Raiden and the years of trekking to the forefront of his mind. He recalled his treatment of Raiden and his rash decision to become a harvester. He'd joined, not caring of the lifestyle. He hadn't been kind to Raiden, who was his only friend. Damn, he owed Raiden hundreds of apologies. He was a terrible person. Now that he remembered their time together, he was surprised Raiden had helped him and Nova at all.

Nova.

He glanced back at the train. His match was on that train and so was his sister. In those boxes were Archer and Dan, with Dawn tied to them. They would die of Snow Flu before either Dawn or Nova could get help. He stopped. His hands tugged on Teagan's arm as the realization of what he did sank in all the way into the pit of his stomach.

"Are you still not well?" Teagan asked. She was forced even with her superior strength to slow down for his dragging steps. "I could carry you but people will stare."

He came to a complete halt while he thought about how to answer her. Teagan was gifted with strength. She was incredibly strong and Mother's slave. He couldn't convince her that he had to go back to save his match.

He needed to buy some time. Think. Nova was smart. What would she do if she were here?

"I'm confused. I know you, Teagan. I don't understand what we're doing. Why did we leave them, Mother?" He did his best to look bewildered. He hoped Mother would stop to explain so he could think. If Mother would launch into her fanatical explanations of The Originals, that would help. She loved to talk about what she considered her blessed work. It was the only thing she ever talked about.

Mother moved to stand directly in front of him. She rested her hands on both his arms still hugging Nova's bag. She gazed lovingly into his eyes.

"We had to leave them, Weaver. It is our holy mission. Mother Earth sent me a vision that Snow Flu is the purifier of Earth. Snow Flu will rid Earth of the unacceptable and deplorable people who don't deserve to live. They didn't deserve to live because they got in our way. You, I, and Teagan, will soon create the cure to Snow Flu. Only the people we deem worthy will live once the world is wiped clean. You'll remember your noble calling."

"Yes, Mother." Noble calling his ass. He never joined The Originals for noble reasons. He'd never bought into her insane beliefs to begin with. The only reason he'd joined was because he was a self-serving asshole. He had only ever listened to Mother because he always looked for whatever would benefit him. Mother had told him if he joined The Originals then she would cure the emptiness that ate at him. On and on she went about how Snow Flu was the remedy to the virus that was humans. How a pure bloodline alone would be the world's salvation.

He never cared about anything other than being able to have sex, and feel human. Back then, it had been the only thing he had thought about. Mother and The Originals had been a self-seeking last-ditch effort to have a normal life.

As much as he wanted to scream at Mother, and say she took him away from the only good and worthy person on the planet, he couldn't say that. Teagan would pick him up and toss him over her shoulder, not caring about the scene they'd make. In the end, Mother was the head of The

Originals, and her needs came before everything and everyone. He had never cared before what her faith system was, but now that Nova's life was forfeited, now he cared.

"Does that help, my American Indian?"

"I guess, I'm not feeling right. Thank you, Mother, for explaining to me." He let his legs drag forward as Mother studied him.

Mother motioned for Teagan to drag him further into the crowds on the platform.

Pausing one more time, Teagan shifted his big duffle on her back. He told her weakly that he could carry the backpack.

She let him have the sack. He held the bag in front of his chest like a safety blanket. It smelled like Nova. He wondered yet again what she would do. If he could get Teagan to let him go, then he could make a run for the base. He wasn't sure if yelling for help would work since, with one hit, he was sure Teagan could knock him out.

As he hugged the back pack, he watched Teagan and Mother ignore him to make plans. The masses of people slowed their walk toward the base entrance.

"We can get on the water base. Once we get past the men at the gate, I have people who will hide us until we can get back to the safe house." Mother strolled past some children playing in front of a trading stall.

"We'll have to lie low if they find the bodies. I'd like to leave before that." Teagan's hand tightened around his waist.

As Arrow listened to them, he realized the only person who had ever made him feel like a real human being, had been Nova. If she died, then a part of him would die too. All that selfishness, which had fueled his actions before, seemed to be stripped away. He had to help Nova, no matter the cost. Before they got on the water base, he had to save her.

He slowed his pace again.

"What's the matter with you?" Teagan had an edge to her voice. It became apparent that they were never going to let him go. Mother wanted her Native American child. She was going to get it whether he was okay with it or not. Mother believed his child was the key to the cure. Teagan was her right hand.

Now that he thought about it, Mother had said "On the path to creating the Snow Flu cure he would find himself healed." In a way, she was correct. He had, for a few precious days, been healed inside and out. Because of all this, he'd met Nova.

Teagan waited for him to answer. He might never get to see Nova again, but he was damn sure Nova wouldn't pay the price for his fucked-up life choices.

"I thought I could walk on my own," he mumbled.

That seemed to appease her, but she didn't let go. He felt like knots were tied around his stomach. He started to scan the platform for someone he could call out to. The place was packed with people. His eyes scanned for the ropes on the pedestrians. He flipped his eyes to Mother and Teagan.

The ropes had vanished. In fact, he only saw them after he met Nova. The knowledge of the ropes, his feelings, and his sex drive, all showed up with Nova. She was the key to his whole life. He grinned. He always needed a key.

Arrow inhaled her backpack as he hugged the straps. He felt the pistol in the bottom. It poked him in the stomach as if calling him an idiot. There was one round left in the Sear-Shot.

Teagan moved to the side as they headed into huddled groups near the water base gate. Individuals milled around, trading and chatting. Stalls with bear meat hung for the public to buy had folks clustered around. Another train pulled in and more people disembarked. He recognized *Windjammer*. The people who got off of it were supposed to make a line to get on the base. No one was doing that. The three of them stood to the side. Mother and Teagan smiled sweetly to a young girl who ran past them to get away from the harvesters.

Arrow's eyes jumped over the men getting off the train. Sadly, he recognized none of them.

He could shoot Teagan with the Sear-Shot. While she was in pain, he could knock Mother down. If Mother was out, he could run for the train Nova was on. He would have to make sure he didn't miss, because if he did, he shuddered to think what would happen to him.

There was a mass of people crushing toward the gate of the base. Everyone was at a standstill as the guards checked people in.

He prayed to the Great Spirit, a thing he used to do when he was a child. He didn't deserve help. He'd never been a good person, but for once, he hoped he would be looked down on and forgiven. Even if he should deserve bad things happening to him, Nova didn't. No matter what a terrible person he was, Nova didn't deserve to be punished for knowing him.

Glancing at the guard up ahead, he slowly unsnapped the button at the top of Nova's bag. Out of the corner of his eye, he saw a man with orange hair. Arrow couldn't believe it. He stepped in front of Teagan as she forced herself closer to the gate. She glared. He ignored her as he scanned more of the men moseying around the train. Once again, he saw orange hair flash between the harvesters who got off *Windjammer*. The Great Spirit had sent him Joe.

"Come along, this way." Mother jerked on his shirt impatiently. Teagan's fingers dug into his ribs.

"My head hurts. I think there are pills in here for head pain." He flipped the top of the bag open.

Mother nodded, but Teagan didn't look pleased. "Mother, we have to move to a safer place. I don't have a good feeling about the men getting off this train. I see blue gears."

"Fucking give me a second," he snapped at Teagan.

While scanning for Joe, Arrow began to rummage through the bag. He was sure he had seen Joe. He prayed it wasn't wishful thinking.

Through the crowd, he saw an old man caring a sign that read "beverages must have lids." When the old man passed in front of him, there stood Joe.

The agent stared at him. With one swift movement, Arrow shoved his hand all the way to the bottom of the bag. He wrapped his fingers around the weapon.

"Help me, Joe," he hollered. He yanked the pistol out.

Like a snowstorm that can deceive the eye, Joe became a blur.

Arrow spun around. He shot Teagan directly in the stomach. He saw the needle go in. She howled with pain. He stumbled backward as Teagan dropped to the floor.

Mother backed away from Teagan. She looked around wildly.

"Help me!" Teagan reached out for her.

"You're on your own." Mother dashed toward one of the trains fading into the crowd.

Joe dove after Mother. That left Arrow with Teagan. Teagan swung her arms crazily. She looked like she'd been lit on fire and was trying to put it out. Her screams reached the ceiling. People gave her a wide berth.

Arrow lost sight of Joe. Distracted, he wasn't ready for the hit. Teagan punched him in the head. He fell to a knee as stars danced across his vision. His palms scraped the cement.

Teagan settled a look of hatred on him. Arrow tried to get up, but Teagan pounced on him. She wasn't a big woman, but her strength overpowered him. Her right hook connected with his face. Blood poured out of his nose.

Arrow fought back as much as he could, but he knew what Teagan was capable of. He threw his hands up to catch her fist. She pried her hands out of his. He swung but she blocked his hit. In his mind, all he could think about was that Teagan was going to kill him. *Goodbye, Nova.*

Teagan wrapped her arms around his waist. She flipped him onto his back. He landed so hard the air was knocked out of his lungs. Teagan sat on him while he tried to strike her stomach. She didn't move. When he felt Teagan's arms around his neck, he knew his life was over. She could snap his neck like a piece of dry kindling. Someone bumped into her from behind. Her hand loosened.

Arrow tried to pry her fingers off his throat. His vision blurred. As he started to lose consciousness, he saw Joe come out of nowhere. Joe tackled Teagan and they flew backward. The mass on the platform parted. He blinked to get his vision back. He gulped for air.

Gasping, he called to Joe. "We have to save Nova. She's on *Frigate*. There are agents with Snow Flu."

The words "Snow Flu" sent everyone into a panic. The platform morphed into an all-out frenzy. Someone stepped on his hand as he tried to get up. He struggled to regain his balance. A huge harvester pushed him to the floor again.

Arrow finally stood and spotted Joe. He shoved men and women out of his way on his mission to reach the agent. Joe fought for air as Teagan tried to strangle him from behind. She hung on him like a backpack. Joe came to his feet, but Teagan brought him to his knees.

As he dashed between the terrified swarm, he shoved more people aside. Finally, he reached Joe. Arrow jumped on Teagan. He pried her hands from the agent's neck. The three of them hit the floor rolling around on the cement.

More hands joined the fray. Finally, Joe pinned Teagan. A beast of a man, who must have been an H.S.P.C. agent, injected Teagan with a needle.

Once held down, Teagan started to scream. The sound was a blood-curdling shriek.

"Mother!" Teagan hollered. Arrow tried to hold her leg, but his left shoulder got pulled out of its socket.

At last, Joe released Teagan when she slumped to the ground. Two men put wide metal cuffs on her. Joe rolled away, then sat on the floor. Arrow sat next to him. The agent's chest heaved as he caught his breath. Arrow dropped his head into his hand.

While Joe and the two men held a subdued Teagan, another agent appeared at Arrow's side.

"I'm Agent Reskin." He was a large heavyset man with a fluffy black beard. He showed Arrow a bracelet with a blue LED light glowing behind a set of gears in the center. The bracelet was the mark of the H.S.P.C. Agent Reskin offered his hand to Arrow. Arrow took the help. The agent got him to his feet. "Are you Weaver?"

A bit distraught over Nova, Arrow nodded. He turned to talk to Joe when the agent put his hand out. He gripped Arrow's upper arm. His fingers dug in and Arrow's heart sank. Arrow didn't think the hold was an offer of aid. He didn't care what happened now as long as Joe or these men saved Nova.

"Yea, I'm Weaver, but you have to save Nova. She's on the train *Frigate* with two other H.S.P.C. agents." He tried to pull away to explain to Joe, but Agent Reskin didn't let go of him.

Arrow looked around wildly as two more men walked up. They held Mother's limp form. She was handcuffed just like Teagan.

Another agent appeared. He was surrounded. So, this is how it would end for him. Fine, he would die and he didn't care as long as they made sure Nova was safe.

"This is Weaver." Agent Reskin turned to the others. One by one, Arrow looked to their solemn faces. Arrow comprehended that they were here for him just as much as they wanted to capture Mother and Teagan. He understood but fear squeezed his stomach.

One of the agents handed another needle to Agent Reskin. Teagan and he had done some immoral and illegal things for Mother. He expected nothing less than to face the consequences. His past had finally caught up with him. He would pay for the crimes he'd committed with The Originals. When the agent to his right grabbed his arm, he gave one last plea.

"I don't matter, just please make sure Nova's alive. Save her."

Chapter 25

Nova drummed her fingertips on the frame of the massive square mirror in the Snow Flu Study Wing.

She glared at the mirror, but she wasn't looking at the light-blue room behind her. She wasn't looking at the narrow hospital bed or the wooden screen that hid the toilet. Nova scowled straight ahead because she knew this was a two-way mirror. There were doctors and research assistants on the other side watching her. She hoped she made them squirm. For once, she wished she had her red-colored eyes back.

"I don't have Snow Flu. I'm immune." Nova repeated the same thing she'd said every day to the mirror. Why was no one listening?

She sighed. Her hot breath left a fog ring. She'd been sitting here staring blankly for two days now, specifically because she wanted them to see her displeasure at being stuck in quarantine for no reason.

Her fingers drummed again making a tapping sound. To her surprise, she heard her door open. A mousy woman with a rounded middle put a tray of food on the pale-blue blanket then hurried out.

Nova heard the lock snap back into place. It didn't look like she would be let out anytime soon.

While arranging the long white robe she was forced to wear, she stared at the food. The mush was some sort of grain with added vitamins. The goo tasted bland. After plopping on the bed, she ate some of the paste even though she wasn't hungry. If she were home, she would be eating better food. She shoved the tray away. It wouldn't matter if she were home having a feast. Right now, food had no taste. Comfort didn't matter. Over all, it felt like she floated in a sea of abysmal nothing. Everything before her was a bland lifeless bog ever since Arrow had left her.

Rising from her bed, she traversed the tiny holding room while she thought about his betrayal for the hundredth time. Where were the tears or the rage? She'd been here for two days. Normally, she would've raged over that at least. Oddly enough, she didn't even have it in her to feel manic or depressed. She was hollow. Her emotions were missing. Or perhaps, her emotions were taken.

Could Arrow have stolen a part of her? Her heart perhaps? She missed him. That thought made her rub her forehead. How could she want him back in her life? How could she miss a man who had left her to die on a harvester train? She'd been back and forth over what happened. Still, she didn't know how she felt.

She walked over to the bedside stand that held a pitcher of water and filled a glass. She guessed that soon everyone would come to see her. When Clare got here, Nova would have to explain what happened. She would have to apologize for the mess she'd made. Her mother, Luna, would show up. She hoped Luna could forgive her for what happened to Archer and Dan. She felt responsible that Archer and Dan had Snow Flu. If she had never let

Arrow out of the locked room in the first place, none of this would've happened.

A part of her wondered if that was true or not, but in the end, she decided it didn't matter. No matter whose fault it was, she felt it would be fair for everyone to blame her.

When Clare came to get her, she hoped she would tell her how her brother was. She was worried about him and Sky. Her mind drifted to her patient. What if Sky was dead because she'd been gone so long?

She took some tiny sips of water as she thought about what to do now. It felt like nothing could ever be put right again. She missed Arrow, but she should hate him. She missed Sky, but she might have killed him. And she had gotten involved with people who gave her brother Snow Flu.

"This is the kind of crap that happens to me," she whispered to herself. Maybe she should simply stay in quarantine. It seemed like a fitting place for someone for whom everything she touched turned into a disaster. "Add a rapist and some thieves, and I could finish off everyone I love."

A rap on the door made her set her water glass down and turn around. They probably came to collect her tray.

To her surprise her father walked in. He shuffled his feet while he pushed his glasses up his noise. He looked tired and… wonderful. She was so happy to see him. Relief that someone had come for her filled her even though she knew he would be angry. He'd probably been worrying about her. She felt terrible about that. Normally guilt over bothering her dad would've had her bawling, but she only felt a vague concern, more emptiness. She couldn't even sum up joy that she might be able to leave the room soon.

"May I come in?"

"Of course, you can. I'm so happy to see you, Dad."
She hurried over to him. Gears hugged her then patted her
shoulder. He always gave her that awkward pat. It
reminded her of how lucky she was that he was her dad.
She was blessed that he and his match Luna took her in
when her parents died. He might not always be comfortable
with her wild emotional side, but he loved her. He was also
brilliant. Somehow just talking to him reminded her he
could help, even if no one else could.

"I'm stuck in quarantine. How did you get those
assholes to let you in here?"

"Nonsense." He snickered like she had told him a joke.
He flapped his hand at her before wandering over to the
bed. He sat next to her food tray. His hand pushed up his
glasses while he bent over the mush. Picking up her fork,
he moved some of the left-over paste around like he had
never seen it before.

"What is this?"

"Food," she answered. She felt like smiling. Leave it
to her dad to be studying the meal.

The door where her father had entered moments ago,
opened again. A woman appeared in the doorway.

"Dr. Gears? You forgot this," the woman called to
him. She stopped about two steps into the room. She looked
at Nova like Nova might give her Snow Flu at any moment.

"Yes, Bartlett?" Her dad addressed the young
assistant.

Nova assumed she was an assistant since she lacked
any authority about her. Bartlett held out a bag, then in a
hushed voice muttered that another patient was being
moved to a Healing Booth down from this one. Her father
nodded before he politely took the bag. He picked up the
dinner tray.

Nova meandered back to her water glass while they had a short conversation about the food quality. While they talked, Nova thought about the term "Healing Booth." Most of the time, these booths were for people who got Snow Flu, and were about to die. They had big mirrors so the doctors could study the people as their lives ended. No part of being in these rooms had anything to do with healing. Most would never walk out of them, except for her.

She was put here for observation after agents had got her off the train with Dan and Archer, but she would be one of the rare people who would leave. These pale-blue walls wouldn't be the last thing she saw.

Too bad. The idea of living seemed overwhelming. Without Arrow in her life, it seemed like having Snow Flu and dying might be for the best. At least if she were dead, then the pain and emptiness would no longer plague her.

"They say, 'You've got questions, we've got answers.' I think we should talk, my Super-Nova," her father addressed her now that the assistant had left. When her dad used the term "they," it brought warm memories of Arrow.

"They?"

"One of my other patients told me that. I like it." Her father held out the bag the assistant had left with him. "I think there's a lot going on in that head of yours."

Nova took the sack and looked inside. In the paper sack were her favorite jeans, the ones with the holes in the knees. There was also her tank top and a small cream-colored cardigan.

"Clare put that bag together for you. They incinerated all your other clothes." Her father had a smile that teased his lips. "I told her to give you real pants. Ones that didn't look like they belonged in the garbage. She didn't listen to me."

"She rarely does." Nova nodded, but the unspoken words about what happened hung between them.

Nova walked behind the screen that hid the toilet from the rest of the room. While she pulled on her underwear, and then her jeans, she leaned her head to the side. Gears sat on the bed with his back to the screen.

"Once I get dressed, are we going home?"

Her father stood up from the bed as he pushed his glasses up in the reflection of the mirror. She slapped on a bra, then a shirt.

"I had to talk to a lot of people in the H.S.P.C. to get you out of here, Nova. After being exposed to Snow Flu, you have a mandatory quarantine of two weeks. They want you to stay for observation."

"I know the normal protocol, but I can't stay here. What about Sky?" She came back out from behind the screen fully clothed.

Dad frowned at her jeans. "They should've incinerated those as well. They look like rags."

"I want to know about Sky." Nova had to know if Sky was alive. Sky was the only thing that kept her from falling into the dark hole that threatened to devour her. She swallowed hard while she wondered if her father didn't want to tell her what happened. Would he tell her she had been gone so long that Sky had died while waiting for her return? He was so weak. "Is Sky alive?" She asked the question even though she was afraid of the answer.

"I came in here and got some blood from you when you were given your sleeping drug. I did that when they first brought you here. Sky's alive. Weak but stable. So are Archer and Dan. Clare is with Dan and Luna is with your brother."

Nova exhaled the air trapped painfully in her lungs. Once she left here, she would check on Sky. After that she would have to face her sister-in-law and her mother. She wasn't ready for that, but then again, she wasn't ready for anything. She felt like climbing back into bed and never getting out again. She didn't know what was wrong with her, but it was as if she couldn't even sum up enough energy to cry, or scream, or be excited over her freedom.

"Nova, is something wrong? You're different. The Nova I know would've reacted to that news." Her father paused. "One of the doctors told me how calm you've been. I think he used the word *salubrious*. I had to look it up. Other than saying you didn't have Snow Flu, he also told me you didn't talk at all. I asked how much you swore at him. A nurse laughed and stated she never heard you swear. I thought they were talking about someone else when they described you with brown eyes. I considered that this might be a mix-up."

"No mix-up. It's me." She didn't know what to say to that. She didn't feel calm, but then again, she didn't feel anything. Yes, she was different and she knew it, but how could she explain what she herself didn't understand?

"I'd like for you to talk to me about what happened before we leave here." Her father eyed her after the silence between them stretched on. He crossed his arms over his chest. The look in his eye was that of a man who wouldn't be deterred.

"I don't know where to start."

"Clare told me that she had to do a lot of convincing to get you to leave, but I'd like to hear it from you what happened after you got on the train." Her father pushed up his glasses.

"I don't know what happened," she whispered sadly. "I feel like where my heart used to be, now there's just an open wound. I feel like I'll never heal. I'll forever have a scar where my heart should be."

Her dad, with all his wisdom, seemed to know what she meant. He nodded encouraging.

"It's a good thing I'm a brilliant doctor because I can put hearts back together."

Tears welled up in Nova's eyes. One tear slid down her cheek.

Placing one word at a time on her tongue, she began haltingly. She felt like someone who placed their foot on thin ice, a step at a time, to see if it would crack. At first, she thought to hold back some of the story, especially her having sex with Arrow, but when her father questioned her about her eyes changing color, she knew the scientist in him would never accept less than the entire narrative.

When she finished her tale, she couldn't look him in the eye. She was afraid she might see judgments in the reflection. Instead, she stared at her image in the mirror. She studied her pale features and her red-brown eyes that now matched her red-brown hair. She looked the same, yet everything had changed.

She waited for her father to ask her more or tell her she could go back to their apartment, but he did neither of those things.

"That's quite a story," he said. "But it doesn't have an end, does it? People with unfinished business can go crazy when there's no end."

"I'm already crazy, remember?"

"Maybe wherever this guy Arrow is, he cares that there is so much left unsaid between you. Maybe he cares about unfinished business."

"Arrow could be anywhere. He picked The Originals." Nova shook her head.

"Maybe he's somewhere worrying about you." Her father raised his eyebrows.

"I doubt he even remembers me. Arrow became someone else with the injection of that antidote. Now, all that's left is my heart shattered into pieces. That's all the end there is."

Nova couldn't understand it, but Arrow had changed the second that needle entered his body. She had been over what happened in her head dozens of times. It was like he forgot her. She wanted to scratch out Mother's eyes for what she did to him. How could he want to be with The Originals anyway? Mother was evil. From everything she had learned about The Originals in the last two days, all she could say was there was a group of people more insane than her.

Who was Arrow that he would want to be a part of that?

Nova wanted to laugh at herself that she had been trying so hard to not talk about a future with him. All that time she'd been thinking he couldn't fit into her life, yet now that he was gone, she felt like she'd been cheated. Everything that happened between Arrow and her had disintegrated her life like a storm that rolls in out of nowhere and decimates everything in its path.

"Maybe you don't care about endings, but I do. Maybe it's the scientist in me, but I don't like untested theories and holes in a story. Things need to make sense. I don't like unfinished business."

"Unfinished business? After everything that happened, that's all Arrow and I will ever be." Maybe her dad was right. Maybe not knowing the end could make you lose your mind.

"I have a story with no end as well. Would you like to hear it?" Her father pushed his glasses up waiting for her response.

"I suppose."

"To start with, two days ago, the strangest thing happened to me. I was thinking my daughter was relaxing on the equator, and I come to find out I was lied to. Luna and I were awoken in the middle of the night by a hysterical Clare who told a bizarre story about you, trains, and the NEDs."

"I'm sorry."

"And then out of the blue my friend Mac shows up. He tells me his youngest son needs my help arguing for a man on trial in front of the H.S.P.C. council."

"What?" Her dad's last sentence seemed to pull her from her melancholy like nothing else could.

"As you know, even though I don't see Mac as often as I would like, I'm still close to him. I gladly went to help. I headed to the trial. When I found Joe, he was going insane trying to defend a man from the council. Let me tell you I've never seen Joe that animated before. The last time I saw Joe, he was little. I didn't think that kid possessed a heart. But here, I found him distraught over a guy named Weaver. The charges against Weaver were impossible to defend, yet Joe was giving it his all. He begged me to sway the council."

"What happened?" She thought Arrow had left with The Originals and Mother. This strange story gave her a smidgen of hope that maybe he'd remembered her.

"According to Joe, the man named Weaver helped him capture two influential people from The Originals that the H.S.P.C. had been after for years. At the trial, Joe stated passionately that Weaver told them where to find you, Archer and Dan, and another woman. He claimed they wouldn't have looked for you hidden on that train. Joe told everyone he saved your lives and saved Joe's life when he was almost strangled."

"Did the council listen?" A giddy feeling bubbled up inside of her. For a moment, all that emptiness fell away. If she could see Arrow again, then she would tell him she might forgive him. Maybe they could work it out now that he was no longer wearing his ass like a hat.

"No. I'm sorry but the council wouldn't be moved. They claimed his past crimes were too horrendous."

She'd been flying. Now she crashed.

"But couldn't you do something, Dad?"

"I showed up at the end of the trial. They said Weaver was party to a crime in which The Originals left a woman dying of Snow Flu on the train tracks. They told me she was carrying an unborn baby. Weaver and a woman named Teagan left the pregnant woman to die. The death of a baby is serious, Nova."

Nova swallowed painfully. She remembered that incident. She didn't know Arrow was involved. She recalled how a year ago, Dan showed up at headquarters with a baby. He gave the child to Clare. Dan had found the kid on the tracks near a dead woman. Dan told Clare he'd been looking for an Original member and had come across the baby by accident. The woman must have held on long enough to have the boy, then she died. Dan didn't know what to do with the child, so he brought the baby to his sister.

The baby had Snow Flu, but oddly enough for how sick he was, he never passed the virus to anyone. Clare, with so much to do at the time, gave the child to Nova. Nova had fallen in love with him the moment she looked into his eyes. She'd been caring for him ever since. She'd named him Sky.

"Dad, did you tell them about Sky? I mean if the baby is alive then doesn't that change things?"

"You know I couldn't tell them about Sky. If the council knew Dan had waltzed into HQ with no precautions carrying a baby with Snow Flu, he'd be in a lot of trouble. In fact, trouble isn't even the right word."

"But Dan didn't know Sky had Snow Flu. Damn it, Sky isn't contagious! This is fucking crap."

Her father smiled. "Now you sound like my Super-Nova."

"Couldn't we tell them that the baby isn't contagious?" Nova stomped her foot.

"None of these things matter, Nova. In the end, I never got a chance to speak at the trial. The crime of being party to the death of a pregnant woman and her unborn child is punishable by death."

"But the H.S.P.C. can't put people to death. We're an endangered species. It's against the law in the NEDs and the C.T.O.N.A. The United Nations said so."

Her dad looked uncomfortable. "Weaver, Mother and Teagan, were sentenced to receive Snow Flu for study. It's not written down as 'Death,' It's marked as 'Medical Testing.'"

It felt like someone had belted her in the stomach. Nova bent over, then wrapped her arms around her stomach.

"The H.S.P.C. protects life." Her father pushed his glasses up before he reached out to pat her shoulder. "But there are consequences for people's actions. Killing a child is one of the worse offences. For the greater good, he and the others were given Snow Flu so that we can all learn more. You seem as upset as Joe was about this news. Joe was forlorn at the trial."

Nova thought the term "forlorn" didn't even cover how she felt. Pain radiated all over her body. She tugged away from her dad, then sank, broken, to the bed.

So, this was the end of the story. Arrow would die somewhere alone. She would never see him again. He'd tried to save her in the end. Arrow had been somewhat of the man she had met.

He'd tried for her, but she would never get the opportunity to tell him she forgave him for what happened.

She pictured him in a room like this one while they all stood on the other side of the window watching him fight Snow Flu until the virus drained his life away. From her experiences, she knew how it would go. Arrow would sweat and perspire like his body was wringing all the moisture from his pores. Then he would lose all bodily functions then start to vomit until it came up blood. With no ability to keep fluids in his system, he would then basically die of severe dehydration. As she pictured his body wracked with pain, she felt like she couldn't breathe.

Tears that had refused to fall for the last few days gathered on her lashes. Her father came over to awkwardly sit next to her on the bed.

"So much for being able to fix my heart, Dad."

"That's not fair," Gears blustered at her comment. "I'm just getting started. You must always be patient with brilliant doctors like myself."

Nova looked up at him through her tears.

"The first thing we'll do is talk, get some answers." Her father pushed his glasses up his nose as he rose from the bed. "I think it'd be best if you talk to Arrow. I think he owes you an apology for leaving you on that train. I know I'd feel better if he apologized about that."

"He's alive?" Nova jumped to her feet. Her tears scattered around her face like glitter.

"You're a research assistant." Her dad gave her a look like she was completely empty headed. "Now think. You know someone cannot die of Snow Flu in two days. Except that one isolated incident, but he also had a lung tumor. I think that was more of the tumor actually."

"But where will we find Arrow? What if I don't find him in time? I have to talk to him." Nova mentally started reviewing all the research labs the H.S.P.C. had in the C.T.O.N.A.

"You just heard Bartlett tell me they moved him to this wing." Again, her dad's look was that she was a simpleton. "He's two doors down in a Healing Booth. I asked for him to be my study. It was the only thing I could do for poor Joe. Besides, I thought I could study him because I have time. My raccoon died. I'm not working on anything."

Nova didn't believe the last of that sentence at all. Her father was always working on either a gadget or healing an illness.

"I think the best thing for the end of your story is if you get an apology. You need to clear up your unfinished business. You wouldn't want to go crazy, after all."

Nova threw herself into his arms. She hugged him as feelings of happiness swamped her.

"No, I wouldn't want that." She smiled. It appeared her father could fix hearts like he said he could.

"If you're going to become my assistant for this patient, Nova, you need to know that he's at stage two." She felt her dad tug on her arms. She leaned back to look at him. His face was solemn. "Are you able to manage this? It's rough in there."

Nova knew what her dad told her. He wanted to protect her from the fact that Arrow would die. She knew the move from stage two to stage three was quick. In stage three, most patients died. No amount of IV fluids could win over Snow Flu. The body rejected water.

"How long will he live?"

"You know that I can't tell you how long anyone will live. Only God knows, but I can tell you one thing."

"What?"

"He asks for you when he's asleep. He calls for you in his dreams."

"He does?"

"Well, I think it's you. When he's in a lot of pain he calls out for his, 'angel-with-demon-eyes.' I think you're the only one who'd fit that description."

Chapter 26

The condensation on the glass beaded and droplets fell on the white table just out of his reach.

Arrow stared at the pitcher. The ice bobbed. He'd tried to get the old man with the glasses to give him a drink, simply a sip of water, but the doctor refused. Doctor Gears stated it would start him vomiting all over again. That was yesterday. He glanced at a black-edged clock mounted high on the wall above the exit. It was 2:05 a.m. He wasn't sure how long he'd been asleep, but no matter, right now he could drink water. He was positive.

Looking at the glass longingly, Arrow didn't care if he threw up or not. He wanted a drink so bad that he even considered getting up out of bed. He strained, but his body was so weak he couldn't even sit up.

"Nova," he breathed then relaxed against the mattress. She was his mantra. The only thing that kept the pain at bay. "Angel," he whispered to the empty blue walls. His lips were chapped. His dry tongue licked them as he stared at the IV bag dripping into his arm. The doctor had insisted on the bag even when the young assistant said the IV was against the H.S.P.C rules for prisoners.

A prison is what he was in. No bars or chains, but he was locked to this bed all the same. It was merely him here dying. He was too weak to even sit up. He was too weak even to reach the water pitcher.

The reality of the situation hit him. He wished he was asleep again. He wasn't a patient to be cared for. He was here to die so they could study his downhill spiral. Hopefully, at least, they might find answers to Snow Flu. If there was a cure, then his death wouldn't be for nothing. A cure might save Nova.

Joe told him, as he was hauled out of court, that Nova had been taken to the Healing Booths with Dan, Archer, and Dawn. At that point, he didn't care about anything as long as Nova was alive. Doctor Gears explained that she slept in a Healing Booth like this one. He didn't know if that meant she was sick or well, but he did know her brother Archer and Dan both had Snow Flu.

At the trial, he'd been blamed for giving the agents the sickness. Mother had gladly pinned as much on him and Teagan as she could. He forced the trial out of his head. He didn't care about any of that. If only he knew if Nova was alive or dead. If she was safe, then it would make up for some of his rotten life.

A gathering of some drips of water fell again to the table. This might be hell. His skin was on fire but he could no longer sweat. As the heat made him feel like he was being cooked, he felt like he deserved this. Even though knowing Nova was the highlight of his life, he figured it was probably rock-bottom for her. He couldn't believe he had left her chained to her brother in a box. If only he could tell her how sorry he was. Guilt was cooking him like the searing heat. What he had done to her and to lots of people he wished he could atone for. Everything he had done for

Mother was all things he wanted to go back in time and erase.

He closed his eyes and pictured Nova. She said sometimes you do things that are crazy and out of control, then you have to let them go. She told him he had to forgive himself. After that he'd have to find that next peaceful moment. Just picturing her in that moment back on the train, was like thinking about heaven. He visualized her eyes, her hair. The way she would rub her forehand while she thought. When he closed his eyes, he could taste her on his lips. Even with his body so battered, his cock tried to stir to life.

"They say, 'There is no way to peace. Peace is the way.'"

Arrow's eyes popped open. He'd been imagining her so hard that he could hear her voice. His heart started to pound as he turned his head to the door.

In the doorway stood Nova.

She stepped lightly into the room. The door behind her closed with a click. Her hands held a bucket, a bag, and what looked like white sheets. The light-colored lab coat with big pockets that she wore swished against the items she held. The coat wasn't buttoned. He could see the dark tank top as well as the sweater that molded to her body. As she walked toward him, he noticed the tight little jeans that had holes ripped in the knees.

"They?" His voice was hoarse. He wasn't sure if it was because he was in shock or because of the illness. "There is no *they*. *They* don't exist." He tried to sit up to see her better, but his entire body disregarded his order.

"Don't say that. I met this guy on a train who had a bunch of smart sayings." Nova came closer. She set the items down next to the water pitcher. Her eyes studied him.

"That guy is gone. He was a terrible person. You won't miss him."

Arrow felt her eyes survey him. He was painfully aware that his hair was tangled from dried sweat. The strands were unbraided and sticking to his bare shoulders. He'd pissed himself too.

A voice from the intercom next to the mirror abruptly drew his thoughts from his embarrassment.

"Doctor Gears' assistant," a woman intoned over the speakers. "You must be in attire that'll protect from Snow Flu. This patient is a level one. Please return to Lab B for further briefings."

"Briefings my ass." Nova's eyes flashed with annoyance. "This is the kind of crap that happens to—" She stopped suddenly then shook her head.

Arrow's eyes grew big. Nova wasn't in the protective plastic outfits like the old man Gears or the other girl he remembered. Panic made his muscles flex.

"Nova, I'm dying. You have to get out of here." He croaked as he tried again to rise, thinking only of getting her to safety, but he only shifted in the bed.

Nova gave him a reassuring smile then walked over to the intercom. Her fingers held the red switch down as she spoke.

"Look what you did," she barked into the speaker. "It's his first day awake and you got him panicked. I swear your brains are made of monkey crap. You have my paper work. If you're not able to read, I don't think you should work here." Nova snapped the switch up. "Why do I even bother? No one listens," she dug into one of her pockets. Pausing, she gave him a sweet smile before producing a screw driver.

"What are you—"

"I thought we might need this." Quickly she opened the intercom box. With a tug, she yanked out two wires which silenced the machine. When she was done, she returned to his side. "I'm fine. Don't panic."

"I'm not panicking," he argued, but worry washed through him. His emotions must have showed on his face.

"Yes, I remember. You don't panic." Nova chuckled at him. "I'm fine, Arrow, or should I call you Weaver? On the trial document, the name says Weaver Yazzie."

"Weaver's not my name." As he spoke, she put a thermometer under his arm. Even with her reassurances, he didn't want her to touch him. "Angel, you have to leave. I'm sick."

"I thought you agreed to be the silent companion on this trip. Silent is the important word." She arranged her items she'd brought next to the bed then she checked the IV bag. "I'm immune to Snow Flu. I always have been. I can't get it even if I want to. Trust me, Clare has tried a bunch of ways to give it to me." As she talked, she moved the screen that was set in front of the toilet to place the divider in front of the mirror. "I could lick you from head to toe and never get it," she added as she arranged the panel.

"I don't think they'll like that, angel," Arrow said when he figured out that she made sure no one could see in.

"They wouldn't like it if I licked you?"

"No, not lick me." He grinned. "I meant to put the screen there." Even though it was painful to laugh, the chuckle came out.

"I know. I was teasing you, but we'll save licking you for another time." She smiled.

Arrow felt her smile like a warm cloak wrapped around him on a cold train. It struck him that he didn't deserve her making him feel better or making him laugh. What he deserved was her yelling at him for what he had done to her. He looked at the water, then at Nova. Both of them were out of his reach.

"You want a drink?" Nova must have caught the fugitive glance he gave the pitcher.

"I'm not supposed to. The old man said I'll start vomiting again."

Nova fished a metal pan out from under the bed.

"I bet he'd love to hear you call him the 'old man.'" She plopped the bedpan on his lap, then returned to the water. She poured only a small amount of water in a glass before she came to his side.

Wrapping an arm around his shoulders, she helped him sit up. The glass pressed to his lips. He paused.

"You really are an angel."

"I know I told you not to call me that, but I changed my mind. I missed it." She held the glass. "I missed you."

He paused for another second. He didn't want to vomit up blood again.

"I missed you too." The idea of receiving a loving declaration from Nova then hurling made him cringe. That would be the worst thing that could happen today. What would she say after? He stared at the glass.

"The 'old man' as you call him is my dad." Nova must have noticed his pause. "He's a brilliant doctor. If he told you that you'll vomit you probably will, but then again that was a week ago. You might keep the liquid down. We'll see."

"A week ago? Who's been caring for me all this time?" He hoped it wasn't Nova. He was so embarrassed she saw him like this. He was covered with his own urine and sweat.

"I have been here every day caring for you, but you mostly sleep." She nodded to the glass again.

He licked his lips before he took a sip. He didn't want her to see him throw up, but he wanted the drink desperately. He took one sip, then two, then drained the glass. He let her settle him back down on the pillow.

Arrow braced for the worst, but his body seemed to accept the water. He felt nauseous, but he held it down. He thanked the Great Sprit she didn't see him disgrace himself any more than he had already.

Nova took the bedpan off his lap.

"I only remember the old man a week ago. So, that's your father?" he asked after he was sure he wasn't going to hurl. "He doesn't look like you."

"Yes. He's my guardian. He isn't my biological father, but he's my dad. I came here when I was a baby. He named me and everything."

"He's a doctor here?" Arrow had a hard time absorbing the idea that he'd slept for a week. Most of the time he'd been dreaming of Nova, but now he wondered if those were not dreams.

"Yes. He's a doctor and a scientist."

"You work for him?"

"Yes, I'm his assistant, but," Nova sat on the bed near his ribs, "I feel like it's not that you should be learning about me, but instead you should tell me about who you are, Weaver." Her eyes dropped to her lap then she rubbed her forehead. "I'd like to know about the kind of man who'd leave me on a train to die."

She stood up as if the subject was painful. He wished she had not brought it up. He knew that they couldn't forget what happened. To be able to ever forgive or move on, they would have to talk about what he did to her. Even with talking, he figured she might never be able to forgive him. He had to pay for sins committed.

As she paced, he was now annoyed more than ever that he was drained. He wanted to pull her into his arms. While holding her, he would beg for forgiveness. He could tell she was hurt. She had every right to be. He wanted her to yell at him, not pace in silence. She should call him names or strike him. She shouldn't have been caring for him for a week. Shame washed through him as he considered that he received all of her attention while he gave her nothing.

"The kind of man who would leave you on a train to die doesn't deserve your care. I can never apologize enough for what I've done to you or your brother. I know I'll never be able to make it up to you. I can't even get out of this bed to hold you. I can tell you how sorry I am, but I don't think I can ever make it right. I'm a terrible person exactly like Raiden said. I don't know who Weaver is, but you should leave me here. I should die."

"Why would you do it, Arrow?"

"I was so confused after they gave me the drug and—"

"I mean why join The Originals?"

He'd been thinking about that question ever since he'd gotten all his memories back, as well as all through the trial. He'd reviewed his decision every waking moment he wasn't in pain with Snow Flu. The only thing he could do was be honest. Maybe she could find it in her heart to at least consider forgiving him one day.

"Mother saved my life when I first returned from a trek above ground with Raiden. I was sick with Snow Flu. She healed me. While I was so ill, I promised her a baby. When I healed, she claimed she could make my life everything I wanted. Mother said if I promised to give her a baby from my body, then that child would cure Snow Flu one day. She stated I'd be able to have sex and feel things like a normal person. Most of my life, Nova, I've felt hollow. I felt like I was missing something."

"I understand."

"No, you don't. Please don't be understanding. Stop being kind to me. I was horrible. I was selfish. I let her extract my sperm. I said nothing while she impregnated a young girl. I did that just to have the chance to get off. Right away..." He paused because he didn't want to admit this to her, but he couldn't keep it from her either, so he plunged on, "After the girl got pregnant, she somehow got Snow Flu. Mother announced that this was Earth telling us the child and the mother were unworthy. She had The Originals kick her out. Teagan and I dropped her on the train tracks in the tunnels to die." His admittance brought tears to his eyes. He swallowed hard.

Nova gave a sharp intake of breath.

If ever he was sure he'd lost Nova completely, it was now. She could never be with someone like him. She would never forgive him for this. He couldn't even forgive himself.

"It was the worst thing I've ever done. It's unforgivable. After that, Mother discovered I had a sister, so she used me to track her so my own sister could carry the next baby. She told me this baby would cure Snow Flu. As long as The Originals had the cure, then we could stop the evil plan of the H.S.P.C."

"But there is no evil plan." Nova stopped pacing. "All the H.S.P.C. does is protect life. Fuck, their name stands for Human Survival and Population Care."

"In many of Mother's insane rants she claimed that if the H.S.P.C. had the cure then they'd create ultimate despair." Arrow shook his head when Nova slapped her hands on her hips. He hurried on. "I know it's bizarre. I knew it at the time. To tell you the truth, I didn't care. All

I wanted was to be normal. She promised me that on the path with her at the end I'd be normal with children, family, and life inside of my soul. I wanted that… I wanted to have sex. So, I agreed to capture Dawn."

"You had sex with your sister?" Nova's voice dripped with shock and disgust. He wished he didn't have to tell her all of this.

"No." Reaching deep for courage, he doggedly continued, "When Raiden said, I couldn't have sex, he wasn't lying. I couldn't perform. It was a huge embarrassment for me in some ways, yet in others I used it to my advantage as best I could. I did create that game we played. I've seen a lot of sexual acts. I tried over and over again but it never worked. Mother knew I couldn't ejaculate, so she extracted sperm from me a second time. She planned to put my sperm inside of Dawn's body."

"We never had a problem." She gave a tiny shrug.

"No, we didn't." Arrow had thought about that too. The only thing he could come up with was that Nova was his perfect match. Mother called it a *conpar*, some Latin word for finding the right connection. Since he left her side, he'd not seen any golden ropes. He guessed he'd no longer be able to have an erection. With her around he knew she brought those things to his life.

"So, you and Mother impregnated Dawn?"

"We were all ready to do it." Again, he cringed at his past. "But Dan burst in. He saved Dawn. Dan took her. I was given the memory drug. While Mother and Teagan tried to fix me, Archer showed up and they captured him. It was such a mess that Mother and Teagan took Archer. They decided to come back for me later. I was out of it so they left me, thinking they could finish the antidote, get rid of Archer, and I'd be fine waiting for them. But things changed with the cave in."

"The H.S.P.C. closed the base."

"Yea, Mother was worried about being caught. They were working on a plan when you showed up." Arrow couldn't look at her.

"And they didn't know where you'd gone."

Arrow sighed.

"Every day I wonder why you got mixed up with me. I have to say you were right about us not being together." Arrow felt like this was his time to tell her goodbye. "I'm no good for you. You should leave me here to die, like I should've in that cage." Arrow closed his eyes briefly. He couldn't watch her go, but he deserved to see her leave. He got up enough courage to look her in the eye.

"It wasn't a cage. It was a locked room." She hadn't left.

"Is this a potato, potatoes thing?"

Nova could make even his darkest moments brighten with a few words.

"You survived Snow Flu once. Don't you think you'll do it again?" She began to pace again. He'd missed that.

"I don't have Mother's magical healing powers this time."

Nova burst out laughing. The sound startled him. It wasn't a joyful laugh, but dark and sharp.

"I'd love to kick Mother in the teeth. She was *not* magical. You can survive. You healed last time on your own, Arrow. She gave you nothing more than sips of water. All you have to do is want to live. She gave you a reason. A goal to get through the pain."

"I don't want to live unless you forgive me."

He held his breath. If she told him she was done with him, then there was no point in living.

"Did you know, around here they nicknamed me Nutty-Nova? So, I have a nutty idea. I've thought about it, and you can make it up to me for leaving me to die on the train. I'll forgive you, but only on one condition."

"What condition?"

"You can promise to survive Snow Flu. When you're well, you can marry me."

"Marry you?" Arrow felt glee and misery simultaneously. Nova came to sit next to him on the bed.

"Maybe it's a bad idea. I know I can be volatile and insane sometimes, and I swear a lot. I only thought…"

Arrow worked to raise his hand to touch her, but it didn't lift.

"Nova, I'd love to marry you. I want to be with you every day. I want to make up for all the wrongs I've done, but I can't promise you I can beat this, and what about Sky? I thought you couldn't fit me in your life with him, too. You and Troy broke up because of this other man. Maybe it'd be best if you let him be your everything. He'd be a better man then I. Hell, anyone is a better choice than me. Anyone who did not leave you to die on a train is a better choice, even Troy. No one should start out a relationship this way."

She was silent. It made his heart hurt to think he'd convinced her to leave.

Finally, Nova spoke. "My dad said that a relationship can start in all sorts of ways. He told me that his friend was shot by his wife." She paused. "It's true, Sky has never left me on a train, but then again he can't walk yet, so I figure that'd be hard for him. Besides, once you marry me you can take your place in his life where you belong."

"As what?"

"As his father."

Stunned silence blanketed him.

"What?" Arrow was glad he was on this bed. His legs would collapse.

"Sky was found near the tracks with a woman in a tunnel. She'd delivered a baby before she died. My dad already checked the DNA. He's yours. Dad's put a lot of this together. Just as sex with you changed my eye color. My blood transfusions changed Sky's hair color."

"He lived. My baby? My baby lived?"

"My blood keeps him alive. I named him Sky because his eyes are a beautiful shade of blue. When the Snow Flu cure is finished, I'm thinking of calling it Sky-Serum. What do you think?"

"I don't understand."

"Serum means—"

"Not about that, about the baby. Why will Sky have the cure?"

"Sky won't have it directly. I mean not right away. He's only one piece of the whole puzzle. Clare and Dad are working on the cure, but basically Sky has Snow Flu, but with my blood in his body he never gets sicker, but he never gets better, either. Also, Sky doesn't pass it on. With me, I can never get it. With you, you can survive it. The idea is all three pieces of us will make a cure."

"Will I be able to meet Sky if I get better?"

"Yes, if you survive, but you were saying you needed Mother for that."

"For you and for my son, I'd do anything, angel."

"I'll remember that."

"I'm sure you will." Arrow paused. "Where is he? I have to make it up to him. I have to make amends."

Nova put her cool hand on his forehead.

"Sky has always been kept with me and Clare, in our apartments. It's a room like this, but it's close to us so we care for him exclusively. What you need to do is rest. Leave Sky to me."

Arrow wrinkled his brow as he recalled his dreams. "Are the walls white?"

"Yes."

"Is he in a crib with wooden bars on the side? Sometimes you come in to sing to him? It's a tune you hum when you kiss and nuzzle his cheeks."

"How do you know that?"

"I finally know why I know you. I've been seeing thorough Sky's eyes. It's why at first you were blurry, then you came into focus. I used to see you a lot in my dreams. I still do." Arrow grinned. "There is so much I want to share with you. I want you to tell me everything about Sky."

She laughed. "We'll have a time for all of that, but right now you promised me you'd heal. You said for me and Sky. You need to get cleaned up, then you're going back to sleep. This was a lot of conversation for someone who just woke up and can barely keep down half a glass of water."

Arrow looked at the forgotten water. "I feel like I could take on the world."

"You might feel like that, but you look like a limp rag could whoop your ass."

He smiled, then frowned as she touched his arm that was slick with sweat again. She stood up, then headed over to the supplies she'd set down.

"I'm going to turn you over so I can strip your bed. I'll give you another glass of water. See if you can drink it before you take on the world."

Arrow felt oddly exposed being naked and helpless. He didn't want her touching his sheets covered with his sweat and piss. He only wanted Nova to see him at his best. After all that happened, the least he could do is spare her caring for him.

"I don't want you to see me like this. Come back when I'm healed. I want you to leave."

"No, you don't." Nova rolled him over. "'I want you to leave' says the man who can hardly move." Nova muttered as she swiftly changed his wet sheets. He couldn't do anything to stop her.

"Yes, I do," he argued feebly. The clean sheets felt like heaven.

"No, you don't. You need me."

He couldn't help but smile that she fought with him. He'd missed that so much. When she set his head down on a clean pillow case, he thought he could smell her sent of flowers.

"You're right. I don't want you to leave me. I do need you. Maybe I'll rest and take on the world another day. You're always right."

"Not always." She squeezed a damp cloth then started to gently mop his brow. She moved to his neck, then his chest. His eyes closed.

"Really?"

"You were right about us being together. We belong together. I love you."

"I was right? That's so amazing I need a banner to celebrate." He yawned. "I love you too."

"I'll get you a banner."

"Yea, one that says, 'Arrow was right.' After this, I can roll it back up and stick the paper into the closet until I'm right again. Maybe in a few years."

Epilogue

Five years later…

Nova threw her extra paperwork as well as her sweater on the floor of the entryway into their apartment. She was ready for the day to be finished.

She glanced around for Arrow, Sky, and Cosmo.

"I'm home," she called into the welcoming apartment.

When she didn't get an answer, she walked down the short hallway off of the kitchen area. The last room on her right was her final destination.

She spotted Arrow bent over his desk jotting notes on the architectural designs he'd been obsessing over for the last two weeks. She figured he would be there.

"I'm home," Nova repeated. She leaned on the door frame. Arrow spun around in his gray office chair.

"I'm sorry I didn't hear you come in. I was distracted." His face lit up when he looked at her. He patted his knee. She grinned as she moved closer, then she let him pull her onto his lap. He kissed her soundly.

"How was work?"

Nova tried to come up with a nice thing to say about Clare and Archer's son. She swore that kid's only purpose in life was to make it impossible for her to get anything done.

"On the up side, my office wasn't destroyed this morning when I got there," she said brightly.

"And the down side?"

"It was destroyed by the time I left."

Arrow laughed before hugging her. "Did you get off early then? What time is it?"

"It's almost three."

"He's just a child, Nova. I can't believe you let Clare's little boy chase you out of work. You're tougher than that, angel."

Nova laughed. "You're one to talk. Cosmo runs circles around you." Nova paused when he kissed her again for his agreement. When she surfaced from his inviting mouth, she continued, "I'm here because I told you this morning that we have to meet Dawn and Dan for dinner. I also thought that you were supposed to drop those plans off to Dad tonight for Clare to look over."

Nova gestured to Arrow's layout of a new care center he designed specifically for women. He'd been working on his idea for the last year with her father and Clare. Now it was finally getting to the stage where the first one would be built. Since the death of the mother of his child, Arrow worked nonstop to make a place that was safe for women. Nova thought that he worked so hard on it to make up for some of his past. A piece of forgiving himself would be given to him when the project was completed.

She leaned over to look at some of the papers when he didn't respond to her right away.

The layout for what he called a Female Care Center or a FCC looked finished to her.

"I remembered that I had to give these to Clare tonight, but I thought I had time to add a few more details before you got home. I guess, I'm fixated on this, but I want it to be safe. I'm nervous. What do you think?"

Nova glanced at the layouts of gardens, rooms, and offices. He'd forgotten nothing. She gave him a reassuring smile.

"I think it will be amazing when it's done. Any woman who needs help, or is all alone in the world, would be lucky to end up in a place like this." She tried to rise, but he stopped her.

He put his arm tightly around her waist. His hand brushed her jean pocket. The action made a crinkle sound.

"I almost forgot." Nova leaned back to pull out a crushed letter from her pocket. She handed the paper to Arrow. "This is for you. It came today, actually it came for a man named Weaver, but I told the messenger according to our documents Weaver Yazzie was given Snow Flu five years ago, and no one survives Snow Flu."

Arrow gave her a half-smile. "I told Raiden twice to make sure he addressed it right, but I guess he forgot again. What did the messenger say?"

"The messenger said it was fine. I told him I'd get rid of the letter."

Arrow set the message down on the desk. He put his arms back around her again. "I think they want to come here to visit. We can read it after we go to dinner unless—" His smile was mischievous. "We skip dinner tonight and go to bed early." He kissed her neck until she squirmed on his lap.

"We could skip it." Nova tilted her head to give him better access. She gave a husky laugh while she slipped her hand up under his white shirt. The look he gave her was first intense, then his eyes drifted closed. Suddenly his eyes opened. His face fell.

"I forgot we can't skip it because Joe is bringing a woman for me to meet. He wants to see if their ropes match. Gears is really into studying my gift. Gears and your mom asked to watch."

"Damn," Nova exhaled.

"Damn," a little voice piped up from the doorway.

Nova spun around to see Cosmo jumping up and down in the hall. His red-brown hair flopped as he bounced.

"Don't swear, Cosmo," she stated automatically. "Mommy shouldn't either."

As she surveyed her son, Nova tried to untangle herself from Arrow's arms, but he was having none of that. Nova's brow crinkled as she noticed their boy wore only white cotton underwear.

"Arrow, where are his clothes?"

Arrow threw his hands up in the air and then patted her bottom so she would get off his lap.

"I swear, I got him dressed this morning before you left for work. He has been dressed all day." Arrow bent down to pick Cosmo up. He threw the three-year-old in the air. They laughed. Nova slapped her hands on her hips.

"Right, Cos?" Arrow hugged his son. "Tell Mommy I dressed you."

"Here are his clothes, Father." Nova looked past Arrow and Cosmo to Sky who had come down the hallway from his bedroom.

Sky was carrying all the articles Cosmo had removed. He gripped them like delivering the articles was an annoying task. Nova held her smile at the seriousness of their older son. With great care, Sky handed Arrow Cosmo's lost attire, then gave him a look of mild displeasure.

"Good evening, Sky. How are you?" Nova could never keep the twinkle out of her eye when she was conversing with her six-year-old. Sky liked it when she was polite. Her older son was the exact opposite of Cosmo in every way. Their three-year-old was wild and unpredictable. Sky was serious and punctual. Their eldest was always impeccably dressed. Most of the time Cosmo was running around in his underwear.

As it was now, Cosmo was fighting to stay unclothed. Sky was dressed superbly in slacks and a gray cardigan. Arrow was struggling to smooth down Cosmo's red-brown mop while Sky's white locks were flawlessly braided like his fathers.

"I had a fine day. Thank you for asking." Sky hugged her before giving Cosmo another look of grim irritation.

Nova held her giggle at his proper tone. In the years since she'd watched him grow, she'd never seen him any other way.

"Nooooooo!" The blood curdling scream drew Nova away from Sky. She gave him another quick hug before returning to the battle that Arrow was having with their youngest.

Arrow held the clothes. Her son only had one arm in the shirt sleeve. He was trying to toss the other clothes down the hall.

"Cosmo!" She clapped cheerfully to distract him from the budding tantrum. "I've an idea. If you get dressed, I'll read you your favorite book before we go to dinner."

"Okay."

Before Nova could get out another word, Cosmo squirmed out of Arrow's arms. He ran off like a shot down the hall. He came back in record time carrying a book that Gears insisted needed to go in the trash. She had to agree the book had seen better days, but there was no way Cosmo would give it up. The full title wasn't even readable anymore. All you could see was "Oscar the grouch." The rest of the words were peeled off.

Cosmo handed her the stapled papers. She saw Sky lift one white eyebrow. It was the most childlike thing she had seen him do all week.

"Not your favorite book, Sky?" she asked playfully then smiled when he gave her his look that stated he shouldn't have to explain his feelings.

"It's silly. I don't know why Oscar is green or why he lives in the trash. Is he supposed to be some type of plant? I can't tell if that's fur. If he has green fur, what animal is green?"

"I don't know. Ask Grandpa Gears. He's a scientist." Arrow pulled a shirt over Cosmo's head. "Sky, they say, 'Challenge everything.' I think it's good you have such an inquisitive mind."

Sky looked at Arrow thoughtfully, but only for a second.

"The book is dumb," Sky announced with authority.

Arrow tried to hide his laugh by averting his head. He helped put Cosmo's pants on. It appeared Arrow wasn't insulted by Sky not being in the mood for his sayings.

Arrow shrugged at Sky, then he stood.

"It's not dumb," Cosmo called out. Arrow pretended to pat his brow like getting Cosmo dressed was hard work.

"Is too."

"Is not."

"Is too."

Cosmo stuck out his tongue. Nova held up her hand for them to stop.

"Mommy?" Cosmo decided her hand gesture meant he had won that round.

"Can we name Sky, Oscar? I like the name better."

"No," Arrow and she responded in unison. Cosmo's little shoulders dropped, crestfallen. Sky shook his head when he saw tears in Cosmo's eyes. He took immediate pity on his brother.

"You can name your child Oscar when you're older, and you have your own children," Sky explained earnestly.

Arrow leaned in to kiss her again while the two boys interacted. When he pulled away, his eyes danced.

"What's so amusing?" she asked.

Arrow turned to Sky and Cosmo instead of answering to her. His voice had a hint of mirth.

"When you're older, Cosmo, you might want to name your kid Oscar, but if your wife says she has another name picked out, then you might have to go with what she wants. They say, 'Have it your way.' If your wonderful wife is right, sometimes you have to let her have it her way."

Nova laughed. "Women are right most of the time but, every once and awhile, we have to listen to some sage advice. Even if it's from a fast food billboard." Nova faced Arrow. "You, my love, know when I'm being a little…" She wrapped her arms around his waist.

"A little what?" Arrow asked when she paused.

"Crazy."

~ The End ~

Thank you for reading **2:05 a.m.** If you enjoyed this book and would like to give back to the authors, please consider writing a review! Reviews are a tremendous help for authors. So, if you were moved and enjoyed this book enough to write even one sentence of encouragement, it would be a huge boon.

Connect with C.M. Moore:

Facebook:

https://www.facebook.com/profile.php?id=100010442116825

Twitter:

https://twitter.com/time_for_snow

Google+:

https://plus.google.com/101755128915251195131

AUTHOR WEBSITE:

www.authorcmmoore.com

About C.M.Moore

C.M. Moore is a retired soldier, and a romantic at heart. After being blown up in Afghanistan and receiving a purple heart, he began writing with his wife. Connor's first book *1:05 am* is a mixture of love, sex, and action. Today if you are looking for Connor, you can find him volunteering with veteran organizations, and harassing his military buddies. You can also find him attempting to "hunt" in the woods and ponds of Minnesota. In the event you find him in the woods, don't be scared, he can't hit anything. If you want to contact him message him at c.m.moore.author@gmail.com

Other Books by C.M.Moore

1:05 a.m. (An Ice Era Chronicle) Book 1

Griding My Gears (1:30 a.m.)
An Off-The-Rails Ice Era Chronicle
Book 1.5